SHORT STORIES, PLEASE!

everyone's favourite short stories

Selected by HILARY LAURIE

PHŒNIX

A PHOENIX PAPERBACK

First published in 1998
by Phoenix, a division of Orion Books Ltd
Orion House, 5 Upper St Martin's Lane, London WC2H 9EA

A CIP catalogue record for this book
is available from the British Library.

ISBN 0 75380 450 6

Typeset by Deltatype Ltd, Birkenhead, Merseyside
Printed in Great Britain by
The Guernsey Press Co. Ltd., Guernsey, C. I.

Contents

Note on the Editor

Hilary Laurie was for five years the Publishing Director of Everyman Paperbacks. She has worked for the Queen's University, Belfast, the West African Examinations Council and the British Council. She has researched and written on George Moore and other Anglo-Irish writers.

SHORT STORIES, PLEASE!
Everyone's Favourite Short Stories

EDGAR ALLAN POE

The Pit and the Pendulum

Impia tortorum longas hic turba furores
Sanguinis innocui, non satiata, aluit.
Sospite nunc patria, fracto nunc funeris antro,
Mors ubi dira fuit vita salusque patent.

Quatrain composed for the gates of a market to be erected upon the site of the Jacobin Club House at Paris

I was sick – sick unto death with that long agony; and when they at length unbound me, and I was permitted to sit, I felt that my senses were leaving me. The sentence – the dread sentence of death – was the last of distinct accentuation which reached my ears. After that the sound of the inquisitorial voices seemed merged in one dreamy indeterminate hum. It conveyed to my soul the idea of *revolution* – perhaps from its association in fancy with the burr of a mill-wheel. This only for a brief period, for presently I heard no more. Yet, for a while, I saw – but with how terrible an exaggeration! I saw the lips of the black-robed judges. They appeared to me white – whiter than the sheet upon which I trace these words – and thin even to grotesqueness; thin with the intensity of their expression of firmness – of immovable resolution – of stern contempt of human torture. I saw that the decrees of what to me was Fate were still issuing from those lips. I saw them writhe with a deadly locution. I saw them fashion the syllables of my name; and I shuddered because no sound succeeded. I saw, too, for a few moments of delirious horror, the soft and nearly imperceptible waving of the sable draperies which enwrapped the walls of the apartment. And then my vision fell upon the seven tall candles upon the table. At first they wore the aspect of charity, and seemed white slender angels who would save me; but then, all at once, there came a most deadly nausea over my spirit, and I felt every fibre in my frame thrill as if I had touched the wire of a galvanic battery, while the angel forms became meaningless spectres, with heads of flame, and I saw that from them there would be no help. And then there stole into my fancy, like a rich musical note, the thought of what sweet rest there must be in the grave. The thought came gently and stealthily, and it seemed long before it attained full appreciation; but just as my spirit came at length properly to feel and entertain it, the figures of the judges vanished, as if magically, from before me; the tall candles sank into nothingness; their flames went out utterly; the blackness of darkness supervened; all sensations appeared swallowed up in a mad rushing descent as of the soul into Hades. Then silence, and stillness, and night were the universe.

I had swooned; but still will not say that all of consciousness was lost. What of it remained I will not attempt to define, or even to describe; yet all was not lost. In the deepest slumber – no! In delirium – no! In a swoon – no! In death – no! even in the grave all *is not* lost. Else there is no immortality for man. Arousing from the most profound of slumbers, we break the gossamer web of *some* dream. Yet in a second afterward (so frail may that web have been) we remember not that we have dreamed. In the return to life from the swoon there are two stages: first, that of the sense of mental or spiritual; secondly, that of the sense of physical, existence. It seems probable that if, upon reaching the second stage, we could recall the impressions of the first, we should find these impressions eloquent in memories of the gulf beyond. And that gulf is – what? How at least shall we distinguish its shadows from those of the tomb? But if the impressions of what I have termed the first stage, are not at will, recalled, yet, after long interval, do they not come unbidden, while we marvel whence they come? He who has never swooned, is not he who finds strange palaces and wildly familiar faces in coals that glow; is not he who beholds floating in mid-air the sad visions that the many may not view; is not he who ponders over the perfume of some novel flower; is not he whose brain grows bewildered with the meaning of some musical cadence which has never before arrested his attention.

Amid frequent and thoughtful endeavours to remember, amid earnest struggles to regather some token of the state of seeming nothingness into which my soul had lapsed, there have been moments when I have dreamed of success; there have been brief, very brief periods when I conjured up remembrances which the lucid reason of a later epoch assures me could have had reference only to that condition of seeming unconsciousness. These shadows of memory tell, indistinctly, of tall figures that lifted and bore me in silence down – down – still down – till a hideous dizziness oppressed me at the mere idea of the interminableness of the descent. They tell also of a vague horror at my heart, on account of that heart's unnatural stillness. Then comes a sense of sudden motionlessness throughout all things; as if those who bore me (a ghastly train!) had outrun, in their descent, the limits of the limitless, and paused from the wearisomeness of their toil. After this I call to mind flatness and dampness; and then all is *madness* – the madness of a memory which busies itself among forbidden things.

Very suddenly there came back to my soul motion and sound – the tumultuous motion of my heart, and, in my ears, the sound of its beating. Then a pause in which all is blank. Then again sound, and motion, and touch – a tingling sensation pervading my frame. Then the mere consciousness of existence, without thought – a condition which lasted long. Then very suddenly, *thought*, and shuddering terror, and earnest endeavour to comprehend my true state. Then a strong desire to lapse into insensibility. Then a rushing revival of soul and a successful effort to move. And now a full memory of the trial, of the judges, of the sable draperies, of the sentence, of the sickness, of the swoon. Then entire forgetfulness of all that followed; of all that a later day and much earnestness of endeavour have enabled me vaguely to recall.

So far, I had not opened my eyes. I felt that I lay upon my back, unbound. I reached out my hand, and it fell heavily upon something damp and hard. There I suffered it to remain for many minutes, while I strove to imagine where and *what* I could be. I longed, yet dared not, to employ my vision. I dreaded the first glance at objects around me. It was not that I feared to look upon things horrible, but that I grew aghast lest there should be *nothing* to see. At length, with a wild desperation at heart, I quickly unclosed my eyes. My worst thoughts, then, were confirmed. The blackness of eternal night encompassed me. I struggled for breath. The intensity of the darkness seemed to oppress and stifle me. The atmosphere was intolerably close. I still lay quietly, and made effort to exercise my reason. I brought to mind the inquisitorial proceedings, and attempted from that point to deduce my real condition. The sentence had passed; and it appeared to me that a very long interval of time had since elapsed. Yet not for a moment did I suppose myself actually dead. Such a supposition, notwithstanding what we read in fiction, is altogether inconsistent with real existence; – but where and in what state was I? The condemned to death, I knew, perished usually at the *auto-da-fés*, and one of these had been held on the very night of the day of my trial. Had I been remanded to my dungeon, to await the next sacrifice, which would not take place for many months? This I at once saw could not be. Victims had been in immediate demand. Moreover, my dungeon, as well as all the condemned cells at Toledo, had stone floors, and light was not altogether excluded.

A fearful idea now suddenly drove the blood in torrents upon my heart, and for a brief period I once more relapsed into insensibility. Upon recovering, I at once started to my feet, trembling convulsively in every fibre. I thrust my arms wildly above and around me in all directions. I felt nothing; yet dreaded to move a step, lest I should be impeded by the walls of a *tomb*. Perspiration burst from every pore, and stood in cold big beads upon my forehead. The agony of suspense grew at length intolerable, and I cautiously moved forward, with my arms extended, and my eyes straining from their sockets in the hope of catching some faint ray of light. I proceeded for many paces; but still all was blackness and vacancy. I breathed more freely. It seemed evident that mine was not, at least, the most hideous of fates.

And now, as I still continued to step cautiously onward, there came thronging upon my recollection a thousand vague rumours of the horrors of Toledo. Of the dungeons there had been strange things narrated – fables I had always deemed them – but yet strange, and too ghastly to repeat, save in a whisper. Was I left to perish of starvation in this subterranean world of darkness; or what fate, perhaps even more fearful, awaited me? That the result would be death, and a death of more than customary bitterness, I knew too well the character of my judges to doubt. The mode and the hour were all that occupied or distracted me.

My outstretched hands at length encountered some solid

obstruction. It was a wall, seemingly of stone masonry – very smooth, slimy, and cold. I followed it up; stepping with all the careful distrust with which certain antique narratives had inspired me. This process, however, afforded me no means of ascertaining the dimensions of my dungeon, as I might make its circuit and return to the point whence I set out without being aware of the fact, so perfectly uniform seemed the wall. I therefore sought the knife which had been in my pocket when led into the inquisitorial chamber; but it was gone; my clothes had been exchanged for a wrapper of coarse serge. I had thought of forcing the blade in some minute crevice of the masonry, so as to identify my point of departure. The difficulty, nevertheless, was but trivial; although, in the disorder of my fancy, it seemed at first insuperable. I tore a part of the hem from the robe and placed the fragment at full length, and at right angles to the wall. In groping my way around the prison, I could not fail to encounter this rag upon completing the circuit. So, at least, I thought; but I had not counted upon the extent of the dungeon, or upon my own weakness. The ground was moist and slippery. I staggered onward for some time, when I stumbled and fell. My excessive fatigue induced me to remain prostrate; and sleep soon overtook me as I lay.

Upon awaking, and stretching forth an arm, I found beside me a loaf and a pitcher with water. I was too much exhausted to reflect upon this circumstance, but ate and drank with avidity. Shortly afterwards, I resumed my tour around the prison, and with much toil, came at last upon the fragment of the serge. Up to the period when I fell, I had counted fifty-two paces, and, upon resuming my walk, I had counted forty-eight more – when I arrived at the rag. There were in all, then, a hundred paces; and, admitting two paces to the yard, I presumed the dungeon to be fifty yards in circuit. I had met, however, with many angles in the wall, and thus I could form no guess at the shape of the vault, for vault I could not help supposing it to be.

I had little object – certainly no hope – in these researches; but a vague curiosity prompted me to continue them. Quitting the wall, I resolved to cross the area of the enclosure. At first, I proceeded with extreme caution, for the floor, although seemingly of solid material, was treacherous with slime. At length, however, I took courage, and did not hesitate to step firmly –

endeavouring to cross in as direct a line as possible. I had advanced some ten or twelve paces in this manner, when the remnant of the torn hem of my robe became entangled between my legs. I stepped on it, and fell violently on my face.

In the confusion attending my fall, I did not immediately apprehend a somewhat startling circumstance, which yet, in a few seconds afterward, and while I still lay prostrate, arrested my attention. It was this: my chin rested upon the floor of the prison, but my lips, and the upper portion of my head, although seemingly at a less elevation than the chin, touched nothing. At the same time, my forehead seemed bathed in a clammy vapour, and the peculiar smell of decayed fungus arose to my nostrils. I put forward my arm, and shuddered to find that I had fallen at the very brink of a circular pit, whose extent, of course, I had no means of ascertaining at the moment. Groping about the masonry just below the margin, I succeeded in dislodging a small fragment, and let it fall into the abyss. For many seconds I harkened to its reverberations as it dashed against the sides of the chasm in its descent; at length, there was a sullen plunge into water, succeeded by loud echoes. At the same moment, there came a sound resembling the quick opening and as rapid closing of a door overhead, while a faint gleam of light flashed suddenly through the gloom, and as suddenly faded away.

I saw clearly the doom which had been prepared for me, and congratulated myself upon the timely accident by which I had escaped. Another step before my fall, and the world had seen me no more. And the death just avoided was of that very character which I had regarded as fabulous and frivolous in the tales respecting the Inquisition. To the victims of its tyranny, there was the choice of death with its direct physical agonies, or death with its most hideous moral horrors. I had been reserved for the latter. By long suffering my nerves had been unstrung, until I trembled at the sound of my own voice, and had become in every respect a fitting subject for the species of torture which awaited me.

Shaking in every limb, I groped my way back to the wall – resolving there to perish rather than risk the terrors of the wells, of which my imagination now pictured many in various positions about the dungeon. In other conditions of mind, I might have had courage to end my misery at once, by a plunge into one of these abysses; but now I was the veriest of cowards. Neither could I forget what I had read of these pits – that the *sudden* extinction of life formed no part of their most horrible plan.

Agitation of spirit kept me awake for many long hours, but at length I again slumbered. Upon arousing, I found by my side, as before, a loaf and a pitcher of water. A burning thirst consumed me, and I emptied the vessel at a draught. It must have been drugged – for scarcely had I drunk, before I became irresistibly drowsy. A deep sleep fell upon me – a sleep like that of death. How long it lasted, of course I knew not; but when, once again, I unclosed my eyes, the objects around me were visible. By a wild, sulphurous lustre, the origin of which I could not at first determine, I was enabled to see the extent and aspect of the prison.

In its size I had been greatly mistaken. The whole circuit of its walls did not exceed twenty-five yards. For some minutes this fact occasioned me a world of vain trouble; vain indeed – for what could be of less importance, under the terrible circumstances which environed me, than the mere dimensions of my dungeon? But my soul took a wild interest in trifles, and I busied myself in endeavours to account for the error I had committed in my measurement. The truth at length flashed upon me. In my first attempt at exploration I had counted fifty-two paces, up to the period when I fell: I must then have been within a pace or two of the fragment of serge; in fact, I had nearly performed the circuit of the vault. I then slept – and upon awaking, I must have turned upon my steps – thus supposing the circuit nearly double what it actually was. My confusion of mind prevented me from observing that I began my tour with the wall to the left, and ended with the wall to the right.

I had been deceived, too, in respect to the shape of the enclosure. In feeling my way I had found many angles, and thus deduced an idea of great irregularity; so potent is the effect of total darkness upon one arousing from lethargy or sleep! The angles were simply those of a few slight depressions, or niches at odd intervals. The general shape of the prison was square. What I had taken for masonry seemed now to be iron, or some other metal, in huge plates, whose sutures or joints occasioned the depression. The entire surface of this metallic enclosure was rudely daubed in all the hideous and repulsive devices to which the charnel superstitions of the monks had given rise. The figures of fiends in aspects of menace, with skeleton forms, and other more really fearful images, overspread and disfigured the walls. I observed that the outlines of these monstrosities were sufficiently distinct, but that the colours seemed faded and blurred, as if from the effects of a damp atmosphere. I now noticed the floor, too, which was of stone. In the centre yawned the circular pit from whose jaws I had escaped; but it was the only one in the dungeon.

All this I saw indistinctly and by much effort – for my personal condition had been greatly changed during slumber. I now lay upon my back, and at full length, on a species of low framework of wood. To this I was securely bound by a long strap resembling a surcingle. It passed in many convolutions about my limbs and body, leaving at liberty only my head, and my left arm to such extent, that I could, by dint of much exercise, supply myself with food from an earthen dish which lay by my side on the floor. I saw, to my horror, that the pitcher had been removed. I say to my horror – for I was consumed with intolerable thirst. This thirst it appeared to be the design of my persecutors to stimulate – for the food in the dish was meat pungently seasoned.

Looking upward, I surveyed the ceiling of my prison. It was some thirty or forty feet overhead, and constructed much as the side walls. In one of its panels a very singular figure riveted my whole attention. It was the painted figure of Time as he is commonly represented, save that, in lieu of a scythe, he held what, at a casual glance, I supposed to be the pictured image of a huge pendulum, such as we see on antique clocks. There was something, however, in the appearance of this machine which caused me to regard it more attentively. While I gazed directly upward at it (for its position was immediately over my own) I fancied that I saw it in motion. In an instant afterward the fancy was confirmed. Its sweep was brief, and of course slow. I watched it for some minutes somewhat in fear, but more in wonder. Wearied at length with observing its dull movement, I turned my eyes upon the other objects in the cell.

A slight noise attracted my notice, and, looking to the floor, I saw several enormous rats traversing it. They had issued from the well which lay just within view to my right. Even then, while I gazed, they came up in troops, hurriedly, with ravenous eyes, allured by the scent of the meat. From this it required much effort and attention to scare them away.

It might have been half an hour, perhaps even an hour (for I could take but imperfect note of time), before I again cast my eyes upward. What I then saw confounded and amazed me. The sweep of the pendulum had increased in extent by nearly a yard. As a natural consequence its velocity was also much greater. But what mainly disturbed me was the idea that it had perceptibly descended. I now observed – with what horror it is needless to say – that its nether extremity was formed of a crescent of glittering steel, about a foot in length from horn to horn; the horns upward, and the under edge evidently as keen as that of a razor. Like a razor also, it seemed massive and heavy, tapering from the edge into a solid and broad structure above. It was appended to a weighty rod of brass, and the whole *hissed* as it swung through the air.

I could no longer doubt the doom prepared for me by monkish ingenuity in torture. My cognizance of the pit had become known to the inquisitorial agents – *the pit*, whose horrors had been destined for so bold a recusant as myself – *the pit*, typical of hell and regarded by rumour as the Ultima Thule of all their punishments. The plunge into this pit I had avoided by the merest of accidents, and I knew that surprise, or entrapment into torment, formed an important portion of all the grotesquerie of these dungeon deaths. Having failed to fall, it was no part of the demon plan to hurl me into the abyss; and thus (there being no alternative) a different and a milder destruction awaited me. Milder! I half smiled in my agony as I thought of such application of such a term.

What boots it to tell of the long, long hours of horror more than mortal, during which I counted the rushing oscillations of the steel! Inch by inch – line by line – with a descent only appreciable at intervals that seemed ages – down and still down it came! Days passed – it might have been that many days passed – ere it swept so closely over me as to fan me with its acrid breath. The odour of the sharp steel forced itself into my nostrils. I prayed – I wearied heaven with my prayer for its more speedy descent. I grew frantically mad, and struggled to force myself upward against the sweep of the fearful scimitar. And then I fell suddenly calm, and lay smiling at the glittering death, as a child at some rare bauble.

There was another interval of utter insensibility; it was brief; for upon again lapsing into life, there had been no perceptible descent in the pendulum. But it might have been long – for I knew there were demons who took note of my swoon, and who could have arrested the vibration at pleasure. Upon my recovery, too, I felt very – oh! inexpressibly – sick and weak, as if through long inanition. Even amid the agonies of that period the human nature craved food. With painful effort I outstretched my left arm as far as my bonds permitted, and took possession of the small remnant which had been spared me by the rats. As I put a portion of it within my lips, there rushed to my mind a half-formed thought of joy – of hope. Yet what business had *I* with hope? It was, as I say, a half-formed thought – man has many such, which are never completed. I felt that it was of joy – of hope; but I felt also that it had perished in its formation. In vain I struggled to perfect – to regain it. Long suffering had nearly annihilated all my ordinary powers of mind. I was an imbecile – an idiot.

The vibration of the pendulum was at right angles to my length. I saw that the crescent was designed to cross the region of the heart. It would fray the serge of my robe – it would return and repeat its operations – again – and again. Notwithstanding its terrifically wide sweep (some thirty feet or more), and the hissing vigour of its descent, sufficient to sunder these very walls of iron, still the fraying of my robe would be all that, for several minutes, it would accomplish. And at this thought I paused. I dared not go further than this reflection. I dwelt upon it with a pertinacity of attention – as if, in so dwelling, I could arrest *here* the descent of the steel. I forced myself to ponder upon the sound of the crescent as it should pass across the garment – upon the peculiar thrilling sensation which the friction of cloth produces on the nerves. I pondered over all this frivolity until my teeth were on edge.

Down – steadily down it crept. I took a frenzied pleasure in contrasting its downward with its lateral velocity. To the right – to the left – far and wide – with the shriek of a damned spirit! to my heart, with the stealthy pace of the tiger! I alternately laughed and howled, as the one or the other idea grew predominant.

Down – certainly, relentlessly down! It vibrated within three inches of my bosom! I struggled violently – furiously – to free my left arm. This was free only from the elbow to the hand. I could reach the latter, from the platter beside me, to my mouth, with great effort, but no farther. Could I have broken the fastenings above the elbow, I would have seized and attempted to arrest the pendulum. I might as well have attempted to arrest an avalanche!

Down – still unceasingly – still inevitably down! I gasped and struggled at each vibration. I shrunk convulsively at its every sweep. My eyes followed its outward or upward whirls with the eagerness of the most unmeaning despair; they closed themselves spasmodically at the descent, although death would have been a relief, oh, how unspeakable! Still I quivered in every nerve to think how slight a sinking of the machinery would precipitate that keen, glistening axe upon my bosom. It was *hope* that prompted the nerve to quiver – the frame to shrink. It was *hope* – the hope that triumphs on the rack – that whispers to the death-condemned even in the dungeons of the Inquisition.

I saw that some ten or twelve vibrations would bring the steel in actual contact with my robe – and with this observation there suddenly came over my spirit all the keen, collected calmness of despair. For the first time during many hours – or perhaps days – I *thought*. It now occurred to me, that the bandage, or surcingle which, enveloped me, was *unique*. I was tied by no separate cord. The first stroke of the razor-like crescent athwart any portion of the band would so detach it that it might be unwound from my person by means of my left hand. But how fearful, in that case, the proximity of the steel! The result of the slightest struggle, how deadly! Was it likely, moreover, that the minions of the torturer had not foreseen and provided for this possibility? Was it probable that the bandage crossed my bosom in the track of the pendulum? Dreading to find my faint and, as it seemed, my last hope frustrated, I so far elevated my head as to obtain a distinct view of my breast. The surcingle enveloped my limbs and body close in all directions – *save in the path of the destroying crescent.*

Scarcely had I dropped my head back into its original position, when there flashed upon my mind what I cannot better describe than as the unformed half of that idea of deliverance to which I have previously alluded, and of which a moiety only floated indeterminately through my brain when I raised food to my burning lips. The whole thought was now present – feeble, scarcely sane, scarcely definite – but still entire. I proceeded at once, with the nervous energy of despair, to attempt its execution.

For many hours the immediate vicinity of the low framework upon which I lay had been literally swarming with rats. They were wild, bold, ravenous – their red eyes glaring upon me as if they waited but for motionlessness on my part to make me their prey. 'To what food,' I thought, 'have they been accustomed in the well?'

They had devoured, in spite of all my efforts to prevent them, all but a small remnant of the contents of the dish. I had fallen into an habitual see-saw or wave of the hand about the platter; and, at length, the unconscious uniformity of the movement deprived it of effort. In their voracity, the vermin frequently fastened their sharp fangs in my fingers. With the particles of the oily and spicy viand which now remained, I thoroughly rubbed the bandage wherever I could reach it; then, raising my hand from the floor, I lay breathlessly still.

At first, the ravenous animals were startled and terrified at the change – at the cessation of movement. They shrank alarmedly back; many sought the well. But this was only for a moment. I had not counted in vain upon their voracity. Observing that I remained without motion, one or two of the boldest leaped upon the framework, and smelt at the surcingle. This seemed the signal for a general rush. Forth from the well they hurried in fresh troops. They clung to the wood – they overran it, and leaped in hundreds upon my person. The measured movement of the pendulum disturbed them not at all. Avoiding its strokes, they busied themselves with the anointed bandage. They pressed – they swarmed upon me in ever accumulating heaps. They writhed upon my throat; their cold lips sought my own; I was half stifled by their thronging pressure; disgust, for which the world has no name, swelled my bosom, and chilled, with a heavy clamminess, my heart. Yet one minute, and I felt that the struggle would be over. Plainly I perceived the loosening of the bandage. I knew that in more than one place it must be already severed. With a more than human resolution I lay *still.*

Nor had I erred in my calculations – nor had I endured in vain. I at length felt that I was *free*. The surcingle hung in ribands from my body. But the stroke of the pendulum already pressed upon my bosom. It had divided the serge of the robe. It had cut through the linen beneath. Twice again it swung, and a sharp sense of pain shot through every nerve. But the moment of escape had arrived. At a wave of my hand my deliverers hurried tumultuously away. With a steady movement – cautious, sidelong, shrinking, and slow – I slid from the embrace of the bandage and beyond the reach of the scimitar. For the moment, at least, *I was free.*

Free! – and in the grasp of the Inquisition! I had scarcely stepped from my wooden bed of horror upon the stone floor of the prison, when the motion of the hellish machine ceased, and I beheld it drawn up, by some invisible force, through the ceiling. This was a lesson which I took desperately to heart. My every motion was undoubtedly watched. Free! – I had but escaped death in one form of agony, to be delivered unto worse than death in some other. With that thought I rolled my eyes nervously around on the barriers of iron that hemmed me in. Something unusual – some change, which, at first, I could not appreciate distinctly – it was obvious, had taken place in the apartment. For many minutes of a dreamy and trembling abstraction, I busied myself in vain, unconnected conjecture. During this period, I became aware, for the first time, of the origin of the sulphurous light which illumined the cell. It proceeded from a fissure, about half an inch in width, extending entirely around the prison at the base of the walls, which thus appeared, and were completely separated from the floor. I endeavoured, but of course in vain, to look through the aperture.

As I arose from the attempt, the mystery of the alteration in the chamber broke at once upon my understanding. I have observed that, although the outlines of the figures upon the walls were sufficiently distinct, yet the colours seemed blurred and indefinite. These colours had now assumed, and were momentarily assuming, a startling and most intense brilliancy, that gave to the spectral and fiendish portraitures an aspect that might have thrilled even firmer nerves than my own. Demon eyes, of a wild and ghastly vivacity, glared upon me in a thousand directions, where none had been visible before, and gleamed with the lurid lustre of a fire that I could not force my imagination to regard as unreal.

Unreal! – Even while I breathed there came to my nostrils the breath of the vapour of heated iron! A suffocating odour pervaded the prison! A deeper glow settled each moment in the eyes that glared at my agonies! A richer tint of crimson diffused itself over the pictured horrors of blood. I panted! I gasped for breath! There could be no doubt of the design of my tormentors – oh! most unrelenting! oh! most demoniac of men! I shrank from the glowing metal to the centre of the cell. Amid the thought of the fiery destruction that impended, the idea of the coolness of the well came over my soul like balm. I rushed to its deadly brink. I threw my straining vision below. The glare from the enkindled roof illumined its inmost recesses. Yet, for a wild moment, did my spirit refuse to comprehend the meaning of what I saw. At length it forced – it wrestled its way into my soul – it burned itself in upon my shuddering reason. Oh! for a voice to speak! – oh! horror! – oh! any horror but this! With a shriek, I rushed from the margin, and buried my face in my hands – weeping bitterly.

The heat rapidly increased, and once again I looked up, shuddering as with a fit of the ague. There had been a second change in the cell – and now the change was obviously in the *form*. As before, it was in vain that I at first endeavoured to appreciate or understand what was taking place. But not long was I left in doubt. The inquisitorial vengeance had been hurried by my two-fold escape, and there was to be no more dallying with the King of Terrors. The room had been square. I saw that two of its iron angles were now acute – two, consequently, obtuse. The fearful difference quickly increased with a low rumbling or moaning sound. In an instant the apartment had shifted its form into that of a lozenge. But the alteration stopped not here – I neither hoped or desired it to stop. I could have clasped the red walls to my bosom as a garment of eternal peace. 'Death,' I said, 'any death but that of the pit! Fool! might I not have known that *into the pit* it was the object of the burning iron to urge me? Could I resist its glow? or if even that, could I withstand its pressure? And now, flatter and flatter grew the lozenge, with a rapidity that left me no time for contemplation.

Its centre, and of course its greatest width, came just over the yawning gulf. I shrank back – but the closing walls pressed me resistlessly onward. At length for my seared and writhing body there was no longer an inch of foothold on the firm floor of the prison. I struggled no more, but the agony of my soul found vent in one loud, long, and final scream of despair. I felt that I tottered upon the brink – I averted my eyes –

There was a discordant hum of human voices! There was a loud blast as of many trumpets! There was a harsh grating as of a thousand thunders! The fiery walls rushed back! An outstretched arm caught my own as I fell, fainting, into the abyss. It was that of General Lasalle. The French army had entered Toledo. The Inquisition was in the hands of its enemies.

GUY DE MAUPASSANT

Boule de Suif

For several consecutive days, the remnants of a shattered army had been passing through the town. They were no longer a disciplined body, but a disorganized rabble. Their beards unkempt and neglected, their uniforms ragged, and the men, separated from their colours and their regiments, marched listlessly. All of them seemed crushed and worn out, incapable of thought or initiative. They marched on from mere force of habit and, as soon as a man stopped moving, he collapsed. The bulk of them were civilians who had been called to the colours, easy-going citizens, who seemed bent down by the weight of their rifles, or undersized conscripts of the last line, quick of apprehension, as prone to panic as to enthusiasm, as ready for attack as for flight. Some regular soldiers in red breeches, sole survivors of a division ground to powder in a great battle, and some sombre gunners, mingled with these nondescript infantry men, and here and there appeared the flashing helmet of a booted dragoon, with difficulty keeping pace with the more lightly shod foot-soldier.

Detachments of *francs-tireurs*, who looked like bandits but bore grandiloquent names, such as 'Avengers of Defeat,' 'Citizens of the Grave,' 'The Brotherhood of Death,' passed through in their turn. Their leaders, all flannel and gold lace and armed to the teeth, were retired drapers, corn chandlers, dealers in soap and tallow, who had turned soldier by force of circumstance, and had been elected officers by virtue of their money or their moustaches. In loud, braggart tones, they discussed plans of campaign, as though they alone were sustaining France in her death agony upon their vainglorious shoulders. But they went in fear of their own men, who were a ruffianly gang and, though often desperately brave, could not be withheld from looting and debauchery.

There was a rumour that the Prussians were about to enter Rouen. The National Guard, who, for the last two months, had been engaged in reconnoitring cautiously the neighbouring woods, sometimes shooting their own sentries, and preparing for action every time a rabbit stirred in a bush, had returned to their firesides. Their arms, their uniforms, all the apparatus of slaughter, with which they had formerly terrorized every milestone within a radius of three leagues, had suddenly vanished.

The last of the French army had just crossed the Seine, making for Pont-Audemer by way of Saint-Sever and Bourg-Achard. The rear was brought up by the general marching on foot between two aides-de-camp. In despair, unable to attempt anything with this medley of broken units, he felt overwhelmed in the utter ruin of a people, hitherto accustomed to victory, but now, despite its heroic prestige, disastrously defeated.

And now, a deep calm, an atmosphere of shuddering, silent apprehension brooded over the city. Many a plump citizen, whose manhood had been sapped by commerce, anxiously awaited the conquerors, in dread lest his spits and his big kitchen knives should be regarded as weapons. Life seemed at a standstill. The shops were closed; the streets silent. Here and there a stray citizen, awed by the stillness, hurried along, keeping close to the wall. Such was the agony of suspense that the arrival of the enemy was looked forward to as a relief.

On the afternoon of the day following the departure of the French troops, some Uhlans, sprung no one knew whence, galloped through the town. A little later, dark masses of troops came pouring down the hill of St Catherine, while two further torrents of invaders streamed along the roads from Darnetal and Boisguillaume. The advance guards of the three corps effected a well-timed junction in the square before the town hall, and down every street leading to the square the German army poured in, battalion after battalion, while the paved streets rang under their hard, measured tread.

Orders, shouted in strange guttural voices, resounded along the walls of houses, which seemed dead and deserted, though behind the closed shutters eyes were spying upon the victors, who by the rules of war were masters of the city, masters of the property and lives of all. In their darkened rooms, the inhabitants had succumbed to that dazed condition produced by natural cataclysms, devasting convulsions of the earth, against which neither strength nor wisdom avails. This sensation is experienced whenever the established order of things is over-turned, when no feeling of security remains, and all that is usually protected by the laws of men or nature is at the mercy of blind and brutal force. The earthquake burying a whole nation beneath the ruins of their houses; the river bursting its banks, drowning peasants and their cattle, tearing rafters from roofs and sweeping all away; the triumphant army slaughtering all who resist, making prisoners of the rest, pillaging in the name of the sword and giving thanks to God amid the roar of cannon: all alike are terrifying visitations which shatter our belief in eternal justice and the confidence we have been taught to place in divine protection and human reason.

Small squads of men knocked at the door of every house and disappeared inside. This was the occupation, the sequel of the invasion. It was now the duty of the vanquished to show themselves courteous to the conquerors.

When the first panic had subsided, a new sort of calm succeeded. In many families, the Prussian officer sat at table with his hosts. If he happened to be a well-bred man, he politely deplored the woes of France and expressed his personal repugnance to the war. His hosts were grateful for these generous sentiments, and, besides, any day they might need his protection. If they humoured him, they might perhaps have fewer men billeted on them. Why should they hurt the man's feelings when they were entirely in his power? To do so would be an act of foolhardiness rather than courage, and foolhardiness is no longer a defect in the character of the burgesses of Rouen, however it might have been in the days of the heroic defences which made their city illustrious. Eventually, appealing to the traditions of French urbanity, they reasoned that it was quite permissible to treat the alien soldier with courtesy within doors, provided that there was no fraternization in public. Though they did not recognize him in the street, at home they were ready to talk to him, and the German soldier sat longer and longer every evening, warming himself at the domestic hearth.

Little by little, the town itself began to resume its normal appearance. For the present, the French population remained indoors, but the streets were swarming with Prussian soldiers. After all, the officers of the Blue Hussars, arrogantly trailing their great sabres along the pavement, did not treat the plain townsmen so very much more contemptuously than did their own light cavalry officers, who had sat drinking in the same cafés the year before.

Yet for all that there was something in the air, some indefinable and subtle quality, a strange and intolerable atmosphere, a diffused exhalation – the effluvium of invasion. It penetrated into private houses and public places, tainting the food, producing an unhomelike feeling, as of exile in distant lands among tribes of hostile savages.

The victorious army demanded money, vast sums of money. The inhabitants went on paying up, and indeed they could afford to do so. But the wealthier he is, the more keenly the Norman trader feels the smallest sacrifice, the transfer of the least fraction of his property into the hands of another.

It was true that a few miles down the Seine, in the vicinity of Croisset, Dieppedalle or Biessart, bargemen and fishermen often brought up from the bottom the bloated corpse of a German soldier in uniform, who had been stabbed or kicked to death, or pushed into the water off a bridge, or had had his head battered in by a stone. The mud of the river engulfed the victims of these surreptitious acts of vengeance, savage yet justifiable, these deeds of obscure heroism, these secret assaults, more perilous than open battle and without the meed of fame. Hatred of the foreigner will always nerve some valiant soul to die for an idea.

At length, finding that the invaders, although subjecting the town to rigorous discipline, had not perpetrated any of the atrocities with which rumour had credited them throughout the whole course of their triumphant march, the population plucked up courage and the tradesmen's business instincts began to revive. Some of them had weighty interests at Havre, which was still held by the French, and were anxious to make an attempt to reach that port, travelling overland to Dieppe and embarking there. Through the influence of German officers, whose acquaintance they had made, a permit for leaving Rouen could be obtained from the general in command.

A large four-horse coach was accordingly engaged for the journey; ten persons had reserved seats in it, and it was agreed to set out one Tuesday morning, before daybreak, so as to avoid exciting attention. For some time there had been a hard frost; on the Monday afternoon great black clouds gathered from the north, and snow fell incessantly all that evening and the following night.

At half-past four in the morning, the travellers met in the yard of the Hôtel de Normandie, where they were to take the coach. They were still half asleep and shivered with cold under their wraps. It was too dark for them to see one another clearly. Under their accumulations of heavy winter clothes, they all resembled corpulent priests in long cassocks. Two men, however, recognized each other; a third joined them, and they entered into conversation.

'I have brought my wife,' said one.

'So have I.'

'And I, too.'

The first speaker added: 'We don't intend returning to Rouen. If the Prussians advance on Havre we shall make our way to England.'

All three were of the same pattern and had the same plans.

Meanwhile, there was no sign of the horses. An ostler carrying a little lantern emerged from time to time from one mysterious door only to disappear through another. Horses' hoofs could be heard stamping on the ground, the noise muffled by stable litter, and from the far end of the building came the voice of a man talking to the animals and swearing. The tinkling of little bells proclaimed that the harness was being got ready, and this sound soon developed into a clear, continuous jingling, in rhythm with the horses' movements, now and then ceasing, only to begin again with a sudden jerk, to the accompaniment of the dull clang of an iron-shod hoof on the stable floor. The door suddenly closed and everything was still. The half-frozen travellers stopped talking and stood there stiff and motionless. A curtain of glistening snow-flakes descended towards the earth, veiling every human form and covering inanimate objects with an icy fleece. In the intense stillness of the town, plunged in the deep repose of winter, no sound was audible save that vague, indefinable, fluttering whisper of the falling snow, felt rather than heard, the mingling of airy atoms, which seemed to fill all space and envelop the whole world.

The man with the lantern reappeared, dragging along by a rope a dejected and reluctant horse. He put the horse along-side the carriage-pole and spent a long time adjusting the harness, for he could only use one hand, as the other held the light. As he was going off to fetch the second horse, he noticed the travellers all standing there motionless and already white with snow.

'Why don't you get inside the coach?' he said. 'You would at least be under cover.'

Apparently this had not occurred to them, and they made a rush for the coach. The three husbands installed their wives at the far end and seated themselves beside them. The other veiled and vague forms took the remaining places without uttering a word.

Their feet sank into the straw which covered the floor. The ladies at the far end had brought little copper foot-warmers with a chemical preparation of charcoal which they lighted, and for some time, in subdued voices, they dwelt upon the advantages of these apparatuses, assuring one another of facts of which they had all long been aware.

At last the coach was ready. It had a team of six horses instead of four in consideration of the bad state of the roads. A voice from without asked: 'Is every one in?' A voice from within replied: 'Yes,' and they set off.

The progress of the coach was laborious and very slow. The wheels sank into the snow. Every joint in the whole structure creaked and moaned. The smoking horses slipped and panted, the driver's immense whip cracked incessantly, flickering in all directions, now tying itself into knots and uncoiling itself again like a slender snake, now stinging a bulging hind quarter and inciting its owner to more strenuous efforts. Imperceptibly, day began to dawn. The fall of ethereal snow-flakes, which one of the travellers, a true-born native of Rouen, had compared to a shower of cotton, had ceased. A livid light filtered through the dense and lowering clouds, whose blackness set off the dazzling whiteness of the landscape. Here and there stood out a row of tall, frosted trees, or a cottage under a hood of snow.

Inside the carriage, the passengers scrutinized one another inquisitively by the melancholy light of dawn.

Dozing opposite each other in the best places at the end sat Monsieur and Madame Loiseau, wholesale wine merchants of the Rue Grand-pont. Originally a clerk in an office, after his employer's bankruptcy, Loiseau had bought the business and made a fortune. He sold very bad wine at very low prices to small retailers in country places. He was regarded by his friends and acquaintances as a knowing rascal and a true Norman, a jovial fellow, up to every dodge. His reputation for sharp practice was so notorious that one evening at a party at the Prefecture, Monsieur Tournel, a local celebrity, author of some songs and stories and a man of shrewd and caustic wit, proposed to the ladies, who seemed to him somewhat drowsy, a game of *Loiseau vole*, 'The bird steals away.' The jest flew through the Prefect's drawing-rooms and thence to all the other drawing-rooms in the town, and for a month it set the whole province laughing. Loiseau himself was famous for practical jokes of all kinds, good-natured and otherwise, so that no one mentioned his name without adding: 'That fellow Loiseau is really priceless.' He was short, his stomach bulged like a balloon and was surmounted by a red face fringed with grizzled whiskers. His wife, a tall, stout, determined woman, loud-voiced and positive, was the methodical and financial factor in the business, while he brought to it his own exuberant vitality.

Next to them, with the dignity of a higher class, sat Monsieur Carré-Lamadon, a man of good standing in the cotton business, owner of three spinning-mills, officer of the Legion of Honour and member of the Conseil Général. Under the Empire, he posed as leader of a benevolent opposition, solely in order to sell at a higher price his desertion to the side against which he had fought, though always, as he said, with weapons of courtesy. Madame Carré-Lamadon was much younger than her husband. She had been a great comfort to officers of good family, garrisoned at Rouen. A slight, dainty figure, muffled in furs, she sat opposite her husband, staring disconsolately at the deplorable interior of the coach.

Their neighbours were the Count and Countess Hubert de Bréville, who bore one of the oldest and most aristocratic names in Normandy. The count, an old nobleman of dignified demeanour, took pains to accentuate by tricks of the toilet his natural likeness to King Henry IV. According to a legend of which the family were very proud, that monarch had seduced a Madame de Bréville, and in return, had made her husband a count and governor of a province. He was associated with Monsieur Carré-Lamadon on the Conseil Général, and was the local representative of the Orléanist party. The story of his marriage with the daughter of a petty shipowner of Nantes had always been a mystery. But thanks to her stately air, her genius for entertaining, and the rumour that one of the sons of Louis Philippe had been her lover, all the local *noblesse* paid court to her. Her *salon* held its own as the first in the neighbourhood. Access to it was not easy, and it was the only drawing-room where old-world courtesy survived. The fortune of the Brévilles, all in landed estate, was said to yield an income of half a million francs.

These six were the backbone of the party. They represented the wealthy, placid, solid element of society, respectable, influential persons of religion and principle.

It so happened that all the women were seated on the same side. Next to the countess sat two nuns telling their long rosaries and muttering paternosters and aves. One of them was old; her skin was deeply pitted with smallpox as if she had received a charge of shot full in the face. Her companion was a puny creature with a pretty but sickly face and the narrow chest of a consumptive, a prey to that burning faith which creates visionaries and martyrs.

Opposite the two nuns sat a man and a woman who excited every one's interest. The man was Cornudet, a notorious democrat, the terror of all respectable people. For the last twenty years he had been dipping his long red beard in mugs of beer at every democratic pothouse. With the help of his boon companions, he had frittered away a respectable fortune which he had inherited from his father, a retired confectioner; and he looked forward eagerly to the coming of the Republic, when he would enter upon the office he had earned by all his libations to the Revolution. On the fourth of September, probably in consequence of a practical joke, he got the idea into his head that he had been elected prefect; but when he essayed to take up his duties, the clerks at the prefecture, who remained in sole possession, refused to recognize him and he was forced to beat a retreat. For all that, he was a very good fellow, harmless and obliging, and he had thrown himself heart and soul into organizing the defence of the town. He had had pits dug in the open country, had had all the young trees in the neighbouring forests cut down and traps set on all the roads, and, satisfied with his preparations, he had, at the approach of the enemy, scuttled back to the city. He felt now that he would be more useful at Havre, where fresh entrenchments would be needed.

The woman beside him was one of those who are technically called gay. She was famous for her premature portliness, which had earned for her the nickname of Boule de Suif, ball of lard, 'tallow-keech.' Short, perfectly spherical, fat as dripping, with puffy fingers, dented at the joints like strings of sausages, her skin shining and smooth, her enormous breasts swelling beneath her bodice, she had nevertheless remained so fresh and blooming that she continued to fascinate and allure. Her face was like a ruddy apple or a peony bud ready to burst into flower. Her magnificent black eyes were shaded and deepened by long, thick lashes. Her charming, pouting mouth, ripe for kisses, revealed two rows of tiny dazzling teeth. It was whispered that she had many other priceless qualities.

As soon as they recognized her, the respectable women began to murmur among themselves, and the words 'prostitute,' 'open shame' were whispered so audibly that she looked up. She bestowed upon her companions a glance so bold and challenging that a deep silence ensued and every one sat with downcast eyes, except Loiseau, who stole arch glances at her.

But very soon, the three ladies, united in a sudden friendship verging on intimacy by the intrusion of that brazen hussy, resumed their conversation. They felt that they must ensconce themselves behind the dignity of their wedded estate in face of this shameless hireling. For legalized love always assumes airs of superiority over its random brother.

The three husbands, on the other hand, were drawn together by a common defensive instinct at the sight of Cornudet. They discussed money matters in tones that implied their scorn of poorer folk. Count Hubert alluded to the losses in stolen cattle and ruined crops he had sustained at the hands of the Prussians in the negligent manner of a magnate worth ten millions, who is fully aware that the inconvenience will hardly be felt in a year's time.

Monsieur Carré-Lamadon, a cotton merchant of wide experience, had taken the precaution to send to England six hundred thousand francs as a provision for a rainy day. As for Loiseau, he had arranged to sell to the French Commissariat all the common wines still in his cellars, so that the State owed him a handsome sum which he counted on receiving at Havre.

The three men exchanged quick, friendly glances. Though of different standing, they were linked together by the common tie of money, members of that wide freemasonry of the well-to-do who can thrust their hands into their trouser pockets and jingle the gold there.

The coach moved so slowly that by ten o'clock they had not accomplished more than ten miles. On three occasions, the men got out and walked up the hills. They all began to feel uneasy. They had intended to lunch at Tôtes, but they had small hopes now of arriving there before nightfall. Every one was on the look out for a wayside inn, when the diligence plunged into a snowdrift from which they were not extricated for two hours. Their increasing hunger began to depress their spirits. There was no sign of the meanest tavern or wine shop; all the tradespeople had fled in terror before the advance of the Prussians and the retreat of the starving French troops. The men tried to get food from the farm-houses by the roadside, but could not obtain even plain bread, for the cautious peasants had hidden away their stores for fear of being plundered by the soldiers, desperate with hunger, who seized by force anything they could lay their hands on. Towards one o'clock, Loiseau announced that he was distinctly conscious of a painful vacuum in his interior. For some time every one had been suffering from the same complaint, and the steadily increasing pangs of hunger had put a stop to conversation. From time to time, one of the travellers yawned; and another would follow suit. One after the other, in accord with individual character, manners, and social position, they opened their mouths, some noisily, others quietly, hastily putting their hands up to hide the gaping chasm from which the breath issued in a cloud of steam.

Boule de Suif stooped down now and then as if looking for something under her petticoats. She would hesitate for a moment, glance at her neighbours, then quietly sit up again. The faces of all the travellers were pale and drawn. Loiseau vowed that he would give a thousand francs for a knuckle of ham. His wife made as if to protest but restrained herself. It was always painful to her to hear of money being squandered and she could not bear even a joke on that subject.

'I don't feel at all well,' said the count. 'Why didn't I think of bringing some provisions?'

Every one blamed himself for the same omission. Cornudet, however, had a flask of rum; he offered it to his companions, but they coldly declined. Loiseau alone took a couple of sips and thanked him as he returned the flask:

'That's some good, anyhow; it warms one up and cheats one's hunger.'

The spirits put him in a good humour, and he suggested that they should do as they did in the song about the little boat, eat the fattest of the company. This sly allusion to Boule de Suif shocked his more refined companions. They made no reply; only Cornudet smiled. The two nuns had left off telling their beads; they sat motionless, their hands thrust into their long sleeves; their eyes steadfastly downcast, doubtless offering as a sacrifice to Heaven the sufferings which it had imposed upon them.

At last, at three o'clock, when the coach was making its way across an interminable plain without a village in sight, Boule de Suif briskly bent down and drew from under the seat a large basket covered with a white napkin. First she took from it a little earthenware plate, next a dainty silver cup, and then a large dish containing two carved fowls embedded in their jelly. The basket revealed glimpses of other good things carefully packed – pies, fruit, dainties, sufficient provisions for a three days' journey without having to fall back on the cookery of the inns.

The necks of four bottles protruded from among the parcels of food. Taking the wing of a chicken, she began daintily to eat it, with one of those rolls of bread called *régence* in Normandy.

All eyes were fixed on her. The pleasant aroma of food was wafted abroad, and the result was seen in distended nostrils, watering mouths, and spasmodic contractions of the muscles of the jaw.

The ladies' contempt for the hussy rose to a fury; they were yearning to kill her or throw her out of the carriage into the snow, her, and her cup and her basket and her provisions.

Loiseau's eyes devoured the dish of fowls.

'Congratulations!' he said. 'Madame has been more foreseeing than the rest of us. Some people always think of everything.'

She turned towards him.

'Will you have some, sir?' she asked. 'It is hard to go fasting all day.'

He bowed.

'Frankly,' he replied, 'I cannot refuse; I am at my last gasp. Any port in a storm, as they say.' And casting a glance around him, he added: 'One is lucky to find a friend in need on an occasion like this.'

He spread a newspaper over his knees to save his trousers, and, with the point of a knife which he always carried in his pocket, he transfixed a leg of chicken thickly coated with jelly, tore at it with his teeth, and chewed it with such obvious enjoyment that his companions could not restrain a deep sigh of anguish.

In a low, gentle voice, Boule de Suif invited the two nuns to share her meal. They accepted with alacrity and, without raising their eyes, murmured their thanks and quickly set to work. Nor did Cornudet decline his neighbour's invitation, and between them they made a sort of table by spreading newspapers on their knees. Their jaws worked feverishly; they chewed and swallowed the food with ravenous haste.

Loiseau, busy in his corner, quietly pressed his wife to follow his example. She held out for a long time, but at last a piercing pang of hunger induced her to give way. Her husband with a well-turned phrase asked his 'charming companion' if he might offer Madame Loiseau a small portion.

'Why, certainly, sir,' she replied, with a pleasant smile, and handed him the dish.

A difficulty arose when the first bottle of Bordeaux was opened; there was only one cup. But they passed it round, each wiping it in turn. Cornudet alone, in a spirit of gallantry, set his lips to the rim still moist from the lips of his fair neighbour.

With people eating and drinking all around them, the Count and Countess de Bréville and Monsieur and Madame Carré-Lamadon, enveloped in the odour of food, endured the torments of Tantalus. Suddenly the manufacturer's wife gave a sigh which drew every one's attention. She was as white as the snow outside; her eyes closed, her head drooped, she had fainted. Her distracted husband uttered a general appeal for help. The other passengers were utterly at a loss, but the elder nun raised the patient's head, held Boule de Suif's cup to her lips, and induced her to swallow a few drops of wine. The pretty creature moved, opened her eyes, smiled, and in a faint voice declared that she felt perfectly well again. But, as a precaution, the nun made her drink a whole glass of Bordeaux, saying:

'It is nothing but sheer hunger.'

Blushing in confusion, Boule de Suif looked at the four travellers who were still fasting, and stammered out:

'Oh, dear, if only I might venture to offer these ladies and gentlemen . . .' She broke off, in dread of a snub.

Loiseau took the floor:

'Upon my soul, in cases like this, we are all brothers and should help one another. Come, ladies, the devil take ceremony; accept her offer. Why, we don't know whether we shall even find a night's lodging. At this rate, we shan't be at Tôtes before midday to-morrow.'

They all hesitated, no one caring to take the responsibility of saying 'Yes.'

It was the count who cut the knot. Turning to the embarrassed young women, and assuming his grandest air, he said:

'Madame, we gratefully accept your offer.'

The first step was the only difficulty. The Rubicon once crossed, they fell to with a will. The basket was emptied. It still contained a *pâté de foie gras*, a *pâté* of larks, smoked tongue, some Crassane pears, a Pont l'Évêque cheese, some little cakes, and a jar of pickled gherkins and onions. For, like all women, Boule de Suif had a taste for crude flavours.

It was impossible to eat the woman's food and not talk to her. They entered into conversation, at first with some reserve, but presently, in view of her admirable behaviour, with increasing freedom. Madame de Bréville and Madame Carré-Lamadon, who were women of the world, were tactful and courteous. The countess, in particular, treated Boule de Suif with the gracious condescension of very great ladies, whom no touch can soil, and was charming to her. Only stout Madame Loiseau, who had the soul of a gendarme, remained obdurate, saying little but eating all the more.

The conversation turned naturally upon the war, the horrors perpetrated by the Prussians, and the gallant deeds of the French. All these people, who were running away, paid tribute to the courage of those who remained behind. Presently they came to personal experiences, and Boule de Suif, with real feeling and that fervent eloquence that sometimes characterizes her class when carried away by emotion, gave her reasons for leaving Rouen:

'At first, I thought I could stay. My house was well stocked with food and I preferred to feed a few soldiers rather than go into exile, God knows where. But when I saw those Prussians, it was too much for me. They made my blood boil, and I cried with shame all day long. Oh, if only I were a man! I watched them out of my window, those fat swine with their spiked helmets, and my maid had to hold my hands to stop me from hurling chairs and tables on their heads. Then some of them were billeted on me. I sprang at the throat of the first one; they are no more difficult to strangle than any one else. I should have done for him too if they had not dragged me off by my hair. After that I had to hide. So when I saw a chance, I came away, and here I am.'

They congratulated her warmly. She rose in the estimation of her companions, who had not shown such pluck. Cornudet listened to her with a benevolent and apostolic smile, like a priest who hears one of his flock praising God, for these long-bearded democrats think they have the monopoly of patriotism just as the men in cassocks are monopolists in religion. Speaking in his turn, he laid down the law with a pomposity borrowed from the proclamations posted up on the walls day after day; and he wound up with a burst of eloquence, in which he inveighed magisterially against that blackguard Badinguet, as he designated Napoleon III.

But Boule de Suif at once fired up, for she was a Bonapartist. She flushed as red as a cherry and stammered with rage: 'I should just like to see fellows like you in his position. A nice mess you would have made of it. It's your sort who betrayed the man. There would be nothing for it but to leave France if it were governed by scoundrels like you.'

Cornudet was unmoved and continued to smile his disdainful superior smile. But a violent outburst of abuse was only averted by the count, who, not without difficulty, contrived to pacify the angry young woman, authoritatively declaring that all sincere opinions were entitled to respect. But the countess and Madame Carré-Lamadon, who cherished the unreasonable hatred felt by all respectable people for the Republic, and the instinctive devotion with which every woman regards despotic governments with their pomps and ceremonies, felt themselves involuntarily drawn towards this prostitute of unbending convictions and sentiments so closely allied to their own.

The basket was empty. Ten hungry people had made short work of its contents. Their only regret was that it had not been larger. Conversation continued for a while, but it grew more constrained when the repast was over.

Night fell; the darkness gradually deepened, and the cold, always more keenly felt after a meal, made Boule de Suif shiver, well-covered though she was. At this, Madame de Bréville offered her her foot-warmer, in which the charcoal had been renewed several times since the morning. Boule de Suif accepted it with alacrity as her feet were like ice. Madame Carré-Lamadon and Madame Loiseau gave their foot-warmers to the two nuns.

The driver had lighted the lamps, which cast a vivid glare upon the cloud of steam rising from the reeking quarters of the wheelers, and upon the roadside snow which seemed to be unrolling itself under the shifting radiance. Within the carriage all was dark, but suddenly there was some by-play between Boule de Suif and Cornudet. Loiseau, straining his eyes through the gloom, thought he saw the man with the long beard start violently away, as if he had received a forcible but noiseless cuff.

On the road ahead, little points of light began to twinkle. It was Tôtes. They had been thirteen hours on the way, including four halts of half an hour each to rest and feed the horses. They entered the town and drew up at the Hôtel du Commerce.

The door of the carriage was flung open. A familiar sound made all the travellers shudder. It was the jingling of a scabbard on the ground. At the same time they heard an exclamation in a German voice.

Though the coach had stopped, no one got out. It was as if the travellers expected to be massacred as soon as they emerged. Then the driver came to the door, flashing his lamps into the farthest recesses of the coach and lighting up two rows of frightened faces with open mouths and eyes bulging with surprise and terror. Beside the driver, in the full glare of the lamp, stood a German officer, a tall, fair young man, extremely slender, squeezed into his uniform like a girl into her corset, wearing on one side his polished flat cap which gave him the appearance of a porter at an English hotel. His huge, long, straight moustache tapered on either side to a point consisting of a single yellow hair, so fine that the extremity was invisible. Its weight seemed to depress the corners of his mouth and by dragging down his cheeks to give to his lips the appearance of drooping. In the French of Alsace, he invited the travellers to alight, saying in a severe voice:

'Will you get out, ladies and gentlemen?'

The two nuns were the first to obey, with the docility of women habituated by their vows to implicit obedience. Next came the count and countess, followed by the manufacturer and his wife; then Loiseau, pushing his better half before him. When he set foot on the ground, Loiseau, from prudence rather than politeness, said to the officer: 'Good evening, sir.' The latter, with the insolence of authority, stared at him without reply. Boule de Suif and Cornudet, though nearest to the door, were the last to emerge, confronting the enemy with a grave and lofty air. The stout young woman endeavoured to control herself and to remain calm. The democrat twisted his long red beard with a histrionic gesture, defiant, yet timid. Conscious that in an encounter such as this, each individual is in some measure the representative of his country, they were anxious to preserve their dignity. Both alike were disgusted at their companions' servility. Boule de Suif desired to prove herself of loftier spirit than those honest women, her fellow-travellers, while Cornudet, realizing that it behoved him to set an example, continued by his attitude the task of resistance which he had begun when he dug up the roads. They went into the great kitchen of the inn, where the German officer, having demanded their permit for departure, signed by the general in command, in which were set forth the names, description, and profession of each of the travellers, minutely examined them all, comparing their appearance with the written record. Then he said abruptly: 'All right!' and disappeared.

They breathed once more. Being still hungry, they ordered supper. It was promised in half an hour; and while two maids were busy preparing it, they went to look at the bedrooms, all of which opened into a long passage, with a glazed door at the end.

Just as they were sitting down to supper, the host appeared. He was a retired horse-dealer, a stout man troubled with asthma, constantly wheezing, coughing and clearing his throat. His father had bequeathed to him the name of Follenvie.

'Mademoiselle Élisabeth Rousset?' he asked.

Boule de Suif turned to him in alarm.

'Yes?'

'Mademoiselle, the Prussian officer wishes to speak to you at once.'

'To me?'

'Yes, if you are really Mademoiselle Élisabeth Rousset?'

She hesitated for a moment in dismay, then she said roundly: 'He may want me, but I shan't go.'

This caused a sensation among the company. Every one gave his opinion, discussing the reason for the summons. The count went up to Boule de Suif:

'You are wrong, madam; for your refusal may have serious consequences, not only for yourself but all your companions. One should never resist those who have the upper hand. Compliance surely cannot involve you in any danger; no doubt it is on account of some formality which has been omitted.'

The others seconded him; they begged, urged, and lectured Boule de Suif till finally they persuaded her. For they dreaded the complications which might result from her rashness. At last she said:

'Well, remember it's for your sakes I do.'

The countess clasped her hand.

'You have our grateful thanks,' she said.

Boule de Suif left the room. The others awaited her return before sitting down to supper. Every one regretted not having been sent for instead of that headstrong, passionate girl, and each rehearsed in his mind suitable platitudes in case he should be summoned in his turn. In ten minutes' time, she returned breathless, scarlet in the face, choking with rage and gasping out: 'The cad! The cad!'

They were eager to hear what had happened, but she would not say a word. And when the count insisted, she replied with much dignity:

'No, it doesn't concern you; I can't tell you.'

They gathered round a large soup-tureen which emitted a a smell of cabbage. In spite of the disturbing incident, it was a merry supper. The cider was good. Monsieur and Madame

Loiseau and the nuns drank it from motives of economy. All the others sent for wine, except Cornudet, who demanded beer. He had his own way of opening the bottle, frothing up the liquor and contemplating it, first tilting his glass, then holding it up to the light to admire the colour. When he drank, his long beard, which was tinged with the colour of his favourite beverage, seemed to quiver with emotion; he squinted in his anxiety not to lose sight of his mug, and it seemed as if he were discharging the one function for which he had been created. One felt that he was effecting in his mind a junction; establishing an affinity between the two ruling passions of his life: Pale Ale and the Revolution. Clearly he could not taste the one without thinking of the other.

Monsieur and Madame Follenvie supped at the other end of the table. The innkeeper, wheezing like a broken-winded engine, suffered from a constriction of the chest, which prevented him from talking while he ate; but his wife's tongue clacked without ceasing. She gave a detailed account of all her feelings on the arrival of the Prussians; of everything they had done and said, abusing them first because they cost her money, next because she had two sons in the army. She addressed most of her remarks to the countess, flattered by the thought that she was speaking to a lady of quality. Presently she lowered her voice and entered upon such delicate topics, that her husband, every now and then, interrupted her with: 'You had much better keep quiet, Madame Follenvie!' But she paid no attention to him, and went on:

'Yes, madam, those fellows do nothing but eat potatoes and pork, and then more pork and potatoes. And they have filthy habits, and if you could only see them drilling in a field, hour after hour, day after day, marching and wheeling and turning in all directions. It isn't as if they worked on the land or mended the roads in their own country. No, madam, these soldiers are of no use to any one. And yet the poor have to support them, simply for them to learn how to slaughter people. It's true I'm only an ignorant old woman; but when I see these men wearing themselves out, tramping about from morning till night, I say to myself: "When there are people finding out so many useful things, why should others take all that trouble to destroy? Isn't it really abominable to kill people, whether they are Prussians or English or Poles or French? If you take revenge on someone who has wronged you, it's a crime, or you wouldn't be punished; but if you shoot down our lads like game, I suppose it's all right, as those who kill most are given decorations." I tell you, it's a thing I shall never understand.'

Cornudet raised his voice:

'War is barbarous when it's an attack on a peaceful neighbour. It is a sacred duty in the defence of one's country.'

The old woman nodded:

'Oh, yes, self-defence is quite another thing. But wouldn't it be better to kill all the kings, who make war for their own pleasure?'

Cornudet's eyes flashed.

'Bravo, citizeness,' he cried.

Monsieur Carré-Lamadon was plunged in deep thought. Though he had a passionate admiration for great soldiers, this peasant woman's common sense made him think of all the wealth that would accrue to a country, if all these idle hands, now a drain on its finances, all the sterile power it had to maintain, were employed on vast industrial enterprises, which in the present circumstances it would take centuries to achieve.

Loiseau, however, left his chair for a quiet talk with the fat innkeeper, who laughed and coughed and spat; his enormous paunch quivered with joy at his neighbour's jests, and he gave him an order for six half-hogsheads of Bordeaux to be delivered in the spring after the Prussians had gone.

Supper was hardly finished when the travellers, tired to death, went off to bed.

But Loiseau had been taking everything in. He sent his wife to bed and then applied ear and eye by turns to the keyhole with a view to discovering what he called 'the mysteries of the corridor.'

After about an hour, he heard a rustling sound, and hastily peeping out he saw Boule de Suif, looking fatter than ever in a blue cashmere dressing-gown, trimmed with white lace. She carried a candle and was making for the glazed door at the end of the corridor. Another door was cautiously opened, and when she presently returned, Cornudet came out in his shirtsleeves and followed her. There was a whispered conversation; then they came to a standstill. Boule de Suif seemed to be protesting energetically against Cornudet's entry into her bedroom. Loiseau was unfortunately unable to hear all that was said, but as they raised their voices, he at last caught a word here and there. Cornudet was insisting eagerly.

'Come now, don't be silly,' he said. 'What can it matter to you?'

She answered indignantly:

'No, my dear, there are times when these things are not done. Just now, it would be scandalous!'

Evidently he did not see her point, and pressed her for a reason. Roused to wrath, she exclaimed in still louder tones:

'You ask why? Don't you see why? When there are Prussians in the house, perhaps even in the next room!'

He was silenced. The patriotic delicacy of this poor outcast, who would not submit to an embrace while the enemy was within the gates, must have revived his waning sense of decency; for, after one kiss, he tiptoed back to his own room.

His senses stirred, Loiseau left the key-hole, cut a caper about the room, put on his night-cap, and turning back the sheet which covered the gaunt form of his spouse, woke her with a kiss, murmuring:

'Do you love me, darling?'

Silence then fell on the house. But soon there arose from some quarter difficult to define, which might have been the cellar or the garret, a powerful, monotonous, rhythmic snore, long drawn out, and vibrant as an engine boiler under pressure. Monsieur Follenvie slept.

As it had been arranged to start at eight o'clock the next morning, the party assembled in the kitchen at an early hour. But the coach, its top covered with snow, stood forlornly in the middle of the courtyard without horses or driver. They hunted vainly for the latter in stables, granary, and coach-house. The men then decided to go out and scour the country for him. They reached the market-place with the church at its far end, and on either side a row of low-roofed houses, where they caught sight of Prussian soldiers. The first one they saw was peeling potatoes. The next, a little farther on, was washing down the barber's shop. Another bearded warrior was petting a tiny child and endeavouring to check its tears by rocking it on his knees. The buxom peasant women, whose men had gone to the war, indicated by means of signs what tasks they desired their docile conquerors to undertake: wood to be split, or the coffee to be ground, or the soup to be poured on the bread. One soldier was actually doing the washing for his hostess, a helpless old grandam.

In surprise, the count questioned the beadle as he came out of the presbytery. The old church rat replied:

'Oh, this lot are not at all bad; they are not Prussians, I'm told, but come from farther off, I don't exactly know where. And every man of them has left a wife and children in his own country. The war is no joke to them, I'll be bound. Their women, too, are crying for their men-folk and are every bit as miserable as our own women here. However, just now we are not so badly off; the soldiers do no harm and are ready for any odd job just as if they were at home. You see, sir, poor folk must help one another. It is the great ones who make the wars.'

Cornudet felt indignant at the friendly feeling that united conquerors and conquered, and went off, preferring to shut himself up in the inn. Loiseau had his little joke:

'They are restocking the country.'

But Monsieur Carré-Lamadon solemnly said:

'They are making reparation.'

The driver was nowhere to be seen. At last they ran him to earth in the village café, fraternizing with the officer's orderly. The count addressed him:

'Weren't you ordered to have the carriage ready by eight o'clock?'

'Yes, to be sure, but I had another order afterwards.'

'What order?'

'Not to get ready at all.'

'Who gave you that order?'

'Why, the Prussian commandant.'

'For what reason?'

'I don't know. Go and ask him. I was told not to get it ready. So I didn't, and there you are.'

'Did he give you the order in person?'

'No, sir, it was through the innkeeper.'

'When was that?'

'Yesterday evening, as I was going to bed.'

The three men returned to the inn, feeling very uneasy. They asked for Monsieur Follenvie, but the maid answered that her master, on account of his asthma, never got up before ten o'clock. He had given strict orders that he was never to be called at an earlier hour, except in case of fire. They then desired to see the officer, but that was absolutely out of the question, although he was staying in the hotel. Monsieur Follenvie alone was authorized to speak to him on civil business. So they had to wait. The ladies went back to their rooms and passed the time in trifling occupations.

Cornudet installed himself in the kitchen chimney corner, where a mighty fire was blazing. A pot of beer stood on a table in front of him; and he took out his pipe which, in democratic circles, was regarded with almost as much respect as its owner, as if in serving Cornudet it served the State. It was a fine meerschaum with a curved stem, beautifully coloured, as black as its master's teeth, redolent and shining, an old friend and a characteristic adjunct to his physiognomy. He sat perfectly still, his eyes now on the blazing hearth, now on the froth of his mug of beer, and whenever he had taken a pull he would pass his long, lean fingers through his greasy locks, while he sucked the froth from his moustache with an air of content.

Under pretext of stretching his legs, Loiseau went out to sell his wine to the local retailers. The count and the manufacturer talked politics and speculated as to the future of France. The one believed in the house of Orleans, the other looked for an unknown saviour, a hero who would come to the rescue when all seemed lost, a du Guesclin, perhaps, or a Joan of Arc, or a second Napoleon. Ah, if only the Prince Imperial were not so young! Cornudet listened with the smile of one who knows the secrets of destiny. The aroma of his pipe filled the kitchen.

On the stroke of ten, Monsieur Follenvie appeared. To their eager questions, he had only one reply, which he repeated two or three times.

'The officer said to me just like this: "Monsieur Follenvie, you will give orders not to have the carriage ready to-morrow for those travellers. I do not wish them to proceed without my consent. You understand? . . . Very good!"'

They then asked to see the officer. The count sent in his card, on which Monsieur Carré-Lamadon had written his name and all his distinctions. The Prussian sent word that he would receive them after luncheon, about one o'clock.

The ladies came down and, in spite of their uneasiness, they partook of a light meal. Boule de Suif seemed out of sorts and terribly worried. As they were finishing their coffee, the orderly came for the two gentlemen, and Loiseau joined the count and Monsieur Carré-Lamadon. They tried to enlist Cornudet to add weight to the deputation, but he declared haughtily that he was resolved never to hold any communication with Germans; and he sat down again in his chimney corner, and called for another pot of beer.

The three men went upstairs and were ushered into the best room of the inn, where the officer received them. Lolling in an arm-chair, with both feet on the mantelpiece, he was smoking a long porcelain pipe and was wrapped in a gaudy dressing-gown, doubtless looted from the deserted house of some middle-class person of execrable taste. He neither rose nor saluted, nor even looked at them. He was a perfect specimen of the insolence which is natural to a victorious soldiery.

At last, after some moments had elapsed, he said:

'What do you want?'

The count was the spokesman:

'Sir, we wish to continue our journey.'

'You can't.'

'Might I venture to ask the reason of your refusal?'

'I don't wish you to go.'

'I would respectfully bring to your notice, sir, that the general in command has given us a permit to go to Dieppe; I am not aware that we have done anything to deserve this harsh treatment.'

'I don't wish it. That's all. You may go.'

The three delegates bowed and withdrew.

They spent a melancholy afternoon. Unable to interpret the capricious behaviour of the German officer, they were tormented by the most fantastic ideas. Gathered in the kitchen, they engaged in endless discussions and hazarded the wildest conjectures. Perhaps it was intended to keep them as hostages – but for what purpose? – or to take them away as prisoners, or, more likely still, to exact a substantial ransom? . . . At this suggestion they were panic-stricken. The wealthier they were the more they were horrified. They saw themselves forced to purchase their lives with bags of gold poured into the lap of that insolent soldier. They racked their brains to devise plausible falsehoods for disguising their wealth, and for passing themselves off for very poor people indeed. Loiseau took off his watch chain and hid it in his pocket. With nightfall, their fears increased. The lamp was lit, and as there were still two hours till dinner, Madame Loiseau proposed a game of *trente-et-un* to pass the time. Every one welcomed this suggestion, including Cornudet, who, out of politeness, extinguished his pipe.

The count shuffled the cards and dealt. Boule de Suif in the very first round held thirty-one. Very soon, in the excitement of the game, their haunting fears subsided. Cornudet, however, noticed that the two Loiseaus were helping each other to cheat.

Just as they were sitting down to dinner, Monsieur Follenvie came in. In his husky voice, he said:

'The Prussian officer wishes to know if Mademoiselle Élisabeth Rousset has changed her mind yet.'

Boule de Suif turned pale. She remained standing. But suddenly she flushed crimson, choking with rage, unable to utter a word. At last she broke out:

'You may tell that blackguard, that dirty scoundrel, that filthy Prussian, that I never will. Have you got it? Never, never, never.'

The fat innkeeper went off. The others gathered round Boule de Suif, teasing her with questions, imploring her to reveal the mystery of her interview with the Prussian. At first she stood out, but finally, carried away by her resentment, she cried:

'What does he want? . . . What does he want? . . . He wants to sleep with me!'

So keen was their indignation that no one was shocked at the phrase. Cornudet brought his mug so violently down on the table that he broke it. There was a general outcry against this ruffianly soldier. Swept by a common gust of anger, they resolved unanimously upon resistance, as if each of them had been called upon to contribute to the sacrifice.

With an air of disgust, the count declared that these fellows were behaving like the barbarians of old. The ladies, in particular, lavished upon Boule de Suif vehement demonstrations of sympathy. The nuns, who appeared only at meal times, bowed their heads and held their peace.

After the first burst of anger had subsided, they dined, but conversation languished; every one was pensive.

The ladies retired early; the men smoked and got up a game of écarté in which they invited Monsieur Follenvie to join, with the object of skilfully eliciting from him the best means of overcoming the officer's opposition. But he devoted his whole attention to the cards, listened to no questions, and made no reply; calling out continually: 'Play, gentlemen, play!' His attention was so closely fixed that he even forgot to spit, an omission which was liable to produce organ effects in his chest. His wheezing lungs ran through the whole asthmatical gamut, from deep bass notes to the shrill squawk of a cockerel trying to crow. He declined to go to bed when his wife, dropping with fatigue, came to look for him. So she went off alone, for she was an early bird, always up with the sun; while her husband preferred late hours and was always ready to make a night of it with his friends. He called out to her: 'Put my egg-flip before the fire,' and went on with the game.

When they saw that they could get nothing out of him, they declared that it was time for them to stop, and they all went off to bed.

They were up early again next morning, filled with a vague hope, an increasing desire to be gone, and a dread of another day in that horrible little inn.

Alas! the horses remained in the stable, and the driver was still invisible. For want of anything better to do, they hung about the coach.

Luncheon was a gloomy meal. A certain coldness began to manifest itself towards Boule de Suif. Taking counsel of their pillows had somewhat modified her companions' view of the case. By this time, they were almost ready to blame the girl for not having secretly sought out the Prussian officer, with a view to providing a pleasant surprise for her fellow-travellers the next morning. Could anything have been simpler? After all, who would have been the wiser? She could have saved her face by letting the officer know that she had taken pity on her fellow-travellers' distress. It would have been such a small matter for her. But as yet no one uttered these thoughts aloud.

In the afternoon, to relieve their devastating boredom, the count suggested a walk on the outskirts of the village. Carefully wrapped up, the little party set out, with the exception of Cornudet, who preferred to stay by the fire, and the nuns who were spending their days in church or at the parsonage. The cold, which was daily increasing in intensity, sharply nipped their ears and noses; their feet ached so painfully that each step was torture. And the open country, under its pall of snow, stretching away beyond range of sight, produced upon them such a terrible impression of dreariness that they turned home, chilled and oppressed in heart and soul. The four women walked on ahead, while the three men followed at a little distance.

Loiseau, who had grasped the situation, suddenly asked if the 'wench' meant to keep them hanging on much longer like this. Chivalrous as ever, the count declared that they could not ask a woman to make so painful a sacrifice; it must be voluntary. Monsieur Carré-Lamadon observed that if the French, as was thought likely, turned and took the offensive by way of Dieppe, the engagement could only take place at Tôtes, a reflection which made the others uneasy.

'Suppose we escape on foot?' said Loiseau.

'Out of the question in all this snow, and with our wives too,' said the count shrugging his shoulders. 'Besides, they would be after us in no time; we should be caught within ten minutes and brought back as prisoners at the mercy of the soldiers.'

There was no answer to this, and they relapsed into silence. The ladies discussed fashions, but a feeling of constraint seemed to disturb the harmony.

Suddenly, the Prussian officer appeared at the end of the street. His tall, wasp-waisted, uniformed figure stood out sharply against the snowy background. He walked with his knees well apart, with the gait characteristic of military men who are anxious not to splash their beautifully polished boots. He bowed as he passed the ladies, but glanced contemptuously at the men, who, for their part, did not lower themselves so far as to take off their hats, though Loiseau made as if to do so.

Boule de Suif blushed up to the eyes, and the three married women felt deeply mortified at having been seen by the officer in the company of the young woman whom he had treated so cavalierly.

Then they discussed him, criticizing his face and figure. Madame Carré-Lamadon, who had known a great many officers and spoke with the authority of an expert, declared that he was not at all unprepossessing. It was a pity, she actually said, that he was not a Frenchman; he would have made a very smart hussar, and all the women would have been crazy about him.

When they returned to the inn, they were at their wits' end for something to do. Sharp words were exchanged on the slightest provocation. Dinner was a short and silent meal, and every one went to bed, hoping to kill time by going to sleep. The next morning they came downstairs with jaded looks and nerves on edge. The women would hardly speak to Boule de Suif.

The church bell rang for a christening. Boule de Suif had a child of her own, who was being brought up in a peasant family at Yvetot. She saw it scarcely once a year and never troubled her head about it. But now the thought of the infant about to be christened awoke in her a sudden burst of tender feeling towards her own baby, and nothing would do but she must be present at the ceremony.

As soon as she had left the inn, the others exchanged glances and drew their chairs close together, for they felt that it was really time they came to some decision. Loiseau had an inspiration. His suggestion was to invite the officer to keep back Boule de Suif by herself and to let the others go. Monsieur Follenvie undertook to convey this message, but he came back almost at once. The German, who knew what men were, had turned him out of the room. He intended to keep the whole party till he had attained his desire.

At this, the innate vulgarity of Madame Loiseau broke out:

'Anyhow, we are not going to stay here till we die of old age. It's the wretched creature's trade. One man is as good as another from her point of view. What right has she to pick and choose? I ask you. She never refused any one who came along at Rouen, not even coachmen. Yes, indeed, madam, she carried on with the mayor's coachman. I know all about it because he buys his wine from us. And now, when it's a question of getting us out of a mess, she put on airs, the slut. Really, I think the officer is behaving very well. He has probably had no opportunities for a long time; and here are we three whom he would no doubt have preferred. But no, he is ready to content himself with a common woman. He has a proper respect for married women. Remember, he is master here. He has only to raise a finger, and his soldiers would seize us for him by force.'

The other women gave a little shudder. Pretty Madame Carré-Lamadon's eyes sparkled and she turned a little pale, as if she already felt herself forcibly seized by the officer.

The men, who had been privately conferring, now joined the ladies. Loiseau, in a fury, was for delivering the wretch, bound hand and foot, to the enemy. But the count, who was sprung from three generations of ambassadors and was himself a diplomat by instinct, counselled strategy.

'We must persuade her,' he said.

So they proceeded to concoct a plan.

The women put their heads together. Voices were lowered and the discussion became general, every one giving an opinion. It was all conducted with the utmost propriety. The ladies displayed a special aptitude for expressing the most outrageous ideas by polite euphemisms and refined phrases. They were so careful of the conventions of speech that a stranger would have understood nothing. But since the veneer of modesty with which every woman is provided is purely superficial, they threw themselves heart and soul into this unsavoury affair, secretly revelling in it, perfectly in their element and dallying with the idea of the liaison with all the sensual emotion of a cook, himself a gourmand, preparing another person's supper.

Their spirits rose again at the humorous aspect of the adventure. The count ventured upon some rather risky jokes which were so neatly turned that no one could help smiling. Loiseau indulged in broader pleasantries, and even these were not resented. Every one was thinking of Madame Loiseau's brutally frank remark: 'It's her trade, so why should she pick and choose?' Indeed, charming Madame Carré-Lamadon seemed to think that if she were in her place she would rather have him than another.

A plan of blockade was carefully considered, as if for the investment of a fortress. To each conspirator a separate role was assigned, including appropriate arguments and manoeuvres. A plan of attack, with strategic openings and surprise methods of assault, was agreed upon with a view to forcing this citadel of flesh and blood to admit the enemy.

They were so deeply engrossed that they did not hear Boule de Suif come in, till, at the count's whispered 'Hush!' every one looked up and saw her.

Conversation ceased abruptly and at first a feeling of embarrassment deterred them from addressing her. The countess, however, was more of an adept than her companions in social insincerity.

'Was it a pretty christening?' she asked.

Not without emotion, Boule de Suif described the whole proceedings, the congregation, the ceremony, and the church itself. She added:

'It does one good to say one's prayers now and then.'

Up to luncheon-time the ladies contented themselves with being pleasant to her, with the object of gaining her confidence and making her amenable to their advice. But as soon as they sat down to table the siege was opened. They began with a vague discussion of the virtue of self-sacrifice. Instances from antiquity were quoted: Judith and Holofernes, then, with utter inconsequence, Lucretia and Sextus, and Cleopatra, admitting to her bed all the enemy generals and making them her obedient slaves. Next was unfolded a fantastic story, hatched in the imagination of these ignorant plutocrats, of how the Roman women betook themselves to Capua and lulled to sleep in their arms Hannibal, his officers, and his phalanxes of mercenaries. They told of women who had stayed the tide of conquest, offering their persons as a battlefield and making of their own beauty an effective weapon; heroines whose caresses had compassed the overthrow of the vilest and most hateful of mankind, and who had sacrificed their chastity in a fervour of vengeance and self-immolation.

All these stories were told with due regard to propriety and good taste, with frequent outbursts of studied enthusiasm calculated to excite to emulation.

By the time they had finished, one would have supposed that the whole duty of woman here below was the repeated sacrifice of her person, a continual surrender of herself to a licentious soldiery.

Deep in their meditations, the two nuns did not seem to be listening, and Boule de Suif said not a word.

All that afternoon they left her to her own reflections. Only, instead of addressing her as 'Madame,' as they had hitherto done, they now said simply 'Mademoiselle,' no one quite knew why, unless it was to detract from the position of respect to which she had attained, and to bring home to her the shame of her calling.

While the soup was being served, Monsieur Follenvie appeared again, and repeated the question of the previous evening:

'The Prussian officer wishes to know if Mademoiselle Élisabeth Rousset has changed her mind yet.'

'No,' said Boule de Suif, curtly.

During dinner, the coalition showed signs of weakening. Loiseau made two or three unfortunate remarks. All the conspirators vainly racked their brains in search of fresh examples, when the countess, probably without design, and simply with a vague idea of showing respect to religion, questioned the elder nun about the main incidents in the lives of the saints. It appeared that many of the saints had been guilty of deeds which would be considered crimes in our eyes. But the Church makes no difficulty about granting absolution for heinous offences, provided that they are committed for the glory of God or the good of one's neighbour. Here was a powerful argument, and the countess jumped at it. It was either a case of that tacit understanding, that veiled connivance, for which all who wear the garb of the Church develop a special faculty, or simply the result of a fortunate lack of intelligence, an opportune stupidity. Whatever the cause, the old nun rendered yeoman's service to the intriguers. In spite of her apparent timidity, she showed herself bold, eloquent, forcible. She, for one, did not trouble to grope among the mazes of casuistry; her doctrine was as rigid as an iron bar; her faith was unswerving; her conscience knew no scruple. She regarded Abraham's sacrifice as perfectly natural, for she herself would have had no hesitation in slaying both father and mother at a command from on high. No act, she believed, could be displeasing to the Lord if the intention was praiseworthy. Taking advantage of the pious authority of this unexpected ally, the countess induced her to deliver an edifying exposition of the moral axiom: 'The end justifies the means.'

'Then, sister,' she said, 'you believe that all means are acceptable to God and that He will pardon any act if only the motive be pure?'

'Who can doubt it, madam? An act culpable in itself often becomes meritorious because of the idea which inspires it.'

And they continued in this strain, interpreting the will of God, anticipating His judgments, and involving Him in matters which were really no concern of His. And the whole drift of their discussion was veiled, insidious, discreet. Every word uttered by the holy woman in the nun's coif made a breach in the courtesan's fierce resistance. Presently the conversation took a somewhat different turn. She of the rosary spoke of the houses of her order, her superior, herself, her charming companion, dear Sister Saint-Nicéphore. They had been summoned to Havre to nurse in the hospitals hundreds of soldiers suffering from smallpox. She depicted these poor fellows, giving a detailed description of their disease. And while they were held up on their journey for a whim of this Prussian, scores of Frenchmen were perhaps dying, whom their ministrations might have saved. Nursing soldiers was her speciality. She had been in the Crimea, in Italy, in Austria. In relating her campaigns, she suddenly revealed herself as one of those nuns of fife and drum, whose destiny it is to follow the armies and bring in the wounded, cast up by the back-wash of battles, and whose word is more effective than a general's in subduing undisciplined soldiers. She was a real Sister Rub-a-dub, and her worn face, seamed with countless wrinkles, was like a symbol of the havoc of war.

The effect of her speech seemed so admirable that when she ceased no one said another word. As soon as dinner was over, the whole party retired at once to their rooms and did not come down till rather late the next morning. Luncheon passed quietly. The seed, which had been sown on the previous evening, was given time to germinate and bear fruit.

In the afternoon, the countess suggested a walk. The count, as had been arranged, gave his arm to Boule de Suif and lingered with her behind the others. He adopted towards her that familiar, paternal, somewhat supercilious manner, with which men of a certain position treat young women of her class, calling her 'my dear child' with the condescension arising from his social rank and his unquestioned respectability.

He went straight to the root of the matter:

'Then, you prefer to keep us here, exposed like yourself to all the outrages which would ensue if the Prussian troops suffered a reverse, rather than grant a favour which you have conceded so often as a matter of course?'

Boule de Suif made no reply.

He tried her with kindness, argument, appeals to sentiment, yet he never forgot his rank, even though obliged to pay court, to lavish compliments – in short, to make himself agreeable. He magnified the service she would render her companions and spoke of their gratitude; finally, with gay familiarity, he exclaimed:

'And you know, my dear, he will be able to boast of having enjoyed a prettier girl than he could often find in his own country.'

Boule de Suif still made no reply and caught up the others. As soon as she returned home she withdrew to her room and did not come down again. The rest of the party were greatly perturbed. What did she mean to do? If she still held out, it would be very awkward.

The dinner hour came, but they waited for her in vain. Then Monsieur Follenvie appeared and said that Mademoiselle Rousset was indisposed and that they might begin. They all pricked up their ears. The count went up to the innkeeper and asked in a whisper; 'Is it all right?' 'Yes,' he was told. From a sense of propriety, he said nothing to his companions, but he slightly nodded his head. Every one uttered a sigh of relief and every face lighted up. Loiseau exclaimed: 'Glory be! I'll stand champagne, if there is any in the house!' and Madame Loiseau writhed in agony when the host came back with four bottles. Every one at once became voluble and noisy. They were bubbling over with joy. The count appeared to awake to Madame Carré-Lamadon's charms; the manufacturer addressed compliments to the countess. The tone of the conversation grew lively, merry, and racy.

Suddenly, Loiseau raised his hands with an air of anxiety, and shouted: 'Silence!' Surprised, almost frightened, the whole party sat mute. He made a sign to them to keep still; stood in an attitude of attention, his eyes raised to the ceiling, and listened again. Then in his ordinary voice, he said: 'Be easy; all is well.' Slowly his meaning dawned upon them and they exchanged smiles.

A quarter of an hour later he went through the same performance, which he repeated at intervals throughout the evening. He pretended to be addressing questions to someone on the floor above, and proffering advice, which had a double meaning characteristic of his bagman's wit. With a sorrowful expression, he would sigh: 'Poor girl,' or he would murmur between his teeth as in a fury: 'Get out, you Prussian brute.'

Sometimes, when the others were off their guard, he would cry repeatedly in a thrilling voice: 'Have done! Have done!' adding, as if to himself: 'I only hope we may see her again and that that scoundrel won't be the death of her.'

Though these jests were in deplorable taste, every one enjoyed them and no one was shocked. Like any other sentiment, virtuous indignation is the result of environment, and gradually an atmosphere had been created which was laden with obscene suggestion. At dessert, even the women, who had drunk a good deal and whose eyes were sparkling, made discreet but waggish allusions.

The count, who preserved, even when he fell from grace, his grave and lofty bearing, drew a comparison, which was much relished, between their condition and that of ice-bound mariners at the Pole, rejoicing because winter is over and the way to the south open once more.

Loiseau jumped up, a glass of champagne in his hand: 'I drink to our deliverance!' Every one rose and drank the toast with acclamation. Even the two nuns yielded to the importunity of the other ladies and took a sip of the bubbling wine, which they had never tasted before. They said it was like effervescent lemonade, but admitted that it had a finer flavour.

Loiseau summed up the situation:

'What a pity we haven't a piano; we might have managed a quadrille.'

Cornudet had not uttered a word or made a sign. He seemed, indeed, as if plunged in serious thought, and now and then with a furious gesture he tugged at his great beard, as if he wished to make it longer still. At last, towards midnight, as the party was about to break up, Loiseau reeled up to him and poked him in the ribs.

'You're not in good form this evening, old chap. Have you lost your tongue?'

Cornudet raised his head sharply and, glaring ferociously at the company, said:

'I tell you all that you have done an infamous thing.' He rose and made his way to the door.

'Infamous!' he repeated and disappeared.

The immediate effect of his words was to cast a blight on every one. Loiseau was utterly taken aback and stood there like a fool.

But he quickly recovered himself. Convulsed with laughter, he exclaimed:

'The grapes are sour, old boy; the grapes are sour.'

As no one understood, he told his story of the mysteries of the corridor. There was a fresh outburst of gaiety. The ladies nearly died of laughing. The count and Monsieur Carré-Lamadon laughed till they cried. They could not believe their ears.

'What! are you sure? He really wanted to—?'

'I tell you I saw it!'

'And she refused?'

'Yes, because the Prussian was in the next room.'

'Is it possible?'

'I'll take my oath.'

The count suffocated with laughter and the manufacturer held his sides. Loiseau resumed:

'And now you know why he didn't think it at all funny this evening!'

The three men exploded again, until they were out of breath and weak with laughing. Then they all went upstairs and the party dispersed.

Madame Loiseau, who was as spiteful as a stinging nettle, said to her husband as soon as they were in bed:

'That affected little minx, Madame Carré-Lamadon, was laughing on the wrong side of her mouth all the evening. When it comes to a uniform, you know, some women don't care whether it is French or Prussian; it's all one to them. Good Lord, isn't it revolting?'

All that night the darkened corridor was alive with rustling sounds, so light as to be almost inaudible, the pattering of bare feet, the faint creaking of boards. From the gleams of light that showed beneath the doors for a long time, it was obvious that no one went to sleep till a late hour. Champagne is said to make one restless.

Next morning, the snow glittered dazzlingly in the bright winter sun. The coach, ready at last, was standing at the door, while a flock of white pigeons, pink-eyed with black pupils, were preening their luxuriant plumage and stalking solemnly in and out between the legs of the six horses, picking up their sustenance.

Wrapped in his sheepskin, the driver was seated on the box,

pulling at his pipe, and the delighted travellers were all of them busy packing up provisions for the rest of the journey. All they were now waiting for was Boule de Suif.

Presently she appeared. She seeemed somewhat ill at ease and ashamed, and as she moved timidly towards her fellow-travellers, they all unanimously turned away as if they had not seen her. The count, with a dignified air, took his wife's arm and drew her away from that contaminating contact.

Boule de Suif stood for a moment in amazement, then plucking up courage, she greeted the manufacturer's wife with a humble 'Good morning, madam.' The latter, however, merely returned an insolent little nod and a glance of virtuous indignation. Every one seemed to have a great deal to do and held aloof from her, as if she carried some infection in her petticoats. Then they made a rush for the coach. Boule de Suif was the last to reach it, and quietly slipped into the seat she had occupied during the first stage of her journey.

They pretended not to see or recognize her, but Madame Loiseau shot an indignant glance at her from a distance, and whispered audibly to her husband: 'I'm glad I'm not sitting next to her.'

The heavy coach lurched off and the journey was resumed. At first every one was silent. Boule de Suif did not venture to look up. She was disgusted with her companions and at the same time ashamed of having submitted to the defiling embraces of the Prussian officer, into whose arms she had been flung by these hypocrites.

Presently, turning to Madame Carré-Lamadon, the countess broke the painful silence:

'I think you know Madame d'Étrelles?'

'Yes, she is a friend of mine.'

'What a charming woman!'

'Perfectly delightful! Really distinguished, well-educated, and artistic to the finger-tips. She sings divinely and draws exquisitely.'

The manufacturer talked to the count; above the rattling of the windows, a word was now and then audible: 'dividend warrant – fall due – premium – mature.'

Loiseau, who had annexed from the inn its pack of old cards, greasy with five years' contact with dirty tables, played bezique with his wife.

The nuns, taking the long rosaries hanging at their waists, crossed themselves, and their lips began to move with ever increasing speed, as though their muttered prayers were running a race. Every now and then they kissed a medallion, crossed themselves again, and resumed their rapid, continuous babbling.

Cornudet sat motionless, plunged in thought.

After they had been three hours or so on the way, Loiseau gathered up the cards, saying:

'I feel hungry!'

His wife produced a packet tied with string from which she took a piece of cold veal. She cut it into neat, thin slices and they both began to eat.

'Suppose we do the same,' said the countess. Her husband agreed and she unpacked the provisions brought for themselves and the Carré-Lamadons. They consisted of an oblong dish with a hare in earthenware on the lid, which was an indication of the contents, a savoury hare-pie, in which the dark flesh, mixed with other finely chopped meat, was set off by streaks of white fat. There was also a fine piece of Gruyère, wrapped in a newspaper, with *Faits divers* impressed on its unctuous surface.

The two nuns took out a piece of sausage smelling of garlic; while Cornudet, thrusting both hands at once into the wide pockets of his loose greatcoat, extracted from one four hard-boiled eggs, from the other a crust of bread. Throwing the shells into the straw at his feet, he set to work on the eggs, scattering on his spreading beard yellow specks of yolk, which shone there like stars.

When she got up that morning Boule de Suif had been too much flustered and agitated to think of anything. Choking with rage and indignation, she watched all these people calmly eating away. Seething with fury, she opened her mouth to tell them what she thought of them, and a torrent of abuse rose to her lips; but her exasperation strangled her utterance. No one gave her a look or a thought. She felt overwhelmed by the contempt of these miserable churls, these respectable people, who had first sacrificed her and then flung her away like a thing useless and unclean. And then she remembered her big basket full of good things which they had greedily devoured, her two fowls in shining jelly, her *pâtés*, her pears, her four bottles of Bordeaux. Her rage suddenly gave way like a snapping cord and she felt on the verge of tears. She made a violent effort to brace herself and swallowed down her sobs as a child does; but tears rose to her eyes, glistened on her eyelashes, and soon two great drops rolled slowly down her cheeks. Then the tears came faster and faster, like drops of water trickling from a rock, and falling in regular succession on to her swelling bosom. She sat erect and looked straight before her, her face pale and set, in the hope that her distress would pass unnoticed. But the countess remarked it and with a gesture drew her husband's attention to it. He shrugged his shoulders as if to say: 'Well, what of it? It's not my fault.'

Madame Loiseau, with a silent laugh of mockery, murmured:

'She is crying for shame.'

After wrapping up the remainder of their sausage, the two nuns returned to their prayers.

Cornudet, who was digesting his eggs, put up his long legs on the opposite seat, leant back with folded arms, and smiled like a man who has thought of a good joke. He began to whistle the *Marseillaise*.

Every face grew overcast. The song of the people certainly did not appeal to his companions in the least. They fidgeted nervously, and each looked ready to howl, like a dog at the sound of a barrel-organ. He realized this, and went on for all that. He even hummed a verse:

Amour sacré de la patrie,
Conduis, soutiens nos bras vengeurs,
Liberté, liberté, chérie,
Combats avec tes défenseurs!

As the snow hardened, their progress became more rapid. All the way to Dieppe, throughout the long weary hours of the journey; above the jolting of the coach, in the gathering gloom, in the subsequent deep darkness which filled the carriage, with savage resolution he kept up his monotonous, vindictive whistling. He forced their jaded, exasperated brains to follow the song from end to end, word by word, and note by note. All the time Boule de Suif never ceased to weep, and now and then, at a pause in the song, a sob that she could not repress was heard in the darkness.

RUDYARD KIPLING

Baa Baa, Black Sheep

Baa Baa, Black Sheep,
Have you any wool?
Yes, Sir, yes, Sir, three bags full.
One for the Master, one for the Dame—
None for the Little Boy that cries down the lane.

NURSERY RHYME

THE FIRST BAG

'When I was in my father's house, I was in a better place.'

They were putting Punch to bed – the *ayah* and the *hamal* and Meeta, the big *Surti* boy, with the red-and-gold turban. Judy, already tucked inside her mosquito-curtains, was nearly asleep. Punch had been allowed to stay up for dinner. Many privileges had been accorded to Punch within the last ten days, and a greater kindness from the people of his world had encompassed his ways and works, which were mostly obstreperous. He sat on the edge of his bed and swung his bare legs defiantly.

'Punch-*baba* going to bye-lo?' said the *ayah* suggestively.

'No,' said Punch. 'Punch-*baba* wants the story about the Ranee that was turned into a tiger. Meeta must tell it, and the *hamal* shall hide behind the door and make tiger-noises at the proper time.'

'But Judy-*baba* will wake up,' said the *ayah*.

'Judy-*baba* is waked,' piped a small voice from the mosquito-curtains. 'There was a Ranee that lived at Delhi. Go on, Meeta,' and she fell fast asleep again while Meeta began the story.

Never had Punch secured the telling of that tale with so little opposition. He reflected for a long time. The *hamal* made the tiger-noises in twenty different keys.

''Top!' said Punch authoritatively. 'Why doesn't Papa come in and say he is going to give me *put-put?*'

'Punch-*baba* is going away,' said the *ayah*. 'In another week there will be no Punch-*baba* to pull my hair any more.' She sighed softly, for the boy of the household was very dear to her heart.

'Up the Ghauts in a train?' said Punch, standing on his bed. 'All the way to Nassick where the Ranee-Tiger lives?'

'Not to Nassick this year, little Sahib,' said Meeta, lifting him on his shoulder. 'Down to the sea where the coconuts are thrown, and across the sea in a big ship. Will you take Meeta with you to *Belait?*'

'You shall all come,' said Punch, from the height of Meeta's strong arms. 'Meeta and the *ayah* and the *hamal* and Bhini-in-the-Garden, and the salaam-Captain-Sahib-snake-man.'

There was no mockery in Meeta's voice when he replied: 'Great is the Sahib's favour,' and laid the little man down in the bed, while the *ayah*, sitting in the moonlight at the doorway, lulled him to sleep with an interminable canticle such as they sing in the Roman Catholic Church at Parel. Punch curled himself into a ball and slept.

Next morning Judy shouted that there was a rat in the nursery, and thus he forgot to tell her the wonderful news. It did not much matter, for Judy was only three and she would not have understood. But Punch was five; and he knew that going to England would be much nicer than a trip to Nassick.

Papa and Mamma sold the brougham and the piano, and stripped the house, and curtailed the allowance of crockery for the daily meals, and took long counsel together over a bundle of letters bearing the Rocklington postmark.

'The worst of it is that one can't be certain of anything,' said Papa, pulling his moustache. 'The letters in themselves are excellent, and the terms are moderate enough.'

'The worst of it is that the children will grow up away from me,' thought Mamma; but she did not say it aloud.

'We are only one case among hundreds,' said Papa bitterly. 'You shall go Home again in five years, dear.'

'Punch will be ten then – and Judy eight. Oh, how long and

long and long the time will be! And we have to leave them among strangers.'

'Punch is a cheery little chap. He's sure to make friends wherever he goes.'

'And who could help loving my Ju?'

They were standing over the cots in the nursery late at night, and I think that Mamma was crying softly. After Papa had gone away, she knelt down by the side of Judy's cot. The *ayah* saw her and put up a prayer that the Memsahib might never find the love of her children taken away from her and given to a stranger.

Mamma's own prayer was a slightly illogical one. Summarized it ran: 'Let strangers love my children and be as good to them as I should be, but let *me* preserve their love and their confidence for ever and ever. Amen.' Punch scratched himself in his sleep, and Judy moaned a little.

Next day they all went down to the sea, and there was a scene at the Apollo Bunder when Punch discovered that Meeta could not come too, and Judy learned that the *ayah* must be left behind. But Punch found a thousand fascinating things in the rope, block, and steam-pipe line on the big P. & O. steamer long before Meeta and the *ayah* had dried their tears.

'Come back, Punch-*baba*,' said the *ayah*.

'Come back,' said Meeta, 'and be a *Burra Sahib* [a big man].'

'Yes,' said Punch, lifted up in his father's arms to wave good-bye. 'Yes, I will come back, and I will be a *Burra Sahib Bahadur* [a very big man indeed]!'

At the end of the first day Punch demanded to be set down in England, which he was certain must be close at hand. Next day there was a merry breeze, and Punch was very sick. 'When I come back to Bombay,' said Punch on his recovery, 'I will come by the road – in a broom-*gharri*. This is a very naughty ship.'

The Swedish boatswain consoled him, and he modified his opinions as the voyage went on. There was so much to see and to handle and ask questions about that Punch nearly forgot the *ayah* and Meeta and the *hamal*, and with difficulty remembered a few words of the Hindustani once his second speech.

But Judy was much worse. The day before the steamer reached Southampton, Mamma asked her if she would not like to see the *ayah* again. Judy's blue eyes turned to the stretch of sea that had swallowed all her tiny past, and she said: '*Ayah! What ayah?*'

Mamma cried over her and Punch marvelled. It was then that he heard for the first time Mamma's passionate appeal to him never to let Judy forget Mamma. Seeing that Judy was young, ridiculously young, and that Mamma, every evening for four weeks past, had come into the cabin to sing her and Punch to sleep with a mysterious rune that he called 'Sonny, my soul,' Punch could not understand what Mamma meant. But he strove to do his duty; for, the moment Mamma left the cabin, he said to Judy: 'Ju, you bemember Mamma?'

''Torse I do,' said Judy.

'Then *always* bemember Mamma, 'r else I won't give you the paper ducks that the red-haired Captain Sahib cut out for me.'

So Judy promised always to 'bemember Mamma.'

Many and many a time was Mamma's command laid upon Punch, and Papa would say the same thing with an insistence that awed the child.

'You must make haste and learn to write, Punch,' said Papa, 'and then you'll be able to write letters to us in Bombay.'

'I'll come into your room,' said Punch, and Papa choked.

Papa and Mamma were always choking in those days. If Punch took Judy to task for not 'bemembering,' they choked. If Punch sprawled on the sofa in the Southampton lodging-house and sketched his future in purple and gold, they choked; and so they did if Judy put up her mouth for a kiss.

Through many days all four were vagabonds on the face of the earth – Punch with no one to give orders to, Judy too young for anything, and Papa and Mamma grave, distracted, and choking.

'Where,' demanded Punch, wearied of a loathsome contrivance on four wheels with a mound of luggage atop – '*where* is our broom-*gharri*? This thing talks so much that *I* can't talk. Where is our *own* broom-*gharri*? When I was at Bandstand before we comed away, I asked Inverarity Sahib why he was sitting in it, and he said it was his own. And I said, "I will *give* it you" – I like Inverarity Sahib – and I said, "Can you put your legs through the pully-wag loops by the windows?" And Inverarity Sahib said No, and laughed. *I* can put my legs through the pully-wag loops. I can put my legs through *these* pully-wag loops. Look! Oh, Mamma's crying again! I didn't know I wasn't not to do *so*.'

Punch drew his legs out of the loops of the four-wheeler: the door opened and he slid to the earth, in a cascade of parcels, at the door of an austere little villa whose gates bore the legend 'Downe Lodge.' Punch gathered himself together and eyed the house with disfavour. It stood on a sandy road, and a cold wind tickled his knickerbockered legs.

'Let us go away,' said Punch. 'This is not a pretty place.'

But Mamma and Papa and Judy had left the cab, and all the luggage was being taken into the house. At the doorstep stood a woman in black, and she smiled largely, with dry chapped lips. Behind her was a man, big, bony, grey, and lame as to one leg – behind him a boy of twelve, black-haired and oily in appearance. Punch surveyed the trio, and advanced without fear, as he had been accustomed to do in Bombay when callers came and he happened to be playing in the veranda.

'How do you do?' said he. 'I am Punch.' But they were all looking at the luggage – all except the grey man, who shook hands with Punch, and said he was 'a smart little fellow.' There was much running about and banging of boxes, and Punch curled himself up on the sofa in the dining-room and considered things.

'I don't like these people,' said Punch. 'But never mind. We'll go away soon. We have always went away soon from everywhere. I wish we was gone back to Bombay *soon*.'

The wish bore no fruit. For six days Mamma wept at intervals, and showed the woman in black all Punch's clothes – a liberty which Punch resented. 'But p'raps she's a new white *ayah*,' he thought. 'I'm to call her Antirosa, but she doesn't call *me* Sahib. She says just Punch,' he confided to Judy. 'What is Antirosa?'

Judy didn't know. Neither she nor Punch had heard anything of an animal called an aunt. Their world had been Papa and Mamma, who knew everything, permitted everything, and loved everybody – even Punch when he used to go into the garden at Bombay and fill his nails with mould after the weekly nail-cutting, because, as he explained between two strokes of the slipper to his sorely-tried father, his fingers 'felt so new at the ends.'

In an undefined way Punch judged it advisable to keep both parents between himself and the woman in black and the boy with black hair. He did not approve of them. He liked the grey man, who had expressed a wish to be called 'Uncleharri.' They nodded at each other when they met, and the grey man showed him a little ship with rigging that took up and down.

'She is a model of the *Brisk* – the little *Brisk* that was sore exposed that day at Navarino.' The grey man hummed the last words and fell into a reverie. 'I'll tell you about Navarino, Punch, when we go for walks together; and you mustn't touch the ship, because she's the *Brisk*.'

Long before that walk, the first of many, was taken, they roused Punch and Judy in the chill dawn of a February morning to say Good-bye; and of all people in the wide earth to Papa and Mamma – both crying this time. Punch was very sleepy and Judy was cross.

'Don't forget us,' pleaded Mamma. 'Oh, my little son, don't forget us, and see that Judy remembers too.'

'I've told Judy to bemember,' said Punch, wriggling, for his father's beard tickled his neck, 'I've told Judy – ten – forty – 'leven thousand times. But Ju's so young – quite a baby – isn't she?'

'Yes,' said Papa, 'quite a baby, and you must be good to Judy, and make haste to learn to write and – and – and—'

Punch was back in his bed again. Judy was fast asleep, and there was the rattle of a cab below. Papa and Mamma had gone away. Not to Nassick; that was across the sea. To some place much nearer, of course, and equally of course they would return. They came back after dinner-parties, and Papa had come back after he had been to a place called 'The Snows,' and Mamma with him, to Punch and Judy at Mrs Inverarity's house in Marine Lines. Assuredly they would come back again. So Punch fell asleep till the true morning, when the black-haired boy met him with the information that Papa and Mamma had gone to Bombay, and that he and Judy were to stay at Downe Lodge 'for ever.' Antirosa, tearfully appealed to for a contradiction, said that Harry had spoken the truth, and that it behoved Punch to fold up his clothes neatly on going to bed. Punch went out and wept bitterly with Judy, into whose fair head he had driven some ideas of the meaning of separation.

When a matured man discovers that he has been deserted by Providence, deprived of his God, and cast without help, comfort, or sympathy, upon a world which is new and strange to him, his despair, which may find expression in evil living, the writing of his experiences, or the more satisfactory diversion of suicide, is generally supposed to be impressive. A child, under exactly similar circumstances as far as its knowledge goes, cannot very well curse God and die. It howls till its nose is red, its eyes are sore, and its head aches. Punch and Judy, through no fault of their own, had lost all their world. They sat in the hall and cried; the black-haired boy looking on from afar.

The model of the ship availed nothing, though the grey man assured Punch that he might pull the rigging up and down as much as he pleased; and Judy was promised free entry into the kitchen. They wanted Papa and Mamma, gone to Bombay beyond the seas, and their grief while it lasted was without remedy.

When the tears ceased the house was very still. Antirosa had decided that it was better to let the children 'have their cry out,' and the boy had gone to school. Punch raised his head from the floor and sniffed mournfully. Judy was nearly asleep. Three short years had not taught her how to bear sorrow with full knowledge. There was a distant, dull boom in the air – a repeated heavy thud. Punch knew that sound in Bombay in the monsoon. It was the sea – the sea that must be traversed before anyone could get to Bombay.

'Quick, Ju!' he cried. 'We're close to the sea. I can hear it! Listen! That's where they've went. P'raps we can catch them if we was in time. They didn't mean to go without us. They've only forgot.'

'Iss,' said Judy. 'They've only forgotted. Less go to the sea.'

The hall-door was open and so was the garden-gate.

'It's very, very big, this place,' he said, looking cautiously down the road, 'and we will get lost. But *I* will find a man and order him to take me back to my house – like I did in Bombay.'

He took Judy by the hand, and the two ran hatless in the direction of the sound of the sea. Downe Lodge was almost the last of a range of newly-built houses running out, through a field of brick-mounds, to a heath where gipsies occasionally camped and where the Garrison Artillery of Rocklington practised. There were few people to be seen, and the children might have been taken for those of the soldiery who ranged far. Half an hour the wearied little legs tramped across heath, potato-patch, and sand-dune.

'I'se so tired,' said Judy, 'and Mamma will be angry.'

'Mamma's *never* angry. I suppose she is waiting at the sea now while Papa gets tickets. We'll find them and go along with them. Ju, you mustn't sit down. Only a little more and we'll come to the sea. Ju, if you sit down I'll *thmack* you!' said Punch.

They climbed another dune, and came upon the great grey sea at low tide. Hundreds of crabs were scuttling about the beach, but there was no trace of Papa and Mamma, not even of a ship upon the waters – nothing but sand and mud for miles and miles.

And 'Uncleharri' found them by chance – very muddy and very forlorn – Punch dissolved in tears, but trying to divert Judy with an 'ickle trab,' and Judy wailing to the pitiless horizon for 'Mamma, Mamma!' – and again 'Mamma!'

THE SECOND BAG

> Ah, well-a-day, for we are souls bereaved!
> Of all the creatures under Heaven's wide scope
> We are most helpless, who had once most hope,
> And most beliefless, who had most believed.
>
> THE CITY OF DREADFUL NIGHT

All this time not a word about Black Sheep. He came later, and Harry, the black-haired boy, was mainly responsible for his coming.

Judy – who could help loving little Judy? – passed, by special permit, into the kitchen and thence straight to Aunty Rosa's heart. Harry was Aunty Rosa's one child, and Punch was the extra boy about the house. There was no special place for him or his little affairs, and he was forbidden to sprawl on sofas and explain his ideas about the manufacture of this world and his hopes for his future. Sprawling was lazy and wore out sofas, and little boys were not expected to talk. They were talked to, and the talking-to was intended for the benefit of their morals. As the unquestioned despot of the house at Bombay, Punch could not quite understand how he came to be of no account in this his new life.

Harry might reach across the table and take what he wanted; Judy might point and get what she wanted. Punch was forbidden to do either. The grey man was his great hope and stand-by for many months after Mamma and Papa left, and he had forgotten to tell Judy to 'bemember Mamma.'

This lapse was excusable, because in the interval he had been introduced by Aunt Rosa to two very impressive things – an abstraction called God, the intimate friend and ally of Aunty Rosa, generally believed to live behind the kitchen-range because it was hot there – and a dirty brown book filled with unintelligible dots and marks. Punch was always anxious to oblige everybody. He therefore welded the story of the Creation on to what he could recollect of his Indian fairy tales, and scandalized Aunty Rosa by repeating the result to Judy. It was a sin, a grievous sin, and Punch was talked to for a quarter of an hour. He could not understand where the iniquity came in, but was careful not to repeat the offence, because Aunty Rosa told him that God had heard every word he had said and was very angry. If this were true why didn't God come and say so, thought Punch, and dismissed the matter from his mind. Afterwards he learned to know the Lord as the only thing in the world more awful than Aunty Rosa – as a Creature that stood in the background and counted the strokes of the cane.

But the reading was, just then, a much more serious matter than any creed. Aunty Rosa sat him upon a table and told him that A B meant ab.

'Why?' said Punch. 'A is a and B is bee. *Why* does A B mean ab?'

'Because I tell you it does,' said Aunty Rosa, 'and you've got to say it.'

Punch said it accordingly, and for a month, hugely against his will, stumbled through the brown book, not in the least comprehending what it meant. But Uncle Harry, who walked much and generally alone, was wont to come into the nursery and suggest to Aunty Rosa that Punch should walk with him. He seldom spoke, but he showed Punch all Rocklington, from the mud-banks and the sand of the back-bay to the great harbours where ships lay at anchor, and the dockyards where the hammers were never still, and the marine-store shops, and the shiny brass counters in the Offices where Uncle Harry went once every three months with a slip of blue paper and received sovereigns in exchange; for he held a wound-pension. Punch heard, too, from his lips the story of the battle of Navarino, where the sailors of the Fleet, for three days afterwards, were deaf as posts and could only sign to each other. 'That was because of the noise of the guns,' said Uncle Harry, 'and I have got the wadding of a bullet somewhere inside me now.'

Punch regarded him with curiosity. He had not the least idea what wadding was, and his notion of a bullet was a dockyard cannon-ball bigger than his own head. How could Uncle Harry keep a cannon-ball inside him? He was afraid to ask, for fear Uncle Harry might be angry.

Punch had never known what anger – real anger – meant until one terrible day when Harry had taken his paint-box to paint a boat with, and Punch had protested. Then Uncle Harry had appeared on the scene and, muttering something about 'strangers' children,' had with a stick smitten the black-haired boy across the shoulders till he wept and yelled, and Aunty Rosa came in and abused Uncle Harry for cruelty to his own flesh and blood, and Punch shuddered to the tips of his shoes. 'It wasn't my fault,' he explained to the boy, but both Harry and Aunty Rosa said that it was, and that Punch had told tales, and for a week there were no more walks with Uncle Harry.

But that week brought a great joy to Punch.

He had repeated till he was thrice weary the statement that 'The Cat lay on the Mat and the Rat came in.'

'Now I can truly read,' said Punch, 'and now I will never read anything in the world.'

He put the brown book in the cupboard where his school-books lived and accidentally tumbled out a venerable volume, without covers, labelled *Sharpe's Magazine*. There was the most portentous picture of a Griffin on the first page, with verses below. The Griffin carried off one sheep a day from a German village, till a man came with a 'falchion' and split the Griffin open. Goodness only knew what a falchion was, but there was the Griffin, and his history was an improvement upon the eternal Cat.

'This,' said Punch, 'means things, and now I will know all about everything in all the world.' He read till the light failed, not understanding a tithe of the meaning, but tantalized by glimpses of new worlds hereafter to be revealed.

'What is a "falchion"? What is a "e-wee lamb"? What is a

"base *uss*urper"? What is a "verdant me-ad"?' he demanded, with flushed cheeks, at bedtime, of the astonished Aunty Rosa.

'Say your prayers and go to sleep,' she replied, and that was all the help Punch then or afterwards found at her hands in the new and delightful exercise of reading.

'Aunty Rosa only knows about God and things like that,' argued Punch. 'Uncle Harry will tell me.'

The next walk proved that Uncle Harry could not help either; but he allowed Punch to talk, and even sat down on a bench to hear about the Griffin. Other walks brought other stories as Punch ranged farther afield, for the house held large store of old books that no one ever opened – from *Frank Fairlegh* in serial numbers, and the earlier poems of Tennyson, contributed anonymously to *Sharpe's Magazine*, to '62 Exhibition Catalogues, gay with colours and delightfully incomprehensible, and odd leaves of *Gulliver's Travels*.

As soon as Punch could string a few pot-hooks together he wrote to Bombay, demanding by return of post 'all the books in all the world.' Papa could not comply with this modest indent, but sent *Grimm's Fairy Tales* and a *Hans Andersen*. That was enough. If he were only left alone Punch could pass, at any hour he chose, into a land of his own, beyond reach of Aunty Rosa and her God, Harry and his teasements, and Judy's claims to be played with.

'Don't disturve me, I'm reading. Go and play in the kitchen,' grunted Punch. 'Aunty Rosa lets *you* go there.' Judy was cutting her second teeth and was fretful. She appealed to Aunty Rosa, who descended on Punch.

'I was reading,' he explained, 'reading a book. I *want* to read.'

'You're only doing that to show off,' said Aunty Rosa. 'But we'll see. Play with Judy now, and don't open a book for a week.'

Judy did not pass a very enjoyable playtime with Punch, who was consumed with indignation. There was a pettiness at the bottom of the prohibition which puzzled him.

'It's what I like to do,' he said, 'and she's found out that and stopped me. Don't cry, Ju – it wasn't your fault – *please* don't cry, or she'll say I made you.'

Ju loyally mopped up her tears, and the two played in their nursery, a room in the basement and half underground, to which they were regularly sent after the mid-day dinner while Aunty

Rosa slept. She drank wine – that is to say, something from a bottle in the cellaret – for her stomach's sake, but if she did not fall asleep she would sometimes come into the nursery to see that the children were really playing. Now bricks, wooden hoops, ninepins, and china-ware cannot amuse for ever, especially when all Fairyland is to be won by the mere opening of a book, and, as often as not, Punch would be discovered reading to Judy or telling her interminable tales. That was an offence in the eyes of the law, and Judy would be whisked off by Aunty Rosa, while Punch was left to play alone, 'and be sure that I hear you doing it.'

It was not a cheering employ, for he had to make a playful noise. At last, with infinite craft, he devised an arrangement whereby the table could be supported as to three legs on toy bricks, leaving the fourth clear to bring down on the floor. He could work the table with one hand and hold a book with the other. This he did till an evil day when Aunty Rosa pounced upon him unawares and told him that he was 'acting a lie.'

'If you're old enough to do that,' she said – her temper was always worst after dinner – 'you're old enough to be beaten.'

'But – I'm – I'm not a animal!' said Punch aghast. He remembered Uncle Harry and the stick, and turned white. Aunty Rosa had hidden a light cane behind her, and Punch was beaten then and there over the shoulders. It was a revelation to him. The room-door was shut, and he was left to weep himself into repentance and work out his own gospel of life.

Aunty Rosa, he argued, had the power to beat him with many stripes. It was unjust and cruel, and Mamma and Papa would never have allowed it. Unless perhaps, as Aunty Rosa seemed to imply, they had sent secret orders. In which case he was abandoned indeed. It would be discreet in the future to propitiate Aunty Rosa, but then again, even in matters in which he was innocent, he had been accused of wishing to 'show off.' He had 'shown off' before visitors when he had attacked a strange gentleman – Harry's uncle, not his own – with requests for information about the Griffin and the falchion, and the precise nature of the Tilbury in which Frank Fairlegh rode – all points of paramount interest which he was bursting to understand. Clearly it would not do to pretend to care for Aunty Rosa.

At this point Harry entered and stood afar off, eyeing Punch, a dishevelled heap in the corner of the room, with disgust.

'You're a liar – a young liar,' said Harry, with great unction, 'and you're to have tea down here because you're not fit to speak to us. And you're not to speak to Judy again till Mother gives you leave. You'll corrupt her. You're only fit to associate with the servant. Mother says so.'

Having reduced Punch to a second agony of tears, Harry departed upstairs with the news that Punch was still rebellious.

Uncle Harry sat uneasily in the dining-room. 'Damn it all, Rosa,' said he at last, 'can't you leave the child alone? He's a good enough little chap when I meet him.'

'He puts on his best manners with you, Henry,' said Aunty Rosa, 'but I'm afraid, I'm very much afraid, that he is the Black Sheep of the family.'

Harry heard and stored up the name for future use. Judy cried till she was bidden to stop, her brother not being worth tears; and the evening concluded with the return of Punch to the upper regions and a private sitting at which all the blinding horrors of Hell were revealed to Punch with such store of imagery as Aunty Rosa's narrow mind possessed.

Most grievous of all was Judy's round-eyed reproach, and Punch went to bed in the depths of the Valley of Humiliation. He shared his room with Harry and knew the torture in store. For an hour and a half he had to answer that young gentleman's questions as to his motives for telling a lie, and a grievous lie, the precise quantity of punishment inflicted by Aunty Rosa, and had also to profess his deep gratitude for such religious instruction as Harry thought fit to impart.

From that day began the downfall of Punch, now Black Sheep.

'Untrustworthy in one thing, untrustworthy in all,' said Aunty Rosa, and Harry felt that Black Sheep was delivered into his hands. He would wake him up in the night to ask him why he was such a liar.

'I don't know,' Punch would reply.

'Then don't you think you ought to get up and pray to God for a new heart?'

'Y-yess.'

'Get out and pray, then!' And Punch would get out of bed with raging hate in his heart against all the world, seen and unseen.

He was always tumbling into trouble. Harry had a knack of cross-examining him as to his day's doings, which seldom failed to lead him, sleepy and savage, into half-a-dozen contradictions – all duly reported to Aunty Rosa next morning.

'But it *wasn't* a lie,' Punch would begin, charging into a laboured explanation that landed him more hopelessly in the mire. 'I said that I didn't say my prayers *twice* over in the day, and *that* was on Tuesday. *Once* I did. I *know* I did, but Harry said I didn't,' and so forth, till the tension brought tears, and he was dismissed from the table in disgrace.

'You usen't to be as bad as this,' said Judy, awe-stricken at the catalogue of Black Sheep's crimes. 'Why are you so bad now?'

'I don't know,' Black Sheep would reply. 'I'm not, if I only wasn't bothered upside-down. I knew what I *did*, and I want to say so; but Harry always makes it out different somehow, and Aunty Rosa doesn't believe a word I say. Oh, Ju! Don't *you* say I'm bad too.'

'Aunty Rosa says you are,' said Judy. 'She told the Vicar so when he came yesterday.'

'Why does she tell all the people outside the house about me? It isn't fair,' said Black Sheep. 'When I was in Bombay, and was bad – *doing* bad, not made-up bad like this – Mamma told Papa, and Papa told me he knew, and that was all. *Outside* people didn't know too – even Meeta didn't know.'

'I don't remember,' said Judy wistfully. 'I was all little then. Mamma was just as fond of you as she was of me, wasn't she?'

''Course she was. So was Papa. So was everybody.'

'Aunty Rosa likes me more than she does you. She says that you are a Trial and a Black Sheep, and I'm not to speak to you more than I can help.'

'Always? Not outside of the times when you mustn't speak to me at all?'

Judy nodded her head mournfully. Black Sheep turned away in despair, but Judy's arms were round his neck.

'Never mind, Punch,' she whispered. 'I *will* speak to you just the same as ever and ever. You're my own own brother though you are – though Aunty Rosa says you're bad, and Harry says you are a little coward. He says that if I pulled your hair hard, you'd cry.'

'Pull, then,' said Punch.

Judy pulled gingerly.

'Pull harder – as hard as you can! There! I don't mind how much you pull it *now*. If you'll speak to me same as ever I'll let you pull it as much as you like – pull it out if you like. But I know if Harry came and stood by and made you do it I'd cry.'

So the two children sealed the compact with a kiss, and Black Sheep's heart was cheered within him, and by extreme caution and careful avoidance of Harry he acquired virtue, and was allowed to read undisturbed for a week. Uncle Harry took him for walks, and consoled him with rough tenderness, never calling him Black Sheep. 'It's good for you, I suppose, Punch,' he used to say. 'Let us sit down. I'm getting tired.' His steps led him now not to the beach, but to the Cemetery of Rocklington, amid the potato-fields. For hours the grey man would sit on a tombstone, while Black Sheep would read epitaphs, and then with a sigh would stump home again.

'I shall lie there soon,' said he to Black Sheep, one winter evening, when his face showed white as a worn silver coin under the light of the lych-gate. 'You needn't tell Aunty Rosa.'

A month later he turned sharp round, ere half a morning walk was completed, and stumped back to the house. 'Put me to bed, Rosa,' he muttered. 'I've walked my last. The wadding has found me out.'

They put him to bed, and for a fortnight the shadow of his sickness lay upon the house, and Black Sheep went to and from unobserved. Papa had sent him some new books, and he was told to keep quiet. He retired into his own world, and was perfectly happy. Even at night his felicity was unbroken. He could lie in bed and string himself tales of travel and adventure while Harry was downstairs.

'Uncle Harry's going to die,' said Judy, who now lived almost entirely with Aunty Rosa.

'I'm very sorry,' said Black Sheep soberly. 'He told me that a long time ago.'

Aunty Rosa heard the conversation. 'Will nothing check your wicked tongue?' she said angrily. There were blue circles round her eyes.

Black Sheep retreated to the nursery and read *Cometh up as a Flower* with deep and uncomprehending interest. He had been forbidden to open it on account of its 'sinfulness,' but the bonds of the Universe were crumbling, and Aunty Rosa was in great grief.

'I'm glad,' said Black Sheep. 'She's unhappy now. It wasn't a lie, though. *I* knew. He told me not to tell.'

That night Black Sheep woke with a start. Harry was not in the room, and there was a sound of sobbing on the next floor. Then the voice of Uncle Harry, singing the song of the Battle of Navarino, came through the darkness:

> *'Our vanship was the Asia—*
> *The* Albion *and* Genoa*!'*

'He's getting well,' thought Black Sheep, who knew the song through all its seventeen verses. But the blood froze at his little heart as he thought. The voice leapt an octave, and rang shrill as a boatswain's pipe:

> *And next came on the lovely* Rose,
> *The* Philomel, *her fire-ship, closed,*
> *And the little* Brisk *was sore exposed*
> *That day at Navarino.'*

'That day at Navarino, Uncle Harry!' shouted Black Sheep, half wild with excitement and fear of he knew not what.

A door opened, and Aunty Rosa screamed up the staircase: 'Hush! For God's sake hush, you little devil! Uncle Harry is *dead*!'

THE THIRD BAG

Journeys end in lovers' meeting,
Every wise man's son doth know.

'I wonder what will happen to me now,' thought Black Sheep, when semi-pagan rites peculiar to the burial of the Dead in middleclass houses had been accomplished, and Aunty Rosa, awful in black crape, had returned to this life. 'I don't think I've done anything bad that she knows of. I suppose I will soon. She will be very cross after Uncle Harry's dying, and Harry will be cross too. I'll keep in the nursery.'

Unfortunately for Punch's plans, it was decided that he should be sent to a day-school which Harry attended. This meant a morning walk with Harry, and perhaps an evening one; but the prospect of freedom in the interval was refreshing. 'Harry'll tell everything I do, but I won't do anything,' said Black Sheep. Fortified with this virtuous resolution, he went to school only to find that Harry's version of his character had preceded him, and that life was a burden in consequence. He took stock of his associates. Some of them were unclean, some of them talked in dialect, many dropped their h's, and there were two Jews and a negro, or someone quite as dark, in the assembly. 'That's a *hubshi*,' said Black Sheep to himself. 'Even Meeta used to laugh at a *hubshi*. I don't think this is a proper place.' He was indignant for at least an hour, till he reflected that any expostulation on his part would be by Aunty Rosa construed into 'showing off,' and that Harry would tell the boys.

'How do you like school?' said Aunty Rosa at the end of the day.

'I think it is a very nice place,' said Punch quietly.

'I suppose you warned the boys of Black Sheep's character?' said Aunty Rosa to Harry.

'Oh yes,' said the censor of Black Sheep's morals. 'They know all about him.'

'If I was with my father,' said Black Sheep, stung to the quick, 'I shouldn't *speak* to those boys. He wouldn't let me. They live in shops. I saw them go into shops – where their fathers live and sell things.'

'You're too good for that school, are you?' said Aunty Rosa, with a bitter smile. 'You ought to be grateful, Black Sheep, that those boys speak to you at all. It isn't every school that takes little liars.'

Harry did not fail to make much capital out of Black Sheep's ill-considered remark; with the result that several boys, including the *hubshi*, demonstrated to Black Sheep the eternal equality of the human race by smacking his head, and his consolation from Aunty Rosa was that it 'served him right for being vain.' He learned, however, to keep his opinions to himself, and by propitiating Harry in carrying books and the like to get a little peace. His existence was not too joyful. From nine till twelve he was at school, and from two to four, except on Saturdays. In the evenings he was sent down into the nursery to prepare his lessons for the next day, and every night came the dreaded cross-questionings at Harry's hand. Of Judy he saw but little. She was deeply religious – at six years of age Religion is easy to come by – and sorely divided between her natural love for Black Sheep and her love for Aunty Rosa, who could do no wrong.

The lean woman returned that love with interest, and Judy, when she dared, took advantage of this for the remission of Black Sheep's penalties. Failures in lessons at school were punished at home by a week without reading other than school-books, and Harry brought the news of such a failure with glee. Further, Black Sheep was then bound to repeat his lessons at bedtime to Harry, who generally succeeded in making him break down, and consoled him by gloomiest forebodings for the morrow. Harry was at once spy, practical joker, inquisitor, and Aunty Rosa's deputy executioner. He filled his many posts to admiration. From his actions, now that Uncle Harry was dead, there was no appeal. Black Sheep had not been permitted to keep any self-respect at school: at home he was, of course, utterly discredited, and grateful for any pity that the servant-girls – they changed frequently at Downe Lodge because they, too, were liars – might show. 'You're just fit to row in the same boat with Black Sheep,' was a sentiment that each new Jane or Eliza might expect to hear, before a month was over, from Aunty Rosa's lips; and Black Sheep was used to ask new girls whether they had yet been compared to him. Harry was 'Master Harry' in their mouths; Judy was officially 'Miss Judy'; but Black Sheep was never anything more than Black Sheep *tout court*.

As time went on and the memory of Papa and Mamma became wholly overlaid by the unpleasant task of writing them letters, under Aunty Rosa's eye, each Sunday, Black Sheep forgot what manner of life he had led in the beginning of things. Even Judy's appeals to 'try and remember about Bombay' failed to quicken him.

'I can't remember,' he said. 'I know I used to give orders and Mamma kissed me.'

'Aunty Rosa will kiss you if you are good,' pleaded Judy.

'Ugh! I don't want to be kissed by Aunty Rosa. She'd say I was doing it to get something more to eat.'

The weeks lengthened into months, and the holidays came; but just before the holidays Black Sheep fell into deadly sin.

Among the many boys whom Harry had incited to 'punch

Black Sheep's head because he daren't hit back,' was one more aggravating than the rest, who, in an unlucky moment, fell upon Black Sheep when Harry was not near. The blows stung, and Black Sheep struck back at random with all the power at his command. The boy dropped and whimpered. Black Sheep was astounded at his own act, but, feeling the unresisting body under him, shook it with both his hands in blind fury and then began to throttle his enemy; meaning honestly to slay him. There was a scuffle, and Black Sheep was torn off the body by Harry and some colleagues, and cuffed home tingling but exultant. Aunty Rosa was out. Pending her arrival, Harry set himself to lecture Black Sheep on the sin of murder – which he described as the offence of Cain.

'Why didn't you fight him fair? What did you hit him when he was down for, you little cur?'

Black Sheep looked up at Harry's throat and then at a knife on the dinner-table.

'I don't understand,' he said wearily. 'You always set him on me and told me I was a coward when I blubbed. Will you leave me alone until Aunty Rosa comes in? She'll beat me if you tell her I ought to be beaten; so it's all right.'

'It's all wrong,' said Harry magisterially. 'You nearly killed him, and I shouldn't wonder if he dies.'

'Will he die?' said Black Sheep.

'I daresay,' said Harry, 'and then you'll be hanged, and go to Hell.'

'All right,' said Black Sheep, picking up the table-knife. 'Then I'll kill *you* now. You say things and do things and – and *I* don't know how things happen, and you never leave me alone – and I don't care *what* happens!'

He ran at the boy with the knife, and Harry fled upstairs to his room, promising Black Sheep the finest thrashing in the world when Aunty Rosa returned. Black Sheep sat at the bottom of the stairs, the table-knife in his hand, and wept for that he had not killed Harry. The servant-girl came up from the kitchen, took the knife away, and consoled him. But Black Sheep was beyond consolation. He would be badly beaten by Aunty Rosa; then there would be another beating at Harry's hands; then Judy would not be allowed to speak to him; then the tale would be told at school, and then—

There was no one to help and no one to care, and the best way out of the business was by death. A knife would hurt, but Aunty Rosa had told him, a year ago, that if he sucked paint he would die. He went into the nursery, unearthed the now disused Noah's Ark, and sucked the paint off as many animals as remained. It tasted abominably, but he had licked Noah's Dove clean by the time Aunty Rosa and Judy returned. He went upstairs and greeted them with: 'Please, Aunty Rosa, I believe I've nearly killed a boy at school, and I've tried to kill Harry, and when you've done all about God and Hell, will you beat me and get it over?'

The tale of the assault as told by Harry could only be explained on the ground of possession by the Devil. Wherefore Black Sheep was not only most excellently beaten, once by Aunty Rosa, and once, when thoroughly cowed down, by Harry, but he was further prayed for at family prayers, together with Jane, who had stolen a cold rissole from the pantry, and snuffled audibly as her sin was brought before the Throne of Grace. Black Sheep was sore and stiff but triumphant. He would die that very night and be rid of them all. No, he would ask for no forgiveness from Harry, and at bed-time would stand no questioning at Harry's hands, even though addressed as 'Young Cain.'

'I've been beaten,' said he, 'and I've done other things. I don't care what I do. If you speak to me tonight, Harry, I'll get out and try to kill you. Now you can kill me if you like.'

Harry took his bed into the spare room, and Black Sheep lay down to die.

It may be that the makers of Noah's Arks know that their animals are likely to find their way into young mouths, and paint them accordingly. Certain it is that the common, weary next morning broke through the windows and found Black Sheep quite well and a good deal ashamed of himself, but richer by the knowledge that he could, in extremity, secure himself against Harry for the future.

When he descended to breakfast on the first day of the holidays, he was greeted with the news that Harry, Aunty Rosa, and Judy were going away to Brighton, while Black Sheep was to stay in the house with the servant. His latest outbreak suited Aunty Rosa's plans admirably. It gave her good excuse for leaving the extra boy behind. Papa in Bombay, who really seemed to know a young sinner's wants to the hour, sent, that week, a package of new books. And with these, and the society of Jane on board-wages, Black Sheep was left alone for a month.

The books lasted for ten days. They were eaten too quickly in long gulps of twelve hours at a time. Then came days of doing absolutely nothing, of dreaming dreams and marching imaginary armies up and down stairs, of counting the number of banisters, and of measuring the length and breadth of every room in handspans – fifty down the side, thirty across, and fifty back again. Jane made many friends, and, after receiving Black Sheep's assurance that he would not tell of her absences, went out daily for long hours. Black Sheep would follow the rays of the sinking sun from the kitchen to the dining-room and thence upward to his own bedroom until all was grey dark, and he ran down to the kitchen fire and read by its light. He was happy in that he was left alone and could read as much as he pleased. But, later, he grew afraid of the shadows of window-curtains and the flapping of doors and the creaking of shutters. He went out into the garden, and the rustling of the laurel-bushes frightened him.

He was glad when they all returned – Aunty Rosa, Harry, and Judy – full of news, and Judy laden with gifts. Who could help loving loyal little Judy? In return for all her merry babblement, Black Sheep confided to her that the distance from the hall-door to the top of the first landing was exactly one hundred and eighty-four hand-spans. He had found it out himself!

Then the old life recommenced; but with a difference, and a new sin. To his other iniquities Black Sheep had now added a phenomenal clumsiness – was as unfit to trust in action as he was in word. He himself could not account for spilling everything he touched, upsetting glasses as he put his hand out, and bumping his head against doors that were manifestly shut. There was a grey haze upon all his world, and it narrowed month by month, until at last it left Black Sheep almost alone with the flapping curtains that were so like ghosts, and the nameless terrors of broad daylight that were only coats on pegs after all.

Holidays came and holidays went, and Black Sheep was taken to see many people whose faces were all exactly alike; was beaten when occasion demanded, and tortured by Harry on all possible occasions; but defended by Judy through good and evil report, though she hereby drew upon herself the wrath of Aunty Rosa.

The weeks were interminable and Papa and Mamma were clean forgotten. Harry had left school and was a clerk in a Banking-Office. Freed from his presence, Black Sheep resolved that he should no longer be deprived of his allowance of pleasure-reading. Consequently when he failed at school he reported that all was well, and conceived a large contempt for Aunty Rosa as he saw how easy it was to deceive her. 'She says I'm a little liar when I don't tell lies, and now I do, she doesn't know,' thought Black Sheep. Aunty Rosa had credited him in the past with petty cunning and stratagem that had never entered into his head. By the light of the sordid knowledge that she had revealed to him he paid her back full tale. In a household where the most innocent of his motives, his natural yearning for a little affection, had been interpreted into a desire for more bread and jam, or to ingratiate himself with strangers and so put Harry into the background, his work was easy. Aunty Rosa could penetrate certain kinds of hypocrisy, but not all. He set his child's wits against hers and was no more beaten. It grew monthly more and more of a trouble to read the school-books, and even the pages of the open-print story-books danced and were dim. So Black Sheep brooded in the shadows that fell about him and cut him off from the world, inventing horrible punishments for 'dear Harry,' or plotting another line of the tangled web of deception that he wrapped round Aunty Rosa.

Then the crash came and the cobwebs were broken. It was impossible to foresee everything. Aunty Rosa made personal inquiries as to Black Sheep's progress and received information that startled her. Step by step, with a delight as keen as when she convicted an underfed housemaid of the theft of cold meats, she followed the trail of Black Sheep's delinquencies. For weeks and weeks, in order to escape banishment from the book-shelves, he had made a fool of Aunty Rosa, of Harry, of God, of all the world! Horrible, most horrible, and evidence of an utterly depraved mind.

Black Sheep counted the cost. 'It will only be one big beating and then she'll put a card with "Liar" on my back, same as she did before. Harry will whack me and pray for me, and she will pray for me at prayers and tell me I'm a Child of the Devil and give me hymns to learn. But I've done all my reading and she never knew. She'll say she knew all along. She's an old liar too,' said he.

For three days Black Sheep was shut in his own bedroom – to prepare his heart. 'That means two beatings. One at school and one here. *That* one will hurt most.' And it fell even as he thought. He was thrashed at school before the Jews and the *hubshi* for the heinous crime of carrying home false reports of progress. He was thrashed at home by Aunty Rosa on the same count, and then the placard was produced. Aunty Rosa stitched it between his shoulders and bade him go for a walk with it upon him.

'If you make me do that,' said Black Sheep very quietly, 'I shall burn this house down, and perhaps I'll kill you. I don't know whether I *can* kill you – you're so bony – but I'll try.'

No punishment followed this blasphemy, though Black Sheep held himself ready to work his way to Aunty Rosa's withered throat and grip there till he was beaten off. Perhaps Aunty Rosa was afraid, for Black Sheep, having reached the Nadir of Sin, bore himself with a new recklessness.

In the midst of all the trouble there came a visitor from over the seas to Downe Lodge, who knew Papa and Mamma, and was commissioned to see Punch and Judy. Black Sheep was sent to the drawing-room and charged into a solid tea-table laden with china.

'Gently, gently, little man,' said the visitor, turning Black Sheep's face to the light slowly. 'What's that big bird on the palings?'

'What bird?' asked Black Sheep.

The visitor looked deep down into Black Sheep's eyes for half a minute, and then said suddenly: 'Good God, the little chap's nearly blind!'

It was a most businesslike visitor. He gave orders, on his own responsibility, that Black Sheep was not to go to school or open a book until Mamma came home. 'She'll be here in three weeks, as you know, of course,' said he, 'and I'm Inverarity Sahib. I ushered you into this wicked world, young man, and a nice use you seem to have made of your time. You must do nothing whatever. Can you do that?'

'Yes,' said Punch in a dazed way. He had known that Mamma was coming. There was a chance, then, of another beating.

Thank Heaven, Papa wasn't coming too. Aunty Rosa had said of late that he ought to be beaten by a man.

For the next three weeks Black Sheep was strictly allowed to do nothing. He spent his time in the old nursery looking at the broken toys, for all of which account must be rendered to Mamma. Aunty Rosa hit him over the hands if even a wooden boat were broken. But that sin was of small importance compared to the other revelations, so darkly hinted at by Aunty Rosa. 'When your Mother comes, and hears what I have to tell her, she may appreciate you properly,' she said grimly, and mounted guard over Judy lest that small maiden should attempt to comfort her brother, to the peril of her soul.

And Mamma came – in a four-wheeler – fluttered with tender excitement. Such a Mamma! She was young, frivolously young, and beautiful, with delicately flushed cheeks, eyes that shone like stars, and a voice that needed no appeal of outstretched arms to draw little ones to her heart. Judy ran straight to her, but Black Sheep hesitated. Could this wonder be 'showing off'? She would not put out her arms when she knew of his crimes. Meantime was it possible that by fondling she wanted to get anything out of Black Sheep? Only all his love and all his confidence; but that Black Sheep did not know. Aunty Rosa withdrew and left Mamma, kneeling between her children, half laughing, half crying, in the very hall where Punch and Judy had wept five years before.

'Well, chicks, do you remember me?'

'No,' said Judy frankly, 'but I said, "God bless Papa and Mamma" ev'vy night.'

'A little,' said Black Sheep. 'Remember I wrote to you every week, anyhow. That isn't to show off, but 'cause of what comes afterwards.'

'What comes after? What should come after, my darling boy?' And she drew him to her again. He came awkwardly, with many angles. 'Not used to petting,' said the quick Mother-soul. 'The girl is.'

'She's too little to hurt anyone,' thought Black Sheep, 'and if I said I'd kill her, she'd be afraid. I wonder what Aunty Rosa will tell.'

There was a constrained late dinner, at the end of which Mamma picked up Judy and put her to bed with endearments manifold. Faithless little Judy had shown her defection from Aunty Rosa already. And that lady resented it bitterly. Black Sheep rose to leave the room.

'Come and say good night,' said Aunty Rosa, offering a withered cheek.

'Huh!' said Black Sheep. 'I never kiss you, and I'm not going to show off. Tell that woman what I've done, and see what she says.'

Black Sheep climbed into bed feeling that he had lost Heaven after a glimpse through the gates. In half an hour 'that woman' was bending over him. Black Sheep flung up his right arm. It wasn't fair to come and hit him in the dark. Even Aunty Rosa never tried that. But no blow followed.

'Are you showing off? I won't tell you anything more than Aunty Rosa has, and *she* doesn't know everything,' said Black Sheep as clearly as he could for the arms round his neck.

'Oh, my son – my little, little son! It was my fault – *my* fault, darling – and yet how could we help it? Forgive me, Punch.' The voice died out in a broken whisper, and two hot tears fell on Black Sheep's forehead.

'Has she been making you cry too?' he asked. 'You should see Jane cry. But you're nice, and Jane is a Born Liar – Aunty Rosa says so.'

'Hush, Punch, hush! My boy, don't talk like that. Try to love me a little bit – a little bit. You don't know how I want it. Punch-*baba*, come back to me! I am your Mother – your own Mother – and never mind the rest. I know – yes, I know, dear. It doesn't matter now. Punch, won't you care for me a little?'

It is astonishing how much petting a big boy of ten can endure when he is quite sure that there is no one to laugh at him. Black Sheep had never been made much of before, and here was this beautiful woman treating him – Black Sheep, the Child of the Devil and the inheritor of undying flame – as though he were a small God.

'I care for you a great deal, Mother dear,' he whispered at last, 'and I'm glad you've come back; but are you sure Aunty Rosa told you everything?'

'Everything. What *does* it matter? But—' the voice broke with a sob that was also laughter – 'Punch, my poor, dear, half-blind darling, don't you think it was a little foolish of you?'

'*No*. It saved a lickin'.'

Mamma shuddered and slipped away in the darkness to write a long letter to Papa. Here is an extract:

> '... Judy is a dear, plump little prig who adores the woman, and wears with as much gravity as her religious opinions – only eight, Jack! – a venerable horse-hair atrocity which she calls her Bustle! I have just burnt it, and the child is asleep in my bed as I write. She will come to me at once. Punch I cannot quite understand. He is well nourished, but seems to have been worried into a system of small deceptions which the woman magnifies into deadly sins. Don't you recollect our own upbringing, dear, when the Fear of the Lord was so often the beginning of falsehood? I shall win Punch to me before long. I am taking the children away into the country to get them to know me, and, on the whole, I am content, or shall be when you come home, dear boy, and then, thank God, we shall be all under one roof again at last!'

Three months later, Punch, no longer Black Sheep, has discovered that he is the veritable owner of a real, live, lovely Mamma, who is also a sister, comforter, and friend, and that he must protect her till the Father comes home. Deception does not suit the part of a protector, and, when one can do anything without question, where is the use of deception?

'Mother would be awfully cross if you walked through that ditch,' says Judy, continuing a conversation.

'Mother's never angry,' says Punch. 'She'd just say, "You're a little *pagal* [idiot]"; and that's not nice, but I'll show.'

Punch walks through the ditch and mires himself to the knees. 'Mother dear,' he shouts, 'I'm just as dirty as I can pos-*sib*-ly be!'

'Then change your clothes as quickly as you pos-*sib*-ly can!' Mother's clear voice rings out from the house. 'And don't be a little *pagal*!'

'There! Told you so,' says Punch. 'It's all different now, and we are just as much Mother's as if she had never gone.'

Not altogether, O Punch, for when young lips have drunk deep of the bitter waters of Hate, Suspicion, and Despair, all the Love in the world will not wholly take away that knowledge; though it may turn darkened eyes for a while to the light, and teach Faith where no Faith was.

THOMAS HARDY

On The Western Circuit

1

The man who played the disturbing part in the two quiet feminine lives hereunder depicted – no great man, in any sense, by the way – first had knowledge of them on an October evening, in the city of Melchester. He had been standing in the Close, vainly endeavouring to gain amid the darkness a glimpse of the most homogeneous pile of mediaeval architecture in England, which towered and tapered from the damp and level sward in front of him. While he stood the presence of the Cathedral walls was revealed rather by the ear than by the eyes; he could not see them, but they reflected sharply a roar of sound which entered the Close by a street leading from the city square, and, falling upon the building, was flung back upon him.

He postponed till the morrow his attempt to examine the deserted edifice, and turned his attention to the noise. It was compounded of steam barrel-organs, the clanging of gongs, the ringing of hand-bells, the clack of rattles, and the undistinguishable shouts of men. A lurid light hung in the air in the direction of the tumult. Thitherward he went, passing under the arched gateway, along a straight street, and into the square.

He might have searched Europe over for a greater contrast between juxtaposed scenes. The spectacle was that of the eighth chasm of the Inferno as to colour and flame, and, as to mirth, a development of the Homeric heaven. A smoky glare, of the complexion of brass-filings, ascended from the fiery tongues of innumerable naphtha lamps affixed to booths, stalls, and other temporary erections which crowded the spacious market-square. In front of this irradiation scores of human figures, more or less in profile, were darting athwart and across, up, down, and around, like gnats against a sunset.

Their motions were so rhythmical that they seemed to be moved by machinery. And it presently appeared that they were moved by machinery indeed; the figures being those of the patrons of swings, see-saws, flying-leaps, above all of the three steam round-abouts which occupied the centre of the position. It was from the latter that the din of steam-organs came.

Throbbing humanity in full light was, on second thoughts, better than architecture in the dark. The young man, lighting a short pipe, and putting his hat on one side and one hand in his pocket, to throw himself into harmony with his new environment, drew near to the largest and most patronized of the steam circuses, as the roundabouts were called by their owners. This was one of brilliant finish, and it was now in full revolution. The musical instrument around which and to whose tones the riders revolved, directed its trumpet-mouths of brass upon the young man, and the long plate-glass mirrors set at angles, which revolved with the machine, flashed the gyrating personages and hobby-horses kaleidoscopically into his eyes.

It could now be seen that he was unlike the majority of the crowd. A gentlemanly young fellow, one of the species found in large towns only, and London particularly, built on delicate lines, well, though not fashionably dressed, he appeared to belong to the professional class; he had nothing square or practical about his look, much that was curvilinear and sensuous. Indeed some would have called him a man not altogether typical of the middle-class male of a century wherein sordid ambition is the master-passion that seems to be taking the time-honoured place of love.

The revolving figures passed before his eyes with an unexpected and quiet grace in a throng whose natural movements did not suggest gracefulness or quietude as a rule. By some contrivance there was imparted to each of the hobby-horses a motion which was really the triumph and perfection of roundabout inventiveness – a galloping rise and fall, so timed that, of each pair of steeds, one was on the spring while the other was on the pitch. The riders were quite fascinated by these equine undulations in this most delightful holiday-game of our times. There were riders as young as six, and as old as sixty years, with every age between. At first it was difficult to catch a personality, but by and by the observer's eyes centred on the prettiest girl out of the several pretty ones revolving.

It was not that one with the light frock and light hat whom he had been at first attracted by; no, it was the one with the black cape, gray skirt, light gloves and – no, not even she, but the one behind her; she with the crimson skirt, dark jacket, brown hat and brown gloves. Unmistakably that was the prettiest girl.

Having finally selected her, this idle spectator studied her as well as he was able during each of her brief transits across his visual field. She was absolutely unconscious of everything save the act of riding: her features were rapt in an ecstatic dreaminess; for the moment she did not know her age or her history or her lineaments, much less her troubles. He himself was full of vague latter-day glooms and popular melancholies, and it was a refreshing sensation to behold this young thing then and there, absolutely as happy as if she were in a Paradise.

Dreading the moment when the inexorable stoker, grimily lurking behind the glittering rococo-work, should decide that this set of riders had had their pennyworth, and bring the whole concern of steam-engine, horses, mirrors, trumpets, drums, cymbals, and such-like to pause and silence, he waited for her every reappearance, glancing indifferently over the intervening forms, including the two plainer girls, the old woman and child, the two youngsters, the newly-married couple, the old man with a clay pipe, the sparkish youth with a ring, the young ladies in the charriot, the pair of journeyman-carpenters, and others, till his select country beauty followed on again in her place. He had never seen a fairer product of nature, and at each round she made a deeper mark in his sentiments. The stoppage then came, and the sighs of the riders were audible.

He moved round to the place at which he reckoned she would alight; but she retained her seat. The empty saddles began to refill, and she plainly was deciding to have another turn. The young man drew up to the side of her steed, and pleasantly asked her if she had enjoyed her ride.

'O yes!' she said with dancing eyes. 'It has been quite unlike anything I have ever felt in my life before!'

It was not difficult to fall into conversation with her. Unreserved – too unreserved – by nature, she was not experienced enough to be reserved by art, and after a little coaxing she answered his remarks readily. She had come to live in Melchester from a village on the Great Plain, and this was the first time that she had ever seen a steam-circus; she could not understand how such wonderful machines were made. She had come to the city on the invitation of Mrs Harnham, who had taken her into her household to train her as a servant, if she showed any aptitude. Mrs Harnham was a young lady who before she married had been Miss Edith White, living in the country near the speaker's cottage; she was now very kind to her through knowing her in childhood so well. She was even taking the trouble to educate her. Mrs Harnham was the only friend she had in the world, and being without children had wished to have her near her in preference to anybody else, though she had only lately come; allowed her to do almost as she liked, and to have a holiday whenever she asked for it. The husband of this kind young lady was a rich wine-merchant of the town, but Mrs Harnham did not care much about him. In the daytime you could see the house from where they were talking. She, the speaker, liked Melchester better than the lonely country, and she was going to have a new hat for next Sunday that was to cost fifteen and ninepence.

Then she inquired of her acquaintance where he lived, and he told her in London, that ancient and smoky city, where everybody lived who lived at all, and die because they could not live there. He came into Wessex two or three times a year for professional reasons; he had arrived from Wintoncester yesterday, and was going on into the next county in a day or two. For one thing he did like the country better than the town, and it was because it contained such girls as herself.

Then the pleasure-machine started again, and, to the light-hearted girl, the figure of the handsome young man, the market-square with its lights and crowd, the houses beyond, and the world at large, began moving round as before, countermoving in the revolving mirrors on her right hand, she being as it were the fixed point in an undulating, dazzling, lurid universe, in which loomed forward most prominently of all the form of her late interlocutor. Each time that she approached the half of her orbit that lay nearest him they gazed at each other with smiles, and with that unmistakable expression which means so little at the moment, yet so often leads up to passion, heartache, union, disunion, devotion, over-population, drudgery, content, resignation, despair.

When the horses slowed anew he stepped to her side and proposed another heat. 'Hang the expense for once,' he said. 'I'll pay!'

She laughed till the tears came.

'Why do you laugh, dear?' said he.

'Because – you are so genteel that you must have plenty of money, and only say that for fun!' she returned.

'Ha-ha!' laughed the young man in unison, and gallantly producing his money she was enabled to whirl on again.

As he stood smiling there in the motley crowd, with his pipe in his hand, and clad in the rough pea-jacket and wideawake that he had put on for his stroll, who would have supposed him to be Charles Bradford Raye, Esquire, stuff-gownsman, educated at Wintoncester, called to the Bar at Lincoln's Inn, now going the Western Circuit, merely detained in Melchester by a small arbitration after his brethren had moved on to the next county-town?

2

The square was overlooked from its remoter corner by the house of which the young girl had spoken, a dignified residence of considerable size, having several windows on each floor. Inside one of these, on the first floor, the apartment being a large drawing-room, sat a lady, in appearance from twenty-eight to thirty years of age. The blinds were still undrawn, and the lady was absently surveying the weird scene without, her cheek resting on her hand. The room was unlit from within, but enough of the glare from the market-place entered it to reveal the lady's face. She was what is called an interesting creature rather than a handsome woman; dark-eyed, thoughtful, and with sensitive lips.

A man sauntered into the room from behind and came forward.

'O, Edith, I didn't see you,' he said. 'Why are you sitting here in the dark?'

'I am looking at the fair,' replied the lady in a languid voice.

'Oh? Horrid nuisance every year! I wish it could be put a stop to.'

'I like it.'

'H'm. There's no accounting for taste.'

For a moment he gazed from the window with her, for politeness' sake, and then went out again.

In a few minutes she rang.

'Hasn't Anna come in?' asked Mrs Harnham.

'No, m'm.'

'She ought to be in by this time. I meant her to go for ten minutes only.'

'Shall I go and look for her, m'm?' said the housemaid alertly.

'No. It is not necessary: she is a good girl and will come soon.'

However, when the servant had gone Mrs Harnham arose, went up to her room, cloaked and bonneted herself, and proceeded downstairs, where she found her husband.

'I want to see the fair,' she said; 'and I am going to look for Anna. I have made myself responsible for her, and must see she comes to no harm. She ought to be indoors. Will you come with me?'

'Oh, she's all right. I saw her on one of those whirligig things, talking to her young man as I came in. But I'll go if you wish, though I'd rather go a hundred miles the other way.'

'Then please do so. I shall come to no harm alone.'

She left the house and entered the crowd which thronged the market-place, where she soon discovered Anna, seated on the revolving horse. As soon as it stopped Mrs Harnham advanced and said severely, 'Anna, how can you be such a wild girl? You were only to be out for ten minutes.'

Anna looked blank, and the young man, who had dropped into the background, came to help her alight.

'Please don't blame her,' he said politely. 'It is my fault that she has stayed. She looked so graceful on the horse that I induced her to go round again. I assure you that she has been quite safe.'

'In that case I'll leave her in your hands,' said Mrs Harnham, turning to retrace her steps.

But this for the moment it was not so easy to do. Something had attracted the crowd to a spot in their rear, and the wine-merchant's wife, caught by its sway, found herself pressed against Anna's acquaintance without power to move away. Their faces were within a few inches of each other, his breath fanned her cheek as well as Anna's. They could do no other than smile at the accident; but neither spoke, and each waited passively. Mrs Harnham then felt a man's hand clasping her fingers, and from the look of consciousness on the young fellow's face she knew the hand to be his: she also knew that from the position of the girl he had no other thought than that the imprisoned hand was Anna's. What prompted her to refrain from undeceiving him she could hardly tell. Not content with holding the hand, he playfully slipped two of his fingers inside her glove, against her palm. Thus matters continued till the pressure lessened; but several minutes passed before the crowd thinned sufficiently to allow Mrs Harnham to withdraw.

'How did they get to know each other, I wonder?' she mused as she retreated. 'Anna is really very forward – and he very wicked and nice.'

She was so gently stirred with the stranger's manner and voice, with the tenderness of his idle touch, that instead of re-entering the house she turned back again and observed the pair from a screened nook. Really she argued (being little less impulsive than Anna herself) it was very excusable in Anna to encourage him, however she might have contrived to make his acquaintance; he was so gentlemanly, so fascinating, had such beautiful eyes. The thought that he was several years her junior produced a reasonless sigh.

At length the couple turned from the roundabout towards the door of Mrs Harnham's house, and the young man could be heard saying that he would accompany her home. Anna, then, had found a lover, apparently a very devoted one. Mrs Harnham was quite interested in him. When they drew near the door of the wine-merchant's house, a comparatively deserted spot by this time, they stood invisible for a little while in the shadow of a wall, where they separated, Anna going on to the entrance, and her acquaintance returning across the square.

'Anna,' said Mrs Harnham, coming up. 'I've been looking at you! That young man kissed you at parting, I am almost sure.'

'Well,' stammered Anna; 'he said, if I didn't mind – it would do me no harm, and – and – him a great deal of good!'

'Ah, I thought so! and he was a stranger till tonight?'

'Yes, ma'am.'

'Yet I warrant you told him your name and everything about yourself?'

'He asked me.'

'But he didn't tell you his?'

'Yes, ma'am, he did!' cried Anna victoriously. 'It is Charles Bradford, of London.'

'Well, if he's respectable, of course I've nothing to say against your knowing him,' remarked her mistress, prepossessed, in spite of general principles, in the young man's favour. 'But I must reconsider all that, if he attempts to renew your acquaintance. A country-bred girl like you, who has never lived in Melchester till this month, who had hardly ever seen a black-coated man till you came here, to be so sharp as to capture a young Londoner like him!'

'I didn't capture him. I didn't do anything,' said Anna, in confusion.

When she was indoors and alone Mrs Harnham thought what a well-bred and chivalrous young man Anna's companion had seemed. There had been a magic in his wooing touch of her hand; and she wondered how he had come to be attracted by the girl.

The next morning the emotional Edith Harnham went to the usual week-day service in Melchester cathedral. In crossing the Close through the fog she again perceived him who had interested her the previous evening, gazing up thoughtfully at the high-piled architecture of the nave: and as soon as she had taken her seat he entered and sat down in a stall opposite hers.

He did not particularly heed her; but Mrs Harnham was continually occupying her eyes with him, and wondered more than ever what had attracted him in her unfledged maid-servant. The mistress was almost as unaccustomed as the maiden herself to the end-of-the-age young man, or she might have wondered less. Raye, having looked about him a while, left abruptly, without regard to the service that was proceeding; and Mrs Harnham – lonely, impressionable creature that she was – took no further interest in praising the Lord. She wished she had married a London man who knew the subtleties of love-making as they were evidently known to him who had mistakenly caressed her hand.

3

The calendar at Melchester had been light, occupying the court only a few hours; and the assizes at Casterbridge, the next county-town on the Western Circuit, having no business for Raye, he had not gone thither. At the next town after that they did not open till the following Monday, trials to begin on Tuesday morning. In the natural order of things Raye would have arrived at the latter place on Monday afternoon; but it was not till the middle of Wednesday that his gown and gray wig, curled in tiers, in the best fashion of Assyrian bas-reliefs, were seen blowing and bobbing behind him as he hastily walked up the High Street from his lodgings. But though he entered the assize building there was nothing for him to do, and sitting at the blue baize table in the well of the court, he mended pens with a mind far away from the case in progress. Thoughts of unpremeditated conduct, of which a week earlier he would not have believed himself capable, threw him into a mood of dissatisfied depression.

He had contrived to see again the pretty rural maiden Anna, the day after the fair, had walked out of the city with her to the earthworks of Old Melchester, and feeling a violent fancy for her, had remained in Melchester all Sunday, Monday, and Tuesday; by persuasion obtaining walks and meeting with the girl six or seven times during the interval; had in brief won her, body and soul.

He supposed it must have been owing to the seclusion in which he had lived of late in town that he had given way so unrestrainedly to a passion for an artless creature whose inexperience had, from the first, led her to place herself unreservedly in his hands. Much he deplored trifling with her feelings for the sake of a passing desire; and he could only hope that she might not live to suffer on his account.

She had begged him to come to her again; entreated him; wept. He had promised that he would do so, and he meant to carry out that promise. He could not desert her now. Awkward as such unintentional connections were, the interspace of a hundred miles – which to a girl of her limited capabilities was like a thousand – would effectually hinder this summer fancy from greatly encumbering his life; while thought of her simple love might do him the negative good of keeping him from idle pleasures in town when he wished to work hard. His circuit journeys would take him to Melchester three or four times a year; and then he could always see her.

The pseudonym, or rather partial name, that he had given her as his before knowing how far the acquaintance was going to carry him, had been spoken on the spur of the moment, without any ulterior intention whatever. He had not afterwards disturbed Anna's error, but on leaving her he had felt bound to give her an address at a stationer's not far from his chambers, at which she might write to him under the initials 'C.B.'

In due time Raye returned to his London abode, having called at Melchester on his way and spent a few additional hours with his fascinating child of nature. In town he lived monotonously every day. Often he and his rooms were enclosed by a tawny fog from all the world besides, and when he lighted the gas to read or write by, his situation seemed so unnatural that he would look into the fire and think of that trusting girl at Melchester again and again. Often, oppressed by absurd fondness for her, he would enter the dim religious nave of the Law Courts by the north door, elbow other juniors habited like himself, and like him unretained; edge himself into this or that crowded court where a sensational case was going on, just as if he were in it, though the police officers at the door knew as well as he knew himself that he had no more concern with the business in hand than the patient idlers at the gallery-door outside, who had waited to enter since eight in the morning because, like him, they belonged to the classes that live on expectation. But he would do these things to no purpose, and think how greatly the characters in such scenes contrasted with the pink and breezy Anna.

An unexpected feature in that peasant maiden's conduct was that she had not as yet written to him, though he had told her she might do so if she wished. Surely a young creature had never before been so reticent in such circumstances. At length he sent her a brief line, postively requesting her to write. There was no answer by the return post, but the day after a letter in a neat feminine hand, and bearing the Melchester post-mark, was handed to him by the stationer.

The fact alone of its arrival was sufficient to satisfy his imaginative sentiment. He was not anxious to open the epistle, and in truth did not begin to read it for nearly half-an-hour, anticipating readily its terms of passionate retrospect and tender adjuration. When at last he turned his feet to the fireplace and unfolded the sheet, he was surprised and pleased to find that neither extravagance nor vulgarity was there. It was the most charming little missive he had ever received from woman. To be sure the language was simple and the ideas were slight; but it was so self-possessed; so purely that of a young girl who felt her womanhood to be enough for her dignity that he read it through twice. Four sides were filled, and a few lines written across, after the fashion of former days; the paper, too, was common, and not of the latest shade and surface. But what of those things? He had received letters from women who were fairly called ladies, but never so sensible, so human a letter as this. He could not single out any one sentence and say it was at all remarkable or clever; the *ensemble* of the letter it was which won him; and beyond the one request that he would write or come to her again soon there was nothing to show her sense of a claim upon him.

To write again and develop a correspondence was the last thing Raye would have preconceived as his conduct in such a situation; yet he did send a short, encouraging line or two, signed with his pseudonym, in which he asked for another letter, and cheeringly promised that he would try to see her again on some near day, and would never forget how much they had been to each other during their short acquaintance.

4

To return now to the moment at which Anna, at Melchester, had received Raye's letter.

It had been put into her own hand by the postman on his morning rounds. She flushed down to her neck on receipt of it, and turned it over and over. 'It is mine?' she said.

'Why, yes, can't you see it is?' said the postman, smiling as he guessed the nature of the document and the cause of the confusion.

'O yes, of course!' replied Anna, looking at the letter, forcedly tittering, and blushing still more.

Her look of embarrassment did not leave her with the

postman's departure. She opened the envelope, kissed its contents, put away the letter in her pocket, and remained musing till her eyes filled with tears.

A few minutes later she carried up a cup of tea to Mrs Harnham in her bed-chamber. Anna's mistress looked at her, and said: 'How dismal you seem this morning, Anna. What's the matter?'

'I'm not dismal. I'm glad; only I –' She stopped to stifle a sob.

'Well?'

'I've got a letter – and what good is it to me, if I can't read a word in it!'

'Why, I'll read it, child, if necessary.'

'But this is from somebody – I don't want anybody to read it but myself!' Anna murmured.

'I shall not tell anybody. Is it from that young man?'

'I think so.' Anna slowly produced the letter, saying: 'Then will you read it to me, ma'am?'

This was the secret of Anna's embarrassment and flutterings. She could neither read nor write. She had grown up under the care of an aunt by marriage at one of the lonely hamlets on the great Mid-Wessex Plain where, even in days of national education, there had been no school within a distance of two miles. Her aunt was an ignorant woman; there had been nobody to investigate Anna's circumstances, nobody to care about her learning the rudiments; though, as often in such cases, she had been well fed and clothed and not unkindly treated. Since she had come to live at Melchester with Mrs Harnham, the latter, who took a kindly interest in the girl, had taught her to speak correctly, in which accomplishment Anna showed considerable readiness, as is not unusual with the illiterate; and soon became quite fluent in the use of her mistress's phraseology. Mrs Harnham also insisted upon her getting a spelling and copy book, and beginning to practice in these. Anna was slower in this branch of her education, and meanwhile here was the letter.

Edith Harnham's large dark eyes expressed some interest in the contents, though, in her character of mere interpreter, she threw into her tone as much as she could of mechanical passiveness. She read the short epistle on to its concluding sentence, which idly requested Anna to send him a tender answer.

'Now – you'll do it for me, won't you, dear mistress?' said

Anna eagerly. 'And you'll do it as well as ever you can, please? Because I couldn't bear him to think I am not able to do it myself. I should sink into the earth with shame if he knew that!'

From some words in the letter Mrs Harnham was led to ask questions, and the answers she received confirmed her suspicions. Deep concern filled Edith's heart at perceiving how the girl had committed her happiness to the issue of this new-sprung attachment. She blamed herself for not interfering in a flirtation which had resulted so seriously for the poor little creature in her charge; though at the time of seeing the pair together she had a feeling that it was hardly within her province to nip young affection in the bud. However, what was done could not be undone, and it behoved her now, as Anna's only protector, to help her as much as she could. To Anna's eager request that she, Mrs Harnham, should compose and write the answer to this young London man's letter, she felt bound to accede, to keep alive his attachment to the girl if possible; though in other circumstances she might have suggested the cook as an amanuensis.

A tender reply was thereupon concocted, and set down in Edith Harnham's hand. This letter it had been which Raye had received and delighted in. Written in the presence of Anna it certainly was, and on Anna's humble note-paper, and in a measure indited by the young girl; but the life, the spirit, the individuality, were Edith Harnham's.

'Won't you at least put your name yourself?' she said. 'You can manage to write that by this time?'

'No, no,' said Anna, shrinking back. 'I should do it so bad. He'd be ashamed of me, and never see me again!'

The note, so prettily requesting another from him, had, as we have seen, power enough in its pages to bring one. He declared it to be such a pleasure to hear from her that she must write every week. The same process of manufacture was accordingly repeated by Anna and her mistress, and continued for several weeks in succession; each letter being penned and suggested by Edith, the girl standing by; the answer read and commented on by Edith, Anna standing by and listening again.

Late on a winter evening, after the dispatch of the sixth letter, Mrs Harnham was sitting alone by the remains of her fire. Her husband had retired to bed, and she had fallen into that fixity of musing which takes no count of hour or temperature. The state of mind had been brought about in Edith by a strange thing which she had done that day. For the first time since Raye's visit Anna had gone to stay over a night or two with her cottage friends on the Plain, and in her absence had arrived, out of its time, a letter from Raye. To this Edith had replied on her own responsibility, from the depths of her own heart, without waiting for her maid's collaboration. The luxury of writing to him what would be known to no consciousness but his was great, and she had indulged herself therein.

Why was it a luxury?

Edith Harnham led a lonely life. Influenced by the belief of the British parent that a bad marriage with its aversions is better than free womanhood with its interests, dignity, and leisure, she had consented to marry the elderly wine-merchant as a *pis aller*, at the age of seven-and-twenty – some three years before this date – to find afterwards that she had made a mistake. That contract had left her still a woman whose deeper nature had never been stirred.

She was now clearly realizing that she had become possessed to the bottom of her soul with the image of a man to whom she was hardly so much as a name. From the first he had attracted her by his looks and voice; by his tender touch; and, with these as generators, the writing of letter after letter and the reading of their soft answers had insensibly developed on her side an emotion which fanned his; till there had resulted a magnetic reciprocity between the correspondents, notwithstanding that one of them wrote in a character not her own. That he had been able to seduce another woman in two days was his crowning though unrecognized fascination for her as the she-animal.

They were her own impassioned and pent-up ideas – lowered to monosyllabic phraseology in order to keep up the disguise – that Edith put into letters signed with another name, much to the shallow Anna's delight, who, unassisted, could not for the world have conceived such pretty fancies for winning him, even had she been able to write them. Edith found that it was these, her own foisted-in sentiments, to which the young barrister mainly responded. The few sentences occasionally added from Anna's own lips made apparently no impression upon him.

The letter-writing in her absence Anna never discovered; but on her return the next morning she declared she wished to see her lover about something at once, and begged Mrs Harnham to ask him to come.

There was a strange anxiety in her manner which did not escape Mrs Harnham, and ultimately resolved itself into a flood of tears. Sinking down at Edith's knees, she made confession that the result of her relations with her lover it would soon become necessary to disclose.

Edith Harnham was generous enough to be very far from inclined to cast Anna adrift at this conjuncture. No true woman ever is so inclined from her own personal point of view, however prompt she may be in taking such steps to safeguard those dear to her. Although she had written to Raye so short a time previously, she instantly penned another Annanote hinting clearly though delicately the state of affairs.

Raye replied by a hasty line to say how much he was concerned at her news: he felt that he must run down to see her almost immediately.

But a week later the girl came to her mistress's room with another note, which on being read informed her that after all he could not find time for the journey. Anna was broken with grief; but by Mrs Harnham's counsel strictly refrained from hurling at him the reproaches and bitterness customary from young women so situated. One thing was imperative: to keep the young man's romantic interest in her alive. Rather therefore did Edith, in the name of her *protégée*, request him on no account to be distressed about the looming event, and not to inconvenience himself to hasten down. She desired above everything to be no weight upon him in his career, no clog upon his high activities. She had wished him to know what had befallen: he was to dismiss it again from his mind. Only he must write tenderly as ever, and when he should come again on the spring circuit it would be soon enough to discuss what had better be done.

It may well be supposed that Anna's own feelings had not been quite in accord with these generous expressions; but the mistress's judgment had ruled, and Anna had acquiesced. 'All I want is that *niceness* you can so well put into your letters, my dear, dear mistress, and that I can't for the life o' me make up out of my own head; though I mean the same thing and feel it exactly when you've written it down!'

When the letter had been sent off, and Edith Harnham was left alone, she bowed herself on the back of her chair and wept.

'I wish his child was mine – I wish it was!' she murmured. 'Yet how can I say such a wicked thing!'

5

The letter moved Raye considerably when it reached him. The intelligence itself had affected him less than her unexpected manner of treating him in relation to it. The absence of any word of reproach, the devotion to his interests, the self-sacrifice apparent in every line, all made up a nobility of character that he had never dreamt of finding in womankind.

'God forgive me!' he said tremulously 'I have been a wicked wretch. I did not know she was such a treasure as this!'

He reassured her instantly – declaring that he would not of course desert her, that he would provide a home for her somewhere. Meanwhile she was to stay where she was as long as her mistress would allow her.

But a misfortune supervened in this direction. Whether an inkling of Anna's circumstances reached the knowledge of Mrs Harnham's husband or not cannot be said, but the girl was compelled, in spite of Edith's entreaties, to leave the house. By her own choice she decided to go back for a while to the cottage on the Plain. This arrangement led to a consultation as to how the correspondence should be carried on; and in the girl's inability to continue personally what had been begun in her name, and in the difficulty of their acting in concert as heretofore, she requested Mrs Harnham – the only well-to-do friend she had in the world – to receive the letters and reply to them off-hand, sending them on afterwards to herself on the Plain, where she might at least get some neighbour to read them to her, if a trustworthy one could be met with. Anna and her box then departed for the Plain.

Thus it befell that Edith Harnham found herself in the strange position of having to correspond, under no supervision by the real woman, with a man not her husband, in terms which were virtually those of a wife, concerning a corporeal condition that was not Edith's at all; the man being one for whom, mainly through the sympathies involved in playing this part, she secretly cherished a predilection, subtle and imaginative truly, but strong and absorbing. She opened each letter, read it as if intended for herself, and replied from the promptings of her own heart and no other.

Throughout this correspondence, carried on in the girl's absence, the high-strung Edith Harnham lived in the ecstasy of fancy; the vicarious intimacy engendered such a flow of passionateness as was never exceeded. For conscience' sake Edith at first sent on each of his letters to Anna, and even rough copies of her replies; but later on these so-called copies were much abridged, and many letters on both sides were not sent on at all.

Though sensuous, and, superficially at least, infested with the self-indulgent vices of artificial society, there was a substratum of honesty and fairness in Raye's character. He had really a tender regard for the country girl, and it grew more tender than ever when he found her apparently capable of expressing the deepest sensibilities in the simplest words. He meditated, he wavered, and finally resolved to consult his sister, a maiden lady much older than himself, of lively sympathies and good intent. In making this confidence he showed her some of the letters.

'She seems fairly educated,' Miss Raye observed. 'And bright in ideas. She expresses herself with a taste that must be innate.'

'Yes. She writes very prettily, doesn't she, thanks to these elementary schools?'

'One is drawn out towards her, in spite of one's self, poor thing.'

The upshot of the discussion was that though he had not been directly advised to do it, Raye wrote, in his real name, what he would never have decided to write on his own responsibility; namely, that he could not live without her, and would come down in the spring and shelve her looming difficulty by marrying her.

This bold acceptance of the situation was made known to Anna by Mrs Harnham driving out immediately to the cottage on the Plain. Anna jumped for joy like a little child. And poor, crude directions for answering appropriately were given to Edith Harnham, who on her return to the city carried them out with warm intensifications.

'O!' she groaned, as she threw down the pen. 'Anna – poor

good little fool – hasn't intelligence enough to appreciate him! How should she? While I – don't bear his child!'

It was now February. The correspondence had continued altogether for four months, and the next letter from Raye contained incidentally a statement of his position and prospects. He said that in offering to wed her he had, at first, contemplated the step of retiring from a profession which hitherto had brought him very slight emolument, and which, to speak plainly, he had thought might be difficult of practice after his union with her. But the unexpected mines of brightness and warmth that her letters had disclosed to be lurking in her sweet nature had led him to abandon that somewhat sad prospect. He felt sure that, with her powers of development, after a little private training in the social forms of London under his supervision, and a little help from a governess if necessary, she would make as good a professional man's wife as could be desired, even if he should rise to the woolsack. Many a Lord Chancellor's wife had been less intuitively a lady than she had shown herself to be in her lines to him.

'O – poor fellow, poor fellow!' mourned Edith Harnham.

Her distress now raged as high as her infatuation. It was she who had wrought him to this pitch – to a marriage which meant his ruin; yet she could not, in mercy to her maid, do anything to hinder his plan. Anna was coming to Melchester that week, but she could hardly show the girl this last reply from the young man; it told too much of the second individuality that had usurped the place of the first.

Anna came, and her mistress took her into her own room for privacy. Anna began by saying with some anxiety that she was glad the wedding was so near.

'O, Anna!' replied Mrs Harnham. 'I think we must tell him all – that I have been doing your writing for you? – lest he should not know it till after you become his wife, and it might lead to dissension and recriminations –'

'O, mis'ess, dear mis'ess – please don't tell him now!' cried Anna in distress. 'If you were to do it perhaps he would not marry me; and what should I do then? It would be terrible what would come to me! And I am getting on with my writing, too. I have brought with me the copybook you were so good as to give me, and I practise every day, and though it so, so hard, I shall do it well at last, I believe, if I keep on trying.'

Edith looked at the copybook. The copies had been set by herself, and such progress as the girl had made was in the way of grotesque facsimile of her mistress's hand. But even if Edith's flowing caligraphy were reproduced the inspiration would be another thing.

'You do it so beautifully,' continued Anna, 'and say all that I want to say so much better than I could say it, that I do hope you won't leave me in the lurch just now!'

'Very well,' replied the other. 'But I – but I thought I ought not to go on!'

'Why?'

Her strong desire to confide her sentiments led Edith to answer truly:

'Because of its effect upon me.'

'But it *can't* have any!'

'Why, child?'

'Because you are married already!' said Anna with lucid simplicity.

'Of course it can't,' said her mistress hastily; yet glad, despite her conscience, that two or three oupourings still remained to her. 'But you must concentrate your attention on writing your name as I write it here.'

6

Soon Raye wrote about the wedding. Having decided to make the best of what he feared was a piece of romantic folly, he had acquired more zest for the grand experiment. He wished the ceremony to be in London, for greater privacy. Edith Harnham would have preferred it at Melchester; Anna was passive. His reasoning prevailed, and Mrs Harnham threw herself with mournful zeal into the preparations for Anna's departure. In a last desperate feeling that she must at every hazard be in at the death of her dream, and see once again the man who by a species of telepathy had exercised such an influence on her, she offered to go up with Anna and be with her through the ceremony – 'to see the end of her', as her mistress put it with forced gaiety; an offer which the girl gratefully accepted; for she had no other friend capable of playing the part of companion and witness, in the presence of a gentlemanly bridegroom, in such a way as not to hasten an opinion that he had made an irremediable social blunder.

It was a muddy morning in March when Raye alighted from a four-wheel cab at the door of a registry-office in the S.W. district of London, and carefully handed down Anna and her companion Mrs Harnham. Anna looked attractive in the somewhat fashionable clothes which Mrs Harnham had helped her to buy, though not quite so attractive as, an innocent child, she had appeared in her country gown on the back of the wooden horse at Melchester Fair.

Mrs Harnham had come up this morning by an early train, and a young man – a friend of Raye's – having met them at the door, all four entered the registry-office together. Till an hour before this time Raye had never known the wine-merchant's wife, except at that first casual encounter, and in the flutter of the performance before them he had little opportunity for more than a brief acquaintance. The contract of marriage at a registry is soon got through; but somehow, during its progress, Raye discovered a strange and secret gravitation between himself and Anna's friend.

The formalities of the wedding – or rather ratification of a previous union – being concluded, the four went in one cab to Raye's lodgings, newly taken in a new suburb in preference to a house, the rent of which he could ill afford just then. Here Anna cut the little cake which Raye had bought at a pastrycook's on his way home from Lincoln's Inn the night before. But she did not do much besides. Raye's friend was obliged to depart almost immediately, and when he had left the only ones virtually present were Edith and Raye, who exchanged ideas with much animation. The conversation was indeed their only, Anna being as a domestic animal who humbly heard but understood not. Raye seemed startled in awakening to this fact, and began to feel dissatisfied with her inadequacy.

At last, more disappointed than he cared to own, he said, 'Mrs Harnham, my darling is so flurried that she doesn't know what she is doing or saying. I see that after this event a little quietude will be necessary before she gives tongue to that tender philosophy which she used to treat me to in her letters.'

They had planned to start early that afternoon for Knollsea, to spend the few opening days of their married life there, and as the hour for departure was drawing near Raye asked his wife if she would go to the writing-desk in the next room and scribble a little note to his sister, who had been unable to attend through indisposition, informing her that the ceremony was over, thanking her for her little present, and hoping to know her well now that she was the writer's sister as well as Charles's.

'Say it in the pretty poetical way you know so well how to adopt,' he added, 'for I want you particularly to win her, and both of you to be dear friends.'

Anna looked uneasy, but departed to her task, Raye remaining to talk to their guest. Anna was a long while absent, and her husband suddenly rose and went to her.

He found her still bending over the writing-table, with tears brimming up in her eyes; and he looked down upon the sheet of note-paper with some interest, to discover with what tact she had expressed her goodwill in the delicate circumstances. To his surprise she had progressed but few lines, in the characters and spelling of a child of eight, and with the ideas of a goose.

'Anna,' he said, staring; 'what's this?'

'It only means – that I can't do it any better!' she answered, through her tears.

'Eh? Nonsense!'

'I can't!' she insisted, with miserable, sobbing hardihood. 'I – I – didn't write those letters, Charles! I only told *her* what to write! And not always that! But I am learning, O so fast, my dear, dear husband! And you'll forgive me, won't you, for not telling you before?' She slid to her knees, abjectly clasped his waist and laid her face against him.

He stood a few moments, raised her, abruptly turned, and shut the door upon her, rejoining Edith in the drawing-room. She saw that something untoward had been discovered, and their eyes remained fixed on each other.

'Do I guess rightly?' he asked, with wan quietude. '*You* were her scribe through all this?'

'It was necessary,' said Edith.

'Did she dictate every word you ever wrote to me?'

'Not every word.'

'In fact, very little?'

'Very little.'

'You wrote a great part of those pages every week from your own conception, though in her name!'

'Yes.'

'Perhaps you wrote many of the letters when you were alone, without communication with her?'

'I did.'

He turned to the bookcase, and leant with his hand over his face; and Edith, seeing his distress, became white as a sheet.

'You have deceived me – ruined me!' he murmured.

'O, don't say it!' she cried in her anguish, jumping up and putting her hand on his shoulder. 'I can't bear that!'

'Delighting me deceptively! Why did you do it – *why* did you!'

'I began doing it in kindness to her! How could I do otherwise than try to save such a simple girl from misery? But I admit that I continued it for pleasure to myself.'

Raye looked up. 'Why did it give you pleasure?' he asked.

'I must not tell,' she said.

He continued to regard her, and saw that her lips suddenly began to quiver under his scrutiny, and her eyes to fill and droop. She started aside, and said that she must go to the station to catch the return train: could a cab be called immediately?

But Raye went up to her, and took her unresisting hand. 'Well, to think of such a thing as this!' he said. 'Why, you and I are friends – lovers – devoted lovers – by correspondence!'

'Yes; I suppose.'

'More.'

'More?'

'Plainly more. It is no use blinking that. Legally I have married her – God help us both! – in soul and spirit I have married you, and no other woman in the world!'

'Hush!'

'But I will not hush! Why should you try to disguise the full truth, when you have already owned half of it? Yes, it is between you and me that the bond is – not between me and her! Now I'll say no more. But, O my cruel one, I think I have one claim upon you!'

She did not say what, and he drew her towards him, and bent over her. 'If it was all pure invention in those letters,' he said emphatically, 'give me your cheek only. If you meant what you said, let it be lips. It is for the first and last time, remember!'

She put up her mouth, and he kissed her long. 'You forgive me?' she said, crying.

'Yes.'

'But you are ruined!'

'What matter!' he said, shrugging his shoulders. 'It serves me right!'

She withdrew, wiped her eyes, entered and bade good-bye to Anna, who had not expected her to go so soon, and was still wrestling with the letter. Raye followed Edith downstairs, and in three minutes she was in a hansom driving to the Waterloo station.

He went back to his wife. 'Never mind the letter, Anna, today,' he said gently. 'Put on your things. We, too, must be off shortly.'

The simple girl, upheld by the sense that she was indeed married, showed her delight at finding that he was as kind as ever after the disclosure. She did not know that before his eyes he beheld as it were a galley, in which he, the fastidious urban, was chained to work for the remainder of his life, with her, the unlettered peasant, chained to his side.

Edith travelled back to Melchester that day with a face that showed the very stupor of grief, her lips still tingling from the desperate pressure of his kiss. The end of her impassioned dream had come. When at dusk she reached the Melchester station her husband was there to meet her, but in his perfunctoriness and her preoccupation they did not see each other, and she went out of the station alone.

She walked mechanically homewards without calling a fly. Entering, she could not bear the silence of the house, and went up in the dark to where Anna had slept, where she remained thinking awhile. She then returned to the drawing-room, and not knowing what she did, crouched down upon the floor.

'I have ruined him!' she kept repeating. 'I have ruined him; because I would not deal treacherously towards her!'

In the course of half an hour a figure opened the door of the apartment.

'Ah – who's that?' she said, starting up, for it was dark.

'Your husband – who should it be?' said the worthy merchant.

'Ah – my husband! – I forgot I had a husband!' She whispered to herself.

'I missed you at the station,' he continued. 'Did you see Anna safely tied up? I hope so, for 'twas time.'

'Yes – Anna is married.'

Simultaneously with Edith's journey home Anna and her husband were sitting at the opposite windows of a second-class carriage which sped along to Knollsea. In his hand was a pocket-book full of creased sheets closely written over. Unfolding them one after another he read them in silence, and sighed.

'What are you doing, dear Charles?' she said timidly from the other window, and drew nearer to him as if he were a god.

'Reading over all those sweet letters to me signed "Anna",' he replied with dreary resignation.

OSCAR WILDE

Lord Arthur Savile's Crime

A STUDY OF DUTY

1

It was Lady Windermere's last reception before Easter, and Bentinck House was even more crowded than usual. Six Cabinet Ministers had come on from the Speaker's Levée in their stars and ribands, all the pretty women wore their smartest dresses, and at the end of the picture-gallery stood the Princess Sophia of Carlsrühe, a heavy Tartar-looking lady, with tiny black eyes and wonderful emeralds, talking bad French at the top of her voice, and laughing immoderately at everything that was said to her. It was certainly a wonderful medley of people. Gorgeous peeresses chatted affably to violent Radicals, popular preachers brushed coat-tails with eminent sceptics, a perfect bevy of bishops kept following a stout prima-donna from room to room, on the staircase stood several Royal Academicians, disguised as artists, and it was said that at one time the supper-room was absolutely crammed with geniuses. In fact, it was one of Lady Windermere's best nights, and the Princess stayed till nearly half-past eleven.

As soon as she had gone, Lady Windermere returned to the picture-gallery, where a celebrated political economist was solemnly explaining the scientific theory of music to an indignant virtuoso from Hungary, and began to talk to the Duchess of Paisley. She looked wonderfully beautiful with her grand ivory throat, her large blue forget-me-not eyes, and her heavy coils of golden hair. *Or pur* they were – not that pale straw colour that nowadays usurps the gracious name of gold, but such gold as is woven into sunbeams or hidden in strange amber; and they gave to her face something of the frame of a saint, with not a little of the fascination of a sinner. She was a curious psychological study. Early in life she had discovered the important truth that nothing looks so like innocence as an indiscretion; and by a series of reckless escapades, half of them quite harmless, she had acquired all the privileges of a personality. She had more than once changed her husband; indeed, Debrett credits her with three marriages: but as she had never changed her lover, the world had long ago ceased to talk scandal about her. She was now forty years of age, childless, and with that inordinate passion for pleasure which is the secret of remaining young.

Suddenly she looked eagerly round the room, and said, in her clear contralto voice, 'Where is my cheiromantist?'

'Your what, Gladys?' exclaimed the Duchess, giving an involuntary start.

'My cheiromantist, Duchess; I can't live without him at present.'

'Dear Gladys! you are always so original,' murmured the Duchess, trying to remember what a cheiromantist really was, and hoping it was not the same as a cheiropodist.

'He comes to see my hand twice a week regularly,' continued Lady Windermere, 'and is most interesting about it.'

'Good heavens!' said the Duchess to herself, 'he is a sort of cheiropodist after all. How very dreadful. I hope he is a foreigner at any rate. It wouldn't be quite so bad then.'

'I must certainly introduce him to you.'

'Introduce him!' cried the Duchess; 'you don't mean to say he is here?' and she began looking about for a small tortoise-shell fan and a very tattered lace shawl, so as to be ready to go at a moment's notice.

'Of course he is here; I would not dream of giving a party without him. He tells me I have a pure psychic hand, and that if my thumb had been the least little bit shorter, I should have been a confirmed pessimist, and gone into a convent.'

'Oh, I see!' said the Duchess, feeling very much relieved; 'he tells fortunes, I suppose?'

'And misfortunes, too,' answered Lady Windermere, 'any amount of them. Next year, for instance, I am in great danger, both by land and sea, so I am going to live in a balloon, and draw up my dinner in a basket every evening. It is all written down on my little finger, or on the palm of my hand, I forget which.'

'But surely that is tempting Providence, Gladys.'

'My dear Duchess, surely Providence can resist temptation by this time. I think every one should have their hands told once a month, so as to know what not to do. Of course, one does it all the same, but it is so pleasant to be warned. Now if some one doesn't go and fetch Mr Podgers at once, I shall have to go myself.'

'Let me go, Lady Windermere,' said a tall handsome young man, who was standing by, listening to the conversation with an amused smile.

'Thanks so much, Lord Arthur; but I am afraid you wouldn't recognise him.'

'If he is as wonderful as you say, Lady Windermere, I couldn't well miss him. Tell me what he is like, and I'll bring him to you at once.'

'Well, he is not a bit like a cheiromantist. I mean he is not mysterious, or esoteric, or romantic-looking. He is a little, stout man, with a funny, bald head, and great gold-rimmed spectacles; something between a family doctor and a country attorney. I'm really very sorry, but it is not my fault. People are so annoying. All my pianists look exactly like poets; and all my poets look exactly like pianists; and I remember last season asking a most dreadful conspirator to dinner, a man who had blown up ever so many people, and always wore a coat of mail, and carried a dagger up his shirt-sleeve; and do you know that when he came he looked just like a nice old clergyman, and cracked jokes all the evening? of course, he was very amusing, and all that, but I was awfully disappointed; and when I asked him about the coat of mail, he only laughed, and said it was far too cold to wear in England. Ah, here is Mr Podgers! Now, Mr Podgers, I want you to tell the Duchess of Paisley's hand. Duchess, you must take your glove off. No, not the left hand, the other.'

'Dear Gladys, I really don't think it is quite right.' said the Duchess, feebly unbuttoning a rather soiled kid glove.

'Nothing interesting ever is,' said Lady Windermere: '*on a fait le monde ainsi.* But I must introduce you. Duchess, this is Mr Podgers, my pet cheiromantist. Mr Podgers, this is the Duchess of Paisley, and if you say that she has a larger mountain of the moon than I have, I will never believe in you again.'

'I am sure, Gladys, there is nothing of the kind in my hand,' said the Duchess gravely.

'Your Grace is quite right,' said Mr Podgers, glancing at the little fat hand with its short square fingers, 'the mountain of the moon is not developed. The line of life, however, is excellent. Kindly bend the wrist. Thank you. Three distinct lines on the *rascette*! You will live to a great age, Duchess, and be extremely happy. Ambition – very moderate, line of intellect not exaggerated, line of heart—'

'Now, do be indiscreet, Mr Podgers,' cried Lady Windermere.

'Nothing would give me greater pleasure,' said Mr Podgers, bowing, 'If the Duchess ever had been, but I am sorry to say that I see great permanence of affection, combined with a strong sense of duty.'

'Pray go on, Mr Podgers,' said the Duchess, looking quite pleased.

'Economy is not the least of your Grace's virtues,' continued Mr Podgers, and Lady Windermere went off into fits of laughter.

'Economy is a very good thing,' remarked the Duchess complacently; 'when I married Paisley he had eleven castles, and not a single house fit to live in.'

'And now he has twelve houses, and not a single castle,' cried Lady Windermere.

'Well, my dear,' said the Duchess, 'I like—'

'Comfort,' said Mr Podgers, 'and modern improvements, and hot water laid on in every bedroom. Your Grace is quite right. Comfort is the only thing our civilisation can give us.'

'You have told the Duchess's character admirably, Mr Podgers, and now you must tell Lady Flora's;' and in answer to a nod from the smiling hostess, a tall girl, with sandy Scotch hair, and high shoulder-blades, stepped awkwardly from behind the sofa, and held out a long, bony hand with spatulate fingers.

'Ah, a pianist! I see,' said Mr Podgers, 'an excellent pianist, but perhaps hardly a musician. Very reserved, very honest, and with a great love of animals.'

'Quite true!' exclaimed the Duchess, turning to Lady Windermere, 'absolutely true! Flora keeps two dozen collie dogs at Macloskie, and would turn our town house into a menagerie if her father would let her.'

'Well, that is just what I do with my house every Thursday evening,' cried Lady Windermere, laughing, 'only I like lions better than collie dogs.'

'Your one mistake, Lady Windermere,' said Mr Podgers, with a pompous bow.

'If a woman can't make her mistakes charming, she is only a female,' was the answer. 'But you must read some more hands for us. Come, Sir Thomas, show Mr Podgers yours;' and a genial-looking old gentleman, in a white waistcoat, came forward, and held out a thick rugged hand, with a very long third finger.

'An adventurous nature; four long voyages in the past, and one to come. Been shipwrecked three times. No, only twice, but in danger of a shipwreck your next journey. A strong Conservative, very punctual, and with a passion for collecting curiosities. Had a severe illness between the ages of sixteen and eighteen. Was left a fortune when about thirty. Great aversion to cats and Radicals.'

'Extraordinary!' exclaimed Sir Thomas; 'you must really tell my wife's hand, too.'

'Your second wife's,' said Mr Podgers quietly, still keeping Sir Thomas's hand in his. 'Your second wife's. I shall be charmed'; but Lady Marvel, a melancholy-looking woman, with brown hair and sentimental eyelashes, entirely declined to have her past or her future exposed; and nothing that Lady Windermere could do would induce Monsieur de Koloff, the Russian Ambassador, even to take his gloves off. In fact, many people seemed afraid to face the odd little man with his stereotyped smile, his gold spectacles, and his bright, beady eyes; and when he told poor Lady Fermor right out before every one, that she did not care a bit for music, but was extremely fond of musicians, it was generally felt that cheiromancy was a most dangerous science, and one that ought not to be encouraged, except in a *tête-à-tête*.

Lord Arthur Savile, however, who did not know anything about Lady Fermor's unfortunate story, and who had been watching Mr Podgers with a great deal of interest, was filled with an immense curiosity to have his own hand read, and feeling somewhat shy about putting himself forward, crossed over the room to where Lady Windermere was sitting, and, with a charming blush, asked her if she thought Mr Podgers would mind.

'Of course, he won't mind,' said Lady Windermere, 'that is what he is here for. All my lions, Lord Arthur, are performing lions, and jump through hoops whenever I ask them. But I must warn you beforehand that I shall tell Sybil everything. She is coming to lunch with me to-morrow, to talk about bonnets, and if Mr Podgers finds out that you have a bad temper, or a tendency to gout, or a wife living in Bayswater, I shall certainly let her know all about it.'

Lord Arthur smiled, and shook his head. 'I am not afraid,' he answered. 'Sybil knows me as well as I know her.'

'Ah! I am a little sorry to hear you say that. The proper basis for marriage is a mutual misunderstanding. No, I am not at all cynical, I have merely got experience, which, however, is very much the same thing. Mr Podgers, Lord Arthur Savile is dying to have his hand read. Don't tell him that he is engaged to one of the most beautiful girls in London, because that appeared in the *Morning Post* a month ago.'

'Dear Lady Windermere,' cried the Marchioness of Jedburgh, 'do let Mr Podgers stay here a little longer. He has just told me I should go on the stage, and I am so interested.'

'If he has told you that, Lady Jedburgh, I shall certainly take him away. Come over at once, Mr Podgers, and read Lord Arthur's hand.'

'Well,' said Lady Jedburgh, making a little *moue* as she rose from the sofa, 'if I am not to be allowed to go on the stage, I must be allowed to be part of the audience at any rate.'

'Of course; we are all going to be part of the audience,' said Lady Windermere; 'and now, Mr Podgers, be sure and tell us something nice. Lord Arthur is one of my special favourites.'

But when Mr Podgers saw Lord Arthur's hand he grew curiously pale, and said nothing. A shudder seemed to pass through him, and his great bushy eyebrows twitched convulsively, in an odd, irritating way they had when he was puzzled. Then some huge beads of perspiration broke out on his yellow forehead, like a poisonous dew, and his fat fingers grew cold and clammy.

Lord Arthur did not fail to notice these strange signs of agitation, and, for the first time in his life, he himself felt fear. His impulse was to rush from the room, but he restrained himself. It was better to know the worst, whatever it was, than to be left in this hideous uncertainty.

'I am waiting, Mr Podgers,' he said.

'We are all waiting,' cried Lady Windermere, in her quick, impatient manner, but the cheiromantist made no reply.

'I believe Arthur is going on the stage,' said Lady Jedburgh, 'and that, after your scolding, Mr Podgers is afraid to tell him so.'

Suddenly Mr Podgers dropped Lord Arthur's right hand, and seized hold of his left, bending down so low to examine it that the gold rims of his spectacles seemed almost to touch the palm. For a moment his face became a white mask of horror, but he soon recovered his *sang-froid*, and looking up at Lady Windermere, said with a forced smile, 'It is the hand of a charming young man.'

'Of course it is!' answered Lady Windermere, 'but will he be a charming husband? That is what I want to know.'

'All charming young men are,' said Mr Podgers.

'I don't think a husband should be too fascinating,' murmured Lady Jedburgh pensively, 'it is so dangerous.'

'My dear child they never are too fascinating,' cried Lady Windermere. 'But what I want are details. Details are the only things that interest. What is going to happen to Lord Arthur?'

'Well, within the next few months Lord Arthur will go a voyage—'

'Oh yes, his honeymoon, of course!'

'And lose a relative.'

'Not his sister, I hope?' said Lady Jedburgh, in a piteous tone of voice.

'Certainly not his sister,' answered Mr Podgers, with a deprecating wave of the hand, 'a distant relative merely.'

'Well, I am dreadfully disappointed,' said Lady Windermere. 'I have absolutely nothing to tell Sybil to-morrow. No one cares about distant relatives nowadays. They went out of fashion years ago. However, I suppose she had better have a black silk by her; it always does for church, you know. And now let us go to supper. They are sure to have eaten everything up, but we may find some hot soup. François used to make excellent soup once, but he is so agitated about politics at present, that I never feel quite certain about him. I do wish General Boulanger would keep quiet. Duchess, I am sure you are tired?'

'Not at all, dear Gladys,' answered the Duchess, waddling towards the door. 'I have enjoyed myself immensely, and the cheiropodist, I mean the cheiromantist, is most interesting. Flora, where can my tortoise-shell fan be? Oh, thank you, Sir Thomas, so much. And my lace shawl, Flora? Oh, thank you, Sir Thomas, very kind, I'm sure'; and the worthy creature finally managed to get downstairs without dropping her scent-bottle more than twice.

All this time Lord Arthur Savile had remained standing by the fireplace, with the same feeling of dread over him, the same sickening sense of coming evil. He smiled sadly at his sister, as she swept past him on Lord Plymdale's arm, looking lovely in her pink brocade and pearls, and he hardly heard Lady Windermere when she called to him to follow her. He thought of Sybil Merton, and the idea that anything could come between them made his eyes dim with tears.

Looking at him, one would have said that Nemesis had stolen the shield of Pallas, and shown him the Gorgon's head. He seemed turned to stone, and his face was like marble in its melancholy. He had lived the delicate and luxurious life of a young man of birth and fortune, a life exquisite in its freedom from sordid care, its beautiful boyish insouciance; and now for the first time he had become conscious of the terrible mystery of Destiny, of the awful meaning of Doom.

How mad and monstrous it all seemed! Could it be that written on his hand, in characters that he could not read himself, but that another could decipher, was some fearful secret of sin, some blood-red sign of crime? Was there no escape possible? Were we no better than chessmen, moved by an unseen power, vessels the potter fashions at his fancy, for honour or for shame? His reason revolted against it, and yet he felt that some tragedy was hanging over him, and that he had been suddenly called upon to bear an intolerable burden. Actors are so fortunate. They can choose whether they will appear in tragedy or in comedy, whether they will suffer or make merry, laugh or shed tears. But in real life it is different. Most men and women are forced to perform parts for which they have no qualifications. Our Guildensterns play Hamlet for us, and our Hamlets have to jest like Prince Hal. The world is a stage, but the play is badly cast.

Suddenly Mr Podgers entered the room. When he saw Lord Arthur he started, and his coarse, fat face became a sort of greenish-yellow colour. The two men's eyes met, and for a moment there was silence.

'The Duchess has left one of her gloves here, Lord Arthur, and has asked me to bring it to her,' said Mr Podgers finally. 'Ah, I see it on the sofa! Good evening.'

'Mr Podgers, I must insist on your giving me a straightforward answer to a question I am going to put to you.'

'Another time, Lord Arthur, but the Duchess is anxious. I am afraid I must go.'

'You shall not go. The Duchess is in no hurry.'

'Ladies should not be kept waiting, Lord Arthur,' said Mr Podgers, with his sickly smile. 'The fair sex is apt to be impatient.'

Lord Arthur's finely-chiselled lips curled in petulant disdain. The poor Duchess seemed to him of very little importance at that moment. He walked across the room to where Mr Podgers was standing, and held his hand out.

'Tell me what you saw there,' he said. 'Tell me the truth. I must know it. I am not a child.'

Mr Podger's eyes blinked behind his gold-rimmed spectacles, and he moved uneasily from one foot to the other, while his fingers played nervously with a flash watch-chain.

'What makes you think that I saw anything in your hand, Lord Arthur, more than I told you?'

'I know you did, and I insist on your telling me what it was. I will pay you. I will give you a cheque for a hundred pounds.'

The green eyes flashed for a moment, and then became dull again.

'Guineas?' said Mr Podgers at last, in a low voice.

'Certainly. I will send you a cheque to-morrow. What is your club?'

'I have no club. That is to say, not just at present. My address is—, but allow me to give you my card'; and producing a bit of gilt-edge pasteboard from his waistcoat pocket, Mr Podgers handed it, with a low bow, to Lord Arthur, who read on it,

Mr SEPTIMUS R. PODGERS
Professional Cheiromantist

103a West Moon Street

'My hours are from ten to four,' murmured Mr Podgers mechanically, 'and I make a reduction for families.'

'Be quick,' cried Lord Arthur, looking very pale, and holding his hand out.

Mr Podgers glanced nervously round, and drew the heavy *portière* across the door.

'It will take a little time, Lord Arthur, you had better sit down.'

'Be quick, sir,' cried Lord Arthur again, stamping his foot angrily on the polished floor.

Mr Podgers smiled, drew from his breast-pocket a small magnifying glass, and wiped it carefully with his handkerchief.

'I am quite ready,' he said.

2

Ten minutes later, with face blanched by terror, and eyes wild with grief, Lord Arthur Savile rushed from Bentinck House, crushing his way through the crowd of fur-coated footmen that stood round the large striped awning, and seeming not to see or hear anything. The night was bitter cold, and the gas-lamps round the square flared and flickered in the keen wind; but his hands were hot with fever, and his forehead burned like fire. On and on he went, almost with the gait of a drunken man. A policeman looked curiously at him as he passed, and a beggar, who slouched from an archway to ask for alms, grew frightened, seeing misery greater than his own. Once he stopped under a lamp, and looked at his hands. He thought he could detect the stain of blood already upon them, and a faint cry broke from his trembling lips.

Murder! that is what the cheiromantist had seen there. Murder! The very night seemed to know it, and the desolate wind to howl it in his ear. The dark corners of the streets were full of it. It grinned at him from the roofs of the houses.

First he came to the Park, whose sombre woodland seemed to fascinate him. He leaned wearily up against the railings, cooling his brow against the wet metal, and listening to the tremulous silence of the trees. 'Murder! murder!' he kept repeating, as though iteration could dim the horror of the word. The sound of his own voice made him shudder, yet he almost hoped that Echo might hear him, and wake the slumbering city from its dreams. He felt a mad desire to stop the casual passer-by, and tell him everything.

Then he wandered across Oxford Street into narrow, shameful alleys. Two women with painted faces mocked at him as he went by. From a dark courtyard came a sound of oaths and blows, followed by shrill screams, and, huddled upon a damp door-step, he saw the crooked-backed forms of poverty and eld. A strange pity came over him. Were these children of sin and misery predestined to their end, as he to his? Were they, like him, merely the puppets of a monstrous show?

And yet it was not the mystery, but the comedy of suffering that struck him; its absolute uselessness, its grotesque want of meaning. How incoherent everything seemed! How lacking in all harmony! He was amazed at the discord between the shallow optimism of the day, and the real facts of existence. He was still very young.

After a time he found himself in front of Marylebone Church. The silent roadway looked like a long riband of polished silver, flecked here and there by the dark arabesques of waving shadows. Far into the distance curved the line of flickering gas-lamps, and outside a little walled-in house stood a solitary hansom, the driver asleep inside. He walked hastily in the direction of Portland Place, now and then looking round, as though he feared that he was being followed. At the corner of Rich Street stood two men, reading a small bill upon a hoarding. An odd feeling of curiosity stirred him, and he crossed over. As he came near, the word 'Murder,' printed in black letters, met his eye. He started, and a deep flush came into his cheek. It was an advertisement offering a reward for any information leading to the arrest of a man of medium height, between thirty and forty years of age, wearing a billycock hat, a black coat, and check trousers, and with a scar upon his right cheek. He read it over and over again, and wondered if the wretched man would be caught, and how he had been scarred. Perhaps, some day, his own name might be placarded on the walls of London. Some day, perhaps, a price would be set on his head also.

The thought made him sick with horror. He turned on his heel, and hurried on into the night.

Where he went he hardly knew. He had a dim memory of wandering through a labyrinth of sordid houses, and it was bright dawn when he found himself at last in Piccadilly Circus. As he strolled home towards Belgrave Square, he met the great waggons on their way to Covent Garden. The white-smocked carters, with their pleasant sunburnt faces and coarse curly hair, strode sturdily on, cracking their whips, and calling out now and then to each other; on the back of a huge grey horse, the leader of a jangling team, sat a chubby boy, with a bunch of primroses in his battered hat, keeping tight hold of the mane with his little hands, and laughing; and the great piles of vegetables looked like masses of jade against the morning sky, like masses of green jade against the pink petals of some marvellous rose. Lord Arthur felt curiously affected, he could not tell why. There was something in the dawn's delicate loveliness that seemed to him inexpressibly pathetic, and he thought of all the days that break in beauty, and that set in storm. These rustics, too, with their rough, good-humoured voices, and their nonchalant ways, what a strange London they saw! A London free from the sin of night and the smoke of day, a pallid, ghost-like city, a desolate town of tombs! He wondered what they thought of it, and whether they knew anything of its splendour and its shame, of its fierce, fiery-coloured joys, and its horrible hunger, of all it makes and mars from morn to eve. Probably it was to them merely a mart where they brought their fruit to sell, and where they tarried for a few hours at most, leaving the streets still silent, the houses still asleep. It gave him pleasure to watch them as they went by. Rude as they were, with their heavy, hob-nailed shoes, and their awkward gait, they brought a little of Arcady with them. He felt that they had lived with Nature, and that she had taught them peace. He envied them all that they did not know.

By the time he had reached Belgrave Square the sky was a faint blue, and the birds were beginning to twitter in the gardens.

3

When Lord Arthur woke it was twelve o'clock, and the midday sun was streaming through the ivory-silk curtains of his room. He got up and looked out of the window. A dim haze of heat was hanging over the great city, and the roofs of the houses were like dull silver. In the flickering green of the square below some children were flitting about like white butterflies, and the pavement was crowded with people on their way to the Park.

Never had life seemed lovelier to him, never had the things of evil seemed more remote.

Then his valet brought him a cup of chocolate on a tray. After he had drunk it, he drew aside a heavy *portière* of peach-coloured plush, and passed into the bathroom. The light stole softly from above, through thin slabs of transparent onyx, and the water in the marble tank glimmered like a moonstone. He plunged hastily in, till the cool ripples touched throat and hair, and then dipped his head right under, as though he would have wiped away the stain of some shameful memory. When he stepped out he felt almost at peace. The exquisite physical conditions of the moment had dominated him, as indeed often happens in the case of very finely-wrought natures, for the senses, like fire, can purify as well as destroy.

After breakfast, he flung himself down on a divan and lit a cigarette. On the mantel-shelf, framed in dainty old brocade, stood a large photograph of Sybil Merton, as he had seen her first at Lady Noel's ball. The small, exquisitely-shaped head drooped slightly to one side, as though the thin, reed-like throat could hardly bear the burden of so much beauty; the lips were slightly parted, and seemed made for sweet music; and all the tender purity of girlhood looked out in wonder from the dreaming eyes. With her soft, clinging dress of *crêpe-de-chine*, and her large leaf-shaped fan, she looked like one of those delicate little figures men find in the olive-woods near Tanagra; and there was a touch of Greek grace in her pose and attitude. Yet she was not *petite*. She was simply perfectly proportioned – a rare thing in an age when so many women are either over life-size or insignificant.

Now as Lord Arthur looked at her, he was filled with the terrible pity that is born of love. He felt that to marry her, with the doom of murder hanging over his head, would be a betrayal like that of Judas, a sin worse than any the Borgia had ever dreamed of. What happiness could there be for them, when at any moment he might be called upon to carry out the awful prophecy written in his hand? What manner of life would be theirs while Fate still held this fearful fortune in the scales? The marriage must be postponed, at all costs. Of this he was quite resolved. Ardently though he loved the girl, and the mere touch of her fingers, when they sat together, made each nerve of his body thrill with exquisite joy, he recognised none the less clearly where his duty lay, and was fully conscious of the fact that he had no right to marry until he had committed the murder. This done, he could stand before the altar with Sybil Merton, and give his life into her hands without terror of wrong-doing. This done, he could take her to his arms, knowing that she would never have to blush for him, never have to hang her head in shame. But done it must be first; and the sooner the better for both.

Many men in his position would have preferred the primrose path of dalliance to the steep heights of duty; but Lord Arthur was too conscientious to set pleasure above principle. There was more than mere passion in his love; and Sybil was to him a symbol of all that is good and noble. For a moment he had a natural repugnance against what he was asked to do, but it soon passed away. His heart told him that it was not a sin, but a sacrifice; his reason reminded him that there was no other course open. He had to choose between living for himself and living for others, and terrible though the task laid upon him undoubtedly was, yet he knew that he must not suffer selfishness to triumph over love. Sooner or later we are all called upon to decide on the same issue – of us all the same question is asked. To Lord Arthur it came early in life – before his nature had been spoiled by the calculating cynicism of middle-age, or his heart corroded by the shallow, fashionable egotism of our day, and he felt no hesitation about doing his duty. Fortunately also, for him, he was no mere dreamer, or idle dilettante. Had he been so, he would have hesitated, like Hamlet, and let irresolution mar his purpose. But he was essentially practical. Life to him meant action, rather than thought. He had that rarest of all things, common-sense.

The wild, turbid feelings of the previous night had by this time completely passed away, and it was almost with a sense of shame that he looked back upon his mad wanderings from street to street, his fierce emotional agony. The very sincerity of his sufferings made them seem unreal to him now. He wondered how he could have been so foolish as to rant and rave about the inevitable. The only question that seemed to trouble him was, whom to make away with; for he was not blind to the fact that murder, like the religions of the Pagan world, requires a victim as well as a priest. Not being a genius, he had no enemies and indeed he felt that this was not the time for the gratification of any personal pique or dislike, the mission in which he was engaged being one of great and grave solemnity. He accordingly made out a list of his friends and relatives on a sheet of notepaper, and after careful consideration, decided in favour of Lady Clementina Beauchamp, a dear old lady who lived in Curzon Street, and was his own second cousin by his mother's side. He had always been very fond of Lady Clem, as every one called her, and as he was very wealthy himself, having come into all Lord Rugby's property when he came of age, there was no possibility of his deriving any vulgar monetary advantage by her death. In fact, the more he thought over the matter, the more she seemed to him to be just the right person, and, feeling that any delay would be unfair to Sybil, he determined to make his arrangements at once.

The first thing to be done was, of course, to settle with the cheiromantist; so he sat down at a small Sheraton writing-table that stood near the window, drew a cheque for £105, payable to the order of Mr Septimus Podgers, and, enclosing it in an envelope, told his valet to take it to West Moon Street. He then telephoned to the stables for his hansom, and dressed to go out. As he was leaving the room he looked back at Sybil Merton's photograph, and swore that, come what may, he would never let her know what he was doing for her sake, but would keep the secret of his self-sacrifice hidden always in his heart.

On his way to the Buckingham, he stopped at a florist's, and sent Sybil a beautiful basket of narcissus, with lovely white petals and staring pheasants' eyes, and on arriving at the club went straight to the library, rang the bell, and ordered the waiter to bring him a lemon-and-soda, and a book on Toxicology. He had fully decided that poison was the best means to adopt in this troublesome business. Anything like personal violence was extremely distasteful to him, and besides, he was very anxious not to murder Lady Clementina in any way that might attract public attention, as he hated the idea of being lionised at Lady Windermere's, or seeing his name figuring in the paragraphs of vulgar society-newspapers. He had also to think of Sybil's father and mother, who were rather old-fashioned people, and might possibly object to the marriage if there was anything like a scandal, though he felt certain that if he told them the whole facts of the case they would be the very first to appreciate the motives that had actuated him. He had every reason, then, to decide in favour of poison. It was safe, sure, and quiet, and did away with any necessity for painful scenes, to which, like most Englishmen, he had a rooted objection.

Of the science of poisons, however, he knew absolutely nothing, and as the waiter seemed quite unable to find anything in the library but *Ruff's Guide and Bailey's Magazine* he examined the book-shelves himself, and finally came across a handsomely-bound edition of the *Pharmacopœia*, and a copy of Erskine's *Toxicology*, edited by Sir Matthew Reid, the President of the Royal College of Physicians, and one of the oldest members of the Buckingham, having been elected in mistake for somebody else; a *contretemps* that so enraged the Committee, that when the real man came up they black-balled him unanimously. Lord Arthur was a good deal puzzled at the technical terms used in both books, and had begun to regret that he had not paid more attention to his classics at Oxford, when in the second volume of Erskine, he found a very interesting and complete account of the properties of aconitine, written in fairly clear English. It seemed to him to be exactly the poison he wanted. It was swift – indeed, almost immediate, in its effect – perfectly painless, and when taken in the form of a gelatine capsule, the mode recommended by Sir Matthew, not by any means unpalatable. He accordingly made a note, upon his shirt-cuff, of the amount necessary for a fatal dose, put the books back in their places, and strolled up St James's Street, to Pestle and Humbey's, the great chemists. Mr Pestle, who always attended personally on the aristocracy, was a good deal surprised at the order, and in a very deferential manner murmured something about a medical certificate being necessary. However, as soon as Lord Arthur explained to him that it was for a large Norwegian mastiff that he was obliged to get rid of, as it showed signs of incipient rabies, and had already bitten the coachman twice in the calf of the leg, he expressed himself as being perfectly satisfied, complimented Lord Arthur on his wonderful knowledge of Toxicology, and had the prescription made up immediately.

Lord Arthur put the capsule into a pretty little silver *bonbonnière* that he saw in a shop window in Bond Street, threw away Pestle and Humbey's ugly pill-box, and drove off at once to Lady Clementina's.

'Well, *monsieur le mauvais sujet,*' cried the old lady, as he entered the room, 'why haven't you been to see me all this time?'

'My dear Lady Clem, I never have a moment to myself,' said Lord Arthur, smiling.

'I suppose you mean that you go about all day long with Miss Sybil Merton, buying *chiffons* and talking nonsense? I cannot understand why people make such a fuss about being married. In my day we never dreamed of billing and cooing in public, or in private for that matter.'

'I assure you I have not seen Sybil for twenty-four hours, Lady Clem. As far as I can make out, she belongs entirely to her milliners.'

'Of course; that is the only reason you come to see an ugly old woman like myself. I wonder you men don't take warning. *On a fait des folies pour moi,* and here I am, a poor rheumatic creature, with a false front and a bad temper. Why, if it were not for dear Lady Jansen, who sends me all the worst French novels she can find, I don't think I could get through the day. Doctors are no use at all, except to get fees out of one. They can't even cure my heartburn.'

'I have brought you a cure for that, Lady Clem,' said Lord Arthur gravely. 'It is a wonderful thing, invented by an American.'

'I don't think I like American inventions, Arthur. I am quite sure I don't. I read some American novels lately, and they were quite nonsensical.'

'Oh, but there is no nonsense at all about this, Lady Clem! I assure you it is a perfect cure. You must promise to try it'; and Lord Arthur brought the little box out of his pocket, and handed it to her.

'Well, the box is charming, Arthur. Is it really a present? That is very sweet of you. And is this the wonderful medicine? It looks like a *bonbon.* I'll take it at once.'

'Good heavens! Lady Clem,' cried Lord Arthur, catching hold of her hand, 'you mustn't do anything of the kind. It is a homœopathic medicine, and if you take it without having heartburn, it might do you no end of harm. Wait till you have an attack, and take it then. You will be astonished at the result.'

'I should like to take it now,' said Lady Clementina, holding up to the light the little transparent capsule, with its floating bubble of liquid aconitine. 'I am sure it is delicious. The fact is that, though I hate doctors, I love medicines. However, I'll keep it till my next attack.'

'And when will that be?' asked Lord Arthur eagerly. 'Will it be soon?'

'I hope not for a week. I had a very bad time yesterday morning with it. But one never knows.'

'You are sure to have one before the end of the month then, Lady Clem?'

'I am afraid so. But how sympathetic you are to-day, Arthur! Really, Sybil has done you a great deal of good. And now you must run away, for I am dining with some very dull people, who won't talk scandal, and I know that if I don't get my sleep now I shall never be able to keep awake during dinner. Good-bye, Arthur, give my love to Sybil, and thank you so much for the American medicine.'

'You won't forget to take it, Lady Clem, will you?' said Lord Arthur, rising from his seat.

'Of course I won't, you silly boy. I think it is most kind of you to think of me, and I shall write and tell you if I want any more.'

Lord Arthur left the house in high spirits, and with a feeling of immense relief.

That night he had an interview with Sybil Merton. He told her how he had been suddenly placed in a position of terrible difficulty, from which neither honour nor duty would allow him to recede. He told her that the marriage must be put off for the present, as until he had got rid of his fearful entanglements, he was not a free man. He implored her to trust him, and not to have any doubts about the future. Everything would come right, but patience was necessary.

The scene took place in the conservatory of Mr Merton's house, in Park Lane, where Lord Arthur had dined as usual. Sybil had never seemed more happy, and for a moment Lord Arthur had been tempted to play the coward's part, to write to Lady Clementina for the pill, and to let the marriage go on as if there was no such person as Mr Podgers in the world. His better nature, however, soon asserted itself, and even when Sybil flung herself weeping into his arms, he did not falter. The beauty that stirred his senses had touched his conscience also. He felt that to wreck so fair a life for the sake of a few months' pleasure would be a wrong thing to do.

He stayed with Sybil till nearly midnight, comforting her and being comforted in turn, and early the next morning he left for Venice, after writing a manly, firm letter to Mr Merton about the necessary postponement of the marriage.

4

In Venice he met his brother, Lord Surbiton, who happened to have come over from Corfu in his yacht. The two young men spent a delightful fortnight together. In the morning they rode on the Lido, or glided up and down the green canal in their long black gondola; in the afternoon they usually entertained visitors on the yacht; and in the evening they dined at Florian's, and smoked innumerable cigarettes on the Piazza. Yet somehow Lord Arthur was not happy. Every day he studied the obituary column in the *Times*, expecting to see a notice of Lady Clementina's death, but every day he was disappointed. He began to be afraid that some accident had happened to her, and often regretted that he had prevented her taking the aconitine when she had been so anxious to try its effect. Sybil's letters, too, though full of love, and trust, and tenderness, were often very sad in their tone, and sometimes he used to think that he was parted from her for ever.

After a fortnight Lord Surbiton got bored with Venice, and determined to run down the coast to Ravenna, as he heard that there was some capital cock-shooting in the Pinetum. Lord Arthur at first refused absolutely to come, but Surbiton, of whom he was extremely fond, finally persuaded him that if he stayed at Danielli's by himself he would be moped to death, and on the morning of the 15th they started, with a strong nor'east wind blowing, and a rather choppy sea. The sport was excellent, and the free, open-air life brought the colour back to Lord Arthur's cheek, but about the 22nd he became anxious about Lady Clementina, and, in spite of Surbiton's remonstrances, came back to Venice by train.

As he stepped out of his gondola on to the hotel steps, the proprietor came forward to meet him with a sheaf of telegrams. Lord Arthur snatched them out of his hand, and tore them open.

Everything had been successful. Lady Clementina had died quite suddenly on the night of the 17th.

His first thought was for Sybil, and he sent her off a telegram announcing his immediate return to London. He then ordered his valet to pack his things for the night mail, sent his gondoliers about five times their proper fare, and ran up to his sitting-room with a light step and a buoyant heart. There he found three letters waiting for him. One was from Sybil herself, full of sympathy and condolence. The others were from his mother, and from Lady Clementina's solicitor. It seemed that the old lady had dined with the Duchess that very night, had delighted every one by her wit and *esprit*, but had gone home somewhat early, complaining of heartburn. In the morning she was found dead in her bed, having apparently suffered no pain. Sir Matthew Reid had been sent for at once, but, of course, there was nothing to be done, and she was to be buried on the 22nd at Beauchamp Chalcote. A few days before she died she had made her will, and left Lord Arthur her little house in Curzon Street, and all her furniture, personal effects, and pictures, with the exception of her collection of miniatures, which was to go to her sister, Lady Margaret Rufford, and her amethyst necklace, which Sybil Merton was to have. The property was not of much value; but Mr Mansfield, the solicitor, was extremely anxious for Lord Arthur to return at once, if possible, as there were a great many bills to be paid, and Lady Clementina had never kept any regular accounts.

Lord Arthur was very much touched by Lady Clementina's kind remembrance of him, and felt that Mr Podgers had a great deal to answer for. His love of Sybil, however, dominated every other emotion, and the consciousness that he had done his duty gave him peace and comfort. When he arrived at Charing Cross, he felt perfectly happy.

The Mertons received him very kindly. Sybil made him promise that he would never again allow anything to come between them, and the marriage was fixed for the 7th June. Life seemed to him once more bright and beautiful, and all his old gladness came back to him again.

One day, however, as he was going over the house in Curzon Street, in company with Lady Clementina's solicitor and Sybil herself, burning packages of faded letters, and turning out drawers of odd rubbish, the young girl suddenly gave a cry of delight.

'What have you found, Sybil?' said Lord Arthur, looking up from his work, and smiling.

'This lovely little silver *bonbonnière*, Arthur, Isn't it quaint and Dutch? Do give it to me! I know amethysts won't become me till I am over eighty.'

It was the box that had held the aconitine.

Lord Arthur started, and a faint blush came into his cheek. He had almost entirely forgotten what he had done, and it seemed to him a curious coincidence that Sybil, for whose sake he had gone through all that terrible anxiety, should have been the first to remind him of it.

'Of course you can have it, Sybil. I gave it to poor Lady Clem myself.'

'Oh! thank you, Arthur; and may I have the *bonbon* too? I had no notion that Lady Clementina liked sweets. I thought she was far too intellectual.'

Lord Arthur grew deadly pale, and a horrible idea crossed his mind.

'*Bonbon*, Sybil? What do you mean?' he said in a slow, hoarse voice.

'There is one in it, that is all. It looks quite old and dusty, and I have not the slightest intention of eating it. What is the matter, Arthur? How white you look!'

Lord Arthur rushed across the room, and seized the box. Inside it was the amber-coloured capsule, with its poison-bubble. Lady Clementina had died a natural death after all!

The shock of the discovery was almost too much for him. He flung the capsule into the fire, and sank on the sofa with a cry of despair.

5

Mr Merton was a good deal distressed at the second postponement of the marriage, and Lady Julia, who had already ordered her dress for the wedding, did all in her power to make Sybil break off the match. Dearly, however, as Sybil loved her mother, she had given her whole life into Lord Arthur's hands, and nothing that Lady Julia could say could make her waver in her faith. As for Lord Arthur himself, it took him days to get over his terrible disappointment, and for a time his nerves were completely unstrung. His excellent common sense, however, soon asserted itself, and his sound, practical mind did not leave him long in doubt about what to do. Poison having proved a complete failure, dynamite, or some other form of explosive, was obviously the proper thing to try.

He accordingly looked again over the list of his friends and relatives, and, after careful consideration, determined to blow up his uncle, the Dean of Chichester. The Dean, who was a man of great culture and learning, was extremely fond of clocks, and had a wonderful collection of timepieces, ranging from the fifteenth century to the present day, and it seemed to Lord Arthur that this hobby of the good Dean's offered him an excellent opportunity for carrying out his scheme. Where to procure an explosive machine was, of course, quite another matter. The London Directory gave him no information on the point, and he felt that there was very little use in going to Scotland Yard about it, as they never seemed to know anything about the movements of the dynamite faction till after an explosion had taken place, and not much even then.

Suddenly he thought of his friend Rouvaloff, a young Russian of very revolutionary tendencies, whom he had met at Lady Windermere's in the winter. Count Rouvaloff was supposed to be writing a life of Peter the Great, and to have come over to England for the purpose of studying the documents relating to that Tsar's residence in this country as a ship carpenter; but it was generally suspected that he was a Nihilist agent, and there was no doubt that the Russian Embassy did not look with any favour upon his presence in London. Lord Arthur felt that he was just the man for his purpose, and drove down one morning to his lodgings in Bloomsbury, to ask his advice and assistance.

'So you are taking up politics seriously?' said Count Rouvaloff, when Lord Arthur had told him the object of his mission; but Lord Arthur, who hated swagger of any kind, felt bound to admit to him that he had not the slightest interest in social questions, and simply wanted the explosive machine for a purely family matter, in which no one was concerned but himself.

Count Rouvaloff looked at him for some moments in amazement, and then seeing that he was quite serious, wrote an address on a piece of paper, initialled it, and handed it to him across the table.

'Scotland Yard would give a good deal to know this address, my dear fellow.'

'They shan't have it,' cried Lord Arthur, laughing; and after shaking the young Russian warmly by the hand he ran downstairs, examined the paper, and told the coachman to drive to Soho Square.

There he dismissed him, and strolled down Greek Street, till he came to a place called Bayle's Court. He passed under the archway, and found himself in a curious *cul-de-sac*, that was apparently occupied by a French Laundry, as a perfect network of clothes-lines was stretched across from house to house, and there was a flutter of white linen in the morning air. He walked right to the end, and knocked at a little green house. After some delay, during which every window became a blurred mass of peering faces, the door was opened by a rather rough-looking foreigner, who asked him in very bad English what his business was. Lord Arthur handed him the paper Count Rouvaloff had given him. When the man saw it he bowed, and invited Lord Arthur into a very shabby front parlour on the ground floor, and in a few moments Herr Winckelkopf, as he was called in England, bustled into the room, with a very wine-stained napkin round his neck, and a fork in his left hand.

'Count Rouvaloff has given me an introduction to you,' said Lord Arthur, bowing, 'and I am anxious to have a short interview with you on a matter of business. My name is Smith, Mr Robert Smith, and I want you to supply me with an explosive clock.'

'Charmed to meet you, Lord Arthur,' said the genial little German, laughing. 'Don't look so alarmed, it is my duty to know everybody, and I remember seeing you one evening at Lady Windermere's. I hope her ladyship is quite well. Do you mind sitting with me while I finish my breakfast? There is an excellent *pâté*, and my friends are kind enough to say that my Rhine wine is better than any they get at the German Embassy,' and before Lord Arthur had got over his surprise at being recognised, he found himself seated in the back-room, sipping the most delicious Marcobrünner out of a pale yellow hock-glass marked with the

Imperial monogram, and chatting in the friendliest manner possible to the famous conspirator.

'Explosive clocks,' said Herr Winckelkopf, 'are not very good things for foreign exportation, as, even if they succeed in passing the Custom House, the train service is so irregular, that they usually go off before they have reached their proper destination. If, however, you want one for home use, I can supply you with an excellent article, and guarantee that you will be satisfied with the result. May I ask for whom it is intended? If it is for the police, or for any one connected with Scotland Yard, I am afraid I cannot do anything for you. The English detectives are really our best friends, and I have always found that by relying on their stupidity, we can do exactly what we like. I could not spare one of them.'

'I assure you,' said Lord Arthur, 'that it has nothing to do with the police at all. In fact, the clock is intended for the Dean of Chichester.'

'Dear me! I had no idea that you felt so strongly about religion, Lord Arthur. Few young men do nowadays.'

'I am afraid you overrate me, Herr Winckelkopf,' said Lord Arthur, blushing. 'The fact is, I really know nothing about theology.'

'It is a purely private matter then?'

'Purely private.'

Herr Winckelkopf shrugged his shoulders, and left the room, returning in a few minutes with a round cake of dynamite about the size of a penny, and a pretty little French clock, surmounted by an ormolu figure of Liberty trampling on the hydra of Despotism.

Lord Arthur's face brightened up when he saw it.

'That is just what I want,' he cried, 'and now tell me how it goes off.'

'Ah! there is my secret,' answered Herr Winckelkopf, contemplating his invention with a justifiable look of pride; 'let me know when you wish it to explode, and I will set the machine to the moment.'

'Well, to-day is Tuesday, and if you could send it off at once—'

'That is impossible; I have a great deal of important work on hand for some friends of mine in Moscow. Still, I might send it off to-morrow.'

'Oh, it will be quite time enough!' said Lord Arthur politely, 'if it is delivered to-morrow night or Thursday morning. For the moment of the explosion, say Friday at noon exactly. The Dean is always at home at that hour.'

'Friday, at noon,' repeated Herr Winckelkopf, and he made a note to that effect in a large ledger that was lying on a bureau near the fireplace.

'And now,' said Lord Arthur, rising from his seat, 'pray let me know how much I am in your debt.'

'It is such a small matter, Lord Arthur, that I do not care to make any charge. The dynamite comes to seven and sixpence, the clock will be three pounds ten, and the carriage about five shillings. I am only too pleased to oblige any friend of Count Rouvaloff's.'

'But your trouble, Herr Winckelkopf?'

'Oh, that is nothing! It is a pleasure to me. I do not work for money; I live entirely for my art.'

Lord Arthur laid down £4 2s. 6d. on the table, thanked the little German for his kindness, and, having succeeded in declining an invitation to meet some Anarchists at a meat-tea on the following Saturday, left the house and went off to the Park.

For the next two days he was in a state of the greatest excitement, and on Friday at twelve o'clock he drove down to the Buckingham to wait for news. All the afternoon the stolid hall-porter kept posting up telegrams from various parts of the country giving the results of horse-races, the verdicts in divorce suits, the state of the weather, and the like, while the tape ticked out wearisome details about an all-night sitting in the House of Commons, and a small panic on the Stock Exchange. At four o'clock the evening papers came in, and Lord Arthur disappeared into the library with the *Pall Mall*, the *St James's*, the *Globe*, and the *Echo*, to the immense indignation of Colonel Goodchild, who wanted to read the reports of a speech he had delivered that morning at the Mansion House, on the subject of South African Missions, and the advisability of having black Bishops in every province, and for some reason or other had a strong prejudice against the *Evening News*. None of the papers, however, contained even the slightest allusion to Chichester, and Lord Arthur felt that the attempt must have failed. It was a terrible blow to him, and for a time he was quite unnerved. Herr Winckelkopf, whom he went to see the next day, was full of elaborate apologies, and offered to supply him with another clock free of charge, or with a case of nitro-glycerine bombs at cost price. But he had lost all faith in explosives, and Herr Winckelkopf himself acknowledged that everything is so adulterated nowadays, that even dynamite can hardly be got in a pure condition. The little German, however, while admitting that something must have gone wrong with the machinery, was not without hope that the clock might still go off, and instanced the case of a barometer that he had once sent to the military Governor at Odessa, which, though timed to explode in ten days, had not done so for something like three months. It was quite true that when it did go off, it merely succeeded in blowing a housemaid to atoms, the Governor having gone out of town six weeks before, but at least it showed that dynamite, as a destructive force, was, when under the control of machinery, a powerful, though somewhat unpunctual agent. Lord Arthur was a little consoled by this reflection, but even here he was destined to disappointment, for two days afterwards, as he was going upstairs, the Duchess called him into her boudoir, and showed him a letter she had just received from the Deanery.

'Jane writes charming letters,' said the Duchess; 'you must really read her last. It is quite as good as the novels Mudie sends us.'

Lord Arthur seized the letter from her hand. It ran as follows:—

THE DEANERY, CHICHESTER,
27th May,

MY DEAREST AUNT,

Thank you so much for the flannel for the Dorcas Society, and also for the gingham. I quite agree with you that it is nonsense their wanting to wear pretty things, but everybody is so Radical and irreligious nowadays, that it is difficult to make them see that they should not try and dress like the upper classes. I am sure I don't know what we are coming to. As papa has often said in his sermons, we live in an age of unbelief.

We have had great fun over a clock that an unknown admirer sent papa last Thursday. It arrived in a wooden box from London, carriage paid; and papa feels it must have been sent by some one who had read his remarkable sermon, 'Is Licence Liberty?' for on the top of the clock was a figure of a woman, with what papa said was the cap of Liberty on her head. I don't think it very becoming myself, but papa said it was historical, so I suppose it is all right. Parker unpacked it, and papa put it on the mantelpiece in the library, and we were all sitting there on Friday morning, when just as the clock struck twelve, we heard a whirring noise, a little puff of smoke came from the pedestal of the figure, and the goddess of Liberty fell off, and broke her nose on the fender! Maria was quite alarmed, but it looked so ridiculous, that James and I went off into fits of laughter, and even papa was amused. When we examined it, we found it was a sort of alarm clock, and that, if you set it to a particular hour, and put some gunpowder and a cap under a little hammer, it went off whenever you wanted. Papa said it must not remain in the library, as it made a noise, so Reggie carried it away to the schoolroom, and does nothing but have small explosions all day long. Do you think Arthur would like one for a wedding present? I suppose they are quite fashionable in London. Papa says they should do a great deal of good, as they show that Liberty can't last, but must fall down. Papa says Liberty was invented at the time of the French Revolution. How awful it seems!

I have now to go to the Dorcas, where I will read your most instructive letter. How true, dear aunt, your idea is, that in their rank of life they should wear what is unbecoming. I must say it is absurd, their anxiety about dress, when there are so many more important things in this world, and in the next. I am so glad your flowered poplin turned out so well, and that your lace was not torn. I am wearing my yellow satin, that you so kindly gave me, at the Bishop's on Wednesday, and think it will look all right. Would you have bows or not? Jennings says that every one wears bows now, and that the underskirt should be frilled. Reggie has just had another explosion, and papa has ordered the clock to be sent to the stables. I don't think papa likes it so much as he did at first, though he is very flattered at being sent such a pretty and ingenious toy. It shows that people read his sermons, and profit by them.

Papa sends his love, in which James, and Reggie, and Maria all unite, and, hoping that Uncle Cecil's gout is better, believe me, dear aunt, ever your affectionate niece,

JANE PERCY.

PS. – Do tell me about the bows. Jennings insists they are the fashion.

Lord Arthur looked so serious and unhappy over the letter, that the Duchess went into fits of laughter.

'My dear Arthur,' she cried, 'I shall never show you a young lady's letter again! But what shall I say about the clock? I think it is a capital invention, and I should like to have one myself.'

'I don't think much of them,' said Lord Arthur, with a sad smile, and, after kissing his mother, he left the room.

When he got upstairs, he flung himself on a sofa, and his eyes filled with tears. He had done his best to commit this murder, but on both occasions he had failed, and through no fault of his own. He had tried to do his duty, but it seemed as if Destiny herself had turned traitor. He was oppressed with the sense of the barrenness of good intentions, of the futility of trying to be fine. Perhaps, it would be better to break off the marriage altogether. Sybil would suffer, it is true, but suffering could not really mar a nature so noble as hers. As for himself, what did it matter? There is always some war in which a man can die, some cause to which a man can give his life, and as life had no pleasure for him, so death had no terror. Let Destiny work out his doom. He would not stir to help her.

At half-past seven he dressed, and went down to the club. Surbiton was there with a party of young men, and he was obliged to dine with them. Their trivial conversation and idle jests did not interest him, and as soon as coffee was brought he left them, inventing some engagement in order to get away. As he was going out of the club, the hall-porter handed him a letter. It was from Herr Winckelkopf, asking him to call down the next evening, and look at an explosive umbrella, that went off as soon as it was opened. It was the very latest invention, and had just arrived from Geneva. He tore the letter up into fragments. He had made up his mind not to try any more experiments. Then he wandered down to the Thames Embankment, and sat for hours by the river. The moon peered through a mane of tawny clouds, as if it were a lion's eye, and innumerable stars spangled the hollow vault, like gold dust powdered on a purple dome. Now and then a barge swung out into the turbid stream, and floated away with the tide, and the railway signals changed from green to scarlet as the trains ran shrieking across the bridge. After some time, twelve o'clock boomed from the tall tower at Westminster, and at each stroke of the sonorous bell the night seemed to tremble. Then the railway lights went out, one solitary lamp left gleaming like a large ruby on a giant mast, and the roar of the city became fainter.

At two o'clock he got up, and strolled towards Blackfriars. How unreal everything looked! How like a strange dream! The houses on the other side of the river seemed built out of darkness. One would have said that silver and shadow had fashioned the world anew. The huge dome of St Paul's loomed like a bubble through the dusky air.

As he approached Cleopatra's Needle he saw a man leaning over the parapet, and as he came nearer the man looked up, the gas-light falling full upon his face.

It was Mr Podgers, the cheiromantist! No one could mistake the fat, flabby face, the gold-rimmed spectacles, the sickly feeble smile, the sensual mouth.

Lord Arthur stopped. A brilliant idea flashed across him, and he stole softly up behind. In a moment he had seized Mr Podgers by the legs, and flung him into the Thames. There was a coarse oath, a heavy splash, and all was still. Lord Arthur looked anxiously over, but could see nothing of the cheiromantist but a tall hat, pirouetting in an eddy of moonlit water. After a time it also sank, and no trace of Mr Podgers was visible. Once he thought that he caught sight of the bulky misshapen figure striking out for the staircase by the bridge, and a horrible feeling of failure came over him, but it turned out to be merely a reflection, and when the moon shone out from behind a cloud it passed away. At last he seemed to have realised the decree of destiny. He heaved a deep sigh of relief, and Sybil's name came to his lips.

'Have you dropped anything, sir? said a voice behind him suddenly.

He turned round, and saw a policeman with a bull's-eye lantern.

'Nothing of importance, sergeant,' he answered, smiling, and hailing a passing hansom, he jumped in, and told the man to drive to Belgrave Square.

For the next few days he alternated between hope and fear. There were moments when he almost expected Mr Podgers to walk into the room, and yet at other times he felt that Fate could not be so unjust to him. Twice he went to the cheiromantist's address in West Moon Street, but he could not bring himself to ring the bell. He longed for certainty, and was afraid of it.

Finally it came. He was sitting in the smoking-room of the club having tea, and listening rather wearily to Surbiton's account of the last comic song at the Gaiety, when the waiter came in with the evening papers. He took up the *St James's*, amd was listlessly turning over its pages, when this strange heading caught his eye:

SUICIDE OF A CHEIROMANTIST.

He turned pale with excitement, and began to read. The paragraph ran as follows:

> Yesterday morning, at seven o'clock, the body of Mr Septimus R. Podgers, the eminent cheiromantist, was washed on shore at Greenwich, just in front of the Ship Hotel. The unfortunate gentleman had been missing for some days, and considerable anxiety for his safety had been felt in cheiromantic circles. It is supposed that he committed suicide under the influence of a temporary mental derangement, caused by overwork, and a verdict to that effect was returned this afternoon by the coroner's jury. Mr Podgers had just completed an elaborate treatise on the subject of the Human Hand, that will shortly be published, when it will no doubt attract much attention. The deceased was sixty-five years of age, and does not seem to have left any relations.

Lord Arthur rushed out of the club with the paper still in his hand, to the immense amazement of the hall-porter, who tried in vain to stop him, and drove at once to Park Lane. Sybil saw him from the window, and something told her that he was the bearer of good news. She ran down to meet him, and, when she saw his face, she knew that all was well.

'My dear Sybil,' cried Lord Arthur, 'let us be married tomorrow!'

'You foolish boy! Why, the cake is not even ordered!' said Sybil, laughing through her tears.

6

When the wedding took place, some three weeks later, St Peter's was crowded with a perfect mob of smart people. The service was read in the most impressive manner by the Dean of Chichester, and everybody agreed that they had never seen a handsomer couple than the bridge and bridegroom. They were more than handsome, however – they were happy. Never for a single moment did Lord Arthur regret all that he had suffered for Sybil's sake, while she, on her side, gave him the best things a women can give to any man – worship, tenderness, and love. For them romance was not killed by reality. They always felt young.

Some years afterwards, when two beautiful children had been born to them, Lady Windermere came down on a visit to Alton Priory, a lovely old place; that had been the Duke's wedding present to his son; and one afternoon as she was sitting with Lady Arthur under a lime-tree in the garden, watching the little boy and girl as they played up and down the rose-walk, like fitful sunbeams, she suddenly took her hostess's hand in hers and said, 'Are you happy, Sybil?'

'Dear Lady Windermere, of course I am happy. Aren't you?'

'I have no time to be happy, Sybil. I always like the last person who is introduced to me; but, as a rule, as soon as I know people I get tired of them.'

'Don't your lions satisfy you, Lady Windermere?'

'Oh dear, no! lions are only good for one season. As soon as their manes are cut, they are the dullest creatures going. Besides, they behave very badly, if you are really nice to them. Do you remember that horrid Mr Podgers? He was a dreadful impostor. Of course, I didn't mind that at all, and even when he wanted to borrow money I forgave him, but I could not stand his making love to me. He has really made me hate cheiromancy. I go in for telepathy now. It is much more amusing.'

'You mustn't say anything against cheiromancy here, Lady Windermere; it is the only subject that Arthur does not like people to chaff about. I assure you he is quite serious over it.'

'You don't mean to say that he believes in it, Sybil?'

'Ask him, Lady Windermere, here he is'; and Lord Arthur came up the garden with a large bunch of yellow roses in his hand, and his two children dancing round him.

'Lord Arthur?'

'Yes, Lady Windermere.'

'You don't mean to say that you believe in cheiromancy?'

'Of course I do,' said the young man, smiling.

'But why?'

'Because I owe to it all the happiness of my life,' he murmured, throwing himself into a wicker chair.

'My dear Lord Arthur, what do you owe to it?'

'Sybil,' he answered, handing his wife the roses, and looking into her violet eyes.

'What nonsense!' cried Lady Windermere. 'I never heard such nonsense in all my life.'

ANTON CHEKHOV

The Lady with the Dog

1

It was said that a new person had appeared on the sea-front: a lady with a little dog. Dmitri Gurov, who had by then been a fortnight in Yalta, and so was fairly at home there, had begun to take an interest in new arrivals. Sitting in Verney's pavilion, he saw, walking on the sea-front, a fair-haired young lady of medium height, wearing a beret; a white Pomeranian dog was running behind her.

And afterwards he met her in the public gardens and in the square several times a day. She was walking alone, always wearing the same beret, and always with the same white dog; no one knew who she was; and everyone called her simply 'the lady with the dog'.

'If she is here alone without a husband or friends, it wouldn't be a bad idea to get to know her,' Gurov reflected.

He was under forty, but he had a daughter already twelve years old, and two sons at school. He had been married young, when he was a student in his second year, and by now his wife seemed half as old again as he. She was a tall, erect woman with dark eyebrows, staid and dignified, and, as she said of herself, intellectual. She read a great deal, used phonetic spelling, called her husband not Dmitri, but Dimitri, and he secretly considered her unintelligent, narrow, inelegant, was afraid of her, and did not like to be at home. He had begun being unfaithful to her long ago – had been unfaithful to her often, and, probably on that account, almost always spoke ill of women, and when they were talked about in his presence, used to call them 'the lower race'.

It seemed to him that he had been sufficiently schooled by bitter experience to call them what he liked, and yet he could not get on for two days together without 'the lower race'. In the society of men he was bored and not himself, with them he was cold and uncommunicative; but when he was in the company of women he felt free, and knew what to say to them and how to behave; and he was at ease with them even when he was silent. In his appearance, in his character, in his whole nature, there was something attractive and elusive which allured women and predisposed them towards him; he knew that, and some force seemed to draw him, too, to them.

Frequent experience, truly bitter experience, had taught him long ago that with decent people, especially Moscow people, always slow to move and irresolute, every intimacy, which at first so agreeably diversifies life and appears as a light and charming adventure, inevitably grows into a whole problem of extreme intricacy, and in the long run the situation becomes burdensome. But at every fresh meeting with an interesting woman this experience seemed to slip out of his memory, and he was eager for life, and everything seemed simple and amusing.

One evening he was dining in the gardens, and the lady in the beret came up slowly to take the next table. Her expression, her gait, her dress, and the way she did her hair told him that she was a lady, that she was married, that she was in Yalta for the first time and alone, and that she was bored there . . . The stories told of the immorality in such places as Yalta are to a great extent untrue; he despised them, and knew that such stories were for the most part made up by persons who would themselves have been glad to sin if they had been able; but when the lady sat down at the next table three paces from him, he remembered these tales of easy conquests, of trips to the mountains, and the tempting thought of a swift, fleeting love affair, a romance with an unknown woman, whose name he did not know, suddenly took possession of him.

He beckoned coaxingly to the Pomeranian, and when the dog came up to him he shook his finger at it. The Pomeranian growled, Gurov shook his finger at it again.

The lady looked at him and at once dropped her eyes.

'He doesn't bite,' she said, and blushed.

'May I give him a bone?' he asked; and when she nodded he asked courteously, 'Have you been long in Yalta?'

'About five days.'

'And I have already dragged out a fortnight here.'

There was a brief silence.

'Time goes fast, and yet it is so dull here!' she said, not looking at him.

'That's only the fashion to say it is dull here. A provincial will live in Beliov or Zhizdra and not be dull, and when he comes here it's "Oh, the dullness! Oh, the dust!" You'd think he came from Grenada!'

She laughed. Then both continued eating in silence, like strangers, but after dinner they walked side by side; and there sprang up between them the light jesting conversation of people who are free and satisfied, to whom it does not matter where they go or what they talk about. They walked and talked of the strange light on the sea; the water was of a soft warm lilac hue, and there was a golden streak from the moon upon it. They talked of how sultry it was after a hot day. Gurov told her that he came from Moscow, that he had taken his degree in arts, but had a post in a bank; that he owned two houses in Moscow . . . And from her he learnt that she had grown up in Petersburg, but had lived in S— since her marriage two years before, that she was staying another month in Yalta, and that her husband, who needed a holiday too, might perhaps come and fetch her. She was not sure whether her husband had a post in the governor's office or the provincial rural administration – and was amused by her own ignorance. And Gurov learnt, too, that she was called Anna Sergeyevna.

Afterwards he thought about her in his room at the hotel – thought that she would certainly meet him the next day; it would be sure to happen. As he got into bed he thought how recently she had been a girl at school, studying like his own daughter; he recalled the diffidence, the angularity, that was still manifest in her laugh and her manner of talking to a stranger. This must have been the first time in her life she had been alone in surroundings in which she was followed, looked at, and spoken to entirely for a secret motive which she could not fail to guess. He recalled her slender, delicate neck, her lovely grey eyes.

'There's something pitiful about her, though,' he thought, and started to fall asleep.

2

A week had passed since they had met. It was a holiday. It was suffocatingly hot indoors, while in the street the wind whirled the dust round and round, and blew people's hats off. They were thirsty all day, and Gurov often went into the pavilion, and pressed Anna to have syrup and water or an ice. There was no refuge.

In the evening when the wind had dropped a little, they went out on to the pier to see the steamer come in. There were a great many people walking about the harbour; they had gathered to welcome someone, bringing bouquets. And two pecularities of a well-dressed Yalta crowd were very conspicuous: the elderly ladies were dressed like young ones, and there were great numbers of generals.

Owing to the roughness of the sea, the steamer arrived late, after the sun had set, and it was a long time turning about before it reached the pier. Anna looked through her lorgnette at the steamer and the passengers as though looking for acquaintances, and when she turned to Gurov her eyes were shining. She talked a great deal and asked disconnected questions, forgetting next moment what she had asked; then she dropped her lorgnette in the crush.

The festive crowd began to disperse; it was too dark to see people's faces. The wind had completely dropped, but Gurov and Anna still stood as though waiting to see someone else come from the steamer. Anna was silent now, and sniffed flowers without looking at Gurov.

'The weather is a bit better now that it's evening,' he said. 'Where shall we go now? Shall we drive somewhere?'

She made no answer.

Then he looked at her intently, and all at once put his arm round her and kissed her on the lips, and breathed in the moisture and the fragrance of the flowers; and he immediately looked round him, anxiously wondering whether anyone had seen them.

'Let's go to your place . . .' he said softly. And both walked quickly.

The room was close and smelt of the scent she had bought at the Japanese shop. Gurov looked at her and thought: 'What different people one meets in the world!' From the past he preserved memories of careless, good-natured women, who loved him cheerfully and were grateful to him for the happiness he gave them, however brief it might be; and of women like his wife who loved without any genuine feeling, with superfluous phrases, affectedly, hysterically, with an expression that suggested that it was not love nor passion, but something more significant; and of two or three others, very beautiful, cold women, on whose faces he had caught a glimpse of a rapacious expression – an obstinate desire to snatch from life more than it could give, and these were capricious, unreflecting, domineering, unintelligent women not in their first youth, and when Gurov grew cold to them their beauty excited his hatred and the lace on their linen seemed to him like fish scales.

But in this case there was still the diffidence, the angularity of inexperienced youth, an awkward feeling; and there was an impression of consternation as though someone had suddenly knocked at the door. The attitude of Anna – 'the lady with the dog' – to what had happened was somehow peculiar, very grave, as though it were her fall – so it seemed, and it was strange and out of place. Her face drooped and faded, and on both sides of it her long hair hung down mournfully; she mused in a dejected attitude like 'The Scarlet Woman' in an old-fashioned picture.

'It's wrong,' she said. 'You will be the first not to respect me now.'

There was a water-melon on the table. Gurov cut himself a slice and began eating it without haste. There followed at least half an hour of silence.

Anna was touching; there was about her the purity of a good naive woman who had seen little of life. The solitary candle burning on the table threw a faint light on her face, yet it was clear that she felt unhappy.

'Why should I stop respecting you?' asked Gurov. 'You don't know what you're saying.'

'God forgive me,' she said, and her eyes filled with tears. 'It's awful.'

'You seem to be defending yourself.'

'What defence do I have? No. I am a bad, low woman; I despise myself and don't attempt to justify myself. It's not my husband but myself I have deceived. And not only just now; I have been deceiving myself for a long time. My husband may be a good, honest man, but he is a flunky! I don't know what he does there, what his work is, but I know he is a flunky! I was twenty when I married him. I was tormented by curiosity; I wanted something better. "There must be a different sort of life," I said to myself. I wanted to live! To live, to live! . . . I was fired by curiosity . . . you don't understand it, but, I swear to God, I could not control myself; something happened to me; I could not be restrained. I told my husband I was ill, and came here . . . And here I have been walking about as though I were intoxicated, like a mad creature . . . and now I have become a vulgar, contemptible woman whom anyone may despise.'

Gurov felt bored already with listening to her. He was irritated by the naive tone, by this remorse, so unexpected and inopportune; but for the tears in her eyes, he might have thought she was jesting or playing a part.

'I don't understand,' he said softly. 'What is it you want?'

She hid her face on his breast and pressed close to him.

'Believe me, believe me, I beg you . . .' she said. 'I love a pure, honest life, and sin is loathsome to me. I don't know what I am doing. Simple people say: "The Evil One has beguiled me." And I can say of myself now that the Evil One has beguiled me.'

'Hush, hush . . .' he muttered.

He looked at her fixed scared eyes, kissed her, talked softly and affectionately, and by degrees she was comforted, and her gaiety returned; they both began laughing.

Afterwards when they went out there was not a soul on the sea-front. The town with its cypresses had quite a deathly air, but the sea still broke noisily on the shore; a single launch was rocking on the waves, and a lantern was blinking sleepily on it.

They found a cab and drove to Oreanda.

'I found out your surname in the hall just now; it was written on the board – 'Von Diderits,' said Gurov. 'Is your husband German?'

'No; I believe his grandfather was German, but he is Orthodox Russian himself.'

At Oreanda they sat on a seat not far from the church, looked down at the sea, and were silent. Yalta was hardly visible through the morning mist; white clouds stood motionless on the mountain tops. The leaves did not stir on the trees, cicadas chirruped, and the monotonous hollow sound of the sea, rising up from below, spoke of the peace, of the eternal sleep awaiting us. So it must have sounded before there was a Yalta, an Oreanda here; so it sounds now, and it will sound as indifferently and monotonously when we are no more. And in this constancy, in this complete indifference to the life and death of each of us, there lies hidden, perhaps, a pledge of our eternal salvation, of the unceasing movement of life upon earth, of uninterrupted perfection. Sitting beside a young woman who in the dawn seemed so lovely, tranquil and spellbound in these magical surroundings – the sea, mountains, clouds, the broad sky – Gurov thought how in reality everything is beautiful in this world when one reflects: everything except what we think or do ourselves when we forget the higher aims of our existence and our human dignity.

A man walked up to them – probably a night-watchman – looked at them and walked away. And this detail seemed mysterious and beautiful, too. They saw a steamer come from Feodosia, with its lights out, illuminated by the dawn.

'There's dew on the grass,' said Anna, after a silence.

'Yes. It's time to go home.'

They went back to town.

Then they met every day at twelve o'clock on the sea-front, lunched and dined together, went for walks, admired the sea. She complained that she slept badly, that her heart throbbed violently; asked the same questions, troubled now by jealousy and now by the fear that he did not respect her sufficiently. And often in the square or gardens, when there was no one near them, he suddenly drew her to him and kissed her passionately. Complete idleness, these kisses in broad daylight with circumspection and fear, in case someone saw them, the heat, the smell of the sea, and the continual passing to and fro before him of idle, well-dressed, well-fed people, virtually regenerated him; he told Anna how beautiful she was, how fascinating, he was impatiently passionate, he would not move a step away from her, while she was often pensive and continually urged him to confess that he did not respect her, and did not love her in the least, and thought of her as nothing but a common woman. Rather late almost every evening they drove somewhere out of town, to Oreanda or to the waterfall; and the expedition was always a success, the scenery invariably impressed them as beautiful and majestic.

They were expecting her husband to come, but a letter came

from him, saying that there was something wrong with his eyes, and he entreated his wife to come home as quickly as possible. Anna made haste to go.

'It's a good thing I am going away,' she said to Gurov. 'It's fate itself!'

She went by carriage and he went with her. They spent the whole day driving to Sevastopol. There, when she had got into a compartment of the mail train, and when the second bell had rung, she said:

'Let me look at you once more . . . look at you once again. That's right.'

She did not shed tears, but was so sad that she seemed ill, and her face was quivering.

'I shall remember you . . . think of you,' she said. 'God be with you; be happy. Don't think badly of me. We are parting for ever – it must be so, for we ought never to have met. Well, God be with you.'

The train moved off rapidly, its lights soon vanished from sight, and a minute later there was no sound of it, as though everything had conspired together to end as quickly as possible that sweet delirium, that madness. Left alone on the platform, and gazing into the dark distance, Gurov listened to the chirrup of the grasshoppers and the hum of the telegraph wires, feeling as though he had only just woken up. And he reflected that this had been another episode or adventure in his life, and it, too, was at an end, and nothing was left of it but a memory . . . He was much moved, sad, and conscious of a slight penitence, for this young woman whom he would never meet again had not been happy with him; he had been warm and affectionate with her, but yet in his manner, his tone, and his caresses there had been a shade of light irony, the rough-edged condescension of a happy man who was, besides, almost twice her age. All the time she had called him kind, exceptional, lofty; obviously he had seemed to her different from what he really was, so he had unintentionally deceived her . . .

Here at the station there was already a smell of autumn; it was a cool evening.

'It's time I went north, too,' thought Gurov as he left the platform. 'High time!'

3

At home in Moscow everything was in winter routine; the stoves were stoked, and in the morning it was still dark when the children were having breakfast and getting ready for school, and the nurse would light the lamps for a short time. The frosts had begun already. When the first snow has fallen, on the first day of sledge-driving, it is pleasant to see the white earth, the white roofs, to draw soft delicious breath, and the season brings back the days of your youth. The old limes and birches, white and hoar frost, have a good-natured expression; they are nearer to your heart than cypresses and palms, and near them you no longer want to think of the sea and the mountains.

Gurov was a Muscovite, he arrived in Moscow on a fine frosty day, and when he put on his fur coat and warm gloves, and walked along Petrovka, and when on Saturday evening he heard the ringing of the bells, his recent trip and the places he had seen lost all charm for him. Little by little he became absorbed in Moscow life, greedily read three newspapers a day, and declared he did not read the Moscow papers on principle! He already felt a longing to go to restaurants, clubs, dinner-parties, anniversary celebrations, and he felt flattered at entertaining distinguished lawyers and artists, and at playing cards with a professor at the doctors' club. He could already eat a frying-pan full of 'hot-pot' . . .

In another month, he fancied, the image of Anna would be shrouded in mist in his memory, and only from time to time would visit him in his dreams with a touching smile, as others did. But more than a month passed, real winter had come, and everything was still clear in his memory as though he had parted with Anna only the day before. And his memories were flaring up all the more vividly. When in the evening stillness he heard from his study the voices of his children doing their homework, or when he listened to a song or the organ at the restaurant, or the storm howled in the chimney, suddenly everything would rise up in his memory: what had happened on the pier, and the early morning with the mist on the mountains, and the steamer coming from Feodosia, and the kisses. He would pace a long time about his room, remembering it all and smiling; then his memories passed into dreams, and in his fancy the past was mingled with what was to come. He did not see Anna in his dreams, but she followed him about everywhere like a shadow and haunted him. When he shut his eyes he saw her as though she were as large as life before him, and she seemed to him lovelier, younger, tenderer than she had been; and he imagined himself finer than he had been in Yalta. In the evenings she peeped out at him from the bookcase, from the fireplace, from the corner – he heard her breathing, the caressing rustle of her dress. In the street he watched the women, looking for someone like her.

He was tormented by an intense desire to share his memories with someone. But in his home it was impossible to talk of his love, and he had no one outside; he could not talk to his tenants nor to anyone at the bank. And what had he to talk of? Had he been in love then? Had there been anything beautiful, poetical, or edifying or simply interesting in his feelings for Anna? And there was nothing for him but to talk vaguely of love, of woman, and no one guessed what it meant; only his wife twitched her black eyebrows, and said: 'The part of a lady killer does not suit you at all, Dimitri.'

One evening, coming out of the doctors' club with an official with whom he had been playing cards, he could not resist saying:

'If you only knew what a fascinating woman I got to know in Yalta!'

The official got into his sledge and was driving away, but turned suddenly and shouted:

'Dmitri!'

'What?'

'You were right this evening: the sturgeon was a bit off!'

These words, so ordinary, for some reason moved Gurov to indignation, and struck him as degrading and unclean. What savage manners, what people! What senseless nights, what uninteresting, uneventful days! The rage for playing cards, the gluttony, the drunkenness, the continual talk always about the same thing. Useless pursuits and conversations always about the same things absorb the better part of your time, the better part of your strength, and in the end you are left with a life earthbound and curtailed, just rubbish, and there is no escaping or getting away from it – just as though you were in a madhouse or in penal servitude.

Gurov did not sleep all night, and was filled with indignation, and on the morrow he had a headache the entire day. And the next night he slept badly; he sat up in bed, thinking, or paced up and down his room. He was sick of his children, sick of the bank; he had no desire to go anywhere or to talk of anything.

In the holidays in December he prepared for a journey, and told his wife he was going to Petersburg to do something in the interests of a young friend – and he set off for S—. What for? He did not very well know himself. He wanted to see Anna and to talk with her, to arrange a meeting, if possible.

He reached S— in the morning, and took the best room at the hotel, in which the floor was covered with grey army cloth, and on the table was an inkstand, grey with dust and adorned with a figure on horseback, with its hat in its hand and its head broken off. The hotel porter gave him the necessary information: Von Diderits lived in a house of his own in Old Goncharnaia Street – it was not far from the hotel; he lived well and was rich, he had his own horses, everyone in town knew him. The porter pronounced the name 'Dridirits'.

Gurov went without haste to Old Goncharnaia Street and found the house. Just opposite the house stretched a long grey fence adorned with nails.

'You'd run away from a fence like that,' thought Gurov, looking from the fence to the windows of the house and back again.

He considered: today was a holiday, and the husband would probably be at home, and in any case it would be tactless to go into the house and upset her. If he were to send her a note it might fall into her husband's hands, and that might ruin everything. The best thing was to trust to chance. And he kept walking up and down the street by the fence, waiting for the chance. He saw a beggar go in at the gate and dogs fly at him; then an hour later he heard a piano, and the sounds were faint and indistinct. Probably it was Anna playing. The front door suddenly opened, and an old woman came out, followed by the familiar white Pomeranian. Gurov was on the point of calling to the dog, but his heart began beating violently, and in his excitement he could not remember the dog's name.

He walked up and down, and loathed the grey fence more and more, and by now he thought irritably that Anna had forgotten him and was perhaps already amusing herself with someone else, and that that was very natural in a young woman who had nothing to look at from morning till night but that accursed fence. He went back to his hotel room and sat for a long while on the sofa, not knowing what to do, then he had dinner and a long nap.

'How stupid and upsetting it is!' he thought when he woke and looked at the dark windows: it was already evening. 'Now I've slept my fill for some reason. Now what shall I do at night?'

He sat on the bed, which was covered by a cheap grey blanket, like a hospital blanket, and he taunted himself in his vexation:

'So much for the lady with the dog . . . So much for the adventure . . . So you're stuck in this room.'

That morning at the station a poster in large letters had caught his eye. *The Geisha* was to be performed for the first time. He thought of this and went to the theatre.

'It's quite possible she may go to the first performance,' he thought.

The theatre was full. As in all provincial theatres, there was a fog above the chandelier, the gallery was noisy and restless; in the front row the local dandies were standing up before the beginning of the performance, with their hands behind them; in the governor's box the governor's daughter, wearing a boa, was sitting in the front seat, while the governor himself lurked modestly behind the curtain with only his hands visible; the orchestra was a long time tuning up; the stage curtain swayed. All the time the audience were coming in and taking their seats, Gurov's eyes were searching eagerly.

Anna, too, came in. She sat down in the third row, and when Gurov looked at her his heart contracted, and he understood clearly that for him there was in the whole world no creature so near, so precious, and so important to him; she, this little woman, in no way remarkable, lost in a provincial crowd, with a vulgar lorgnette in her hand, filled his whole life now, was his sorrow and his joy, the one happiness that he now desired for himself, and to the sounds of the inferior orchestra, of the wretched provincial violins, he thought how lovely she was. He thought and dreamed.

A young man with small side-whiskers, tall and stooping, came in with Anna and sat down beside her; he bent his head at every step and seemed to be continually bowing. Most likely this was the husband whom at Yalta, in a rush of bitter feeling, she had called a flunky. And there really was in his long figure, his side-whiskers, and the small bald patch on his head, something of the flunky's obsequiousness; his smile was sugary, and in his buttonhole there was some obscure order's badge, like a waiter's number tag.

During the first interval the husband went out to smoke; she remained alone in her stall. Gurov, who was in the stalls, too, went up to her and said in a trembling voice, with a forced smile:

'Good evening.'

She glanced at him and turned pale, then glanced again with horror, unable to believe her eyes, and tightly gripped the fan and the lorgnette in her hands, evidently struggling with herself not to faint. Both were silent. She was sitting, he was standing, frightened by her turmoil and not venturing to sit down beside her. The violins and the flute began tuning up. He felt suddenly frightened; it seemed as if everyone in the boxes was looking at them. She got up and went quickly to the door; he followed her, and both walked senselessly along passages, and up and down stairs, and figures in legal, scholastic, and civil service uniforms, all wearing badges, flitted before their eyes. They caught glimpses of ladies, of fur coats hanging on pegs; the draughts blew on them, bringing a smell of cigarette ends. And Gurov, whose heart was beating violently, thought:

'Oh Lord! Why are all these people, this orchestra around . . .'

And that minute he suddenly remembered that evening at the station, when he was seeing Anna off, and he had told himself that it was all over and they would never see each other again. But how far off the end still was!

On a narrow, murky staircase, with a sign saying 'Entrance to Circle', she stopped.

'How you've frightened me!' she said, breathing heavily, still all pale and aghast. 'Oh, how you've frightened me! I am half dead. Why have you come? Why?'

'But do understand, Anna, do understand . . .' he said hastily in a low voice. 'I beg you to understand . . .'

She looked at him with dread, with entreaty, with love; she looked at him intently, to keep his features as sharply as she could in her memory.

'I am so wretched,' she went on, not heeding him. 'I have thought of nothing but you all the time; I live only by thinking about you. And I wanted to forget, to forget you; but why, oh why, have you come?'

On the landing above them two schoolboys were smoking and looking down, but Gurov did not care; he drew Anna to him, and began kissing her face, her cheeks, and her hands.

'What are you doing, what are you doing!' she cried in horror, pushing him away. 'We are mad. Go away today; go away at once . . . I beg you by all that is sacred, I implore you . . . People are coming!'

Someone was coming up the stairs.

'You must go away,' Anna went on in a whisper. 'Do you hear, Dmitri? I will come and see you in Moscow, I have never been happy; I am miserable now, and I never, never shall be happy, never! Don't make me suffer still more! I swear I'll come to Moscow. But now let us part. My precious, good, dear one, we must part!'

She pressed his hand and began rapidly going downstairs, looking round at him, and from her eyes he could see that she really was unhappy. Gurov stood for a little while, listened, then, when all sound had died away, he found his coat and left the theatre.

4

And Anna began visiting him in Moscow. Once every two or three months she left S—, telling her husband that she was going to consult a doctor about a gynaecological complaint – and her husband half believed her. In Moscow she stayed at the Slaviansky Bazaar hotel, and at once sent a man in a red cap to Gurov. Gurov went to see her, and no one in Moscow knew of it.

Once he was going to see her in this way on a winter morning (the messenger had come the evening before when he was out). With him walked his daughter, whom he wanted to take to school: it was on the way. Snow was falling in big wet flakes.

'It's three degrees above freezing point, and yet it is snowing,' said Gurov to his daughter. 'The thaw is only on the surface of the earth; there is quite a different temperature at a greater height in the atmosphere.'

'And why are there no thunderstorms in winter, papa?'

He explained that, too. He talked, thinking all the while that he was going to see her, and no living soul knew of it, and probably never would know. He had two lives: one, open, seen and known by all who cared to know, full of conventional truth and of conventional falsehood, exactly like the lives of his friends and acquaintances; and another life running its course in secret. And through some strange, perhaps accidental, conjunction of circumstances, everything that was essential, of interest and of value to him, everything in which he was sincere and did not deceive himself, everything that made the kernel of his life, was kept secret from other people; and all that was false in him, a membrane in which he hid to conceal the truth – such, for instance, as his work in the bank, his discussions at the club, his 'lower race', his presence with his wife at anniversary festivities – all that was open. And he judged of others by himself, not believing what he saw, and always presupposed that every person lived his real, most interesting life under the cover of secrecy, as if under the cover of night. All personal existence rested on privacy, and possibly it was partly on that account that civilised man was so nervously anxious that personal privacy should be respected.

After seeing his daughter to school, Gurov went on to the Slaviansky Bazaar. He took off his fur coat below, went upstairs, and softly knocked at the door. Anna, wearing his favourite grey dress, exhausted by the journey and the suspense, had been expecting him since the evening before. She was pale; she looked at him, and did not smile, and he had hardly come in when she fell on his breast. Their kiss was slow and prolonged, as though they had not met for two years.

'Well, how are you getting on there?' he asked. 'What news?'

'Wait; I'll tell you in a moment . . . I can't talk.'

She could not speak, since she was crying. She turned away from him, and pressed her handkerchief to her eyes.

'Let her have her cry. I'll sit down and wait,' he thought, and he sat down in an arm-chair.

Then he rang and asked for tea to be brought to him, and while he drank his tea she remained standing at the window with her back to him. She was crying from emotion, from the miserable consciousness that their life was so hard for them; they could only meet in secret, hiding themselves from people, like thieves! Their life was shattered, wasn't it?

'Come, do stop!' he said.

It was evident to him that this love of theirs was not going to end for some time, and its end was impossible to foresee. Anna was growing more and more attached to him. She adored him, and it was unthinkable to say to her that it was bound to have an end some day; besides, she would not have believed it.

He went up to her and took her by the shoulders to say something affectionate and cheering, and at that moment he saw himself in the looking-glass.

His hair was already beginning to turn grey. And it seemed strange to him that he had grown so much older, so much plainer during the last few years. The shoulders on which his hands rested were warm and quivering. He felt compassion for this life, still so warm and lovely, but probably already not far from beginning to fade and wither like his own. Why did she love him so much? He always seemed to women different from what he was, and they loved in him not himself, but the man created by their imagination, whom they had been eagerly seeking all their lives; and afterwards, when they noticed their mistake, they loved him all the same. And not one of them had been happy with him. Time passed, he met them, became intimate with them, parted, but he had never once loved; call it what you like, but not love.

And only now when his head was grey he had fallen properly, really in love – for the first time in his life.

Anna and he loved each other like people very close and akin, like husband and wife, like tender friends; it seemed to them that fate itself had meant them for one another, and they could not understand why he had a wife and she a husband; it was as though they were two birds of passage, male and female, caught and forced to live in different cages. They forgave each other for what they were ashamed of in their past, they forgave everything in the present, and felt that this love of theirs had changed them both.

In sad moments in the past he had comforted himself with any arguments that came into his mind, but now he was beyond arguments; he felt profound compassion, he wanted to be sincere and tender . . .

'Don't cry, my darling,' he said. 'You've had your cry; that's enough . . . Let's talk now, let's think of something.'

Thus they spent a long while taking counsel together, talked of how to avoid the necessity for hiding, for lying, for living in different towns and not seeing each other for long periods. How could they get free from these intolerable bonds?

'How? How?' he asked, clutching his head. 'How?'

And it seemed as though in a little while the solution would be found, and then a new and splendid life would begin; and it was clear to both of them that they had still a long, long way to go, and that the most complicated and difficult part of it was only just beginning.

ARTHUR CONAN DOYLE

The Speckled Band

In glancing over my notes of the seventy odd cases in which I have during the last eight years studied the methods of my friend Sherlock Holmes, I find many tragic, some comic, a large number merely strange, but none commonplace; for working as he did rather for the love of his art than for the acquirement of wealth, he refused to associate himself with any investigation which did not tend towards the unusual, and even the fantastic. Of all these varied cases, however, I cannot recall any which presented more singular features than that which was associated with the well-known Surrey family of the Roylotts of Stoke Moran. The events in question occurred in the early days of my association with Holmes, when we were sharing rooms as bachelors, in Baker Street. It is possible that I might have placed them upon record before, but a promise of secrecy was made at the time, from which I have only been freed during the last month by the untimely death of the lady to whom the pledge was given. It is perhaps as well that the facts should now come to light, for I have reasons to know there are widespread rumours as to the death of Dr Grimesby Roylott which tend to make the matter even more terrible than the truth.

It was early in April, in the year '83, that I woke one morning to find Sherlock Holmes standing, fully dressed, by the side of my bed. He was a late riser as a rule, and, as the clock on the mantelpiece showed me that it was only a quarter past seven, I blinked up at him in some surprise, and perhaps just a little resentment, for I was myself regular in my habits.

'Very sorry to knock you up, Watson,' said he, 'but it's the common lot this morning. Mrs Hudson has been knocked up, she retorted upon me, and I on you.'

'What is it, then? A fire?'

'No, a client. It seems that a young lady has arrived in a considerable state of excitement, who insists upon seeing me. She is waiting now in the sitting-room. Now, when young ladies wander about the metropolis at this hour of the morning, and knock sleepy people up out of their beds, I presume that it is something very pressing which they have to communicate. Should it prove to be an interesting case, you would, I am sure, wish to follow it from the outset. I thought at any rate that I should call you, and give you the chance.'

'My dear fellow, I would not miss it for anything.'

I had no keener pleasure than in following Holmes in his professional investigations, and in admiring the rapid deductions, as swift as intuitions, and yet always founded on a logical basic, with which he unravelled the problems which were submitted to him. I rapidly threw on my clothes, and was ready in a few minutes to accompany my friend down to the sitting-room. A lady dressed in black and heavily veiled, who had been sitting in the window, rose as we entered.

'Good morning, madam,' said Holmes cheerily. 'My name is Sherlock Holmes. This is my intimate friend and associate, Dr Watson, before whom you can speak as freely as before myself. Ha, I am glad to see that Mrs Hudson has had the good sense to light the fire. Pray draw up to it, and I shall order you a cup of coffee, for I observe that you are shivering.'

'It is not cold which makes me shiver,' said the woman in a low voice, changing her seat as requested.

'What then?'

'It is fear, Mr Holmes. It is terror.' She raised her veil as she spoke, and we could see that she was indeed in a pitiable state of agitation, her face all drawn and grey, with restless, frightened eyes, like those of some hunted animal. Her features and figure were those of a woman of thirty, but her hair was shot with premature grey, and her expression was weary and haggard. Sherlock Holmes ran her over with one of his quick, all-comprehensive glances.

'You must not fear,' said he soothingly, bending forward and patting her forearm. 'We shall soon set matters right, I have no doubt. You have come in by train this morning, I see.'

'You know me, then?'

'No, but I observe the second half of a return ticket in the palm of your left glove. You must have started early, and yet you had a good drive in a dog-cart, along heavy roads, before you reached the station.'

The lady gave a violent start, and stared in bewilderment at my companion.

'There is no mystery, my dear madam,' said he, smiling. 'The left arm of your jacket is spattered with mud in no less than seven places. The marks are perfectly fresh. There is no vehicle save a dog-cart which throws up mud in that way, and then only when you sit on the lefthand side of the driver.'

'Whatever your reasons may be, you are perfectly correct,' said she. 'I started from home before six, reached Leatherhead at twenty past, and came in by the first train to Waterloo. Sir, I can stand this strain no longer, I shall go mad if it continues. I have no one to turn to – none, save only one, who cares for me, and he, poor fellow, can be of little aid. I have heard of you, Mr Holmes; I have heard of you from Mrs Farintosh, whom you helped in the hour of her sore need. It was from her that I had your address. Oh, sir, do you not think you could help me too, and at least throw a little light through the dense darkness which surrounds me? At present it is out of my power to reward you for your services, but in a month or two I shall be married, with the control of my own income, and then at least you shall not find me ungrateful.'

Holmes turned to his desk, and unlocking it, drew out a small casebook which he consulted.

'Farintosh,' said he. 'Ah, yes, I recall the case; it was concerned with an opal tiara. I think it was before your time, Watson. I can only say, madam, that I shall be happy to devote the same care to your case as I did to that of your friend. As to reward, my profession is its reward; but you are at liberty to defray whatever expenses I may be put to, at the time which suits you best. And now I beg that you will lay before us everything that may help us in forming an opinion upon the matter.'

'Alas!' replied our visitor. 'The very horror of my situation lies in the fact that my fears are so vague, and my suspicions depend so entirely upon small points, which might seem trivial to another, that even he to whom of all others I have a right to look for help and advice looks upon all that I tell him about it as the fancies of a nervous woman. He does not say so, but I can read it from his soothing answers and averted eyes. But I have heard, Mr

Holmes, that you can see deeply into the manifold wickedness of the human heart. You may advise me how to walk amid the dangers which encompass me.'

'I am all attention, madam.'

'My name is Helen Stoner, and I am living with my stepfather, who is the last survivor of one of the oldest Saxon families in England, the Roylotts of Stoke Moran, on the Western border of Surrey.'

Holmes nodded his head. 'The name is familiar to me,' said he.

'The family was at one time among the richest in England, and the estate extended over the borders into Berkshire in the north, and Hampshire in the west. In the last century, however, four successive heirs were of dissolute and wasteful disposition, and the family ruin was eventually completed by a gambler, in the days of the Regency. Nothing was left save a few acres of ground and the 200-year-old house, which is itself crushed under a heavy mortgage. The last squire dragged out his existence there, living the horrible life of an aristocratic pauper; but his only son, my stepfather, seeing that he must adapt himself to the new conditions, obtained an advance from a relative, which enabled him to take a medical degree, and went out to Calcutta, where, by his professional skill and his force of character, he established a large practice. In a fit of anger, however, caused by some robberies which had been perpetrated in the house, he beat his native butler to death, and narrowly escaped a capital sentence. As it was, he suffered a long term of imprisonment, and afterwards returned to England a morose and disappointed man.

'When Dr Roylott was in India he married my mother, Mrs Stoner, the young widow of Major-General Stoner, of the Bengal Artillery. My sister Julia and I were twins, and we were only two years old at the time of my mother's remarriage. She had a considerable sum of money, not less than a thousand a year, and this she bequeathed to Dr Roylott entirely whilst we resided with him, with a provision that a certain annual sum should be allowed to each of us in the event of our marriage. Shortly after our return to England my mother died – she was killed eight years ago in a railway accident near Crewe. Dr Roylott then abandoned his attempts to establish himself in practice in London, and took us to live with him in the ancestral house at

Stoke Moran. The money which my mother had left was enough for all our wants, and there seemed no obstacle to our happiness.

'But a terrible change came over our stepfather about this time. Instead of making friends and exchanging visits with our neighbours, who had at first been overjoyed to see a Roylott of Stoke Moran back in the old family seat, he shut himself up in his house, and seldom came out save to indulge in ferocious quarrels with whoever might cross his path. Violence of temper approaching to mania has been hereditary in the men of the family, and in my stepfather's case it had, I believe, been intensified by his long residence in the tropics. A series of disgraceful brawls took place, two of which ended in the police-court, until at last he became the terror of the village, and the folks would fly at his approach, for he is a man of immense strength, and absolutely uncontrollable in his anger.

'Last week he hurled the local blacksmith over a parapet into a stream and it was only by paying over all the money that I could gather together that I was able to avert another public exposure. He had no friends at all save the wandering gipsies, and he would give these vagabonds leave to encamp upon the few acres of bramble-covered land which represent the family estate, and would accept in return the hospitality of their tents, wandering away with them sometimes for weeks on end. He has a passion also for Indian animals, which are sent over to him by a correspondent, and he has at this moment a cheetah and a baboon, which wander freely over the grounds, and are feared by the villagers almost as much as their master.

'You can imagine from what I say that my poor sister Julia and I had no great pleasure in our lives. No servant would stay with us, and for a long time we did all the work of the house. She was but thirty at the time of her death, and yet her hair had already begun to whiten, even as mine has.'

'Your sister is dead, then?'

'She died just two years ago, and it is of her death that I wish to speak to you. You can understand that, living the life which I have described, we were little likely to see anyone of our own age and position. We had, however, an aunt, my mother's maiden sister, Miss Honoria Westphail, who lives near Harrow, and we were occasionally allowed to pay short visits at this lady's house. Julia went there at Christmas two years ago, and met there a half-pay Major of Marines, to whom she became engaged. My stepfather learned of the engagement when my sister returned, and offered no objections to the marriage; but within a fortnight of the day which had been fixed for the wedding, the terrible event occurred which has deprived me of my only companion.'

Sherlock Holmes had been leaning back in his chair with his eyes closed, and his head sunk in a cushion, but he had opened his lids now, and glanced across at his visitor.

'Pray be precise as to details,' said he.

'It is easy for me to be so, for every event of that dreadful time is seared into my memory. The manor house is, as I have already said, very old, and only one wing is now inhabited. The bedrooms in this wing are on the ground floor, the sitting-rooms being in the central block of the buildings. Of these bedrooms the first is Dr Roylott's, the second is my sister's, and the third my own. There is no communication between them, but they all open out into the same corridor. Do I make myself plain?'

'Perfectly so.'

'The windows of the three rooms open out upon the lawn. That fatal night Dr Roylott had gone to his room early, though we knew that he had not retired to rest, for my sister was troubled by the smell of the strong Indian cigars which it was his custom to smoke. She left her room, therefore, and came into mine, where she sat for some time, chatting about her approaching wedding. At eleven o'clock she rose to leave me, but she paused at the door and looked back.

'"Tell me, Helen," said she, "have you ever heard anyone whistle in the dead of the night."

'"Never," said I.

'"I suppose that you could not possibly whistle yourself in your sleep?"

'"Certainly not. But why?"

'"Because during the last few nights I have always, about three in the morning, heard a low clear whistle. I am a light sleeper, and it has awakened me. I cannot tell where it came from – perhaps from the next room, perhaps from the lawn. I thought that I would just ask you whether you had heard it."

'"No, I have not. It must be those wretched gipsies in the plantation."

'"Very likely. And yet if it were on the lawn I wonder that you did not hear it also."

'"Well, it is of no great consequence, at any rate," she smiled back at me, closed my door, and a few moments later I heard her key turn in the lock.'

'Indeed,' said Holmes. 'Was it your custom always to lock yourselves in at night?'

'Always.'

'And why?'

'I think that I mentioned to you that the Doctor kept a cheetah and a baboon. We had no feeling of security unless our doors were locked.'

'Quite so. Pray proceed with your statement.'

'I could not sleep that night. A vague feeling of impending misfortune impressed me. My sister and I, you will recollect, were twins, and you know how subtle are the links which bind two souls which are so closely allied. It was a wild night. The wind was howling outside, and the rain was beating and splashing against the windows. Suddenly, amidst all the hubbub of the gale, there burst forth the wild scream of a terrified woman. I knew that it was my sister's voice. I sprang from my bed, wrapped a shawl round me, and rushed into the corridor. As I opened my door I seemed to hear a low whistle, such as my sister described, and a few moments later a clanging sound, as if a mass of metal had fallen. As I ran down the passage my sister's door was unlocked, and revolved slowly upon its hinges. I stared at it horror-stricken, not knowing what was about to issue from it. By the light of the corridor lamp I saw my sister appear at the opening, her face blanched with terror, her hands groping for help, her whole figure swaying to and fro like that of a drunkard. I ran to her and threw my arms around her, but at that moment her knees seemed to give way and she fell to the ground. She writhed as one who is in terrible pain, and her limbs were dreadfully convulsed. At first I thought that she had not recognized me, but as I bent over her she suddenly shrieked out in a voice which I shall never forget, "Oh, my God Helen! It was the band! The speckled band!" There was something else which she would fain have said, and she stabbed with her finger into the air in the direction of the Doctor's room, but a fresh convulsion seized her and choked her words. I rushed out, calling loudly for my stepfather, and I met him hastening from his room in his dressing-gown. When he reached my sister's side she was unconscious, and though he poured brandy down her throat, and sent for medical aid from the village, all efforts were in vain, for she slowly sank and died without having recovered her consciousness. Such was the dreadful end of my beloved sister.'

'One moment,' said Holmes; 'are you sure about this whistle and metallic sound? Could you swear to it?'

'That was what the county coroner asked me at the inquiry. It is my strong impression that I heard it, and yet among the crash of the gale, and the creaking of an old house, I may possibly have been deceived.'

'Was your sister dressed?'

'No, she was in her nightdress. In her right hand was found the charred stump of a match, and in her left a matchbox.'

'Showing that she had struck a light and looked about her when the alarm took place. That is important. And what conclusions did the coroner come to?'

'He investigated the case with great care, for Dr Roylott's conduct had long been notorious in the county, but he was unable to find any satisfactory cause of death. My evidence showed that the door had been fastened upon the inner side, and the windows were blocked by old-fashioned shutters with broad iron bars, which were secured every night. The walls were carefully sounded, and were shown to be quite solid all round, and the flooring was also thoroughly examined, with the same result. The chimney is wide, but is barred up by four large staples. It is certain, therefore, that my sister was quite alone when she met her end. Besides, there were no marks of any violence upon her.'

'How about poison?'

'The doctors examined her for it, but without success.'

'What do you think that this unfortunate lady died of, then?'

'It is my belief that she died of pure fear and nervous shock, though what it was which frightened her I cannot imagine.'

'Were there gipsies in the plantation at that time?'

'Yes, there are nearly always some there.'

'Ah, and what did you gather from this allusion to a band – a speckled band?'

'Sometimes I have thought that it was merely the wild talk of delirium, sometimes that it may have referred to some band of people, perhaps to these very gipsies in the plantation. I do not know whether the spotted handkerchief which so many of them wear over their heads might have suggested the strange adjective which she used.'

Holmes shook his head like a man who is far from being satisfied.

'These are very deep waters,' said he; 'pray go on with your narrative.'

'Two years have passed since then, and my life has been until lately lonelier than ever. A month ago, however, a dear friend, whom I have known for many years, has done me the honour to ask my hand in marriage. His name is Armitage – Percy Armitage – the second son of Mr Armitage, of Crane Water, near Reading. My stepfather has offered no opposition to the match, and we are to be married in the course of the spring. Two days ago some repairs were started in the west wing of the building, and my bedroom wall has been pierced, so that I have had to move into the chamber in which my sister died, and so sleep in the very bed in which she slept. Imagine, then, my thrill of terror when last night, as I lay awake, thinking over her terrible fate, I suddenly heard in the silence of the night the low whistle which had been the herald of her own death. I sprang up and lit the lamp, but nothing was to be seen in the room. I was too shaken to go to bed again, however, so I dressed, and as soon as it was daylight slipped down, got a dogcart at the Crown Inn, which is opposite, and drove to Leatherhead, from whence I have come on this morning, with the one object of seeing you and asking your advice.'

'You have done wisely,' said my friend. 'But have you told me all?'

'Yes, all.'

'Miss Stoner, you have not. You are screening your stepfather.'

'Why, what do you mean?'

For answer Holmes pushed back the frill of black lace which fringed the hand that lay upon our visitor's knee. Five little livid spots, the marks of four fingers and a thumb, were printed upon the white wrist.

'You have been cruelly used,' said Holmes.

The lady coloured deeply, and covered over her injured wrist.

'He is a hard man,' she said, 'and perhaps he hardly knows his own strength.'

There was a long silence, during which Holmes leaned his chin upon his hands and stared into the crackling fire.

'This is very deep business,' he said at last. 'There are a thousand details which I should desire to know before I decide upon our course of action. Yet we have not a moment to lose. If we were to come to Stoke Moran today, would it be possible for us to see over these rooms without the knowledge of your stepfather?'

'As it happens, he spoke of coming into town today upon some most important business. It is probable that he will be away all day, and that there would be nothing to disturb you. We have a housekeeper now, but she is old and foolish, and I could easily get her out of the way.'

'Excellent. You are not averse to this trip, Watson?'

'By no means.'

'Then we shall both come. What are you going to do yourself?'

'I have one or two things which I would wish to do now that I am in town. But I shall return by the twelve o'clock train, so as to be there in time for your coming.'

'And you may expect us early in the afternoon. I have myself some small business matters to attend to. Will you not wait and breakfast?'

'No, I must go. My heart is lightened already since I have confided my trouble to you. I shall look forward to seeing you again this afternoon.' She dropped her thick black veil over her face, and glided from the room.

'And what do you think of it all, Watson?' asked Sherlock Holmes, leaning back in his chair.

'It seems to me to be a most dark and sinister business.'

'Dark enough and sinister enough.'

'Yet if the lady is correct in saying that the flooring and walls are sound; and that the door, window, and chimney are impassable, then her sister must have been undoubtedly alone when she met her mysterious end.'

'What becomes, then, of these nocturnal whistles, and what of the very peculiar words of the dying woman?'

'I cannot think.'

'When you combine the ideas of whistles at night, the presence of a band of gipsies who are on intimate terms with this old doctor, the fact that we have every reason to believe that the doctor has an interest in preventing his stepdaughter's marriage, the dying allusion to a band, and finally, the fact that Miss Helen Stoner heard a metallic clang, which might have been caused by one of those metal bars which secured the shutters falling back into their place, I think there is good ground to think that the mystery may be cleared along those lines.'

'But what, then, did the gipsies do?'

'I cannot imagine.'

'I see many objections to any such a theory.'

'And so do I. It is precisely for that reason that we are going to Stoke Moran this day. I want to see whether the objections are fatal, or if they may be explained away. But what, in the name of the devil?'

The ejaculation had been drawn from my companion by the fact that our door had been suddenly dashed open, and that a huge man framed himself in the aperture. His costume was a peculiar mixture of the professional and the agricultural, having a black top-hat, long frock-coat, and a pair of high gaiters, with a hunting-crop swinging in his hand. So tall was he that his hat actually brushed the cross-bar of the doorway, and his breadth seemed to span it across from side to side. A large face, seared with a thousand wrinkles, burned yellow with the sun, and marked with every evil passion, was turned from one to the other of us, while his deep-set, bile-shot eyes, and the high thin fleshless nose, gave him somewhat the resemblance to a fierce old bird of prey.

'Which of you is Holmes?' asked this apparition.

'My name, sir, but you have the advantage of me,' said my companion quietly.

'I am Dr Grimesby Roylott, of Stoke Moran.'

'Indeed, Doctor,' said Holmes blandly. 'Pray take a seat.'

'I will do nothing of the kind. My stepdaughter has been here. I have traced her. What has she been saying to you?'

'It is a little cold for the time of the year,' said Holmes.

'What has she been saying to you?' screamed the old man furiously.

'But I have heard that the crocuses promise well,' continued my companion imperturbably.

'Ha! You put me off, do you?' said our new visitor, taking a step forward, and shaking his hunting-crop. 'I know you, you scoundrel! I have heard of you before. You are Holmes the meddler.'

My friend smiled.

'Holmes the busybody.'

His smile broadened.

'Holmes the Scotland Yard jack-in-office.'

Holmes chuckled heartily. 'Your conversation is most entertaining,' said he. 'When you go out close the door, for there is a decided draught.'

'I will go when I have had my say. Don't you dare to meddle with my affairs. I know that Miss Stoner has been here – I traced her! I am a dangerous man to fall foul of! See here.' He stepped swiftly forward, seized the poker, and bent it into a curve with his huge brown hands.

'See that you keep yourself out of my grip,' he snarled, and hurling the twisted poker into the fireplace, he strode out of the room.

'He seems a very amiable person,' said Holmes, laughing, 'I am not quite so bulky, but if he had remained I might have shown him that my grip was not much more feeble than his own.' As he spoke he picked up the steel poker, and with a sudden effort straightened it out again.

'Fancy his having the insolence to confound me with the official detective force! This incident gives zest to our investigation, however, and I only trust that our little friend will not suffer from her imprudence in allowing this brute to trace her. And now, Watson, we shall order breakfast, and afterwards I shall walk down to Doctors' Commons, where I hope to get some data which may help us in this matter.'

It was nearly one o'clock when Sherlock Holmes returned from his excursion. He held in his hand a sheet of blue paper, scrawled over with notes and figures.

'I have seen the will of the deceased wife,' said he. 'To determine its exact meaning I have been obliged to work out the present prices of the investments with which it is concerned. The total income, which at the time of the wife's death was little short of £1,100, is now through the fall in agricultural prices not more than £750. Each daughter can claim an income of £250, in case of marriage. It is evident therefore, that if both girls had married, this beauty would have had a mere pittance, while even one of them would cripple him to a serious extent. My morning's work has not been wasted, since it has proved that he has the very strongest motives for standing in the way of anything of the sort. And now, Watson, this is too serious for dawdling, especially as the old man is aware that we are interesting ourselves in his affairs, so if you are ready we shall call a cab and drive to Waterloo. I should be very much obliged if you would slip your revolver into your pocket. An Eley's No. 2 is an excellent argument with gentlemen who can twist steel pokers into knots. That and a toothbrush are, I think, all that we need.'

At Waterloo we were fortunate in catching a train for Leatherhead, where we hired a trap at the station inn, and drove for four or five miles through the lovely Surrey lanes. It was a perfect day, with a bright sun and a few fleecy clouds in the heavens. The trees and wayside hedges were just throwing out their first green shoots, and the air was full of the pleasant smell of the moist earth. To me at least there was a strange contrast between the sweet promise of the spring and this sinister quest upon which we were engaged. My companion sat in front of the trap, his arms folded, his hat pulled down over his eyes, and his chin sunk upon his breast, buried in the deepest thought. Suddenly, however, he started, tapped me on the shoulder, and pointed over the meadows.

'Look here!' said he.

A heavily timbered park stretched up in a gentle slope, thickening into a grove at the highest point. From amidst the branches there jutted out the grey gables and high roof-tree of a very old mansion.

'Stoke Moran?' said he.

'Yes, sir, that be the house of Dr Grimesby Roylott,' remarked the driver.

'There is some building going on there,' said Holmes: 'that is where we are going.'

'There's the village,' said the driver, pointing to a cluster of roofs some distance to the left; 'but if you want to get to the house, you'll find it shorter to go over this stile, and so by the footpath over the fields. There it is, where the lady is walking.'

'And the lady, I fancy, is Miss Stoner,' observed Holmes, shading his eyes. 'Yes, I think we had better do as you suggest.'

We got off, paid our fare, and the trap rattled back on its way to Leatherhead.

'I thought it as well,' said Holmes, as we climbed the stile, 'that this fellow should think we had come here as architects or on some definite business. It may stop his gossip. Good afternoon, Miss Stoner. You see that we have been as good as our word.'

Our client of the morning had hurried forward to meet us with a face which spoke her joy. 'I have been waiting eagerly for you,' she cried, shaking hands with us warmly. 'All has turned out splendidly. Dr Roylott has gone to town and it is unlikely that he will be back before evening.'

'We have had the pleasure of making the Doctor's acquaintance,' said Holmes, and in a few words he sketched out what had occurred. Miss Stoner turned white to the lips as she listened.

'Good heavens!' she cried, 'he has followed me, then.'

'So it appears.'

'He is so cunning that I never know when I am safe from him. What will he say when he returns?'

'He must guard himself, for he may find that there is someone more cunning than himself upon his track. You must lock yourself from him tonight. If he is violent, we shall take you away to your aunt's at Harrow. Now, we must make the best use of our time, so kindly take us at once to the rooms which we are to examine.'

The building was of grey, lichen-blotched stone, with a high central portion, and two curving wings, like the claws of a crab, thrown out on each side. In one of these wings the windows were broken, and blocked with wooden boards, while the roof was partly caved in, a picture of ruin. The central portion was in little better repair, but the right-hand block was comparatively modern, and the blinds in the windows, with the blue smoke curling up from the chimneys showed that this was where the family resided. Some scaffolding had been erected against the end wall, and the stone-work had been broken into, but there were no signs of any workmen at the moment of our visit. Holmes walked slowly up and down the ill-trimmed lawn, and examined with deep attention the outsides of the windows.

'This, I take it, belongs to the room in which you used to sleep, the centre one to your sister's, and the one next to the main building to Dr Roylott's chamber?'

'Exactly so. But I am now sleeping in the middle one.'

'Pending the alterations, as I understand. By the way, there does not seem to be any very pressing need for repairs at that end wall.'

'There were none. I believe that it was an excuse to move me from my room.'

'Ah! that is suggestive. Now, on the other side of this narrow wing runs the corridor from which these three rooms open. There are windows in it, of course?'

'Yes, but very small ones. Too narrow for anyone to pass through.'

'As you both locked your doors at night, your rooms were unapproachable from that side. Now, would you have the kindness to go into your room, and to bar your shutters.'

Miss Stoner did so, and Holmes, after a careful examination through the open window, endeavoured in every way to force the shutter open, but without success. There was no slit through which a knife could be passed to raise the bar. Then with his lens he tested the hinges, but they were of solid iron, built firmly into the massive masonry. 'Hum!' said he, scratching his chin in some perplexity, 'my theory certainly presents some difficulties. No one could pass these shutters if they were bolted. Well, we shall see if the inside throws any light upon the matter.'

A small side-door led into the whitewashed corridor from which the three bedrooms opened. Holmes refused to examine the third chamber, so we passed at once to the second, that in which Miss Stoner was now sleeping, and in which her sister had met her fate. It was a homely little room, with a low ceiling and gaping fireplace, after the fashion of old country houses. A brown chest of drawers stood in one corner, a narrow white-counterpaned bed in another, and a dressing-table on the left-hand side of the window. These articles, with two small wickerwork chairs, made up all the furniture in the room, save for a square of Wilton carpet in the centre. The boards round and the panelling of the walls were brown worm-eaten oak, so old and discoloured that it may have dated from the original building of the house. Holmes drew one of the chairs into a corner and sat silent, while his eyes travelled round and round and up and down, taking in every detail of the apartment.

'Where does that bell communicate with?' he asked at last, pointing to a thick bell-rope which hung down beside the bed, the tassel actually lying upon the pillow.

'It goes to the housekeeper's room.'

'It looks newer than the other things?'

'Yes, it was only put there a couple of years ago.'

'Your sister asked for it, I suppose?'

'No, I never heard of her using it. We used always to get what we wanted for ourselves.'

'Indeed, it seemed unnecessary to put so nice a bell-pull there. You will excuse me for a few minutes while I satisfy myself as to this floor.' He threw himself down upon his face with his lens in his hand, and crawled swiftly backwards and forwards, examining minutely the cracks between the boards. Then he did the same with the woodwork with which the chamber was panelled. Finally he walked over to the bed and spent some time in staring at it, and in running his eye up and down the wall. Finally he took the bell-rope in his hand and gave it a brisk tug.

'Why, it's a dummy,' said he.

'Won't it ring?'

'No, it is not even attached to a wire. This is very interesting. You can see now that it is fastened to a hook just above where the little opening of the ventilator is.'

'How very absurd! I never noticed that before.'

'Very strange!' muttered Holmes, pulling at the rope. 'There are one or two very singular points about this room. For example, what a fool a builder must be to open a ventilator in another room, when with the same trouble, he might have communicated with the outside air!'

'That is also quite modern,' said the lady.

'Done about the same time as the bell-rope?' remarked Holmes.

'Yes, there were several little changes carried out about that time.'

'They seem to have been of a most interesting character – dummy bell-ropes, and ventilators which do not ventilate. With your permission, Miss Stoner, we shall now carry out researches into the inner apartment.'

Dr Grimesby Roylott's chamber was larger than that of his

stepdaughter, but was as plainly furnished. A camp bed, a small wooden shelf full of books, mostly of technical character, an armchair beside the bed, a plain wooden chair against the wall, a round table, and a large iron safe were the principal things which met the eye. Holmes walked slowly round and examined each and all of them with the keenest interest.

'What's in here?' he asked, tapping the safe.

'My stepfather's business papers.'

'Oh! you have seen inside then?'

'Only once, some years ago. I remember that it was full of papers.'

'There isn't a cat in it, for example?'

'No. What a strange idea!'

'Well, look at this!' He took up a small saucer of milk which stood on the top of it.

'No; we don't keep a cat. But there is a cheetah and a baboon.'

'Ah, yes, of course! Well, a cheetah is just a big cat, and yet a saucer of milk does not go very far in satisfying its wants, I daresay. There is one point which I should wish to determine.' He squatted down in front of the wooden chair, and examined the seat of it with the greatest attention.

'Thank you. That is quite settled,' said he, rising and putting his lens in his pocket. 'Hullo! here is something interesting!'

The object which had caught his eye was a small dog lash hung on one corner of the bed. The lash, however, was curled upon itself, and tied so as to make a loop of whipcord.

'What do you make of that, Watson?'

'It's a common enough lash. But I don't know why it should be tied.'

'That is not quite so common, is it? Ah, me! it's a wicked world, and when a clever man turns his brain to crime it is the worst of all. I think that I have seen enough now, Miss Stoner, and, with your permission, we shall walk out upon the lawn.'

I had never seen my friend's face so grim, or his brow so dark, as it was when we turned from the scene of his investigation. We had walked several times up and down the lawn, neither Miss Stoner nor myself liking to break in upon his thoughts before he roused himself from his reverie.

'It is very essential, Miss Stoner,' said he, 'that you should absolutely follow my advice in every respect.'

'I shall most certainly do so.'

'The matter is too serious for any hesitation. Your life may depend upon your compliance.'

'I assure you that I am in your hands.'

'In the first place, both my friend and I must spend the night in your room.'

Both Miss Stoner and I gazed at him in astonishment.

'Yes, it must be so. Let me explain. I believe that that is the village inn over there?'

'Yes, that is the "Crown".'

'Very good. Your windows would be visible from there.'

'Certainly.'

'You must confine yourself to your room, on pretence of a headache, when your stepfather comes back. Then when you hear him retire for the night, you must open the shutters of your windows, undo the hasp, put your lamp there as a signal to us, and then withdraw with everything which you are likely to want into the room which you used to occupy. I have no doubt that, in spite of your repairs, you could manage there for one night.'

'Oh, yes, easily.'

'The rest you will leave in our hands.'

'But what will you do?'

'We shall spend the night in your room, and we shall investigate the cause of this noise which has disturbed you.'

'I believe, Mr Holmes, that you have already made up your mind,' said Miss Stoner, laying her hand upon my companion's sleeve.

'Perhaps I have.'

'Then for pity's sake tell me what was the cause of my sister's death.'

'I should prefer to have clearer proof before I speak.'

'You can at least tell me whether my own thought is correct, and if she died from some sudden fright.'

'No, I do not think so. I think that there was probably some more tangible cause. And now, Miss Stoner, we must leave you, for if Dr Roylott returned and saw us, our journey would be in vain. Goodbye, and be brave, for if you will do what I have told you, you may rest assured that we shall soon drive away the dangers that threaten you.'

Sherlock Holmes and I had no difficulty in engaging a bedroom and sitting-room at the Crown Inn. They were on the upper floor, and from our window we could command a view of the avenue gate, and of the inhabited wing of Stoke Moran Manor House. At dusk we saw Dr Grimesby Roylott drive past, his huge form looming up beside the little figure of the lad who drove him. The boy had some slight difficulty in undoing the heavy iron gates, and we heard the hoarse roar of the Doctor's voice, and saw the fury with which he shook his clenched fists at him. The trap drove on, and a few minutes later we saw a sudden light spring up among the trees as the lamp was lit in one of the sitting-rooms.

'Do you know, Watson,' said Holmes, as we sat together in the gathering darkness, 'I have really some scruples as to taking you tonight. There is a distinct element of danger.'

'Can I be of assistance?'

'Your presence might be invaluable.'

'Then I shall certainly come.'

'It is very kind of you.'

'You speak of danger. You have evidently seen more in these rooms than was visible to me.'

'No, but I fancy that I may have deduced a little more. I imagine that you saw all that I did.'

'I saw nothing remarkable save the bell-rope, and what purpose that could answer I confess is more than I can imagine.'

'You saw the ventilator, too?'

'Yes, but I do not think that it is such a very unusual thing to have a small opening between two rooms. It was so small a rat could hardly pass through.'

'I knew that we should find a ventilator before ever we came to Stoke Moran.'

'My dear Holmes.'

'Oh, yes, I did. You remember in her statement she said that her sister could smell Dr Roylott's cigar. Now, of course that suggests at once that there must be a communication between the two rooms. It could only be a small one, or it would have been remarked upon at the coroner's inquiry. I deduced a ventilator.'

'But what harm can there be in that?'

'Well, there is at least a curious coincidence of dates. A

ventilator is made, a cord is hung, and a lady who sleeps in the bed dies. Does not that strike you?'

'I cannot as yet see any connection.'

'Did you observe anything very peculiar about that bed?'

'No.'

'It was clamped to the floor. Did you ever see a bed fastened like that before?'

'I cannot say that I have.'

'The lady could not move her bed. It must always be in the same relative position to the ventilator and to the rope – for so we may call it, since it was clearly never meant for a bell-pull.'

'Holmes,' I cried, 'I seem to see dimly what you are hitting at. We are only just in time to prevent some subtle and horrible crime.'

'Subtle enough and horrible enough. When a doctor does go wrong he is the first of criminals. He has nerve and he has knowledge. Palmer and Pritchard were among the heads of their profession. This man strikes even deeper, but, I think, Watson, that we shall be able to strike deeper still. But we shall have horrors enough before this night is over: for goodness sake let us have a quiet pipe, and turn our minds for a few hours to something more cheerful.'

About nine o'clock the light among the trees was extinguished, and all was dark in the direction of the Manor House. Two hours passed slowly away, and then, suddenly, just at the stroke of eleven, a single bright light shone out right in front of us.

'That is our signal,' said Holmes, springing to his feet; 'it comes from the middle window.'

As we passed out he exchanged a few words with the landlord, explaining that we were going on a late visit to an acquaintance, and that it was possible that we might spend the night there. A moment later we were out on the dark road, a chill wind blowing in our faces, and one yellow light twinkling in front of us through the gloom to guide us on our sombre errand.

There was little difficulty in entering the grounds, for unrepaired breaches gaped in the old park wall. Making our way among the trees, we reached the lawn, crossed it, and were about to enter through the window, when out from a clump of laurel bushes there darted what seemed to be a hideous and distorted child, who threw itself on the grass with writhing limbs, and then ran swiftly across the lawn into the darkness.

'My God!' I whispered, 'did you see it?'

Holmes was for that moment as startled as I. His hand closed like a vice upon my wrist in his agitation. Then he broke into a low laugh, and put his lips to my ear.

'It is a nice household,' he murmured, 'that is the baboon.'

I had forgotten the strange pets which the doctor affected. There was a cheetah, too; perhaps we might find it upon our shoulders at any moment. I confess that I felt easier in my mind when, after following Holmes's example and slipping off my shoes, I found myself inside the bedroom. My companion noiselessly closed the shutters, moved the lamp on to the table, and cast his eyes round the room. All was as we had seen it in the day-time. Then creeping up to me and making a trumpet of his hand, he whispered into my ear again so gently that it was all that I could do to distinguish the words:

'The least sound would be fatal to our plans.'

I nodded to show that I had heard.

'We must sit without a light. He would see it through the ventilator.'

I nodded again.

'Do not go to sleep; your life may depend upon it. Have your pistol ready in case we should need it. I will sit on the side of the bed, and you in that chair.'

I took out my revolver and laid it on the corner of the table.

Holmes had brought up a long thin cane, and this he placed upon the bed beside him. By it he laid the box of matches and the stump of a candle. Then he turned down the lamp and we were left in darkness.

How shall I ever forget that dreadful vigil? I could not hear a sound, not even a drawing of a breath, and yet I knew that my companion sat open-eyed, within a few feet of me, in the same state of nervous tension in which I was myself. The shutters cut off the least ray of light, and we waited in absolute darkness. From outside came the occasional cry of a nightbird, and once at our very window a long drawn, cat-like whine, which told us that the cheetah was indeed at liberty. Far away we could hear the deep tones of the parish clock, which boomed out every quarter of an hour. How long they seemed, those quarters!

Twelve o'clock, and one, and two, and three, and still we sat waiting silently for whatever might befall.

Suddenly there was the momentary gleam of a light up in the direction of the ventilator, which vanished immediately, but was succeeded by a strong smell of burning oil and heated metal. Someone in the next room had lit a dark lantern. I heard a gentle sound of movement, and then all was silent once more, though the smell grew stronger. For half an hour I sat with straining ears. Then suddenly another sound became audible – a very gentle, soothing sound, like that of a small jet of steam escaping continually from a kettle. The instant that we heard it, Holmes sprang from the bed, struck a match, and lashed furiously with his cane at the bed-pull.

'You see it, Watson?' he yelled. 'You see it?'

But I saw nothing. At the moment when Holmes struck the light I heard a low, clear whistle, but the sudden glare flashing into my weary eyes made it impossible for me to tell what it was at which my friend lashed so savagely. I could, however, see that his face was deadly pale, and filled with horror and loathing.

He had ceased to strike, and was gazing up at the ventilator, when suddenly there broke from the silence of the night the most horrible cry to which I have ever listened. It swelled up louder and louder, a hoarse yell of pain and fear and anger all mingled in the one dreadful shriek. They say that away down in the village, and even in the distant parsonage, that cry raised the sleepers from their beds. It struck cold to our hearts, and I stood gazing at Holmes, and he at me, until the last echoes of it had died away into the silence from which it rose.

'What can it mean?' I gasped.

'It means that it is all over,' Holmes answered. 'And perhaps, after all, it is for the best. Take your pistol, and we shall enter Dr Roylott's room.'

With a grave face he lit the lamp, and led the way down the corridor. Twice he struck at the chamber door without any reply from within. Then he turned the handle and entered, I at his heels, with the cocked pistol in my hand.

It was a singular sight which met our eyes. On the table stood a dark lantern with the shutter half open, throwing a brilliant beam of light upon the iron safe, the door of which was ajar. Beside this table, on the wooden chair, sat Dr Grimesby Roylott, clad in a long grey dressing-gown, his bare ankles protruding beneath, and his feet thrust into red heelless Turkish slippers. Across his lap lay the short stock with the long lash which we had noticed during the day. His chin was cocked upwards, and his eyes were fixed in a dreadful rigid stare at the corner of the ceiling. Round his brow he had a peculiar yellow band, with brownish speckles, which seemed to be bound tight round his head. As we entered he made neither sound nor motion.

'The band! the speckled band!' whispered Holmes.

I took a step forward: in an instant his strange headgear began to move, and there reared itself from among his hair the squat diamond-shaped head and puffed neck of a loathsome serpent.

'It is a swamp adder!' cried Holmes – 'the deadliest snake in India. He has died within ten seconds of being bitten. Violence does, in truth, recoil upon the violent, and the schemer falls into the pit which he digs for another. Let us thrust this creature back into its den, and we can then remove Miss Stoner to some place of shelter, and let the county police know what has happened.'

As he spoke he drew the dog whip swiftly from the dead man's lap, and throwing the noose round the reptile's neck, he drew it from its horrid perch, and, carrying it at arm's length, threw it into the iron safe, which he closed upon it.

Such are the true facts of the death of Dr Grimesby Roylott, of Stoke Moran. It is not necessary that I should prolong a narrative which has already run to too great a length, by telling how we broke the sad news to the terrified girl, how we conveyed her by the morning train to the care of her good aunt at Harrow, of how the slow process of official inquiry came to the conclusion that the Doctor met his fate while indiscreetly playing with a dangerous pet. The little which I had yet to learn of the case was told me by Sherlock Holmes as we travelled back next day.

'I had,' said he, 'come to an entirely erroneous conclusion, which shows, my dear Watson, how dangerous it always is to reason from insufficient data. The presence of the gipsies, and the use of the word "band", which was used by the poor girl, no doubt, to explain the appearance which she had caught a horrid glimpse of by the light of her match, were sufficient to put me upon an entirely wrong scent. I can only claim the merit that I instantly reconsidered my position when, however, it became clear to me that whatever danger threatened an occupant of the room could not come either from the window or the door. My attention was speedily drawn, as I have already remarked to you, to this ventilator, and to the bell-rope which hung down to the bed. The discovery that this was a dummy, and that the bed was clamped to the floor, instantly gave rise to the suspicion that the rope was there as a bridge for something passing through the hole, and coming to the bed. The idea of a snake instantly occurred to me, and when I coupled it with my knowledge that the Doctor was furnished with a supply of creatures from India, I felt that I was probably on the right track. The idea of using a form of poison which could not possibly be discovered by any chemical test was just such a one as would occur to a clever and ruthless man who had had an Eastern training. The rapidity with which such a poison would take effect would also, from his point of view, be an advantage. It would be a sharp-eyed coroner indeed who could distinguish the two little dark punctures which would show where the poison fangs had done their work. Then I thought of the whistle. Of course, he must recall the snake before the morning light revealed it to the victim. He had trained it, probably by the use of the milk which we saw, to return to him when summoned. He would put it through the ventilator at the hour that he thought best with the certainty that it would crawl down the rope, and land on the bed. It might or might not bite the occupant, perhaps she might escape every night for a week, but sooner or later she must fall a victim.

'I had come to these conclusions before ever I had entered his room. An inspection of his chair showed me that he had been in the habit of standing on it, which, of course, would be necessary in order that he should reach the ventilator. The sight of the safe, the saucer of milk, and the loop of whipcord were enough to finally dispel any doubts which may have remained. The metallic clang heard by Miss Stoner was obviously caused by her father hastily closing the door of his safe upon its terrible occupant. Having once made up my mind, you know the steps which I took in order to put the matter to the proof. I heard the creature hiss, as I have no doubt that you did also, and I instantly lit the light and attacked it.'

'With the result of driving it through the ventilator.'

'And also with the result of causing it to turn upon its master at the other side. Some of the blows of my cane came home, and roused its snakish temper, so that it flew upon the first person it saw. In this way I am no doubt indirectly responsible for Dr Grimesby Roylott's death, and I cannot say that it is likely to weigh very heavily upon my conscience.'

H. G. WELLS

The Country of the Blind

Three hundred miles and more from Chimborazo, one hundred from the snows of Cotopaxi, in the wildest wastes of Ecuador's Andes, there lies that mysterious mountain valley, cut off from the world of men, the Country of the Blind. Long years ago that valley lay so far open to the world that men might come at last through frightful gorges and over an icy pass into its equable meadows; and thither indeed men came, a family or so of Peruvian half-breeds fleeing from the lust and tyranny of an evil Spanish ruler. Then came the stupendous outbreak of Mindobamba, when it was night in Quito for seventeen days, and the water was boiling at Yaguachi and all the fish floating dying even as far as Guayaquil; everywhere along the Pacific slopes there were landslips and swift thawings and sudden floods, and one whole side of the old Arauca crest slipped and came down in thunder, and cut off the Country of the Blind for ever from the exploring feet of men. But one of these early settlers had chanced to be on the hither side of the gorges when the world had so terribly shaken itself, and he perforce had to forget his wife and his child and all the friends and possessions he had left up there, and start life over again in the lower world. He started it again but ill, blindness overtook him, and he died of punishment in the mines; but the story he told begot a legend that lingers along the length of the Cordilleras of the Andes to this day.

He told of his reason for venturing back from that fastness, into which he had first been carried lashed to a llama, beside a vast bale of gear, when he was a child. The valley, he said, had in it all that the heart of man could desire – sweet water, pasture, and even climate, slopes of rich brown soil with tangles of a shrub that bore an excellent fruit, and on one side great hanging forests of pine that held the avalanches high. Far overhead, on three sides, vast cliffs of grey-green rock were capped by cliffs of ice; but the glacier stream came not to them but flowed away by the farther slopes, and only now and then huge ice masses fell on the valley side. In this valley it neither rained nor snowed, but the abundant springs gave a rich green pasture, that irrigation would spread over all the valley space. The settlers did well indeed there. Their beasts did well and multiplied, and but one thing marred their happiness. Yet it was enough to mar it greatly. A strange disease had come upon them, and had made all the children born to them there – and, indeed, several older children also – blind. It was to seek some charm or antidote against this plague of blindness that he had with fatigue and danger and difficulty returned down the gorge. In those days, in such cases, men did not think of germs and infections but of sins; and it seemed to him that the reason of this affliction must lie in the negligence of these priestless immigrants to set up a shrine so soon as they entered the valley. He wanted a shrine – a handsome, cheap, effectual shrine – to be erected in the valley; he wanted relics and such-like potent things of faith, blessed objects and mysterious medals and prayers. In his wallet he had a bar of native silver for which he would not account; he insisted there was none in the valley with something of the insistence of an inexpert liar. They had all clubbed their money and ornaments together, having little need for such treasure up there, he said, to buy them holy help against their ill. I figure this dim-eyed young mountaineer, sunburnt, gaunt, and anxious, hat-brim clutched feverishly, a man all unused to the ways of the lower world, telling this story to some keen-eyed, attentive priest before the great convulsion; I can picture him presently seeking to return with pious and infallible remedies against that trouble, and the infinite dismay with which he must have faced the tumbled vastness where the gorge had once come out. But the rest of his story of mischances is lost to me, save that I know of his evil death after several years. Poor stray from that remoteness! The stream that had once made the gorge now bursts from the mouth of a rocky cave, and the legend his poor, ill-told story set going developed into the legend of a race of blind men somewhere 'over there' one may still hear to-day.

And amidst the little population of that now isolated and forgotten valley the disease ran its course. The old became groping and purblind, the young saw but dimly, and the children that were born to them saw never at all. But life was very easy in that snow-rimmed basin, lost to all the world, with neither thorns nor briars, with no evil insects nor any beasts save the gentle breed of llamas they had lugged and thrust and followed up the beds of the shrunken rivers in the gorges up which they had come. The seeing had become purblind so gradually that they scarcely noted their loss. They guided the sightless youngsters hither and thither until they knew the whole valley marvellously, and when at last sight died out among them the race lived on. They had even time to adapt themselves to the blind control of fire, which they made carefully in stoves of stone. They were a simple strain of people at the first, unlettered, only slightly touched with the Spanish civilisation, but with something of a tradition of the arts of old Peru and of its lost philosophy. Generation followed generation. They forgot many things; they devised many things. Their tradition of the greater world they came from became mythical in colour and uncertain. In all things save sight they were strong and able; and presently the chance of birth and heredity sent one who had an original mind and who could talk and persuade among them, and then afterwards another. These two passed, leaving their effects, and the little community grew in numbers and in understanding, and met and settled social and economic problems that arose. Generation followed generation. Generation followed generation. There came a time when a child was born who was fifteen generations from that ancestor who went out of the valley with a bar of silver to seek God's aid, and who never returned. Thereabouts it chanced that a man came into this community from the outer world. And this is the story of that man.

He was a mountaineer from the country near Quito, a man who had been down to the sea and had seen the world, a reader of books in an original way, an acute and enterprising man, and he was taken on by a party of Englishmen who had come out to Ecuador to climb mountains, to replace one of their three Swiss guides who had fallen ill. He climbed here and he climbed there, and then came the attempt on Parascotopetl, the Matterhorn of the Andes, in which he was lost to the outer world. The story of the accident has been written a dozen times. Pointer's narrative is the best. He tells how the party worked their difficult and almost vertical way up to the very foot of the last and greatest precipice, and how they built a night shelter amidst the snow upon a little shelf of rock, and, with a touch of real dramatic power, how presently they found Nunez had gone from them. They shouted, and there was no reply; shouted and whistled, and for the rest of that night they slept no more.

As the morning broke they saw the traces of his fall. It seems impossible he could have uttered a sound. He had slipped eastward towards the unknown side of the mountain; far below he had struck a steep slope of snow, and ploughed his way down it in the midst of a snow avalanche. His track went straight to the edge of a frightful precipice, and beyond that everything was hidden. Far, far below, and hazy with distance, they could see trees rising out of a narrow, shut-in valley – the lost Country of the Blind. But they did not know it was the lost Country of the Blind, nor distinguish it in any way from any other narrow streak of upland valley. Unnerved by the disaster, they abandoned their attempt in the afternoon, and Pointer was called away to the war before he could make another attack. To this day Parascotopetl lifts an unconquered crest, and Pointer's shelter crumbles unvisited amidst the snows.

And the man who fell survived.

At the end of the slope he fell a thousand feet, and came down in the midst of a cloud of snow upon a snow slope even steeper than the one above. Down this he was whirled, stunned and insensible, but without a bone broken in his body; and then at last came to gentler slopes, and at last rolled out and lay still, buried amidst a softening heap of the white masses that had accompanied and saved him. He came to himself with a dim fancy that he was ill in bed; then realised his position with a mountaineer's intelligence, and worked himself loose and, after a rest or so, out until he saw the stars. He rested flat upon his chest for a space, wondering where he was and what had happened to him. He explored his limbs, and discovered that several of his buttons were gone and his coat turned over his head. His knife had gone from his pocket, and his hat was lost, though he had tied it under his chin. He recalled that he had been looking for loose stones to raise his piece of the shelter wall. His ice-axe had disappeared.

He decided he must have fallen, and looked up to see, exaggerated by the ghastly light of the rising moon, the tremendous flight he had taken. For a while he lay, gazing blankly at that vast pale cliff towering above, rising moment by moment out of a subsiding tide of darkness. Its phantasmal, mysterious beauty held him for a space, and then he was seized with a paroxysm of sobbing laughter . . .

After a great interval of time he became aware that he was near the lower edge of the snow. Below, down what was now a moonlit and practicable slope, he saw the dark and broken appearance of rock-strewn turf. He struggled to his feet, aching in every joint and limb, got down painfully from the heaped loose snow about him, went downward until he was on the turf, and there dropped rather than lay beside a boulder, drank deep from the flask in his inner pocket, and instantly fell asleep . . .

He was awakened by the singing of birds in the trees far below.

He sat up and perceived he was on a little alp at the foot of a vast precipice, that was grooved by the gully down which he and his snow had come. Over against him another wall of rock reared itself against the sky. The gorge between these precipices ran east and west and was full of the morning sunlight, which lit to the westward the mass of fallen mountain that closed the descending gorge. Below him it seemed there was a precipice equally steep, but behind the snow in the gully he found a sort of chimney-cleft dripping with snow-water down which a desperate man might venture. He found it easier than it seemed, and came at last to another desolate alp, and then after a rock climb of no particular difficulty to a steep slope of trees. He took his bearings and turned his face up the gorge, for he saw it opened out above upon green meadows, among which he now glimpsed quite distinctly a cluster of stone huts of unfamiliar fashion. At times his progress was like clambering along the face of a wall, and after a time the rising sun ceased to strike along the gorge, the voices of the singing birds died away, and the air grew cold and dark about him. But the distant valley with its houses was all the brighter for that. He came presently to talus, and among the rocks he noted – for he was an observant man – an unfamiliar fern that seemed to clutch out of the crevices with intense green hands. He picked a frond or so and gnawed its stalk and found it helpful.

About midday he came at last out of the throat of the gorge into the plain and the sunlight. He was stiff and weary; he sat down in the shadow of a rock, filled up his flask with water from a spring and drank it down, and remained for a time resting before he went on to the houses.

They were very strange to his eyes, and indeed the whole aspect of that valley became, as he regarded it, queerer and more unfamiliar. The greater part of its surface was lush green meadow, starred with many beautiful flowers, irrigated with extraordinary care, and bearing evidence of systematic cropping piece by piece. High up and ringing the valley about was a wall, and what appeared to be a circumferential water-channel, from which the little trickles of water that fed the meadow plants came, and on the higher slopes above this flocks of llamas cropped the scanty herbage. Sheds, apparently shelters or feeding-places for the llamas, stood against the boundary wall here and there. The irrigation streams ran together into a main channel down the centre of the valley, and this was enclosed on either side by a wall breast high. This gave a singularly urban quality to this secluded place, a quality that was greatly enhanced by the fact that a number of paths paved with black and white stones, and each with a curious little kerb at the side, ran hither and thither in an orderly manner. The houses of the central village were quite unlike the casual and higgledy-piggledy agglomeration of the mountain villages he knew; they stood in a continuous row on either side of a central street of astonishing cleanness; here and there their parti-coloured façade was pierced by a door, and not a solitary window broke their even frontage. They were parti-coloured with extraordinary irregularity; smeared with a sort of plaster that was sometimes grey, sometimes drab, sometimes slate-coloured or dark brown; and it was the sight of this wild plastering first brought the word 'blind' into the thoughts of the explorer. 'The good man who did that,' he thought, 'must have been as blind as a bat.'

He descended a steep place, and so came to the wall and channel that ran about the valley, near where the latter spouted out its surplus contents into the deeps of the gorge in a thin and wavering thread of cascade. He could now see a number of men and women resting on piled heaps of grass, as if taking a siesta, in the remoter part of the meadow, and nearer the village a number of recumbent children, and then nearer at hand three men carrying pails on yokes along a little path that ran from the encircling wall towards the houses. These latter were clad in garments of llama cloth and boots and belts of leather, and they wore caps of cloth with back and ear flaps. They followed one another in single file, walking slowly and yawning as they walked, like men who have been up all night. There was something so reassuringly prosperous and respectable in their bearing that after a moment's hesitation. Nunez stood forward as conspicuously as possible upon his rock, and gave vent to a mighty shout that echoed round the valley.

The three men stopped, and moved their heads as though they were looking about them. They turned their faces this way and that, and Nunez gesticulated with freedom. But they did not appear to see him for all his gestures, and after a time, directing themselves towards the mountains far away to the right, they shouted as if in answer. Nunez bawled again, and then once more, and as he gestured ineffectually the word 'blind' came up to the top of his thoughts. 'The fools must be blind,' he said.

When at last, after much shouting and wrath, Nunez crossed the stream by a little bridge, came through a gate in the wall, and approached them, he was sure that they were blind. He was sure that this was the Country of the Blind of which the legends told. Conviction had sprung upon him, and a sense of great and rather enviable adventure. The three stood side by side, not looking at him, but with their ears directed towards him, judging him by his unfamiliar steps. They stood close together like men a little afraid, and he could see their eyelids closed and sunken, as though the very balls beneath had shrunk away. There was an expression near awe on their faces.

'A man,' one said, in hardly recognisable Spanish – 'a man it is – a man or a spirit – coming down from the rocks.'

But Nunez advanced with the confident steps of a youth who enters upon life. All the old stories of the lost valley and the Country of the Blind had come back to his mind, and through his thoughts ran this old proverb, as if it were a refrain—

'In the Country of the Blind the One-eyed Man is King.'

'In the Country of the Blind the One-eyed Man is King.'

And very civilly he gave them greeting. He talked to them and used his eyes.

'Where does he come from, brother Pedro?' asked one.

'Down out of the rocks.'

'Over the mountains I come,' said Nunez, 'out of the country beyond there – where men can see. From near Bogota, where there are a hundred thousands of people, and where the city passes out of sight.'

'Sight?' muttered Pedro. 'Sight?'

'He comes,' said the second blind man, 'out of the rocks.'

The cloth of their coats Nunez saw was curiously fashioned, each with a different sort of stitching.

They startled him by a simultaneous movement towards him, each with a hand outstretched. He stepped back from the advance of these spread fingers.

'Come hither,' said the third blind man, following his motion and clutching him neatly.

And they held Nunez and felt him over, saying no word further until they had done so.

'Carefully,' he cried, with a finger in his eye, and found they thought that organ, with its fluttering lids, a queer thing in him. They went over it again.

'A strange creature, Correa,' said the one called Pedro. 'Feel the coarseness of his hair. Like a llama's hair.'

'Rough he is as the rocks that begot him,' said Correa, investigating Nunez's unshaven chin with a soft and slightly moist hand. 'Perhaps he will grow finer.' Nunez struggled a little under their examination, but they gripped him firm.

'Carefully,' he said again.

'He speaks,' said the third man. 'Certainly he is a man.'

'Ugh!' said Pedro, at the roughness of his coat.

'And you have come into the world?' asked Pedro.

'*Out* of the world. Over mountains and glaciers; right over above there, half-way to the sun. Out of the great big world that goes down, twelve days' journey to the sea.'

They scarcely seemed to heed him. 'Our fathers have told us men may be made by the forces of Nature,' said Correa. 'It is the warmth of things and moisture, and rottenness – rottenness.'

'Let us lead him to the elders,' said Pedro.

'Shout first,' said Correa, 'lest the children be afraid. This is a marvellous occasion.'

So they shouted, and Pedro went first and took Nunez by the hand to lead him to the houses.

He drew his hand away. 'I can see,' he said.

'See?' said Correa.

'Yes, see,' said Nunez, turning towards him, and stumbled against Pedro's pail.

'His senses are still imperfect,' said the third blind man.

'He stumbles, and talks unmeaning words. Lead him by the hand.'

'As you will,' said Nunez, and was led along, laughing.

It seemed they knew nothing of sight.

Well, all in good time he would teach them.

He heard people shouting, and saw a number of figures gathering together in the middle roadway of the village.

He found it taxed his nerve and patience more than he had anticipated, that first encounter with the population of the Country of the Blind. The place seemed larger as he drew near to it, and the smeared plasterings queerer, and a crowd of children and men and women (the women and girls, he was pleased to note, had some of them quite sweet faces, for all that their eyes were shut and sunken) came about him, holding on to him, touching him with soft, sensitive hands, smelling at him, and listening at every word he spoke. Some of the maidens and children, however, kept aloof as if afraid, and indeed his voice seemed coarse and rude beside their softer notes. They mobbed him. His three guides kept close to him with an effect of proprietorship, and said again and again, 'A wild man out of the rocks.'

'Bogota,' he said. 'Bogota. Over the mountain crests.'

'A wild man – using wild words,' said Pedro. 'Did you hear that – *Bogota?* His mind is hardly formed yet. He has only the beginnings of speech.'

A little boy nipped his hand. 'Bogota!' he said mockingly.

'Ay! A city to your village. I come from the great world – where men have eyes and see.'

'His name's Bogota,' they said.

'He stumbled,' said Correa; 'stumbled twice as we came hither.'

'Bring him to the elders.'

And they thrust him suddenly through a doorway into a room as black as pitch, save at the end there faintly glowed a fire. The crowd closed in behind him and shut out all but the faintest glimmer of day, and before he could arrest himself he had fallen headlong over the feet of a seated man. His arm, outflung, struck the face of someone else as he went down; he felt the soft impact of features and heard a cry of anger, and for a moment he struggled against a number of hands that clutched him. It was a one-sided fight. An inkling of the situation came to him, and he lay quiet.

'I fell down,' he said; 'I couldn't see in this pitchy darkness.'

There was a pause as if the unseen persons about him tried to understand his words. Then the voice of Correa said: 'He is but newly formed. He stumbles as he walks and mingles words that mean nothing with his speech.'

Others also said things about him that he heard or understood imperfectly.

'May I sit up?' he asked, in a pause. 'I will not struggle against you again.'

They consulted and let him rise.

The voice of an older man began to question him, and Nunez found himself trying to explain the great world out of which he had fallen, and the sky and mountains and sight and such-like marvels, to these elders who sat in darkness in the Country of the Blind. And they would believe and understand nothing whatever he told them, a thing quite outside his expectation. They would not even understand many of his words. For fourteen generations these people had been blind and cut off from all the seeing world; the names for all the things of sight had faded and changed; the story of the outer world was faded and changed to a child's story; and they had ceased to concern themselves with anything beyond the rocky slopes above their circling wall. Blind men of genius had arisen among them and questioned the shreds of belief and tradition they had brought with them from their seeing days, and had dismissed all these things as idle fancies, and replaced them with new and saner explanations. Much of their imagination had shrivelled with their eyes, and they had made for themselves new imaginations with their ever more sensitive ears and finger-tips. Slowly Nunez realised this; that his expectation of wonder and reverence at his origin and his gifts was not to be borne out; and after his poor attempt to explain sight to them had been set aside as the confused version of a new-made being describing the marvels of his incoherent sensations, he subsided, a little dashed, into listening to their instruction. And the eldest of the blind men explained to him life and philosophy and religion, how that the world (meaning their valley) had been first an empty hollow in the rocks, and then had come, first, inanimate things without the gift of touch, and llamas and a few other creatures that had little sense, and then men, and at last angels, whom one could hear singing and making fluttering sounds, but whom no one could touch at all, which puzzled Nunez greatly until he thought of the birds.

He went on to tell Nunez how this time had been divided into the warm and the cold, which are the blind equivalents of day and night, and how it was good to sleep in the warm and work during the cold, so that now, but for his advent, the whole town of the blind would have been asleep. He said Nunez must have been specially created to learn and serve the wisdom they had acquired, and for that all his mental incoherency and stumbling behaviour he must have courage, and do his best to learn, and at that all the people in the doorway murmured encouragingly. He said the night – for the blind call their day night – was now far gone, and it behoved every one to go back to sleep. He asked Nunez if he knew how to sleep, and Nunez said he did, but that before sleep he wanted food.

They brought him food – llama's milk in a bowl, and rough salted bread – and led him into a lonely place to eat out of their hearing, and afterwards to slumber until the chill of the mountain evening roused them to begin their day again. But Nunez slumbered not at all.

Instead, he sat up in the place where they had left him, resting his limbs and turning the unanticipated circumstances of his arrival over and over in his mind.

Every now and then he laughed, sometimes with amusement, and sometimes with indignation.

'Unformed mind!' he said. 'Got no senses yet! They little know they've been insulting their heaven-sent king and master. I see I must bring them to reason. Let me think – let me think.'

He was still thinking when the sun set.

Nunez had an eye for all beautiful things, and it seemed to him that the glow upon the snowfields and glaciers that rose about the valley on every side was the most beautiful thing he had ever seen. His eyes went from that inaccessible glory to the village and irrigated fields, fast sinking into the twilight, and suddenly a wave of emotion took him, and he thanked God from the bottom of his heart that the power of sight had been given him.

He heard a voice calling to him from out of the village.

'Ya ho there, Bogota! Come hither!'

At that he stood up smiling. He would show these people once and for all what sight would do for a man. They would seek him, but not find him.

'You move not, Bogota,' said the voice.

He laughed noiselessly, and made two stealthy steps aside from the path.

'Trample not on the grass, Bogota; that is not allowed.'

Nunez had scarcely heard the sound he made himself. He stopped amazed.

The owner of the voice came running up the piebald path towards him.

He stepped back into the pathway. 'Here I am,' he said.

'Why did you not come when I called you?' said the blind man. 'Must you be led like a child? Cannot you hear the path as you walk?'

Nunez laughed. 'I can see it,' he said.

'There is no such word as *see*,' said the blind man, after a pause. 'Cease this folly, and follow the sound of my feet.'

Nunez followed, a little annoyed.

'My time will come,' he said.

'You'll learn,' the blind man answered. 'There is much to learn in the world.'

'Has no one told you, "In the Country of the Blind the One-eyed Man is King"?'

'What is blind?' asked the blind man carelessly over his shoulder.

Four days passed, and the fifth found the King of the Blind still incognito, as a clumsy and useless stranger among his subjects.

It was, he found, much more difficult to proclaim himself than he had supposed, and in the meantime, while he meditated his *coup d'état*, he did what he was told and learned the manners and customs of the Country of the Blind. He found working and going about at night a particularly irksome thing, and he decided that that should be the first thing he would change.

They led a simple, laborious life, these people, with all the elements of virtue and happiness, as these things can be understood by men. They toiled, but not oppressively; they had food and clothing sufficient for their needs; they had days and seasons of rest; they made much of music and singing, and there was love among them, and little children.

It was marvellous with what confidence and precision they went about their ordered world. Everything, you see, had been made to fit their needs; each of the radiating paths of the valley area had a constant angle to the others, and was distinguished by a special notch upon its kerbing; all obstacles and irregularities of path or meadow had long since been cleared away; all their methods and procedure arose naturally from their special needs. Their senses had become marvellously acute; they could hear and judge the slightest gesture of a man a dozen paces away – could hear the very beating of his heart. Intonation had long replaced expression with them, and touches gesture, and their work with hoe and spade and fork was as free and confident as garden work can be. Their sense of smell was extraordinarily fine; they could distinguish individual differences as readily as a dog can, and they went about the tending of the llamas, who lived among the rocks above and came to the wall for food and shelter, with ease and confidence. It was only when at last Nunez sought to assert himself that he found how easy and confident their movements could be.

He rebelled only after he had tried persuasion.

He tried at first on several occasions to tell them of sight. 'Look you here, you people,' he said. 'There are things you do not understand in me.'

Once or twice one or two of them attended to him; they sat with faces downcast and ears turned intelligently towards him, and he did his best to tell them what it was to see. Among his hearers was a girl, with eyelids less red and sunken than the others, so that one could almost fancy she was hiding eyes, whom especially he hoped to persuade. He spoke of the beauties of sight, of watching the mountains, of the sky and the sunrise, and they heard him with amused incredulity that presently became condemnatory. They told him there were indeed no mountains at all, but that the end of the rocks where the llamas grazed was indeed the end of the world; thence sprang a cavernous roof of the universe, from which the dew and the avalanches fell; and when he maintained stoutly the world had neither end nor roof such as they supposed, they said his thoughts were wicked. So far as he could describe sky and clouds and stars to them it seemed to them a hideous void, a terrible blankness in the place of the smooth roof to things in which they believed – it was an article of faith with them that the cavern roof was exquisitely smooth to the touch. He saw that in some manner he shocked them, and gave up that aspect of the matter altogether, and tried to show them the practical value of sight. One morning he saw Pedro in the path called Seventeen and coming towards the central houses, but still too far off for hearing or scent, and he told them as much. 'In a little while,' he prophesied, 'Pedro will be here.' An old man remarked that Pedro had no business on path Seventeen, and then, as if in confirmation, that individual as he drew near turned and went transversely into path Ten, and so back with nimble paces towards the outer wall. They mocked Nunez when Pedro did not arrive, and afterwards, when he asked Pedro questions to clear his character, Pedro denied and outfaced him, and was afterwards hostile to him.

Then he induced them to let him go a long way up the sloping meadows towards the wall with one complacent individual, and to him he promised to describe all that happened among the houses. He noted certain goings and comings, but the things that really seemed to signify to these people happened inside of or behind the windowless houses – the only things they took note of to test him by – and of these he could see or tell nothing; and it was after the failure of this attempt, and the ridicule they could not repress, that he resorted to force. He thought of seizing a spade and suddenly smiting one or two of them to earth, and so in fair combat showing the advantage of eyes. He went so far with that resolution as to seize his spade, and then he discovered a new thing about himself, and that was that it was impossible for him to hit a blind man in cold blood.

He hesitated, and found them all aware that he snatched up the spade. They stood alert, with their heads on one side, and bent ears towards him for what he would do next.

'Put that spade down,' said one, and he felt a sort of helpless horror. He came near obedience.

Then he thrust one backwards against a house wall, and fled past him and out of the village.

He went athwart one of their meadows, leaving a track of trampled grass behind his feet, and presently sat down by the side of one of their ways. He felt something of the buoyancy that comes to all men in the beginning of a fight, but more perplexity. He began to realise that you cannot even fight happily with creatures who stand upon a different mental basis to yourself. Far away he saw a number of men carrying spades and sticks come out of the street of houses, and advance in a spreading line along the several paths towards him. They advanced slowly, speaking frequently to one another, and ever and again the whole cordon would halt and sniff the air and listen.

The first time they did this Nunez laughed. But afterwards he did not laugh.

One struck his trail in the meadow grass, and came stooping and feeling his way along it.

For five minutes he watched the slow extension of the cordon, and then his vague disposition to do something forthwith became frantic. He stood up, went a pace or so towards the circumferential wall, turned, and went back a little way. There they all stood in a crescent, still and listening.

He also stood still, gripping his spade very tightly in both hands. Should he charge them?

The pulse in his ears ran into the rhythm of 'In the Country of the Blind the One-eyed Man is King!'

Should he charge them?

He looked back at the high and unclimbable wall behind – unclimbable because of its smooth plastering, but withal pierced with many little doors, and at the approaching line of seekers. Behind these, others were now coming out of the street of houses.

Should he charge them?

'Bogota!' called one. 'Bogota! where are you?'

He gripped his spade still tighter, and advanced down the meadows towards the place of habitations, and directly he moved they converged upon him. 'I'll hit them if they touch me,' he swore; 'by Heaven, I will. I'll hit.' He called aloud, 'Look here, I'm going to do what I like in this valley. Do you hear? I'm going to do what I like and go where I like!'

They were moving in upon him quickly, groping, yet moving rapidly. It was like playing blind man's buff, with everyone blindfolded except one. 'Get hold of him!' cried one. He found himself in the arc of a loose curve of pursuers. He felt suddenly he must be active and resolute.

'You don't understand,' he cried in a voice that was meant to be great and resolute, and which broke. 'You are blind, and I can see. Leave me alone!'

'Bogota! Put down that spade, and come off the grass!'

The last order, grotesque in its urban familiarity, produced a gust of anger.

'I'll hurt you,' he said, sobbing with emotion. 'By Heaven, I'll hurt you. Leave me alone!'

He began to run, not knowing clearly where to run. He ran from the nearest blind man, because it was a horror to hit him. He stopped, and then made a dash to escape from their closing ranks. He made for where a gap was wide, and the men on either side, with a quick perception of the approach of his paces, rushed in on one another. He sprang forward, and then saw he must be caught, and *swish!* the spade had struck. He felt the soft thud of hand and arm, and the man was down with a yell of pain, and he was through.

Through! And then he was close to the street of houses again, and blind men, whirling spades and stakes, were running with a sort of reasoned swiftness hither and thither.

He heard steps behind him just in time, and found a tall man rushing forward and swiping at the sound of him. He lost his nerve, hurled his spade a yard wide at his antagonist, and whirled about and fled, fairly yelling as he dodged another.

He was panic-stricken. He ran furiously to and fro, dodging when there was no need to dodge, and in his anxiety to see on every side of him at once, stumbling. For a moment, he was down and they heard his fall. Far away in the circumferential wall a little doorway looked like heaven, and he set off in a wild rush for it. He did not even look round at his pursuers until it was gained, and he had stumbled across the bridge, clambered a little way among the rocks, to the surprise and dismay of a young llama, who went leaping out of sight, and lay down sobbing for breath.

And so his *coup d'état* came to an end.

He stayed outside the wall of the valley of the Blind for two nights and days without food or shelter, and meditated upon the unexpected. During these meditations he repeated very frequently and always with a profounder note of decision the exploded proverb: 'In the Country of the Blind the One-eyed Man is King.' He thought chiefly of ways of fighting and conquering these people, and it grew clear that for him no practicable way was possible. He had no weapons, and now it would be hard to get one.

The canker of civilisation had got to him even in Bogota, and he could not find it in himself to go down and assassinate a blind man. Of course, if he did that, he might then dictate terms on the threat of assassinating them all. But – sooner or later he must sleep! . . .

He tried also to find food among the pine trees, to be comfortable under pine boughs while the frost fell at night, and – with less confidence – to catch a llama by artifice in order to try to kill it – perhaps by hammering it with a stone – and so finally, perhaps, to eat some of it. But the llamas had a doubt of him and regarded him with distrustful brown eyes, and spat when he drew near. Fear came on him the second day and fits of shivering. Finally he crawled down to the wall of the Country of the Blind and tried to make terms. He crawled along by the stream, shouting, until two blind men came out to the gate and talked to him.

'I was mad,' he said. 'But I was only newly made.'

They said that was better.

He told them he was wiser now, and repented of all he had done.

Then he wept without intention, for he was very weak and ill now, and they took that as a favourable sign.

They asked him if he still thought he could '*see*.'

'No,' he said. 'That was folly. The word means nothing – less than nothing!'

They asked him what was overhead.

'About ten times ten the height of a man there is a roof above the world – of rock – and very, very smooth.' . . . He burst again into hysterical tears. 'Before you ask me any more, give me some food or I shall die.'

He expected dire punishments, but these blind people were capable of toleration. They regarded his rebellion as but one more proof of his general idiocy and inferiority; and after they had whipped him they appointed him to do the simplest and heaviest work they had for anyone to do, and he, seeing no other way of living, did submissively what he was told.

He was ill for some days, and they nursed him kindly. That refined his submission. But they insisted on his lying in the dark, and that was a great misery. And blind philosophers came and talked to him of the wicked levity of his mind, and reproved him so impressively for his doubts about the lid of rock that covered their cosmic casserole that he almost doubted whether indeed he was not the victim of hallucination in not seeing it overhead.

So Nunez became a citizen of the Country of the Blind, and these people ceased to be a generalised people and became individualities and familiar to him, while the world beyond the mountains became more and more remote and unreal. There was Yacob, his master, a kindly man when not annoyed; there was Pedro, Yacob's nephew; and there was Medina-saroté, who was the youngest daughter of Yacob. She was little esteemed in the world of the blind, because she had a clear-cut face, and lacked that satisfying, glossy smoothness that is the blind man's ideal of feminine beauty; but Nunez thought her beautiful at first, and presently the most beautiful thing in the whole creation. Her closed eyelids were not sunken and red after the common way of the valley, but lay as though they might open again at any moment; and she had long eyelashes, which were considered a grave disfigurement. And her voice was strong, and did not satisfy the acute hearing of the valley swains. So that she had no lover.

There came a time when Nunez thought that, could he win her, he would be resigned to live in the valley for all the rest of his days.

He watched her; he sought opportunities of doing her little services, and presently he found that she observed him. Once at a rest-day gathering they sat side by side in the dim starlight, and the music was sweet. His hand came upon hers and he dared to clasp it. Then very tenderly she returned his pressure. And one day, as they were at their meal in the darkness, he felt her hand very softly seeking him, and as it chanced the fire leaped then and he saw the tenderness of her face.

He sought to speak to her.

He went to her one day when she was sitting in the summer moonlight spinning. The light made her a thing of silver and mystery. He sat down at her feet and told her he loved her, and told her how beautiful she seemed to him. He had a lover's voice, he spoke with a tender reverence that came near to awe, and she had never before been touched by adoration. She made him no definite answer, but it was clear his words pleased her.

After that he talked to her whenever he could take an opportunity. The valley became the world for him, and the world beyond the mountains where men lived in sunlight seemed no more than a fairy tale he would some day pour into her ears. Very tentatively and timidly he spoke to her of sight.

Sight seemed to her the most poetical of fancies, and she listened to his description of the stars and the mountains and her own sweet white-lit beauty as though it was a guilty indulgence. She did not believe, she could only half understand, but she was mysteriously delighted, and it seemed to him that she completely understood.

His love lost its awe and took courage. Presently he was for demanding her of Yacob and the elders in marriage, but she became fearful and delayed. And it was one of her elder sisters who first told Yacob that Medina-saroté and Nunez were in love.

There was from the first very great opposition to the marriage of Nunez and Medina-saroté; not so much because they valued her as because they held him as a being apart, an idiot, incompetent thing below the permissible level of a man. Her sisters opposed it bitterly as bringing discredit on them all; and old Yacob, though he had formed a sort of liking for his clumsy, obedient serf, shook his head and said the thing could not be. The young men were all angry at the idea of corrupting the race, and one went so far as to revile and strike Nunez. He struck back. Then for the first time he found an advantage in seeing, even by twilight, and after that fight was over no one was disposed to raise a hand against him. But they still found his marriage impossible.

Old Yacob had a tenderness for his last little daughter, and was grieved to have her weep upon his shoulder.

'You see, my dear, he's an idiot. He has delusions; he can't do anything right.'

'I know,' wept Medina-saroté. 'But he's better than he was. He's getting better. And he's strong, dear father, and kind – stronger and kinder than any other man in the world. And he loves me – and, father, I love him.'

Old Yacob was greatly distressed to find her inconsolable, and, besides – what made it more distressing – he liked Nunez for many things. So he went and sat in the windowless council-chamber with the other elders and watched the trend of the talk, and said, at the proper time, 'He's better than he was. Very likely, some day, we shall find him as sane as ourselves.'

Then afterwards one of the elders, who thought deeply, had an idea. He was the great doctor among these people, their medicine-man, and he had a very philosophical and inventive mind, and the idea of curing Nunez of his peculiarities appealed to him. One day when Yacob was present he returned to the topic of Nunez.

'I have examined Bogota,' he said, 'and the case is clearer to me. I think very probably he might be cured.'

'That is what I have always hoped,' said old Yacob.

'His brain is affected,' said the blind doctor.

The elders murmured assent.

'Now, *what* affects it?'

'Ah!' said old Yacob.

'*This*,' said the doctor, answering his own question. 'Those queer things that are called the eyes, and which exist to make an agreeable soft depression in the face, are diseased, in the case of Bogota, in such a way as to affect his brain. They are greatly distended, he has eyelashes, and his eyelids move, and consequently his brain is in a state of constant irritation and destruction.'

'Yes?' said old Yacob. 'Yes?'

'And I think I may say with reasonable certainty that, in order to cure him completely, all that we need do is a simple and easy surgical operation – namely, to remove these irritant bodies.'

'And then he will be sane?'

'Then he will be perfectly sane, and a quite admirable citizen.'

'Thank Heaven for science!' said old Yacob, and went forth at once to tell Nunez of his happy hopes.

But Nunez's manner of receiving the good news struck him as being cold and disappointing.

'One might think,' he said, 'from the tone you take, that you did not care for my daughter.'

It was Medina-saroté who persuaded Nunez to face the blind surgeons.

'*You* do not want me,' he said, 'to lose my gift of sight?'

She shook her head.

'My world is sight.'

Her head drooped lower.

'There are the beautiful things, the beautiful little things – the flowers, the lichens among the rocks, the lightness and softness on a piece of fur, the far sky with its drifting down of clouds, the sunsets and the stars. And there is *you*. For you alone it is good to have sight, to see your sweet, serene face, your kindly lips, your dear, beautiful hands folded together . . .. It is these eyes of mine you won, these eyes that hold me to you, that these idiots seek. Instead, I must touch you, hear you, and never see you again. I must come under that roof of rock and stone and darkness, that horrible roof under which your imagination stoops . . .. No; you would not have me do that?'

A disagreeable doubt had arisen in him. He stopped, and left the thing a question.

'I wish,' she said, 'sometimes—' She paused.

'Yes?' said he, a little apprehensively.

'I wish sometimes – you would not talk like that.'

'Like what?'

'I know it's pretty – it's your imagination. I love it, but *now*—'

He felt cold. '*Now?*' he said faintly.

She sat quite still.

'You mean – you think – I should be better, better perhaps—'

He was realising things very swiftly. He felt anger, indeed, anger at the dull course of fate, but also sympathy for her lack of understanding – a sympathy near akin to pity.

'*Dear*,' he said, and he could see by her whiteness how intensely her spirit pressed against the things she could not say. He put his arms about her, he kissed her ear, and they sat for a time in silence.

'If I were to consent to this?' he said at last, in a voice that was very gentle.

She flung her arms about him, weeping wildly. 'Oh, if you would,' she sobbed, 'if only you would!'

For a week before the operation that was to raise him from his servitude and inferiority to the level of a blind citizen, Nunez knew nothing of sleep, and all through the warm sunlit hours, while the others slumbered happily, he sat brooding or wandered aimlessly, trying to bring his mind to bear on his dilemma. He had given his answer, he had given his consent, and still he was not sure. And at last work-time was over, the sun rose in splendour over the golden crests, and his last day of vision began for him. He had a few minutes with Medina-saroté before she went apart to sleep.

'To-morrow,' he said, 'I shall see no more.'

'Dear heart!' she answered, and pressed his hands with all her strength.

'They will hurt you but little,' she said; 'and you are going through this pain-you are going through it, dear lover, for me. . .. Dear, if a woman's heart and life can do it, I will repay you. My dearest one, my dearest with the tender voice, I will repay.'

He was drenched in pity for himself and her.

He held her in his arms, and pressed his lips to hers, and looked on her sweet face for the last time. 'Good-bye!' he whispered at that dear sight, 'good-bye!'

And then in silence he turned away from her.

She could hear his slow retreating footsteps, and something in the rhythm of them threw her into a passion of weeping.

He had fully meant to go to a lonely place where the meadows were beautiful with white narcissus, and there remain until the hour of his sacrifice should come, but as he went he lifted up his eyes and saw the morning, the morning like an angel in golden armour, marching down the steeps . . ..

It seemed to him that before this splendour he, and this blind world in the valley, and his love, and all, were no more than a pit of sin.

He did not turn aside as he had meant to do, but went on, and passed through the wall of the circumference and out upon the rocks, and his eyes were always upon the sunlit ice and snow.

He saw their infinite beauty, and his imagination soared over them to the things beyond he was now to resign for ever.

He thought of that great free world he was parted from, the world that was his own, and he had a vision of those further slopes, distance beyond distance, with Bogota, a place of multitudinous stirring beauty, a glory by day, a luminous mystery by night, a place of palaces and fountains and statues and white houses, lying beautifully in the middle distance. He thought how for a day or so one might come down through passes, drawing ever nearer and nearer to its busy streets and ways. He thought of the river journey, day by day, from great Bogota to the still vaster world beyond, through towns and villages, forest and desert places, the rushing river day by day, until its banks receded and the big steamers came splashing by, and one had reached the sea – the limitless sea, with its thousand islands, its thousands of islands, and its ships seen dimly far away in their incessant journeyings round and about that greater world. And there, unpent by mountains, one saw the sky – the sky, not such a disc as one saw it here, but an arch of immeasurable blue, a deep of deeps in which the circling stars were floating . . ..

His eyes scrutinised the great curtain of the mountains with a keener inquiry.

For example, if one went so, up that gully and to that chimney there, then one might come out high among those stunted pines that ran round in a sort of shelf and rose still higher and higher as it passed above the gorge. And then? That talus might be managed. Thence perhaps a climb might be found to take him up to the precipice that came below the snow; and if that chimney failed, then another farther to the east might serve his purpose better. And then? Then one would be out upon the amber-lit snow there, and half-way up to the crest of those beautiful desolations.

He glanced back at the village, then turned right round and regarded it steadfastly.

He thought of Medina-saroté, and she had become small and remote.

He turned again towards the mountain wall, down which the day had come to him.

Then very circumspectly he began to climb.

When sunset came he was no longer climbing, but he was far and high. He had been higher, but he was still very high. His clothes were torn, his limbs were blood-stained, he was bruised in many places, but he lay as if he were at his ease, and there was a smile on his face.

From where he rested the valley seemed as if it were in a pit and nearly a mile below. Already it was dim with haze and shadow, though the mountain summits around him were things of light and fire, and the little details of the rocks near at hand were drenched with subtle beauty – a vein of green mineral piercing the grey, the flash of crystal faces here and there, a minute, minutely beautiful orange lichen close beside his face. There were deep mysterious shadows in the gorge, blue deepening into purple, and purple into a luminous darkness, and overhead was the illimitable vastness of the sky. But he heeded these things no longer, but lay quite inactive there, smiling as if he were satisfied merely to have escaped from the valley of the Blind in which he had thought to be King.

The glow of the sunset passed, and the night came, and still he lay peacefully contented under the cold stars.

'SAKI'

Tobermory

It was a chill, rain-washed afternoon of a late August day, that indefinite season when partridges are still in security or cold storage, and there is nothing to hunt – unless one is bounded on the north by the Bristol Channel, in which case one may lawfully gallop after fat red stags. Lady Blemley's house-party was not bounded on the north by the Bristol Channel, hence there was a full gathering of her guests round the tea-table on this particular afternoon. And, in spite of the blankness of the season and the triteness of the occasion, there was no trace in the company of that fatigued restlessness which means a dread of the pianola and a subdued hankering for auction bridge. The undisguised open-mouthed attention of the entire party was fixed on the homely negative personality of Mr Cornelius Appin. Of all her guests, he was the one who had come to Lady Blemley with the vaguest reputation. Someone had said he was 'clever', and he had got his invitation in the moderate expectation, on the part of his hostess, that some portion at least of his cleverness would be contributed to the general entertainment. Until tea-time that day she had been unable to discover in what direction, if any, his cleverness lay. He was neither a wit nor a croquet champion, a hypnotic force nor a begetter of amateur theatricals. Neither did his exterior suggest a generous measure of mental deficiency. He had subsided into mere Mr Appin, and the Cornelius seemed a piece of transparent baptismal bluff. And now he was claiming to have launched on the world a discovery beside which the invention of gunpowder, of the printing-press, and of steam locomotion were inconsiderable trifles. Science had made bewildering strides in many directions during recent decades, but this thing seemed to belong to the domain of miracle rather than to scientific achievement.

'And do you really ask us to believe,' Sir Wilfrid was saying, 'that you have discovered a means for instructing animals in the art of human speech, and that dear old Tobermory has proved your first successful pupil?'

'It is a problem at which I have worked for the last seventeen years,' said Mr Appin, 'but only during the last eight or nine months have I been rewarded with glimmerings of success. Of course I have experimented with thousands of animals, but latterly only with cats, those wonderful creatures which have assimilated themselves so marvellously with our civilization while retaining all their highly developed feral instincts. Here and there among cats one comes across an outstanding superior intellect, just as one does among the ruck of human beings, and when I made the acquaintance of Tobermory a week ago I saw at once that I was in contact with a "Beyond-cat" of extraordinary intelligence. I had gone far along the road to success in recent experiments; with Tobermory, as you call him, I have reached the goal.'

Mr Appin concluded his remarkable statement in a voice which he strove to divest of a triumphant inflection. No one said 'Rats', though Clovis's lips moved in a monosyllabic contortion, which probably invoked those rodents of disbelief.

'And do you mean to say,' asked Miss Resker, after a slight pause, 'that you have taught Tobermory to say and understand easy sentences of one syllable?'

'My dear Miss Resker,' said the wonder-worker patiently, 'one teaches little children and savages and backward adults in that piecemeal fashion; when one has once solved the problem of making a beginning with an animal of highly developed intelligence one has no need for those halting methods. Tobermory can speak our language with perfect correctness.'

This time Clovis very distinctly said, 'Beyond-rats!' Sir Wilfrid was more polite, but equally sceptical.

'Hadn't we better have the cat in and judge for ourselves?' suggested Lady Blemley.

Sir Wilfrid went in search of the animal, and the company settled themselves down to the languid expectation of witnessing some more or less adroit drawing-room ventriloquism.

In a minute Sir Wilfrid was back in the room, his face white beneath its tan and his eyes dilated with excitement.

'By Gad, it's true!'

His agitation was unmistakably genuine, and his hearers started forward in a thrill of awakened interest.

Collapsing into an armchair he continued breathlessly; 'I found him dozing in the smoking-room, and called to him to come for his tea. He blinked at me in his usual way, and I said, "Come on Toby; don't keep us waiting;" and, by Gad! he drawled out in a most horribly natural voice that he'd come when he dashed well pleased! I nearly jumped out of my skin!'

Appin had preached to absolutely incredulous hearers; Sir Wilfrid's statement carried instant conviction. A Babel-like chorus of startled exclamation arose, amid which the scientist sat mutely enjoying the first fruit of his stupendous discovery.

In the midst of the clamour Tobermory entered the room and made his way with velvet tread and studied unconcern across to the group seated round the tea-table.

A sudden hush of awkwardness and constraint fell on the company. Somehow there seemed an element of embarrassment in addressing on equal terms a domestic cat of acknowledged dental ability.

'Will you have some milk, Tobermory?' asked Lady Blemley in a rather strained voice.

'I don't mind if I do,' was the response, couched in a tone of even indifference. A shiver of suppressed excitement went through the listeners, and Lady Blemley might be excused for pouring out the saucerful of milk rather unsteadily.

'I'm afraid I've spilt a good deal of it,' she said apologetically.

'After all, it's not my Axminster,' was Tobermory's rejoinder.

Another silence fell on the group, and then Miss Resker, in her best district-visitor manner, asked if the human language had been difficult to learn. Tobermory looked squarely at her for a moment and then fixed his gaze serenely on the middle-distance. It was obvious that boring questions lay outside his scheme of life.

'What do you think of human intelligence?' asked Mavis Pellington lamely.

'Of whose intelligence in particular?' asked Tobermory coldly.

'Oh, well, mine for instance,' said Mavis, with a feeble laugh.

'You put me in an embarrassing position,' said Tobermory, whose tone and attitude certainly did not suggest a shred of embarrassment. 'When your inclusion in this house-party was suggested Sir Wilfrid protested that you were the most brainless woman of his acquaintance, and that there was a wide distinction between hospitality and the care of the feeble-minded. Lady Blemley replied that your lack of brain-power was the precise quality which had earned you your invitation, as you were the only person she could think of who might be idiotic enough to buy their old car. You know, the one they call "The Envy of Sisyphus", because it goes quite nicely up-hill if you push it.'

Lady Blemley's protestations would have had greater effect if she had not casually suggested to Mavis only that morning that the car in question would he just the thing for her down at her Devonshire home.

Major Barfield plunged in heavily to effect a diversion.

'How about your carrying-on with the tortoise-shell puss up at the stables, eh?'

The moment he had said it everyone realized the blunder.

'One does not usually discuss these matters in public,' said Tobermory frigidly. 'From a slight observation of your ways since you've been in this house I should imagine you'd find it inconvenient if I were to shift the conversation on to your own little affairs.'

The panic which ensued was not confined to the Major.

'Would you like to go and see if cook has got your dinner ready?' suggested Lady Blemley hurriedly, affecting to ignore the fact that it wanted at least two hours to Tobermory's dinner-time.

'Thanks,' said Tobermory; 'not quite so soon after my tea. I don't want to die of indigestion.'

'Cats have nine lives, you know,' said Sir Wilfrid heartily.

'Possibly,' answered Tobermory; 'but only one liver.'

'Adelaide!' said Mrs Cornett, 'do you mean to encourage that cat to go out and gossip about us in the servants' hall?'

The panic had indeed become general. A narrow ornamental balustrade ran in front of most of the bedroom windows at the Towers, and it was recalled with dismay that this had formed a favourite promenade for Tobermory at all hours, whence he could watch the pigeons – and heaven knew what else besides. If he intended to become reminiscent in his present outspoken strain the effect would be something more than disconcerting. Mrs Cornett, who spent much time at her toilet table, and whose complexion was reputed to be of a nomadic though punctual disposition, looked as ill at ease as the Major. Miss Scrawen, who wrote fiercely sensuous poetry and led a blameless life, merely displayed irritation; if you are methodical and virtuous in private you don't necessarily want every one to know it. Bertie van Tahn, who was so depraved at seventeen that he had long ago given up trying to be any worse, turned a dull shade of gardenia white, but he did not commit the error of dashing out of the room like Odo Finsberry, a young gentleman who was understood to be reading for the Church and who was possibly disturbed at the thought of scandals he might hear concerning other people. Clovis had the presence of mind to maintain a composed exterior; privately he was calculating how long it would take to procure a box of fancy mice through the agency of the *Exchange and Mart* as a species of hush-money.

Even in a delicate situation like the present, Agnes Resker could not endure to remain too long in the background.

'Why did I ever come down here?' she asked dramatically.

Tobermory immediately accepted the opening.

'Judging by what you said to Mrs Cornett on the croquet-lawn yesterday, you were out for food. You described the Blemleys as the dullest people to stay with that you knew, but said they were clever enough to employ a first-rate cook otherwise they'd find it difficult to get anyone to come down a second time.'

'There's not a word of truth in it! I appeal to Mrs Cornett—' exclaimed the discomfited Agnes.

'Mrs Cornett repeated your remark afterwards to Bertie van Tahn,' continued Tobermory, 'and said "That woman is a regular Hunger Marcher; she'd go anywhere for four square meals a day," and Bertie van Tahn said—'

At this point the chronicle mercifully ceased. Tobermory had caught a glimpse of the big yellow Tom from the Rectory working his way through the shrubbery towards the stable wing. In a flash he had vanished through the open French window.

With the disappearance of his too brilliant pupil Cornelius Appin found himself beset by a hurricane of bitter upbraiding, anxious inquiry, and frightened entreaty. The responsibility for the situation lay with him, and he must prevent matters from becoming worse. Could Tobermory impart his dangerous gift to other cats? was the first question he had to answer. It was possible, he replied, that he might have initiated his intimate friend the stable puss into his new accomplishment, but it was unlikely that his teaching could have taken a wider range as yet.

'Then,' said Mrs Cornett, 'Tobermory may be a valuable cat and a great pet; but I'm sure you'll agree, Adelaide, that both he and the stable cat must be done away with without delay.'

'You don't suppose I've enjoyed the last quarter of an hour, do you?' said Lady Blemley bitterly. 'My husband and I are very fond of Tobermory – at least, we were before this horrible accomplishment was infused into him but now, of course, the only thing is to have him destroyed as soon as possible.'

'We can put some strychnine in the scraps he always gets at dinner-time,' said Sir Wilfrid, 'and I will go and drown the stable cat myself. The coachman will be very sore at losing his pet, but I'll say a very catching form of mange has broken out in cats and we're afraid of it spreading to the kennels.'

'But my great discovery!' expostulated Mr Appin; 'after all my years of experiment—'

'You can go and experiment on the short-horns at the farm, who are under proper control,' said Mrs Cornett, 'or the elephants at the Zoological Gardens. They're said to be highly intelligent, and they have this recommendation, that they don't come creeping about our bedrooms and under chairs, and so forth.'

An archangel ecstatically proclaiming the Millennium, and then finding that it clashed unpardonably with Henley and would have to be indefinitely postponed, could hardly have felt more crestfallen than Cornelius Appin at the reception of his wonderful achievement. Public opinion, however, was against him – in fact, had the general voice been consulted on the subject it is probable that a strong minority vote would have been in favour of including him in the strychnine diet.

Defective train arrangements and a nervous desire to see matters brought to a finish prevented an immediate dispersal of the party, but dinner that evening was not a social success. Sir Wilfrid had had rather a trying time with the stable cat and subsequently with the coachman. Agnes Resker ostentatiously limited her repast to a morsel of dry toast, which she bit as though it were a personal enemy; while Mavis Pellington maintained a vindictive silence throughout the meal. Lady

Blemley kept up a flow of what she hoped was conversation, but her attention was fixed on the doorway. A plateful of carefully dosed fish scraps was in readiness on the sideboard, but sweets and savoury and dessert went their way, and no Tobermory appeared either in the dining-room or kitchen.

The sepulchral dinner was cheerful compared with the subsequent vigil in the smoking room. Eating and drinking had at least supplied a distraction and cloak to the prevailing embarrassment. Bridge was out of the question in the general tension of nerves and tempers, and after Odo Finsberry had given a lugubrious rendering of 'Mélisande in the Wood' to a frigid audience, music was tacitly avoided. At eleven the servants went to bed, announcing that the small window in the pantry had been left open as usual for Tobermory's private use. The guests read steadily through the current batch of magazines, and fell back gradually on the 'Badminton Library' and bound volumes of *Punch*. Lady Blemley made periodic visits to the pantry, returning each time with an expression of listless depression which forestalled questioning.

At two o'clock Clovis broke the dominating silence.

'He won't turn up tonight. He's probably in the local newspaper office at the present moment, dictating the first instalment of his reminiscences. Lady What's-her-name's book won't be in it. It will be the event of the day.'

Having made his contribution to the general cheerfulness, Clovis went to bed. At long intervals the various members of the house-party followed his example.

The servants taking round the early tea made a uniform announcement in reply to a uniform question. Tobermory had not returned.

Breakfast was, if anything, a more unpleasant function than dinner had been, but before its conclusion the situation was relieved. Tobermory's corpse was brought in from the shrubbery, where a gardener had just discovered it. From the bites on his throat and the yellow fur which coated his claws it was evident that he had fallen in unequal combat with the big Tom from the Rectory.

By midday most of the guests had quitted the Towers, and after lunch Lady Blemley had sufficiently recovered her spirits to write an extremely nasty letter to the Rectory about the loss of her valuable pet.

Tobermory had been Appin's one successful pupil, and he was destined to have no successor. A few weeks later an elephant in the Dresden Zoological Garden, which had shown no previous signs of irritability, broke loose and killed an Englishman who had apparently been teasing it. The victim's name was variously reported in the papers as Oppin and Eppelin, but his front name was faithfully rendered Cornelius.

'If he was trying German irregular verbs on the poor beast,' said Clovis, 'he deserved all he got.'

KATHERINE MANSFIELD

Bliss

Although Bertha Young was thirty she still had moments like this when she wanted to run instead of walk, to take dancing steps on and off the pavement, to bowl a hoop, to throw something up in the air and catch it again, or to stand still and laugh at – nothing – at nothing, simply.

What can you do if you are thirty and, turning the corner of your own street, you are overcome, suddenly by a feeling of bliss – absolute bliss! – as though you'd suddenly swallowed a bright piece of that late afternoon sun and it burned in your bosom, sending out a little shower of sparks into every particle, into every finger and toe? . . .

Oh, is there no way you can express it without being 'drunk and disorderly'? How idiotic civilisation is! Why be given a body if you have to keep it shut up in a case like a rare, rare fiddle?

'No, that about the fiddle is not quite what I mean,' she thought, running up the steps and feeling in her bag for the key – she'd forgotten it, as usual – and rattling the letter-box. 'It's not what I mean, because – Thank you, Mary' – she went into the hall. 'Is nurse back?'

'Yes, M'm.'

'And has the fruit come?'

'Yes, M'm. Everything's come.'

'Bring the fruit up to the dining-room, will you? I'll arrange it before I go upstairs.'

It was dusky in the dining-room and quite chilly. But all the same Bertha threw off her coat; she could not bear the tight clasp of it another moment, and the cold air fell on her arms.

But in her bosom there was still that bright glowing place – that shower of little sparks coming from it. It was almost unbearable. She hardly dared to breathe for fear of fanning it higher, and yet she breathed deeply, deeply. She hardly dared to look into the cold mirror – but she did look, and it gave her back a woman, radiant, with smiling, trembling lips, with big, dark eyes and an air of listening, waiting for something . . . divine to happen . . . that she knew must happen . . . infallibly.

Mary brought in the fruit on a tray and with it a glass bowl, and a blue dish, very lovely, with a strange sheen on it as though it had been dipped in milk.

'Shall I turn on the light, M'm?'

'No, thank you. I can see quite well.'

There were tangerines and apples stained with strawberry pink. Some yellow pears, smooth as silk, some white grapes covered with a silver bloom and a big cluster of purple ones. These last she had bought to tone in with the new dining-room carpet. Yes, that did sound rather far-fetched and absurd, but it was really why she had bought them. She had thought in the shop: 'I must have some purple ones to bring the carpet up to the table.' And it had seemed quite sense at the time.

When she had finished with them and had made two pyramids of these bright round shapes, she stood away from the table to get the effect – and it really was most curious. For the dark table seemed to melt into the dusky light and the glass dish and the blue bowl to float in the air. This, of course, in her present mood, was so incredibly beautiful . . .. She began to laugh.

'No, no. I'm getting hysterical.' And she seized her bag and coat and ran upstairs to the nursery.

Nurse sat at a low table giving Little B her supper after her bath. The baby had on a white flannel gown and a blue woollen jacket, and her dark, fine hair was brushed up into a funny little peak. She looked up when she saw her mother and began to jump.

'Now, my lovely, eat it up like a good girl,' said nurse, setting her lips in a way that Bertha knew, and that meant she had come into the nursery at another wrong moment.

'Has she been good, Nanny?'

'She's been a little sweet all the afternoon,' whispered Nanny. 'We went to the park and I sat down on a chair and took her out of the pram and a big dog came along and put its head on my knee and she clutched its ear, tugged it. Oh, you should have seen her.'

Bertha wanted to ask if it wasn't rather dangerous to let her clutch at a strange dog's ear. But she did not dare to. She stood watching them, her hands by her side, like the poor little girl in front of the rich girl with the doll.

The baby looked up at her again, stared, and then smiled so charmingly that Bertha couldn't help crying:

'Oh, Nanny, do let me finish giving her her supper while you put the bath things away.'

'Well, M'm, she oughtn't to be changed hands while she's eating,' said Nanny, still whispering. 'It unsettles her; it's very likely to upset her.'

How absurd it was. Why have a baby if it has to be kept – not in a case like a rare, rare fiddle – but in another woman's arms?

'Oh, I must!' said she.

Very offended, Nanny handed her over.

'Now, don't excite her after her supper. You know you do, M'm. And I have such a time with her after!'

Thank heaven! Nanny went out of the room with the bath towels.

'Now I've got you to myself, my little precious,' said Bertha, as the baby leaned against her.

She ate delightfully, holding up her lips for the spoon and then waving her hands. Sometimes she wouldn't let the spoon go; and sometimes, just as Bertha had filled it, she waved it away to the four winds.

When the soup was finished Bertha turned round to the fire.

'You're nice – you're very nice!' said she, kissing her warm baby. 'I'm fond of you. I like you.'

And indeed, she loved Little B so much – her neck as she bent forward, her exquisite toes as they shone transparent in the firelight – that all her feeling of bliss came back again, and again she didn't know how to express it – what to do with it.

'You're wanted on the telephone,' said Nanny, coming back in triumph and seizing *her* Little B.

Down she flew. It was Harry.

'Oh, is that you, Ber? Look here. I'll be late. I'll take a taxi and come along as quickly as I can, but get dinner put back ten minutes – will you? All right?'

'Yes, perfectly. Oh, Harry!'

'Yes?'

What had she to say? She'd nothing to say. She only wanted to get in touch with him for a moment. She couldn't absurdly cry: 'Hasn't it been a divine day?'

'What is it?' rapped out the little voice.

'Nothing. *Entendu,*' said Bertha, and hung up the receiver, thinking how much more than idiotic civilisation was.

They had people coming to dinner. The Norman Knights – a very sound couple – he was about to start a theatre, and she was awfully keen on interior decoration, a young man, Eddie Warren, who had just published a little book of poems and whom everybody was asking to dine, and a 'find' of Bertha's called Pearl Fulton. What Miss Fulton did, Bertha didn't know. They had met at the club and Bertha had fallen in love with her, as she always did fall in love with beautiful women who had something strange about them.

The provoking thing was that, though they had been about together and met a number of times and really talked, Bertha couldn't make her out. Up to a certain point Miss Fulton was rarely, wonderfully frank, but the certain point was there, and beyond that she would not go.

Was there anything beyond it? Harry said 'No.' Voted her dullish, and 'cold like all blonde women, with a touch, perhaps, of anaemia of the brain.' But Bertha wouldn't agree with him; not yet, at any rate.

'No, the way she has of sitting with her head a little on one side, and smiling, has something behind it, Harry, and I must find out what that something is.'

'Most likely it's a good stomach,' answered Harry.

He made a point of catching Bertha's heels with replies of that kinds . . . 'liver frozen, my dear girl,' or 'pure flatulence,' or 'kidney disease,' . . . and so on. For some strange reason Bertha liked this, and almost admired it in him very much.

She went into the drawing-room and lighted the fire; then, picking up the cushions, one by one, that Mary had disposed so carefully, she threw them back on to the chairs and the couches. That made all the difference; the room came alive at once. As she was about to throw the last one she surprised herself by suddenly hugging it to her, passionately, passionately. But it did not put out the fire in her bosom. Oh, on the contrary!

The windows of the drawing-room opened on to a balcony

overlooking the garden. At the far end, against the wall, there was a tall, slender pear tree in fullest, richest bloom; it stood perfect, as though becalmed against the jade-green sky. Bertha couldn't help feeling, even from this distance, that it had not a single bud or a faded petal. Down below, in the garden beds, the red and yellow tulips, heavy with flowers, seemed to lean upon the dusk. A grey cat, dragging its belly, crept across the lawn, and a black one, its shadow, trailed after. The sight of them, so intent and so quick, gave Bertha a curious shiver.

'What creepy things cats are!' she stammered, and she turned away from the window and began walking up and down . . ..

How strong the jonquils smelled in the warm room. Too strong? Oh, no. And yet, as though overcome, she flung down on a couch and pressed her hands to her eyes.

'I'm too happy – too happy!' she murmured.

And she seemed to see on her eyelids the lovely pear tree with its wide open blossoms as a symbol of her own life.

Really – really – she had everything. She was young. Harry and she were as much in love as ever, and they got on together splendidly and were really good pals. She had an adorable baby. They didn't have to worry about money. They had this absolutely satisfactory house and garden. And friends – modern, thrilling friends, writers and painters and poets or people keen on social questions – just the kind of friends they wanted. And then there were books, and there was music, and she had found a wonderful little dressmaker, and they were going abroad in the summer, and their new cook made the most superb omelettes . . ..

'I'm absurd. Absurd!' She sat up; but she felt quite dizzy, quite drunk. It must have been the spring.

Yes, it was the spring. Now she was so tired she could not drag herself upstairs to dress.

A white dress, a string of jade beads, green shoes and stockings. It wasn't intentional. She had thought of this scheme hours before she stood at the drawing-room window.

Her petals rustled softly into the hall, and she kissed Mrs Norman Knight, who was taking off the most amusing orange coat with a procession of black monkeys round the hem and up the fronts.

'. . . Why! Why! Why is the middle-class so stodgy – so utterly without a sense of humour! My dear, it's only by a fluke that I am here at all – Norman being the protective fluke. For my darling monkeys so upset the train that it rose to a man and simply ate me with its eyes. Didn't laugh – wasn't amused – that I should have loved. No, just stared – and bored me through and through.'

'But the cream of it was,' said Norman, pressing a large tortoiseshell-rimmed monocle into his eye, 'you don't mind me telling this, Face, do you?' (In their home and among their friends they called each other Face and Mug.) 'The cream of it was when she, being full fed, turned to the woman beside her and said: "Haven't you ever seen a monkey before?"'

'Oh, yes!' Mrs Norman Knight joined in the laughter. 'Wasn't that too absolutely creamy?'

And a funnier thing still was that now her coat was off she did look like a very intelligent monkey – who had even made that yellow silk dress out of scraped banana skins. And her amber earrings: they were like little dangling nuts.

'This is a sad, sad fall!' said Mug, pausing in front of Little B's perambulator. 'When the perambulator comes into the hall—' and he waved the rest of the quotation away.

The bell rang. It was lean, pale Eddie Warren (as usual) in a state of acute distress.

'It *is* the right house, *isn't it*?' he pleaded.

'Oh, I think so – I hope so,' said Bertha brightly.

'I have had such a *dreadful* experience with a taxi-man; he was *most* sinister. I couldn't get him to *stop*. The *more* I knocked and called the *faster* he went. And *in* the moonlight this *bizarre* figure with the *flattened* head *crouching* over the *lit-tle* wheel . . .'

He shuddered, taking off an immense white silk scarf. Bertha noticed that his socks were white, too – most charming.

'But how dreadful!' she cried.

'Yes, it really was,' said Eddie, following her into the drawing-room. 'I saw myself *driving* through Eternity in a *timeless* taxi.'

He knew the Norman Knights. In fact, he was going to write a play for N.K. when the theatre scheme came off.

'Well, Warren, how's the play?' said Norman Knight, dropping his monocle and giving his eye a moment in which to rise to the surface before it was screwed down again.

And Mrs Norman Knight: 'Oh, Mr Warren, what happy socks?'

'I *am* so glad you like them,' said he, staring at his feet. 'They seem to have got so *much* whiter since the moon rose.' And he turned his lean sorrowful young face to Bertha. 'There *is* a moon, you know.'

She wanted to cry: 'I am sure there is – often – often!'

He really was a most attractive person. But so was Face, crouched before the fire in her banana skins, and so was Mug, smoking a cigarette and saying as he flicked the ash: 'Why doth the bridegroom tarry?'

'There he is, now.'

Bang went the front door open and shut. Harry shouted: 'Hullo, you people. Down in five minutes.' And they heard him swarm up the stairs. Bertha couldn't help smiling; she knew how he loved doing things at high pressure. What, after all, did an extra five minutes matter? But he would pretend to himself that they mattered beyond measure. And then he would make a great point of coming into the drawing-room, extravagantly cool and collected.

Harry had such a zest for life. Oh, how she appreciated it in him. And his passion for fighting – for seeking in everything that came up against him another test of his power and of his courage – that, too, she understood. Even when it made him just occasionally, to other people, who didn't know him well, a little ridiculous perhaps . . .. For there were moments when he rushed into battle where no battle was . . .. She talked and laughed and positively forgot until he had come in (just as she had imagined) that Pearl Fulton had not turned up.

'I wonder if Miss Fulton has forgotten?'

'I expect so,' said Harry. 'Is she on the 'phone?'

'Ah! There's a taxi now.' And Bertha smiled with that little air of proprietorship that she always assumed while her women finds were new and mysterious. 'She lives in taxis.'

'She'll run to fat if she does,' said Harry coolly, ringing the bell for dinner. 'Frightful danger for blonde women.'

'Harry – don't!' warned Bertha, laughing up at him.

Came another tiny moment, while they waited, laughing and talking, just a trifle too much at their ease, a trifle too unaware. And then Miss Fulton, all in silver, with a silver fillet binding her pale blonde hair, came in smiling, her head a little on one side.

'Am I late?'

'No, not at all,' said Bertha. 'Come along.' And she took her arm and they moved into the dining-room.

What was there in the touch of that cool arm that could fan – fan – start blazing – blazing – the fire of bliss that Bertha did not know what to do with?

Miss Fulton did not look at her; but then she seldom did look at people directly. Her heavy eyelids lay upon her eyes and the strange half-smile came and went upon her lips as though she lived by listening rather than seeing. But Bertha knew, suddenly, as if the longest, most intimate look had passed between them – as if they had said to each other: 'You too?' – that Pearl Fulton, stirring the beautiful red soup in the grey plate, was feeling just what she was feeling.

And the others? Face and Mug, Eddie and Harry, their spoons rising and falling – dabbing their lips with their napkins, crumbling bread, fiddling with the forks and glasses and talking.

'I met her at the Alpha show – the weirdest little person. She'd not only cut off her hair, but she seemed to have taken a dreadfully good snip off her legs and arms and her neck and her poor little nose as well.'

'Isn't she very *liée* with Michael Oat?'

'The man who wrote *Love in False Teeth*?'

'He wants to write a play for me. One act. One man. Decides to commit suicide. Gives all the reasons why he should and why he shouldn't. And just as he has made up his mind either to do it or not to do it – curtain. Not half a bad idea.'

'What's he going to call it – "Stomach Trouble"?'

'I *think* I've come across the *same* idea in a lit-tle French review, *quite* unknown in England.'

No, they didn't share it. They were dears – dears – and she loved having them there, at her table, and giving them delicious food and wine. In fact, she longed to tell them how delightful they were, and what a decorative group they made, how they seemed to set one another off and how they reminded her of a play by Tchekof!

Harry was enjoying his dinner. It was part of his – well, not his nature, exactly, and certainly not his pose – his – something or other – to talk about food and to glory in his 'shameless passion for the white flash of the lobster' and 'the green of pistachio ices – green and cold like the eyelids of Egyptian dancers'.

When he looked up at her and said: 'Bertha, this is a very admirable *soufflé*!' she almost could have wept with child-like pleasure.

Oh, why did she feel so tender towards the whole world tonight? Everything was good – was right. All that happened seemed to fill again her brimming cup of bliss.

And still, in the back of her mind, there was the pear tree. It would be silver now, in the light of poor dear Eddie's moon, silver as Miss Fulton, who sat there turning a tangerine in her slender fingers that were so pale a light seemed to come from them.

What she simply couldn't make out – what was miraculous – was how she should have guessed Miss Fulton's mood so exactly and so instantly. For she never doubted for a moment that she was right, and yet what had she to go on? Less than nothing.

'I believe this does happen very, very rarely between women. Never between men,' thought Bertha. 'But while I am making the coffee in the drawing-room perhaps she will "give a sign".'

What she meant by that she did not know, and what would happen after that she could not imagine.

While she thought like this she saw herself talking and laughing. She had to talk because of her desire to laugh.

'I must laugh or die.'

But when she noticed Face's funny little habit of tucking something down the front of her bodice – as if she kept a tiny, secret hoard of nuts there, too – Bertha had to dig her nails into her hands – so as not to laugh too much.

It was over at last. And: 'Come and see my new coffee machine,' said Bertha.

'We only have a new coffee machine once a fortnight,' said Harry. Face took her arm this time; Miss Fulton bent her head and followed after.

The fire had died down in the drawing-room to a red, flickering 'nest of baby phoenixes', said Face.

'Don't turn up the light for a moment. It is so lovely.' And down she crouched by the fire again. She was always cold . . . 'without her little red flannel jacket, of course,' thought Bertha.

At that moment Miss Fulton 'gave the sign'.

'Have you a garden?' said the cool, sleepy voice.

This was so exquisite on her part that all Bertha could do was to obey. She crossed the room, pulled the curtains apart, and opened those long windows.

'There!' she breathed.

And the two women stood side by side looking at the slender, flowering tree. Although it was so still it seemed, like the flame of a candle, to stretch up, to point, to quiver in the bright air, to grow taller and taller as they gazed – almost to touch the rim of the round, silver moon.

How long did they stand there? Both, as it were, caught in that circle of unearthly light, understanding each other perfectly, creatures of another world, and wondering what they were to do in this one with all this blissful treasure that burned in their bosoms and dropped, in silver flowers, from their hair and hands?

For ever – for a moment? And did Miss Fulton murmur: 'Yes. Just *that*.' Or did Bertha dream it?

Then the light was snapped on and Face made the coffee and Harry said: 'My dear Mrs Knight, don't ask me about my baby. I never see her. I shan't feel the slightest interest in her until she has a lover,' and Mug took his eye out of the conservatory for a moment and then put it under glass again and Eddie Warren drank his coffee and set down the cup with a face of anguish as though he had drunk and seen the spider.

'What I want to do is to give the young men a show. I believe London is simply teeming with first-chop, unwritten plays. What I want to say to 'em is: "Here's the theatre. Fire ahead."'

'You know, my dear, I am going to decorate a room for the Jacob Nathans. Oh, I am so tempted to do a fried-fish scheme, with the backs of the chairs shaped like frying-pans and lovely chip potatoes embroidered all over the curtains.'

'The trouble with our young writing men is that they are still too romantic. You can't put out to sea without being seasick and wanting a basin. Well, why won't they have the courage of those basins?'

'A *dreadful* poem about a girl who was *violated* by a beggar *without* a nose in a lit-tle wood . . .'

Miss Fulton sank into the lowest, deepest chair and Harry handed round the cigarettes.

From the way he stood in front of her shaking the silver box and saying abruptly: 'Egyptian? Turkish? Virginian? They're all mixed up,' Bertha realised that she not only bored him; he really disliked her. And she decided from the way Miss Fulton said: 'No, thank you, I won't smoke,' that she felt it, too, and was hurt.

'Oh, Harry, don't dislike her. You are quite wrong about her. She's wonderful, wonderful. And, besides, how can you feel so differently about someone who means so much to me. I shall try to tell you when we are in bed tonight what has been happening. What she and I have shared.'

At those last words something strange and almost terrifying darted into Bertha's mind. And this something blind and smiling whispered to her: 'Soon these people will go. The house will be quiet – quiet. The lights will be out. And you and he will be alone together in the dark room – the warm bed . . .

She jumped up from her chair and ran over to the piano.

'What a pity someone does not play!' she cried. 'What a pity somebody does not play.'

For the first time in her life Bertha Young desired her husband.

Oh, she'd loved him – she'd been in love with him, of course, in every other way, but just not in that way. And equally, of course, she'd understood that he was different. They'd discussed it so often. It had worried her dreadfully at first to find that she was so cold, but after a time it had not seemed to matter. They were so frank with each other – such good pals. That was the best of being modern.

But now – ardently! ardently! The word ached in her ardent body! Was this what that feeling of bliss had been leading up to? But then, then—

'My dear,' said Mrs Norman Knight, 'you know our shame. We are the victims of time and train. We live in Hampstead. It's been so nice.'

'I'll come with you into the hall,' said Bertha. 'I loved having you. But you must not miss the last train. That's so awful, isn't it?'

'Have a whisky, Knight, before you go?' called Harry.

'No, thanks, old chap.'

Bertha squeezed his hand for that as she shook it.

'Good night, goodbye,' she cried from the top step, feeling that this self of hers was taking leave of them for ever.

When she got back into the drawing-room the others were on the move.

'. . . Then you can come part of the way in my taxi.'

'I shall be *so* thankful *not* to have to face *another* drive *alone* after my *dreadful* experience.'

'You can get a taxi at the rank just at the end of the street. You won't have to walk more than a few yards.'

'That's a comfort. I'll go and put on my coat.'

Miss Fulton moved towards the hall and Bertha was following when Harry almost pushed past.

'Let me help you.'

Bertha knew that he was repenting his rudeness – she let him go. What a boy he was in some ways – so impulsive – so – simple.

And Eddie and she were left by the fire.

'I *wonder* if you have seen Bilks' *new* poem called *Table d'Hôte*,' said Eddie softly. 'It's so wonderful. In the last Anthology. Have you got a copy? I'd *so* like to *show* it to you. It begins with an *incredibly* beautiful line: "Why Must it Always be Tomato Soup?"'

'Yes,' said Bertha. And she moved noiselessly to a table opposite the drawing-room door and Eddie glided noiselessly after her. She picked up the little book and gave it to him; they had not made a sound.

While he looked it up she turned her head towards the hall. And she saw . . . Harry with Miss Fulton's coat in his arms and Miss Fulton with her back turned to him and her head bent. He tossed the coat away, put his hands on her shoulders and turned her violently to him. His lips said: 'I adore you,' and Miss Fulton laid her moonbeam fingers on his cheeks and smiled her sleepy smile. Harry's nostrils quivered; his lips curled back in a hideous grin while he whispered: 'Tomorrow,' and with her eyelids Miss Fulton said: 'Yes.'

'Here it is,' said Eddie. '"Why Must it Always be Tomato Soup?" It's so *deeply* true, don't you feel? Tomato soup is so *dreadfully* eternal.'

'If you prefer,' said Harry's voice, very loud, from the hall, 'I can 'phone you a cab to come to the door.'

'Oh, no. It's not necessary,' said Miss Fulton, and she came up to Bertha and gave her the slender fingers to hold.

'Goodbye. Thank you so much.'

'Goodbye,' said Bertha.

Miss Fulton held her hand a moment longer.

'Your lovely pear tree!' she murmured.

And then she was gone, with Eddie following, like the black cat following the grey cat.

'I'll shut up shop,' said Harry, extravagantly cool and collected.

'Your lovely pear tree – pear tree – pear tree!'

Bertha simply ran over to the long windows.

'Oh, what is going to happen now?' she cried.

But the pear tree was as lovely as ever and as full of flower and as still.

M. R. JAMES

A Warning to the Curious

The place on the east coast which the reader is asked to consider is Seaburgh. It is not very different now from what I remember it to have been when I was a child. Marshes intersected by dykes to the south, recalling the early chapters of *Great Expectations*; flat fields to the north, merging into heath; heath, fir woods, and, above all, gorse, inland. A long sea-front and a street: behind that a spacious church of flint, with a broad, solid western tower and a peal of six bells. How well I remember their sound on a hot Sunday in August, as our party went slowly up the white, dusty slope of road towards them, for the church stands at the top of a short, steep incline. They rang with a flat clacking sort of sound on those hot days, but when the air was softer they were mellower too. The railway ran down to its little terminus farther along the same road. There was a gay white windmill just before you came to the station, and another down near the shingle at the south end of the town, and yet others on higher ground to the north. There were cottages of bright red brick with slate roofs . . . but why do I encumber you with these commonplace details? The fact is that they come crowding to the point of the pencil when it begins to write of Seaburgh. I should like to be sure that I had allowed the right ones to get on to the paper. But I forgot. I have not quite done with the word-painting business yet.

Walk away from the sea and the town, pass the station, and turn up the road on the right. It is a sandy road, parallel with the railway, and if you follow it, it climbs to somewhat higher ground. On your left (you are now going northward) is heath, on your right (the side towards the sea) is a belt of old firs, wind-beaten, thick at the top, with the slope that old seaside trees have; seen on the skyline from the train they would tell you in an instant, if you did not know it, that you were approaching a windy coast. Well, at the top of my little hill, a line of these firs strikes out and runs towards the sea, for there is a ridge that goes that way; and the ridge ends in a rather well-defined mound commanding the level fields of rough grass, and a little knot of fir trees crowns it. And here you may sit on a hot spring day, very well content to look at blue sea, white windmills, red cottages, bright green grass, church tower, and distant martello tower on the south.

As I have said, I began to know Seaburgh as a child; but a gap of a good many years separates my early knowledge from that which is more recent. Still it keeps its place in my affections, and any tales of it that I pick up have an interest for me. One such tale is this: it came to me in a place very remote from Seaburgh, and quite accidentally, from a man whom I had been able to oblige – enough in his opinion to justify his making me his confidant to this extent.

I know all that country more or less (he said). I used to go to Seaburgh pretty regularly for golf in the spring. I generally put up at the 'Bear', with a friend – Henry Long it was, you knew him perhaps – ('Slightly,' I said) and we used to take a sitting-room and be very happy there. Since he died I haven't cared to go there. And I don't know that I should anyhow after the particular thing that happened on our last visit.

It was in April, 19—, we were there, and by some chance we were almost the only people in the hotel. So the ordinary public rooms were practically empty, and we were the more surprised when, after dinner, our sitting-room door opened, and a young man put his head in. We were aware of this young man. He was rather a rabbity anaemic subject – light hair and light eyes – but not unpleasing. So when he said: 'I beg your pardon, is this a private room?' we did not growl and say: 'Yes, it is,' but Long said, or I did – no matter which: 'Please come in.' 'Oh, may I?' he said, and seemed relieved. Of course it was obvious that he wanted company; and as he was a reasonable kind of person – not the sort to bestow his whole family history on you – we urged him to make himself at home. 'I dare say you find the other rooms rather bleak,' I said. Yes, he did: but it was really too good of us, and so on. That being got over, he made some pretence of reading a book. Long was playing Patience, I was writing. It became plain to me after a few minutes that this visitor of ours was in rather a state of fidgets or nerves, which communicated itself to me, and so I put away my writing and turned to at engaging him in talk.

After some remarks, which I forget, he became rather confidential. 'You'll think it very odd of me' (this was the sort of way he began), 'but the fact is I've had something of a shock.' Well, I recommended a drink of some cheering kind, and we had it. The waiter coming in made an interruption (and I thought our young man seemed very jumpy when the door opened), but after a while he got back to his woes again. There was nobody he knew in the place, and he did happen to know who we both were (it turned out there was some common acquaintance in town), and really he did want a word of advice, if we didn't mind. Of course we both said: 'By all means,' or 'Not at all,' and Long put away his cards. And we settled down to hear what his difficulty was.

'It began,' he said, 'more than a week ago, when I bicycled over to Froston, only about five or six miles, to see the church; I'm very much interested in architecture, and it's got one of those pretty porches with niches and shields. I took a photograph of it, and then an old man who was tidying up in the churchyard came and asked if I'd care to look into the church. I said yes, and he produced a key and let me in. There wasn't much inside, but I told him it was a nice little church, and he kept it very clean, "But," I said, "the porch is the best part of it." We were just outside the porch then, and he said, "Ah, yes, that is a nice porch; and do you know, sir, what's the meanin' of that coat of arms there?"

'It was the one with the three crowns, and though I'm not much of a herald, I was able to say yes, I thought it was the old arms of the kingdom of East Anglia.

'"That's right, sir," he said, "and do you know the meanin' of them three crowns that's on it?"

'I said I'd no doubt it was known, but I couldn't recollect to have heard it myself.

'"Well, then," he said, "for all you're a scholard, I can tell you something you don't know. Them's the three 'oly crowns what was buried in the ground near by the coast to keep the Germans from landing – ah, I can see you don't believe that. But I tell you, if it hadn't have been for one of them 'oly crowns bein' there still, them Germans would a landed here time and again, they would.

Landed with their ships, and killed man, woman and child in their beds. Now then, that's the truth what I'm telling you, that is; and if you don't believe me, you ast the rector. There he comes: you ast him, I says."

'I looked round, and there was the rector, a nice-looking old man, coming up the path; and before I could begin assuring my old man, who was getting quite excited, that I didn't disbelieve him, the rector struck in, and said: "What's all this about, John? Good day to you, sir. Have you been looking at our little church?"

'So then there was a little talk which allowed the old man to calm down, and then the rector asked him again what was the matter.

'"Oh," he said, "it warn't nothink, only I was telling this gentleman he'd ought to ast you about them 'oly crowns."

'"Ah, yes, to be sure," said the rector, "that's a very curious matter, isn't it? But I don't know whether the gentleman is interested in our old stories, eh?"

'"Oh, he'll be interested fast enough," says the old man, "he'll put his confidence in what you tells him, sir; why, you known William Ager yourself, father and son too."

'Then I put in a word to say how much I should like to hear all about it, and before many minutes I was walking up the village street with the rector, who had one or two words to say to parishioners, and then to the rectory, where he took me into his study. He had made out, on the way, that I really was capable of taking an intelligent interest in a piece of folklore, and not quite the ordinary tripper. So he was very willing to talk, and it is rather surprising to me that the particular legend he told me has not made its way into print before. His account of it was this: "There has always been a belief in these parts in the three holy crowns. The old people say they were buried in different places near the coast to keep off the Danes or the French or the Germans. And they say that one of the three was dug up a long time ago, and another has disappeared by the encroaching of the sea, and one's still left doing its work, keeping off invaders. Well, now, if you have read the ordinary guides and histories of this county, you will remember perhaps that in 1687 a crown, which was said to be the crown of Redwald, King of the East Angles, was dug up at Rendlesham, and alas! alas! melted down before it was even properly described or drawn. Well, Rendlesham isn't on the coast, but it isn't so very far inland, and it's on a very important line of access. And I believe that is the crown which the people mean when they say that one has been dug up. Then on the south you don't want me to tell you where there was a Saxon royal palace which is now under the sea, eh? Well, there was the second crown, I take it. And up beyond these two, they say, lies the third."

'"Do they say where it is?" of course I asked.

'He said, "Yes, indeed, they do, but they don't tell," and his manner did not encourage me to put the obvious question. Instead of that I waited a moment, and said: "What did the old man mean when he said you knew William Ager, as if that had something to do with the crowns?"

'"To be sure," he said, "now that's another curious story. These Agers – it's a very old name in these parts, but I can't find that they were ever people of quality or big owners – these Agers say, or said, that their branch of the family were the guardians of the last crown. A certain old Nathaniel Ager was the first one I knew – I was born and brought up quite near here – and he, I believe, camped out at the place during the whole of the war of 1870. William, his son, did the same, I know, during the South African War. And young William, *his* son, who has only died fairly recently, took lodgings at the cottage nearest the spot, and I've no doubt hastened his end, for he was a consumptive, by exposure and night watching. And he was the last of that branch. It was a dreadful grief to him to think that he was the last, but he could do nothing, the only relations at all near to him were in the colonies. I wrote letters for him to them imploring them to come over on business very important to the family, but there has been no answer. So the last of the holy crowns, if it's there, has no guardian now."

'That was what the rector told me, and you can fancy how interesting I found it. The only thing I could think of when I left him was how to hit upon the spot where the crown was supposed to be. I wish I'd left it alone.

'But there was a sort of fate in it, for as I bicycled back past the churchyard wall my eye caught a fairly new gravestone, and on it was the name of William Ager. Of course I got off and read it. It said "of this parish, died at Seaburgh, 19—, aged 28." There it was, you see. A little judicious questioning in the right place, and

I should at least find the cottage nearest the spot. Only I didn't quite know what was the right place to begin my questioning at. Again there was fate: it took me to the curiosity-shop down that way – you know – and I turned over some old books, and, if you please, one was a prayer-book of 1740 odd, in a rather handsome binding – I'll just go and get it, it's in my room.'

He left us in a state of some surprise, but we had hardly time to exchange any remarks when he was back, panting, and handed us the book opened at the fly-leaf, on which was, in a straggly hand:

'Nathaniel Ager is my name and England is my nation,
Seaburgh is my dwelling-place and Christ is my Salvation,
When I am dead and in my Grave, and all my bones are rotton,
I hope the Lord will think on me when I am quite forgotton.'

This poem was dated 1754, and there were many more entries of Agers, Nathaniel, Frederick, William, and so on, ending with William, 19—.

'You see,' he said, 'anybody would call it the greatest bit of luck. *I* did, but I don't now. Of course I asked the shopman about William Ager, and of course he happened to remember that he lodged in a cottage in the North Field and died there. This was just chalking the road for me. I knew which the cottage must be: there is only one sizable one about there. The next thing was to scrape some sort of acquaintance with the people, and I took a walk that way at once. A dog did the business for me: he made at me so fiercely that they had to run out and beat him off, and then naturally begged my pardon, and we got into talk. I had only to bring up Ager's name, and pretend I knew, or thought I knew something of him, and then the woman said how sad it was him dying so young, and she was sure it came of him spending the night out of doors in the cold weather. Then I had to say: "Did he go out on the sea at night?" and she said: "Oh, no, it was on the hillock yonder with the trees on it." And there I was.

'I know something about digging in these barrows: I've opened many of them in the down country. But that was with owner's leave, and in broad daylight and with men to help. I had to prospect very carefully here before I put a spade in: I couldn't trench across the mound, and with those old firs growing there I knew there would be awkward tree roots. Still the soil was very light and sandy and easy, and there was a rabbit hole or so that might be developed into a sort of tunnel. The going out and coming back at odd hours to the hotel was going to be the awkward part. When I made up my mind about the way to excavate I told the people that I was called away for a night, and I spent it out there. I made my tunnel: I won't bore you with the details of how I supported it and filled it in when I'd done, but the main thing is that I got the crown.'

Naturally we both broke out into exclamations of surprise and interest. I for one had long known about the finding of the crown at Rendlesham and had often lamented its fate. No one has ever seen an Anglo-Saxon crown – at least no one had. But our man gazed at us with a rueful eye. 'Yes,' he said, 'and the worst of it is I don't know how to put it back.'

'Put it back?' we cried out. 'Why, my dear sir, you've made one of the most exciting finds ever heard of in this country. Of course it ought to go to the Jewel House at the Tower. What's your difficulty? If you're thinking about the owner of the land, and treasure-trove, and all that, we can certainly help you through. Nobody's going to make a fuss about technicalities in a case of this kind.'

Probably more was said, but all he did was to put his face in his hands, and mutter: 'I don't know how to put it back.'

At last Long said: 'You'll forgive me, I hope, if I seem impertinent, but are you *quite* sure you've got it?' I was wanting to ask much the same question myself, for of course the story did seem a lunatic's dream when one thought over it. But I hadn't quite dared to say what might hurt the poor young man's feelings. However, he took it quite calmly – really, with the calm of despair, you might say. He sat up and said: 'Oh, yes, there's no doubt of that: I have it here, in my room, locked up in my bag. You can come and look at it if you like: I won't offer to bring it here.'

We were not likely to let the chance slip. We went with him; his room was only a few doors off. The boots was just collecting shoes in the passage: or so we thought: afterwards we were not sure. Our visitor – his name was Paxton – was in a worse state of shivers than before, and went hurriedly into the room, and beckoned us after him, turned on the light, and shut the door carefully. Then he unlocked his kit-bag, and produced a bundle of clean pocket-handkerchiefs in which something was wrapped, laid it on the bed, and undid it. I can now say I *have* seen an actual Anglo-Saxon crown. It was of silver – as the Rendlesham one is always said to have been – it was set with some gems, mostly antique intaglios and cameos, and was of rather plain, almost rough workmanship. In fact, it was like those you see on the coins and in the manuscripts. I found no reason to think it was later than the ninth century. I was intensely interested, of course, and I wanted to turn it over in my hands, but Paxton prevented me. 'Don't *you* touch it,' he said, 'I'll do that.' And with a sigh that was, I declare to you, dreadful to hear, he took it up and turned it about so that we could see every part of it. 'Seen enough?' he said at last, and we nodded. He wrapped it up and locked it in his bag, and stood looking at us dumbly. 'Come back to our room,' Long said, 'and tell us what the trouble is.' He thanked us, and said: 'Will you go first and see if – if the coast is clear?' That wasn't very intelligible, for our proceedings hadn't been, after all, very suspicious, and the hotel, as I said, was practically empty. However, we were beginning to have inklings of – we didn't know what, and anyhow nerves are infectious. So we did go, first peering out as we opened the door, and fancying (I found we both had the fancy) that a shadow, or more than a shadow – but it made no sound – passed from before us to one side as we came out into the passage. 'It's all right,' we whispered to Paxton – whispering seemed the proper tone – and we went, with him between us, back to our sitting-room. I was preparing, when we got there, to be ecstatic about the unique interest of what we had seen, but when I looked at Paxton I saw that would be terribly out of place, and I left it to him to begin.

'What *is* to be done?' was his opening. Long thought it right (as he explained to me afterwards) to be obtuse, and said: 'Why not find out who the owner of the land is, and inform—' 'Oh, no, no!' Paxton broke in impatiently, 'I beg your pardon: you've been very kind, but don't you see it's *got* to go back, and I daren't be there at night, and daytime's impossible. Perhaps, though, you don't see: well, then, the truth is that I've never been alone since I touched it.' I was beginning some fairly stupid comment, but Long caught my eye, and I stopped. Long said: 'I think I do see, perhaps: but wouldn't it be – a relief – to tell us a little more clearly what the situation is?'

Then it all came out: Paxton looked over his shoulder and beckoned to us to come nearer to him, and began speaking in a low voice: we listened most intently, of course, and compared notes afterwards, and I wrote down our version, so I am confident I have what he told us almost word for word. He said: 'It began when I was first prospecting, and put me off again and again. There was always somebody – a man – standing by one of the firs. This was in daylight, you know. He was never in front of me. I always saw him with the tail of my eye on the left or the right, and he was never there when I looked straight for him. I would lie down for quite a long time and take careful observations, and make sure there was no one, and then when I got up and began prospecting again, there he was. And he began to give me hints, besides; for wherever I put that prayer-book – short of locking it up, which I did at last – when I came back to my room it was always out on my table open at the fly-leaf where the names are, and one of my razors across it to keep it open. I'm sure he just can't open my bag, or something more would have happened. You see, he's light and weak, but all the same I daren't face him. Well, then, when I was making the tunnel, of course it was worse, and if I hadn't been so keen I should have dropped the whole thing and run. It was like someone scraping at my back all the time: I thought for a long time it was only soil dropping on me, but as I got nearer the – the crown, it was unmistakable. And when I actually laid it bare and got my fingers into the ring of it and pulled it out, there came a sort of cry behind me – oh, I can't tell you how desolate it was! And horribly threatening too. It spoilt all my pleasure in my find – cut it off that moment. And if I hadn't been the wretched fool I am, I should have put the thing back and left it. But I didn't. The rest of the time was just awful. I had hours to get through before I could decently come back to the hotel. First I spent time filling up my tunnel and covering my tracks, and all the while he was there trying to thwart me. Sometimes, you know, you see him, and sometimes you don't, just as he pleases, I think: he's there, but he has some power over your eyes. Well, I wasn't off the spot very long before sunrise, and then I had to get to the junction for Seaburgh, and take a train back. And though it was daylight fairly soon, I don't know if that made it much better. There were always hedges, or gorse-bushes, or park fences along the road –

some sort of cover, I mean – and I was never easy for a second. And then when I began to meet people going to work, they always looked behind me very strangely: it might have been that they were surprised at seeing anyone so early; but I didn't think it was only that, and I don't now: they didn't look exactly at *me*. And the porter at the train was like that too. And the guard held open the door after I'd got into the carriage – just as he would if there was somebody else coming, you know. Oh, you may be very sure it isn't my fancy,' he said with a dull sort of laugh. Then he went on: 'And even if I do get it put back, he won't forgive me: I can tell that. And I was so happy a fortnight ago.' He dropped into a chair, and I believe he began to cry.

We didn't know what to say, but we felt we must come to the rescue somehow, and so – it really seemed the only thing – we said if he was so set on putting the crown back in its place, we would help him. And I must say that after what we had heard it did seem the right thing. If these horrid consequences had come on this poor man, might there not really be something in the original idea of the crown having some curious power bound up with it, to guard the coast? At least, that was my feeling, and I think it was Long's too. Our offer was very welcome to Paxton, anyhow. When could we do it? It was nearing half-past ten. Could we contrive to make a late walk plausible to the hotel people that very night? We looked out of the window: there was a brilliant full moon – the Paschal moon. Long undertook to tackle the boots and propitiate him. He was to say that we should not be much over the hour, and if we did find it so pleasant that we stopped out a bit longer we would see that he didn't lose by sitting up. Well, we were pretty regular customers of the hotel, and did not give much trouble, and were considered by the servants to be not under the mark in the way of tips; and so the boots *was* propitiated, and let us out on to the sea-front, and remained, as we heard later, looking after us. Paxton had a large coat over his arm, under which was the wrapped-up crown.

So we were off on this strange errand before we had time to think how very much out of the way it was. I have told this part quite shortly on purpose, for it really does represent the haste with which we settled our plan and took action. 'The shortest way is up the hill and through the churchyard,' Paxton said, as we stood a moment before the hotel looking up and down the front. There was nobody about – nobody at all. Seaburgh out of the season is an early, quiet place. 'We can't go along the dyke by the cottage, because of the dog,' Paxton also said, when I pointed to what I thought a shorter way along the front and across two fields. The reason he gave was good enough. We went up the road to the church, and turned in at the churchyard gate. I confess to having thought that there might be some lying there who might be conscious of our business: but if it was so, they were also conscious that one who was on their side, so to say, had us under surveillance, and we saw no sign of them. But under observation we felt we were, as I have never felt it at another time. Specially was it so when we passed out of the churchyard into a narrow path with close high hedges, through which we hurried as Christian did through that Valley; and so got out into open fields. Then along hedges, though I would sooner have been in the open, where I could see if anyone was visible behind me; over a gate or two, and then a swerve to the left, taking us up on to the ridge which ended in that mound.

As we neared it, Henry Long felt, and I felt too, that there were what I can only call dim presences waiting for us, as well as a far more actual one attending us. Of Paxton's agitation all this time I can give you no adequate picture: he breathed like a hunted beast, and we could not either of us look at his face. How he would manage when we got to the very place we had not troubled to think: he had seemed so sure that that would not be difficult. Nor was it. I never saw anything like the dash with which he flung himself at a particular spot in the side of the mound, and tore at it, so that in a very few minutes the greater part of his body was out of sight. We stood holding the coat and that bundle of handkerchiefs, and looking, very fearfully, I must admit, about us. There was nothing to be seen: a line of dark firs behind us made one skyline, more trees and the church tower half a mile off on the right, cottages and a windmill on the horizon on the left, calm sea dead in front, faint barking of a dog at a cottage on a gleaming dyke between us and it: full moon making that path we know across the sea: the eternal whisper of the Scotch firs just above us, and of the sea in front. Yet, in all this quiet, an acute, an acrid consciousness of a restrained hostility very near us, like a dog on a leash that might be let go at any moment.

Paxton pulled himself out of the hole, and stretched a hand back to us. 'Give it to me,' he whispered, 'unwrapped.' We pulled off the handkerchiefs, and he took the crown. The moonlight just fell on it as he snatched it. We had not ourselves touched that bit of metal, and I have thought since that it was just as well. In another moment Paxton was out of the hole again and busy shovelling back the soil with hands that were already bleeding. He would have none of our help, though. It was much the longest part of the job to get the place to look undisturbed: yet – I don't know how – he made a wonderful success of it. At last he was satisfied, and we turned back.

We were a couple of hundred yards from the hill when Long suddenly said to him: 'I say, you've left your coat there. That won't do. See?' And I certainly did see it – the long dark overcoat lying where the tunnel had been. Paxton had not stopped, however: he only shook his head, and held up the coat on his arm. And when we joined him, he said, without any excitement, but as if nothing mattered any more: 'That wasn't my coat.' And, indeed, when we looked back again, that dark thing was not to be seen.

Well, we got out on the road, and came rapidly back that way. It was well before twelve when we got in, trying to put a good face on it, and saying – Long and I – what a lovely night it was for a walk. The boots was on the look-out for us, and we made remarks like that for his edification as we entered the hotel. He gave another look up and down the sea-front before he locked the front door, and said: 'You didn't meet many people about, I s'pose, sir?' 'No, indeed, not a soul,' I said; at which I remember Paxton looked oddly at me. 'Only I thought I see someone turn up the station road after you gentlemen,' said the boots. 'Still, you was three together, and I don't suppose he meant mischief.' I didn't know what to say; Long merely said 'Good night,' and we went off upstairs, promising to turn out all lights, and to go to bed in a few minutes.

Back in our room, we did our very best to make Paxton take a cheerful view. 'There's the crown safe back,' we said; 'very likely you'd have done better not to touch it' (and he heavily assented to that), 'but no real harm has been done, and we shall never give this away to anyone who would be so mad as to go near it. Besides, don't you feel better yourself? I don't mind confessing,' I said, 'that on the way there I was very much inclined to take your view about – well, about being followed; but going back, it wasn't at all the same thing, was it?' No, it wouldn't do: '*You've* nothing to trouble yourselves about,' he said, 'but I'm not forgiven. I've got to pay for that miserable sacrilege still. I know what you are going to say. The Church might help. Yes, but it's the body that has to suffer. It's true I'm not feeling that he's waiting outside for me just now. But—' Then he stopped. Then he turned to thanking us, and we put him off as soon as we could. And naturally we pressed him to use our sitting-room next day, and said we should be glad to go out with him. Or did he play golf, perhaps? Yes, he did, but he didn't think he should care about that tomorrow. Well, we recommended him to get up late and sit in our room in the morning while we were playing, and we would have a walk later in the day. He was very submissive and *piano* about it all: ready to do just what we thought best, but clearly quite certain in his own mind that what was coming could not be averted or palliated. You'll wonder why we didn't insist on accompanying him to his home and seeing him safe into the care of brothers or someone. The fact was he had nobody. He had had a flat in town, but lately he had made up his mind to settle for a time in Sweden, and he had dismantled his flat and shipped off his belongings, and was whiling away a fortnight or three weeks before he made a start. Anyhow, we didn't see what we could do better than sleep on it – or not sleep very much, as was my case – and see what we felt like tomorrow morning.

We felt very different, Long and I, on as beautiful an April morning as you could desire; and Paxton also looked very different when we saw him at breakfast. 'The first approach to a decent night I seem ever to have had,' was what he said. But he was going to do as we had settled: stay in probably all the morning, and come out with us later. We went to the links; we met some other men and played with them in the morning, and had lunch there rather early, so as not to be late back. All the same, the snares of death overtook him.

Whether it could have been prevented, I don't know. I think he would have been got at somehow, do what we might. Anyhow, this is what happened.

We went straight up to our room. Paxton was there, reading quite peaceably. 'Ready to come out shortly?' said Long, 'say in half an hour's time?' 'Certainly,' he said: and I said we would change first, and perhaps have baths, and call for him in half an hour. I had my bath first, and went and lay down on my bed, and slept for about ten minutes. We came out of our rooms at the same time, and went together to the sitting-room. Paxton wasn't there – only his book. Nor was he in his room, nor in the downstair rooms. We shouted for him. A servant came out and said: 'Why, I thought you gentlemen was gone out already, and so did the other gentleman. He heard you a-calling from the path there, and run out in a hurry, and I looked out of the coffee-room window, but I didn't see you. 'Owever, he run off down the beach that way.'

Without a word we ran that way too – it was the opposite direction to that of last night's expedition. It wasn't quite four o'clock, and the day was fair, though not so fair as it had been, so there was really no reason, you'd say, for anxiety: with people about, surely a man couldn't come to much harm.

But something in our look as we ran out must have struck the servant, for she came out on the steps, and pointed, and said, 'Yes, that's the way he went.' We ran on as far as the top of the shingle bank, and there pulled up. There was a choice of ways: past the houses on the sea-front, or along the sand at the bottom of the beach, which, the tide being now out, was fairly broad. Or of course we might keep along the shingle between these two tracks and have some view of both of them; only that was heavy going. We chose the sand, for that was the loneliest, and someone *might* come to harm there without being seen from the public path.

Long said he saw Paxton some distance ahead, running and waving his stick, as if he wanted to signal to people who were on ahead of him. I couldn't be sure: one of these sea-mists was coming up very quickly from the south. There was someone, that's all I could say. And there were tracks on the sand as of someone running who wore shoes; and there were other tracks made before those – for the shoes sometimes trod in them and interfered with them – of someone not in shoes. Oh, of course, it's only my word you've got to take for all this: Long's dead, we'd no time or means to make sketches or take casts, and the next tide washed everything away. All we could do was to notice these marks as we hurried on. But there they were over and over again, and we had no doubt whatever that what we saw was the track of a bare foot, and one that showed more bones than flesh.

The notion of Paxton running after – after anything like this, and supposing it to be the friends he was looking for, was very dreadful to us. You can guess what we fancied: how the thing he was following might stop suddenly and turn round on him, and what sort of face it would show, half-seen at first in the mist – which all the while was getting thicker and thicker. And as I ran on wondering how the poor wretch could have been lured into mistaking that other thing for us, I remembered his saying, 'He has some power over your eyes.' And then I wondered what the end would be, for I had no hope now that the end could be averted, and – well, there is no need to tell all the dismal and horrid thoughts that flitted through my head as we ran on into the mist. It was uncanny, too, that the sun should still be bright in the sky and we could see nothing. We could only tell that we were now past the houses and had reached that gap there is between them and the old martello tower. When you are past the tower, you know, there is nothing but shingle for a long way – not a house, not a human creature, just that spit of land, or rather shingle, with the river on your right and the sea on your left.

But just before that, just by the martello tower, you remember there is the old battery, close to the sea. I believe there are only a few blocks of concrete left now: the rest has all been washed away, but at this time there was a lot more, though the place was a ruin. Well, when we got there, we clambered to the top as quick as we could to take breath and look over the shingle in front if by chance the mist would let us see anything. But a moment's rest we must have. We had run a mile at least. Nothing whatever was visible ahead of us, and we were just turning by common consent to get down and run hopelessly on, when we heard what I can only call a laugh: and if you can understand what I mean by a breathless, a lungless laugh, you have it: but I don't suppose you can. It came from below, and swerved away into the mist. That was enough. We bent over the wall. Paxton was there at the bottom.

You don't need to be told that he was dead. His tracks showed that he had run along the side of the battery, had turned sharp round the corner of it, and, small doubt of it, must have dashed straight into the open arms of someone who was waiting there. His mouth was full of sand and stones, and his teeth and jaws were broken to bits. I only glanced once at his face.

At the same moment, just as we were scrambling down from the battery to get to the body, we heard a shout, and saw a man running down the bank of the martello tower. He was the caretaker stationed there, and his keen old eyes had managed to descry through the mist that something was wrong. He had seen Paxton fall, and had seen us a moment after, running up – fortunate this, for otherwise we could hardly have escaped suspicion of being concerned in the dreadful business. Had he, we asked, caught sight of anybody attacking our friend? He could not be sure.

We sent him off for help, and stayed by the dead man till they came with the stretcher. It was then that we traced out how he had come, on the narrow fringe of sand under the battery wall. The rest was shingle, and it was hopelessly impossible to tell whither the other had gone.

What were we to say at the inquest? It was a duty, we felt, not to give up, there and then, the secret of the crown, to be published in every paper. I don't know how much you would have told; but what we did agree upon was this: to say that we had only made acquaintance with Paxton the day before, and that he had told us he was under some apprehension of danger at the hands of a man called William Ager. Also that we had seen some other tracks besides Paxton's when we followed him along the beach. But of course by that time everything was gone from the sands.

No one had any knowledge, fortunately, of any William Ager living in the district. The evidence of the man at the martello tower freed us from all suspicion. All that could be done was to return a verdict of wilful murder by some person or persons unknown.

Paxton was so totally without connections that all the inquiries that were subsequently made ended in a No Thoroughfare. And I have never been at Seaburgh, or even near it, since.

DYLAN THOMAS

A Child's Christmas in Wales

One Christmas was so much like another, in those years around the sea-town corner now and out of all sound except the distant speaking of the voices I sometimes hear a moment before sleep, that I can never remember whether it snowed for six days and six nights when I was twelve or whether it snowed for twelve days and twelve nights when I was six.

All the Christmases roll down toward the two-tongued sea, like a cold and headlong moon bundling down the sky that was our street; and they stop at the rim of the ice-edged, fish-freezing waves, and I plunge my hands in the snow and bring out whatever I can find. In goes my hand into that wool-white bell-tongued ball of holidays resting at the rim of the carol-singing sea, and out come Mrs Prothero and the firemen.

It was on the afternoon of the day of Christmas Eve, and I was in Mrs Prothero's garden, waiting for cats, with her son Jim. It was snowing. It was always snowing at Christmas. December, in my memory, is white as Lapland, though there were no reindeers. But there were cats. Patient, cold and callous, our hands wrapped in socks, we waited to snowball the cats. Sleek and long as jaguars and horrible-whiskered, spitting and snarling, they would slink and sidle over the white back-garden walls, and the lynx-eyed hunters, Jim and I, fur-capped and moccasined trappers from Hudson Bay, off Mumbles Road, would hurl our deadly snowballs at the green of their eyes.

The wise cats never appeared. We were so still, Eskimo-footed arctic marksmen in the muffling silence of the eternal snows – eternal, ever since Wednesday – that we never heard Mrs Prothero's first cry from her igloo at the bottom of the garden. Or, if we heard it at all, it was, to us, like the far-off challenge of our enemy and prey, the neighbour's polar cat. But soon the voice grew louder. 'Fire!' cried Mrs Prothero, and she beat the dinner-gong.

And we ran down the garden, with the snowballs in our arms, toward the house; and smoke, indeed, was pouring out of the dining-room, and the gong was bombilating, and Mrs Prothero was announcing ruin like a town crier in Pompeii. This was better than all the cats in Wales standing on the wall in a row. We bounded into the house, laden with snowballs, and stopped at the open door of the smoke-filled room.

Something was burning all right; perhaps it was Mr Prothero, who always slept there after midday dinner with a newspaper over his face. But he was standing in the middle of the room, saying, 'A fine Christmas!' and smacking at the smoke with a slipper. 'Call the fire brigade,' cried Mrs Prothero as she beat the gong.

'They won't be there,' said Mr Prothero, 'it's Christmas.'

There was no fire to be seen, only clouds of smoke and Mr Prothero standing in the middle of them, waving his slipper as though he were conducting.

'Do something,' he said.

And we threw all our snowballs into the smoke – I think we missed Mr Prothero – and ran out of the house to the telephone box.

'Let's call the police as well,' Jim said.

'And the ambulance.'

'And Ernie Jenkins, he likes fires.'

But we only called the fire brigade, and soon the fire engine came and three tall men in helmets brought a hose into the house and Mr Prothero got out just in time before they turned it on. Nobody could have had a noisier Christmas Eve. And when the firemen turned off the hose and were standing in the wet, smoky room, Jim's aunt, Miss Prothero, came downstairs and peered in at them. Jim and I waited, very quietly, to hear what she would say to them. She said the right thing, always. She looked at the three tall firemen in their shining helmets, standing among the smoke and cinders and dissolving snowballs, and she said: 'Would you like anything to read?'

Years and years and years ago, when I was a boy, when there were wolves in Wales, and birds the colour of red-flannel petticoats whisked past the harp-shaped hills, when we sang and wallowed all night and day in caves that smelt like Sunday afternoons in damp front farmhouse parlours, and we chased, with the jawbones of deacons, the English and the bears, before the motor-car, before the wheel, before the duchess-faced horse, when we rode the daft and happy hills bareback, it snowed and it snowed. But here a small boy says: 'It snowed last year, too. I made a snowman and my brother knocked it down and I knocked my brother down and then we had tea.'

'But that was not the same snow,' I say. 'Our snow was not only shaken from whitewash buckets down the sky, it came shawling out of the ground and swam and drifted out of the arms and hands and bodies of the trees; snow grew overnight on the roofs of the houses like a pure and grandfather moss, minutely white-ivied the walls and settled on the postman, opening the gate, like a dumb, numb thunderstorm of white, torn Christmas cards.'

'Were there postmen then, too?'

'With sprinkling eyes and wind-cherried noses, on spread, frozen feet they crunched up to the doors and mittened on them manfully. But all that the children could hear was a ringing of bells.'

'You mean that the postman went rat-a-tat-tat and the doors rang?'

'I mean that the bells that the children could hear were inside them.'

'I only hear thunder sometimes, never bells.'

'There were church bells, too.'

'Inside them?'

'No, no, no, in the bat-black, snow-white belfries, tugged by bishops and storks. And they rang their tidings over the bandaged town, over the frozen foam of the powder and ice-cream hills, over the crackling sea. It seemed that all the churches boomed for joy under my window; and the weather-cocks crew for Christmas, on our fence.'

'Get back to the postmen.'

'They were just ordinary postmen, fond of walking and dogs and Christmas and the snow. They knocked on the doors with blue knuckles . . .'

'Ours has got a black knocker . . .'

'And then they stood on the white Welcome mat in the little, drifted porches and huffed and puffed, making ghosts with their breath, and jogged from foot to foot like small boys wanting to go out.'

'And then the Presents?'

'And then the Presents, after the Christmas box. And the cold postman, with a rose on his button-nose, tingled down the tea-tray-slithered run of the chilly glinting hill. He went in his ice-bound boots like a man on fishmonger's slabs. He wagged his bag like a frozen camel's hump, dizzily turned the corner on one foot, and, by God, he was gone.'

'Get back to the Presents.'

'There were the Useful Presents: engulfing mufflers of the old coach days, and mittens made for giant sloths; zebra scarfs of a substance like silky gum that could be tug-o'-warred down to the galoshes; blinding tam-o'-shanters like patchwork tea cosies and bunny-suited busbies and balaclavas for victims of head-shrinking tribes; from aunts who always wore wool next to the skin there were moustached and rasping vests that made you wonder why the aunts had any skin left at all; and once I had a little crocheted nose bag from an aunt now, alas, no longer whinnying with us. And pictureless books in which small boys, though warned with quotations not to, *would* skate on Farmer Giles' pond and did and drowned; and books that told me everything about the wasp, except why.'

'Go on to the Useless Presents.'

'Bags of moist and many-coloured jelly babies and a folded flag and a false nose and a tram-conductor's cap and a machine that punched tickets and rang a bell; never a catapult; once, by mistake that no one could explain, a little hatchet; and a celluloid duck that made, when you pressed it, a most unduck-like sound, a mewing moo that an ambitious cat might make who wished to be a cow; and a painting book in which I could make the grass, the trees, the sea and the animals any colour I pleased, and still the dazzling sky-blue sheep are grazing in the red field under the rainbow-billed and pea-green birds.

'Hardboileds, toffee, fudge and allsorts, crunches, cracknels, humbugs, glaciers, marzipan, and butterwelsh for the Welsh. And troops of bright tin soldiers who, if they could not fight, could always run. And Snakes-and-Familes and Happy Ladders. And Easy Hobbi-Games for Little Engineers, complete with instructions.

'Oh, easy for Leonardo! And a whistle to make the dogs bark to wake up the old man next door to make him beat on the wall with his stick to shake our picture off the wall.

'And a packet of cigarettes: you put one in your mouth and you stood at the corner of the street and you waited for hours, in vain, for an old lady to scold you for smoking a cigarette, and then with a smirk you ate it. And then it was breakfast under the balloons.'

'Were there Uncles like in our house?'

'There are always Uncles at Christmas.

'The same Uncles. And on Christmas mornings, with dog-disturbing whistle and sugar fags, I would scour the swatched town for the news of the little world, and find always a dead bird by the white Post Office or by the deserted swings; perhaps a robin, all but one of his fires out. Men and women wading or scooping back from chapel, with taproom noses and windbussed cheeks, all albinos, huddled their stiff black jarring . . . feathers against the irreligious snow.

'Mistletoe hung from the gas brackets in all the front parlours; there was sherry and walnuts and bottled beer and crackers by the dessertspoons; and cats in their fur-abouts watched the fires; and the high-heaped fire spat, all ready for the chestnuts and the mulling pokers.

'Some few large men sat in the front parlours, without their collars, Uncles almost certainly, trying their new cigars, holding them out judiciously at arms' length, returning them to their mouths, coughing, then holding them out again as though waiting for the explosion; and some few small Aunts, not wanted in the kitchen, nor anywhere else for that matter, sat on the very edges of their chairs, poised and brittle, afraid to break, like faded cups and saucers.'

Not many those mornings trod the piling streets: an old man always, fawn-bowlered, yellow-gloved and, at this time of year, with spats of snow, would take his constitutional to the white bowling green and back, as he would take it wet or fine on Christmas Day or Doomsday; sometimes two hale young men, with big pipes blazing, no overcoats and wind-blown scarfs, would trudge, unspeaking, down to the forlorn sea, to work up an appetite, to blow away the fumes, who knows, to walk into the waves until nothing of them was left but the two curling smoke clouds of their inextinguishable briars. Then I would be slap-dashing home, the gravy smell of the dinners of others, the bird smell, the brandy, the pudding and mince, coiling up to my nostrils, when out of a snow-clogged side lane would come a boy the spit of myself, with a pink-tipped cigarette and the violet rast of a black eye, cocky as a bullfinch, leering all to himself.

I hated him on sight and sound, and would be about to put my dog whistle to my lips and blow him off the face of Christmas when suddenly he, with a violent wink, put *his* whistle to *his* lips and blew so stridently, so high, so exquisitely loud, that gobbling faces, their cheeks bulged with goose, would press against their tinselled windows, the whole length of the white echoing street. For dinner we had turkey and blazing pudding, and after dinner the Uncles sat in front of the fire, loosened all buttons, put their large moist hands over their watch chains, groaned a little and slept. Mothers, aunts and sisters scuttled to and fro, bearing tureens. Auntie Bessie, who had already been frightened, twice, by a clock-work mouse, whimpered at the sideboard and had some elderberry wine. The dog was sick. Auntie Dosie had to have three aspirins, but Auntie Hannah, who liked port, stood in the middle of the snowbound back yard, singing like a big-bosomed thrush. I would blow up balloons to see how big they would blow up to; and, when they burst, which they all did, the Uncles jumped and rumbled. In the rich and heavy afternoon, the Uncles breathing like dolphins and the snow descending, I would sit among festoons and Chinese lanterns and nibble dates and try to make a model man-o'-war, following the Instructions for Little Engineers, and produce what might be mistaken for a sea-going tramcar.

Or I would go out, my bright new boots squeaking, into the white world, on to the seaward hill, to call on Jim and Dan and Jack and to pad through the still streets, leaving huge deep footprints on the hidden pavements.

'I bet people will think there's been hippos.'

'What would you do if you saw a hippo coming down our street?'

'I'd go like this, bang! I'd throw him over the railings and roll him down the hill and then I'd tickle him under the ear and he'd wag his tail.'

'What would you do if you saw *two* hippos?'

Iron-flanked and bellowing he-hippos clanked and battered through the scudding snow toward us as we passed Mr Daniel's house.

'Let's post Mr Daniel a snowball through his letter-box.'

'Let's write, "Mr Daniel looks like a spaniel" all over his lawn.'

Or we walked on the white shore.

'Can the fishes see it's snowing?'

The silent one-clouded heavens drifted on to the sea. Now we were snow-blind travellers lost on the north hills, and vast dewlapped dogs, with flasks round their necks, ambled and shambled up to us, baying 'Excelsior'. We returned home through the poor streets where only a few children fumbled with bare red fingers in the wheel-rutted snow and cat-called after us, their voices fading away, as we trudged uphill, into the cries of the dock birds and the hooting of ships out in the whirling bay. And then, at tea the recovered Uncles would be jolly; and the ice cake loomed in the centre of the table like a marble grave. Auntie Hannah laced her tea with rum, because it was only once a year.

Bring out the tall tales now that we told by the fire as the gaslight bubbled like a diver. Ghosts whooed like owls in the long nights when I dared not look over my shoulder; animals lurked in the cubbyhole under the stairs where the gas meter ticked. And I remember that we went singing carols once, when there wasn't the shaving of a moon to light the flying streets. At the end of a long road was a drive that led to a large house, and we stumbled up the darkness of the drive that night, each one of us afraid, each one holding a stone in his hand in case, and all of us too brave to say a word. The wind through the trees made noises as of old and unpleasant and maybe webfooted men wheezing in caves. We reached the black bulk of the house.

'What shall we give them? "Hark the Herald"?'

'No,' Jack said, "Good King Wenceslas". I'll count three.'

One, two, three, and we began to sing, our voices high and seemingly distant in the snow-felted darkness round the house that was occupied by nobody we knew. We stood close together, near the dark door.

Good King Wenceslas looked out
On the Feast of Stephen ...

And then a small, dry voice, like the voice of someone who has not spoken for a long time, joined our singing: a small, dry, eggshell voice from the other side of the door: a small dry voice through the keyhole. And when we stopped running we were outside *our* house; the front room was lovely; balloons floated under the hot-water-bottle-gulping gas; everything was good again and shone over the town.

'Perhaps it was a ghost,' Jim said.

'Perhaps it was trolls,' Dan said, who was always reading.

'Let's go in and see if there's any jelly left,' Jack said. And we did that.

Always on Christmas night there was music. An uncle played the fiddle, a cousin sang 'Cherry Ripe', and another uncle sang 'Drake's Drum'. It was very warm in the little house.

Auntie Hannah, who had got on to the parsnip wine, sang a song about Bleeding Hearts and Death, and then another in which she said her heart was like a Bird's Nest; and then everybody laughed again; and then I went to bed. Looking through my bedroom window, out into the moonlight and the unending smoke-coloured snow, I could see the lights in the windows of all the other houses on our hill and hear the music rising from them up the long, steadily falling night. I turned the gas down, I got into bed. I said some words to the close and holy darkness, and then I slept.

ACKNOWLEDGEMENTS

Acknowledgements are due to the following for permission to include the stories which appear in this book: A.P. Watt Ltd for *Baa Baa, Black Sheep* by Rudyard Kipling; Macmillan Publishers Ltd for *On The Western Circuit* by Thomas Hardy; Jonathan Clowes Ltd for *The Speckled Band* by Sir Arthur Conan Doyle; A.P. Watt Ltd for *The Country of the Blind* by H.G. Wells; N.R. James for *A Warning to the Curious* by M.R. James; David Higham Ltd for *A Child's Christmas in Wales* by Dylan Thomas..